THE OTHER SIDE OF HAPPINESS

The 1960s — a decade of mini-skirts, pop music and endless possibilities — are full of promise for typist Sadie Bell. She lives with her parents and brothers in Hammersmith. When she meets Paul Winston at a Cliff Richard concert, they fall head over heels in love, and, impatient to be married, they move in to Paul's parents' home in Surrey, until they can afford their own place. Then, tragically, their joy short-lived, Sadie finds herself returning to London alone, pregnant and heartbroken. However, supported by her family and close friend, Brenda, she finds a new sense of purpose when Rosie is born. But life has more surprises in store for Sadie, and a terrible secret threatens to take everything away from her once more . . .

Books by Pamela Evans
Published by The House of Ulverscroft:

A BARROW IN THE BROADWAY
MAGGIE OF MOSS STREET
STAR QUALITY
THE WILLOW GIRLS
A SONG IN YOUR HEART
THE CAROUSEL KEEPS TURNING
CLOSE TO HOME
SECOND CHANCE OF SUNSHINE
THE SPARROWS OF SYCAMORE ROAD
LAMPLIGHT ON THE THAMES
IN THE DARK STREETS SHINING
WHEN THE BOYS COME HOME
UNDER AN AMBER SKY
THE TIDEWAY GIRLS
HARVEST NIGHTS

PAMELA EVANS

THE OTHER SIDE OF HAPPINESS

Complete and Unabridged

CHARNWOOD
Leicester

First published in Great Britain in 2011 by
Headline Publishing Group
London

First Charnwood Edition
published 2012
by arrangement with
Headline Publishing Group
An Hachette UK Company
London

British Library CIP Data

Evans, Pamela.
The other side of happiness.
1. London (England)- -Social life and customs- -
20th century- -Fiction. 2. Nineteen sixties- -Fiction.
3. Single mothers- -Fiction. 4. Large type books.
I. Title
823.9'14–dc23

ISBN 978–1–4448–0940–4

Published by
F. A. Thorpe (Publishing)
Anstey, Leicestershire

Set by Words & Graphics Ltd.
Anstey, Leicestershire
Printed and bound in Great Britain by
T. J. International Ltd., Padstow, Cornwall

This book is printed on acid-free paper

To my dear and longstanding friend
Dawn Faure, with love and gratitude for her
wit, wisdom and uplifting company.

1

The Bell family was so accustomed to the exuberance of their youngest member, they weren't in the least surprised when eighteen-year-old Sadie came home from work one day in March 1962 in a state of feverish excitement.

'You'll never guess what,' she burst out to her brothers and parents who were gathered in the living room of number 2 Fern Terrace, Hammersmith. 'It's something so absolutely fabulous, you will just never guess.'

'Perhaps you'd better tell us then?' chortled her mother, Marge, who was laying the table for the evening meal. 'What's happened? Did the boss give you a pay rise?'

'Better than that, Mum; much better,' enthused Sadie.

'Spit it out then, for goodness' sake,' urged Marge. 'Before we die of suspense.'

'There are two tickets going spare for a Cliff Richard concert next Wednesday and Brenda and I can have them if we get the money by tomorrow.' The importance she bestowed upon the event was almost on a par with the end of a world war. 'A girl at work is selling them because she and her friend can't go and Brenda and I have first refusal. I called to see Brenda on the way home and she wants to go if she can raise the cash in time.'

'So . . . what are we all supposed to do, dance

1

a tango?' said her brother Derek, teasing her; he was twenty-four and the oldest of the Bell brood.

'I'm talking about Cliff Richard, Derek,' Sadie pointed out, as though speaking of a world leader. 'Surely you must know how important this is to me.'

'I do actually live in this country,' he reminded her, his dark eyes sparkling with fun. 'So I know who Cliff Richard is.'

'Then you'll know that I can't possibly miss this opportunity to see him perform live.'

'None of us are stopping you,' mentioned brother Don, who was a year younger than Derek and so similar in appearance that they were often taken to be twins with their dark, swarthy looks.

'Uh-oh. I get it,' guessed Derek. 'She can't afford the ticket. She's on the flippin' cadge again.'

Sadie made a face that confirmed his theory. 'I'm only a poor filing clerk,' she said, adding an air of tragedy to her tone. 'I don't earn much.'

'And whose fault's that?' put in her mother, a warm-hearted, sensible soul from whom Sadie had inherited her fair complexion and blue eyes. Marge had been a stunner in her day and was still an attractive woman now, her face only lightly feathered with lines and just a smattering of grey in her blonde hair. 'You could have been a shorthand typist if you hadn't bunked off evening classes and gone to the coffee bar round the corner instead. You'd be on a much higher salary now if you'd stuck with it, and there would have been the prospect of getting a job as

2

a personal secretary, maybe even in the West End where secretaries earn good money.'

At least Sadie had the grace to look sheepish. 'We went into all that at the time, Mum,' she reminded her. 'I wasn't any good at shorthand and even worse at typing.'

'You didn't give it a fair chance,' said Marge in a tone of mild admonition. 'After a fortnight you were off enjoying yourself while your Dad and I thought you were safely installed in the classroom two nights a week.'

Sadie bit her lip. She wasn't proud of the fact that her parents had paid for evening classes that she hadn't attended. But the steamy aroma of the espresso machines and the company of her 'with-it' friends had won hands down against the blanked-out keyboards in a row of typewriters and an overwhelming feeling of inadequacy to the task of learning shorthand.

'All right, maybe I didn't give it long enough,' she admitted. 'But I did come clean about it eventually. I said I was sorry hundreds of times; and I was only fifteen.'

'And you're eighteen now and still as irresponsible as you were then. You're old enough to have a more serious attitude towards things, especially money.'

'I know I am, Mum,' she sighed, 'and I will try to improve, especially if I can manage to get a better-paid job.' Sadie made a performance of looking downcast and under-privileged. She was an expert at winning over the men of the family even if her mother was more of a challenge. 'It's just that I would really, *really* love to go to see Cliff.'

Her father, Cyril, lowered his newspaper and peered over his spectacles at his youngest child, a lively blue-eyed blonde with a gorgeous smile that never failed to melt his heart. 'All right, you can quit the drama,' he said with a sigh of resignation. 'I'll come up with the dough.'

'There you go, spoiling her again.' His wife disapproved. 'You'll do her no good in the long run, you know.'

'All right, Marge,' sighed Cyril, a dark-complexioned man with balding black hair and bushy eyebrows. 'Don't go on about it.'

'I have to for Sadie's own good,' she told him. 'She's got to learn that money doesn't grow on trees, and she can't have her own way over every single thing.'

'And I'm sure she will realise that, in time,' he responded.

'Not if you have your way,' riposted his wife.

'Thanks, Dad.' Sadie was all smiles now. 'I'll pay you back as soon as I can.'

This created a roar of laughter because Sadie wasn't renowned for honouring her debts. Her wages passed only fleetingly through her purse. Everything, after she'd paid for her keep, went on the latest clothes, records and dance tickets.

'I will pay it back eventually, Dad, even if it does take me a little time, I promise,' she said, needing to convince herself as well as him. Her generous relatives made it so easy for her to take advantage she was barely aware that she was doing it.

4

'You shouldn't make a promise you know you can't keep,' chipped in her mother, who constantly strove, against strong opposition from the rest of the family, to instil in her daughter a sense of responsibility even if it did make her unpopular. 'If you can't afford the price of a ticket now, you won't be able to in the foreseeable future. There will always be a skirt or dress or a pair of shoes that you just must have, or a dance that you simply *have* to go to.'

Sadie bit her lip. 'It's Cliff Richard, Mum,' she said, as though that excused all her shortcomings.

'I don't care if it's Elvis Presley and the Queen of England singing 'All Shook Up' together at the Albert Hall, if you can't afford a thing you don't have it.'

'Don't be too hard on her, Mum,' urged Derek.

'I'm just trying to do a proper job as a mother.'

'She really does want to go to this show so how about we go halves on the dough she needs, Derek?' suggested brother Don.

'Suits me,' his brother agreed, turning to their father. 'We'll see to it, Dad. You hang on to your dosh.'

'If you're sure,' said Cyril, proud of his sons for their generosity towards their sister.

'Oh boys,' Sadie gushed, rushing over and hugging each man in turn. 'You are the best brothers a girl could possibly have. I'll love you both forever.'

'Or at least until we've handed over the cash,'

laughed Don affectionately. 'And I suppose you'll want a bit extra for something new to wear.'

'Ooh, could I?' she beamed.

Watching this display of extravagance against her wishes, Marge's frown deepened. Being the youngest child by several years and the only girl, it was almost inevitable that Sadie had been spoilt, especially by the men of the family. Her zest for life, sunny personality and sense of fun made it all too easy to pander to her.

Both of Marge's sons had been born before the war and she had almost despaired of having another child because Cyril was abroad for a long time. Then he'd been given leave unexpectedly towards the end of hostilities and their beautiful, much-wanted daughter had been the result. So Marge was just as susceptible to her charm as the others but she considered it her duty as a mother to do her very best for Sadie, which in her opinion meant preparing her to be a well-balanced, unselfish adult. The ease with which Sadie got her own way with the others was a constant headache to Marge. The girl didn't seem to have a serious thought in her head. Life for her outside of work was all fun, friends and fashion.

Of course, Marge realised that she and Cyril had been brought up in much harder times and had been raised to do as they were told, pay their way and live within their means. In these days of hire-purchase and low unemployment, attitudes had changed. Having lived through the dangers and hardship of war and the ensuing austerity, Marge embraced the current vibrant economy, but the principles by which she'd been brought up remained and she'd always believed that too much indulgence led to selfishness and a lack of care for other people's needs and feelings.

Sadie probably wasn't any more selfish than any other young person in this increasingly youth-orientated society but she could be thoughtless at times. She lived for the moment with not a care for tomorrow, and she did tend to take things for granted. Socialising was all she seemed to care about.

That's how it was in these socially liberated times with young people having so much enjoyment available to them; even their own music and fashion. It was a wonder they hadn't made the new contraceptive pill available to everyone but at the moment it was only available to married women. Like all of her generation, Sadie had been raised to believe that decent girls didn't until after they were married. But once they were out on their own with hormones playing havoc there wasn't much a parent could do except hope for the best.

Like many other working-class households in the area, they weren't badly off in the current economic climate, every family member apart from Marge being in paid employment. It was quite common now for married women to go out to work when the children were off their hands. But Marge was happy to stay at home to look after the house and family. Cyril was a self-employed carpenter and the boys were both car mechanics; all well-trained tradesmen. Both the motor trade and the building industry were thriving in Harold Macmillan's Britain so there was plenty of work around, which meant they could afford such modern luxuries as a television and a telephone. A fridge was next on the list but they were still saving up for that.

Marge was recalled to the present by her daughter, whose face was wreathed in smiles. 'Oh Mum, isn't it exciting?' she trilled. 'I can go to see Cliff and the Shadows in real life, thanks to those lovely sons of yours.'

Looking at her shining blue eyes and heartfelt, dimpled smile, a surge of warmth spread through Marge. It was no wonder the men of the family found it impossible to refuse Sadie anything.

'If I have a win on the Bingo, I'll give you a little something too,' she heard herself say, much against her better judgement.

'I'm so lucky to have such a smashing family,' said the girl, wrapping her arms around her mother and hugging her tight. 'What on earth would I do without you?'

Heaven only knows, thought Marge, but she just said, 'Be permanently skint I should think.'

'I would be too,' agreed Sadie lightly, and picking up Pickles, the family tabby, who had been rubbing circles around her legs, she cuddled and stroked him and danced around with him in her arms singing, 'I'm going to see Cliff' to the tune of 'Living Doll'.

★ ★ ★

'Your hair is getting bigger by the day, Sadie,' remarked Derek later that evening as they all sat round the table eating lamb chops with potatoes, cabbage and gravy. 'I've never seen anything like it.'

'Yeah, it's good, isn't it,' she said, taking his remark as a compliment. 'I'm getting to be a dab hand at backcombing and I'm aiming to have the best beehive in the whole of West London. Brenda and I are streets ahead of everyone else. Some girls round here haven't even got into this look yet.'

'What's the point of having it so high and wide and lacquered into place?' Don wondered. 'I thought women's hair was supposed to move about.'

'It's fashion and it's called bouffant,' his sister explained, giving him a pitying look.

'If you were a brunette like us you could get a job as a stand-in for one of the guards at Buckingham Palace with that built-in bearskin,' teased Derek, laughing.

'But because you're blonde it's rather like a miniature haystack,' observed Don, joining in the joke. 'I reckon there's wildlife living in there, don't you, Derek?'

'I certainly do, mate; bees, butterflies, mice. There's room for a whole menagerie.'

'Take no notice of them, love,' advised Marge. Her daughter was indulged, it was true, but she was also teased mercilessly by her brothers, which she always took in good part. 'Your hair looks very nice.'

'She doesn't care what we say as long as we hand over the dosh, do you, kid?' laughed Don.

'I certainly don't,' Sadie confirmed, smiling.

9

'You can say what you like about me. I'm used to your insults.'

'That's what brothers are for,' said Don. 'To keep your feet on the ground.'

'You do that all right,' she grinned.

'Where is the concert anyway?' asked Derek.

'At the ABC cinema in Kingston-upon-Thames.'

'Blimey, that's a bit of a trek from Hammersmith, isn't it?' he suggested.

'No, not really. We'll get the train to Ealing Broadway and the bus from there,' his sister told him breezily. 'It'll be well worth the journey. Anyway, we'd walk there barefoot if it meant seeing Cliff.' She sighed. 'He and the Shadows are fabulous and seeing them for real, ooh, just the thought of it makes me go all weak at the knees.'

'Good grief, you girls don't half get yourselves into a state about pop singers,' remarked Derek, tutting. 'Weak at the knees, I've never heard anything so soft.'

'What's so special about this singer anyway?' enquired her father with interest.

'Nothing that us blokes would appreciate, Dad,' Derek informed him. 'Very good-looking; plays up to the girls and gets 'em all squealing. I prefer Adam Faith myself. He seems a bit more down to earth.' He launched into a tuneless version of the first hit by the aforementioned singer, 'What Do You Want'.

'I hope the real thing sounds better,' said Cyril.

'It does, believe me, Dad,' Don assured him

lightly. 'Even Pickles the cat with his tail caught in the mangle sounds better than Derek in song.'

'You shouldn't be singing at the table anyway,' admonished Marge, in a good-humoured but rather hopeless attempt to keep some sort of order amongst her lively, garrulous family.

'I've never heard of either of them, anyway,' admitted Cyril.

'That's because you're out of date, Dad,' joshed Don. 'The world has moved on a bit since Vera Lynn, you know.'

'Blimin' cheek. Me and your mum aren't all that old-fashioned. We like Frank Sinatra.'

'Exactly,' chuckled his son. 'He's old hat for Sadie's age group.'

'I'm very partial to a spot of Cliff as well,' put in Marge. 'People — adults, that is — say he's a bit suggestive with all that smouldering he does but he's got a good voice. I've heard him when Sadie plays his records on her Dansette in her room.'

'Why did you try and stop her going to see him then?' wondered Cyril, who had never been able to fathom out the workings of a woman's mind.

'Because she can't afford it and I'm trying to teach her to be responsible, something that you lot don't seem to have a clue about,' she came back at him. 'It has nothing to do with the show. I'm all for young people enjoying themselves . . . when they have enough money to pay for it.'

'It's all guitars and rock'n'roll these days,' observed Don rather randomly.

'Hooray for that,' Sadie responded.

11

'I can see that I shall have to get more up to date,' suggested Cyril lightly.

'Don't you dare, Dad. That would be so *embarrassing*,' wailed Sadie. 'The older generation are meant to be behind the times. It would be awful if you started to like Elvis.'

'That's nice, I must say,' quipped her mother with irony. 'We're not even allowed to like their music now, and I do quite like Elvis, as a matter of fact.'

'Oh, I can't have that,' said Sadie, teasing her. 'The war was your era so you stick with 'We'll Meet Again' and 'The White Cliffs of Dover'.'

'Saucy madam,' said Marge but she was smiling. 'Kids, eh. Who'd have 'em?'

When they had finished their meal, Sadie and her mother took the plates to the kitchen and brought in an apple pie straight from the oven accompanied by a jug of warm custard.

'I'll give pudding a miss if you don't mind, Mum,' announced Sadie, making as though to leave. 'I'm going round to Brenda's to play records.' She smiled, her cheeks flushed with pleasure. 'I can't wait to know if she managed to get the money for her ticket. Shouldn't think she'd have a problem. She earns more than me because she works in a factory so her mum and dad won't mind lending it to her.'

'You don't do so badly, having us lot twisted around your little finger,' Marge reminded her.

'I know, Mum, and I love you all to bits,' said Sadie, turning towards the door. 'Ta-ta then. I'll see you all later.'

'You're not going anywhere until you've had

your pudding and helped me with the washing up.'

'Oh, Mum,' Sadie protested. 'I can't stay. I told Brenda I'd get round there early tonight.'

'That's just too bad. You're not getting round me over this one. Oh no,' said her mother in a tone that defied argument. 'You'll go out when you've finished the meal, that I went to time and trouble to cook, and helped with the dishes.'

Sadie exuded a series of eloquent sighs and rolled her eyes dramatically but she knew that victory wouldn't be hers on this issue. So did the rest of them, so there were no pleas for Marge to change her mind.

★   ★   ★

It was a cold and cloudy Saturday afternoon with March winds scurrying around corners, sending street litter scudding and causing the crowds in Shepherds Bush Market to pull up their scarves and coat collars. The trading day was drawing to a close and there was a gathering around the meat stall as the butcher sold off what he had left at a cheap price. A trader marketing a kitchen gadget went through his spiel for the umpteenth time that day and the fruit stalls were almost sold out. The air was infused with the earthy, slightly sour smell of vegetables, frying fat from the cafés, cheap scent and the unmistakable sound of Elvis Presley coming from the record stall.

Sadie and Brenda, both dressed in long winkle-picker boots and short coats, were looking through the rails at one of the clothes stalls, already carrying bags from the dress shops opposite the Green.

'These jeans look nice, Sadie,' observed Brenda, a tall, willowy girl with warm brown eyes and chestnut hair worn bouffant like her friend's. 'They're dead cheap too.'

'I can't afford anything else today,' Sadie told her. 'I've got a new top and a skirt to wear on Wednesday when we go to see Cliff. That's the lot for me.'

'They're not at all expensive and once we've shrunk them in the bath they'll be fantastic.'

'I've spent all the money my brothers gave me for the ticket and something to wear, and I need my own dosh to see me through till pay day,' Sadie informed her. 'You get a pair if you want, though.'

Brenda looked at Sadie sheepishly. They were the same age, had been inseparable since primary school and were very close. 'It doesn't seem right if you're not having a pair,' she said.

'Don't be so daft. You get them,' urged Sadie.

When Brenda had made her purchase, they moved on past stalls selling everything from food and household goods to jewellery, sweets and haberdashery. There were several notices outside the shops that flanked the market advertising ear-piercing at budget prices.

Sadie and Brenda had been out around the town all afternoon as usual on a Saturday. There were some very good boutique-type dress and shoe shops in Shepherds Bush where they stocked cheap clothes aimed at the youth

14

market. These popular stores as well as the market drew crowds from all over West London on a Saturday.

'Shall we go to the record stall to see what he's got in,' suggested Brenda.

'So that you can get an eyeful of your heartthrob,' laughed Sadie, teasing her.

'No, of course not,' Brenda denied, colouring up. 'He isn't my heartthrob.'

'I don't believe you,' challenged Sadie lightly. 'You fancy him rotten.'

She was referring to Ray Smart, who had a stall here selling records, sheet music and second-hand musical instruments. He was a pal of Sadie's brothers and a regular visitor to the Bell house, so Sadie knew him in a casual and fairly indifferent way, whereas Brenda had a massive crush on him.

'I want to go there so we can see what records he's got in, that's all,' insisted Brenda. 'We might get him to play something by Cliff to get us in the mood for Wednesday.'

'Still don't believe you,' laughed Sadie.

'All right, so what if I do fancy him,' retorted Brenda, finally admitting it. 'He's gorgeous, anyone can see that.'

'A bit ancient for my taste,' Sadie pointed out. 'He's the same age as my brother Derek.'

'Only six years older than us,' said Brenda.

'Still puts him in a different age group,' asserted Sadie. 'He isn't part of our scene.'

'I still think he's dead lovely but don't you dare say a word to anyone about it, especially your brothers,' warned Brenda. 'I'd die if they said anything to him.'

'How are you going to get together with him if you're not going to help things along?'

'I'll find a way somehow but I don't want Don and Derek putting their oar in and embarrassing me.'

'They'd accuse him of cradle-snatching, anyway, I expect,' suggested Sadie as they approached the music stall. 'But my lips are sealed, I promise.'

'They'd better be.'

'Wotcha, girls,' Ray Smart greeted them as they hovered near the records on display. 'What are you in the mood for today?'

'Sorry, Ray, but we're not buying,' confessed Sadie, casting her eye over his stock. 'Just looking.'

'Blown all your money on clothes, have you?' guessed Ray, glancing at their bags.

Sadie nodded.

'I'm surprised you don't get your gear in Carnaby Street,' he went on. 'I've heard it's all beginning to happen there for a couple of dolly birds like yourselves.'

'We don't need to go there because some really trendy boutiques have opened around here,' Sadie told him.

'Carnaby's loss is my gain,' he grinned. 'I get two pretty girls coming to see me.'

'Actually, Ray, we wondered if you could play something by Cliff,' said Sadie coaxingly.

'Yeah, sure.'

'We're going to see him perform live next week,' she added excitedly. 'Fabulous, isn't it?'

'Very nice too,' approved Ray, who was tall and well-built with shandy-coloured eyes and wavy brown hair which he wore brushed back in traditional style. 'Is he doing a gig locally then?'

'No. He's doing a show at a cinema out at Kingston,' Sadie informed him.

'Thank God he isn't appearing around here,' laughed Ray. 'I wouldn't want to get trampled to death by crowds of screaming girls.'

'Ooh you fibber, you'd love having lots of girls around,' joshed Brenda.

'We'll be there yelling with the rest of them over in Kingston, won't we, Brenda?' smiled Sadie.

'Not half,' her friend enthused, grinning at Ray, entranced by the way he held his head to the side; sort of cocky but nice with it. He was very self-confident and she liked that in a bloke.

'I bet you're a right pair of horrors when you're let loose at a show like that.'

'We intend to let our hair down if that's what you mean,' Sadie informed him brightly. 'But don't tell Mum and Dad or my brothers. I don't want them knowing what I get up to when I'm out.'

'You watch yourselves,' he warned. 'A couple of good-looking girls like you out on your own at night could be asking for trouble. There's no shortage of villains out there.'

'We're going to Kingston, Ray, not Soho,' Sadie came back at him with a pained expression.

'Even so, you be careful.'

Sadie laughed heartily. 'You sound just like my

17

dad,' she told him. 'You'll be old before your time if you're not careful.'

'Just looking out for you,' he said.

'Course he is,' put in Brenda, impressed. 'It's very nice of him and you should be grateful.'

'I'm glad someone appreciates me,' Ray said, looking at her, and she melted.

'I think you're a real gentleman,' she complimented.

'Ha ha, that's a good one,' he laughed in a confident but self-deprecating manner. 'I don't know if anyone else would agree with you about that.'

'I speak as I find,' declared Brenda, enjoying herself immensely.

Ray turned his attention to Sadie. 'How are they all at home?' he asked. 'I haven't been round this week.'

'They're all fine.'

'Will you tell your brothers I'll meet them down the pub tonight as planned,' he said. 'Then we'll go for a game of billiards.'

'Will do.'

He turned to his portable record player. 'You asked for Cliff so here he is, just for you,' he said and put on their idol singing 'When the Girl in Your Arms is the Girl in Your Heart'.

'Thanks, Ray,' said Sadie, glowing with pleasure when the song ended. 'We're off home now.'

'Behave yourselves at the concert,' he said lightly.

'Not if we can help it,' giggled Sadie and the two girls went on their way, arm in arm.

18

'I don't know how I'm ever going to get a date with him,' sighed Brenda. 'He thinks we're just a couple of kids.'

'We are, compared to him.'

'I wonder if he's got a girlfriend.'

'He's meeting my brothers tonight so he can't have,' Sadie pointed out. 'It's Saturday night. If he had a girl he'd be seeing her.'

'Mmm, that's true.'

'Forget about him and concentrate on boys of your own age,' said Sadie.

'Mmm, I suppose I should,' Brenda agreed reluctantly. 'He's dead nice though. So worldly and confident. Makes boys of our age seem so immature.'

'They are and so are we because we're young, and that's how we're meant to be.' Sadie paused and mulled it over. 'But Ray does have a tough edge about him which some people might find attractive, I suppose. He isn't as good-looking as Cliff though.'

'We can't have Cliff, though, can we,' Brenda pointed out. 'He's well out of our reach. More of a fantasy figure, whereas Ray is real life and living round here.'

'That's true,' agreed Sadie. 'But Cliff will seem more real when we see him in the flesh next week.'

'Roll on Wednesday,' said Brenda.

'I can't wait,' responded Sadie.

★ ★ ★

Even as the girls approached the cinema on Wednesday they could feel the flash of electricity

19

in the atmosphere. Crowds stood outside, queues of teenagers chanted. There were street traders selling souvenirs and dense traffic jams. Inside the auditorium the place was buzzing with expectancy, a warm and happy multitude of voices creating a roar that sent shivers up Sadie's spine.

When the compere came on the stage to get the show started, the audience cheered and when the man they had all come to see appeared the ovation was so deafening that Sadie and Brenda could hear little of Cliff's first song. But it didn't matter; they were here with their peers and part of the experience.

The Shadows were greeted with shrieks of delight too; every knee bend and hip sway caused a further, even louder eruption. Girls were sobbing with emotion. Sadie was enraptured. It was magic; it was joy. It was like one big party. Seeing Cliff in real life made her feel special. He exceeded her expectations a million times over. His talent was abundant every moment he was on stage. He had rhythm, style, good looks and a warm and melodious singing voice that seemed to physically wash over her. She guessed that everyone in the audience felt as she did, as though he was performing for them alone.

Just before the final curtain came down, a shower of embroidered hearts was thrown on to the stage by some fans in the front rows. Then it was over. The lights were up, the performers had gone and the magic along with them, though some of it lived on in Sadie, who felt uplifted and invulnerable. Because of the competitive nature of teenage youth, she sometimes experienced a sense of not being quite a part of the scene; that it was all happening bigger and better somewhere else. But tonight she felt as though the world belonged to her.

'I'll never forget that show,' she sighed to Brenda as they made their way out slowly with the crowds and headed for the bus stop.

'Me neither,' Brenda responded.

'Blimey, look at the length of the bus queue,' Sadie observed. 'We'll have to wait ages.'

'Gawd knows what time we'll get home,' said Brenda.

But neither of them cared really; they were still glowing in the aftermath of the show.

★　★　★

Four buses came, filled up and went and there were still lots of people in front of Sadie and Brenda in the queue but the crowds in the street were beginning to thin out. On the other side of the road there was a group of boys with scooters who looked like mods.

'One of us had better give them the eye, I think,' suggested Brenda. 'Perhaps we might get a lift home then.'

'That's not a bad idea,' agreed Sadie, glancing over at the group, some of them wearing parkas.

Two of them must have noticed the attention they were getting because they left their scooters and came strolling over. 'Have you been to see the show at the ABC?' one of them asked, looking directly at Sadie.

'Yeah, have you?'

'Not likely,' he said. 'We've been to the Cellar Club. That's much more our sort of thing.'

'You're not Cliff fans then?'

'No. He's more a girl's singer.'

'You don't know what you're missing,' said Sadie.

'We've heard his records so I think we do.'

He smiled at Sadie and, although she could only see him in the street lights, she thought he was gorgeous. He had dark hair with a quiff and a look of Elvis about him. He looked dead smart in a suit with a short jacket, a white shirt and dark tie. Unlike his friend, he wasn't wearing a parka.

She feigned a nonchalant shrug. 'Each to their own, I suppose,' she said.

Looking towards the hordes of people waiting for a bus, he said, 'Looks like you're in for quite a wait.'

'Yeah,' she nodded, looking suitably down-hearted.

'Fancy a lift?'

Looking towards Brenda who was talking to the other boy, she said, 'I couldn't leave my friend on her own. Anyway, we're not local. We live at Hammersmith.'

'I'm in the mood for a bit of a spin.' He was so smitten with her he really thought he would have taken her to Scotland if it meant getting to know her better. He turned to his pal. 'How about it then, Brian? Are you going to be a gentleman and take the young lady's friend to Hammersmith?'

'If that's what her friend wants, yeah, certainly,' Brian said, his eyes gleaming with possibilities.

So the girls hitched up their skirts and clambered on to the chrome-sided Lambrettas.

★   ★   ★

'So, how did it go?' asked Brenda the next day when the girls met in the park in their lunch break to eat their sandwiches, something they did most days. It was chilly and blustery with the odd spot of rain in the air so, naturally, their beloved bouffants were heavily sprayed and protected by headscarves.

'Wonderful,' sighed Sadie. 'His name is Paul Weston, he's lovely and I'm seeing him tonight.'

'Tonight! Blimey, he must be keen if he isn't even going to wait until Saturday.'

'I'm keen too,' Sadie confessed. 'It was love at first sight.'

'That's just plain silly,' admonished Brenda. 'You don't even know him.'

'I know enough to be sure that he's the one for me,' she said, hesitating before biting into an egg sandwich. 'I knew the minute I clapped eyes on him.'

'Now you really are being ridiculous,' disapproved Brenda protectively. 'You're asking to be hurt with ideas like that when you've only just met someone.'

'You just wait and see.' Sadie finished chewing and turned to her friend. 'Anyway, how did you get on with the other one?'

'I didn't. He tried it on so I gave him a kick where the sun doesn't shine. Ugh, what a creep. Just because he gave me a lift home he thought he could take liberties.'

'You wouldn't have minded if you'd fancied him.'

'But I didn't, so I did mind.'

'He did give you a lift home though, so he isn't all bad,' Sadie pointed out.

'He only did it for his own ends.'

'No chance of a foursome then,' said Sadie lightly.

'Not blinking likely! Not with him anyway. It would be a different matter if I managed to get things going with Ray Smart,' Brenda laughed. 'I'd make up a foursome with you anytime then.' She finished her sandwiches and rolled the paper bag into a ball. 'Anyway, what about you and whatsisname? Come on, spill the beans. Let's have all the juicy details.'

'Paul is nineteen, he works in a bank and there aren't any juicy details,' Sadie told her. 'Not the sort you mean anyway. We talked and laughed for ages outside my house. We got on really well and I feel as though I've known him for ages but am excited about the prospect of getting to know him better.'

'Nothing physical then.'

'Not yet.'

'He must be ill.'

'No, he's just a decent sort of a bloke who's waiting until we get to know each other better.'

She giggled. 'Though I hope it doesn't take him too long.'

'Where are you meeting him?' Brenda wanted to know.

'He's coming to pick me up from home.'

'All the way from Kingston,' she said in astonishment. 'Wow, he must be as smitten as you are.'

'He lives even further out than Kingston too, apparently. Some village or other in Surrey,' said Sadie. 'It's a good job he's got a scooter or he'd be marooned, living miles from anywhere.'

'Yeah, they're good, those Lambrettas, and very in. I wouldn't mind one myself if I could afford it,' said Brenda.

'I enjoyed the ride home,' remarked Sadie, 'and I can't wait to go on the scooter again tonight.'

'Lucky thing,' sighed Brenda. 'I'll be at home all on my lonesome. I hope you have a nice time though, kid, with your scooter fella.'

'Thanks, Brenda, I'm sure I will.'

★ ★ ★

Not all members of the Bell family were as thrilled at the idea of Sadie going out on a Lambretta as she was.

'They can be dangerous,' stated her father over the evening meal. 'Not to mention noisy.'

'They're the in thing,' Sadie told him.

'You and flippin' fashion,' said her mother. 'If riding an elephant around Hammersmith Broadway became fashionable, you'd want to do it.'

25

'I wouldn't go quite that far,' said Sadie, giggling.

'I shall have a word with this boy when he comes for you,' announced her mother. 'I'll tell him to make sure he takes good care on the dratted thing while you're on it.'

'It isn't a great big beast of a machine that goes about two hundred miles an hour like the boys have,' Sadie pointed out, referring to her brothers who had shared ownership of a BSA. She paused thoughtfully. 'Anyway, why is it that they go out on their motorbike and no one turns a hair, but I want to go out on a little motor scooter and everyone flies into a panic?'

'Who says no one turns a hair?' said Marge, who had terrible fears about her sons when they were out on their bike.

'You never seem to,' said Sadie.

'She knows we can handle ourselves,' Derek put in. 'Anyway, we're grown men. You're going out with some young boy.'

'He's nineteen,' she pointed out.

'There's no protection on those things, love,' said her father.

'I'll be fine,' Sadie said with the confidence of youth. 'Anyway, none of you will get the chance to say anything to him at all because I'm not bringing him into the house so that you can all give him the once-over and take the mickey if you don't like the look of him. As soon as he arrives I'll go straight out.' She looked appealingly at her mother. 'Can I be let off of the wiping up tonight so that I have plenty of time to get ready? I want to look my best.'

Marge thought about it. 'Go on then, just this

26

once.' But she knew as well as Sadie did that it wouldn't be just a single occasion.

★   ★   ★

Looking out of the window, as soon as Sadie saw Paul pull up outside the house, she flew out of the front door and ran up the path.

'You're quick off the mark,' he said with a welcoming smile. 'You're either ashamed of me or keen to see me.'

She didn't want to appear too eager at this early stage so said, 'I wanted to save you from the third degree. My family are a nosy lot. I'm the youngest and the only girl so you can imagine what they're like when I go out on a date.'

'It wouldn't have worried me if they wanted to check me out,' he said. 'I've got nothing to hide.'

'Perhaps another time,' she said, adding quickly, 'if there is one, of course.'

She saw the answer in his eyes and was thrilled. It wasn't yet fully dark so she could get a proper look at him and she liked what she saw. He was no he-man, being a bit on the lean side, but he was fresh-faced and boyish with expressive eyes of the darkest brown. What Sadie wanted she usually got but she'd never wanted anything before as much as she wanted him as her boyfriend.

'If it's up to me there definitely will be,' he told her warmly.

'Oh . . . good.'

'But what do you fancy doing now?' he asked. 'The Palais or the pictures?'

27

'Dancing would be nice.'

'The Palais it is then,' he said, patting the pillion. 'Hop on.'

Behind the net curtains, the family watched as they chugged off down the road, Sadie riding sidesaddle.

★ ★ ★

They jived, twisted and smooched to rock'n'roll, swing, and standard classics. The atmosphere was warm, vibrant and exciting. Sadie was in her element.

'I don't know why people need purple hearts to have a good time,' she remarked in the interval when they went upstairs to the cafeteria for a soft drink. 'I get high on the music and the mood of the place.'

'Me too. But I suppose some people might want an extra buzz,' he suggested.

She shrugged. 'Are you really a mod? Do you go off to Brighton and Margate making trouble?'

He grinned and she melted. 'Not a proper mod. I just like the clothes,' he confessed. 'The scooter is not so much a badge of my allegiance to the mod movement as a necessity where I live. But yes, I have been to the coast with my Lambretta mates, and no, I didn't get into any trouble.'

'I don't belong to any particular fashion group and I enjoy all sorts of modern music,' Sadie said. 'I just like to dig the scene and be part of things. Dolly birds is what I think people call girls like me who wear their skirts short and have bouffant hair.'

'A very beautiful dolly bird, if I may say so.'

'You may,' she said, lapping it up.

He had a more cultured accent than the people she usually mixed with and he worked in a bank so she guessed that he was ex-grammar school. She hoped he wasn't put off by the fact that any grey matter she might have had had mostly gone unused. Mentally lazy had been the verdict of every teacher she'd ever had. They were probably right. She'd known she could have done better at school but didn't have the interest to tackle anything that took too much of an effort so she concentrated on having fun instead. Fun she really was good at. She did hope she didn't lose him when he realised that she couldn't match him intellectually.

★ ★ ★

Sadie's intellect was the last thing on Paul's mind. He could hardly believe that a girl like her would give him a second glance. Not only was she gorgeous, she was also very 'with-it'. All that lovely blonde hair surrounding her face in a huge, high cloud. Very in! She had the tiniest waist and the shortest skirt this side of the Thames with long legs in knee-high boots. He had no illusions about himself; he wasn't bad-looking but not what a girl would call hunky. In fact he was a bit skinny. There was something else too that he would never admit to her at this stage: he had to wear glasses for close work. No one outside of the bank or his home knew about it and he wasn't about to divulge it to Sadie at this point. That really would destroy his chances.

He was recalled to the present by the sound of the music starting up again.

'Shall we go and show them how it's done!' he suggested.

'Yes, please,' she smiled.

* * *

Marge was still up when Sadie got home. She'd been next door for a cup of tea with her neighbour when they'd got back from Bingo, so she'd been later than usual getting in.

'Did you have a good time, love?' she asked.

'Smashing,' replied Sadie and her mother had never seen her so radiant.

'Nice boy then, is he?'

'Very.' Sadie was so full of thoughts and feelings, she wanted to go to bed and hug them to herself. She put her arms around her mother. 'I will tell you all about him tomorrow, Mum, but I want to go to bed now if you don't mind.'

'Course I don't mind. Off you go. Sleep well.'

As Marge washed some cups at the sink she felt an unaccountable sense of change. Her daughter was usually full of it when she'd been out on a date. But there was something different about her tonight. The boy must be very special. She hoped he was a good sort and didn't hurt her. Time will tell, she thought, as she made her way up to bed.

* * *

'Have you had a good time, son?' asked Paul's mother, Harriet, when he got home.

'Yes, very good thanks, Mum,' he said.

'Where did you go?'

'Dancing.' He was preoccupied with thoughts of Sadie and not feeling very talkative.

'You're later than usual,' she commented.

'Mmm, I've been in London. Hammersmith actually.'

'That's a long stretch for a weeknight when you've got to get up for work in the morning, isn't it?' Lately she'd had to be careful to make her tone conversational rather than admonitory because he tended to be overly sensitive about the fact that he was an adult and needed privacy. 'It must have been something a bit special.'

'It was. Very special,' he confirmed.

'Really? Why is that?'

'I've met this wonderful girl,' he replied dreamily. 'She's really fabulous.'

'I see . . . '

'I'm off to bed,' he said, wanting to be on his own. 'Night, Mum.'

A stout woman in a dark red dressing-gown, her iron-grey hair clamped to her head by a heavy brown hairnet, Harriet was frowning as she turned off the lights and went up the stairs. Really fabulous, eh, she thought, as she got into bed. We'll soon see about that!

31

2

'I really miss you, Sadie, since you've been courting and I don't see so much of you,' confessed Brenda. 'It isn't the same going out of an evening with the girls from work.'

'Sorry if I've been neglecting you.' Sadie tried to find time for her friend but her feelings for Paul dominated her life to such an extent, she found it difficult to think about anything else. 'But we do meet most days at lunchtime.'

'It isn't the same as us hanging out together like we used to.' Brenda heaved a wistful sigh. 'Still, I expect I'd be the same if I met someone special.'

'You would if you felt like I do,' she told her. 'I'm absolutely besotted with him, Bren.'

'You're telling me. Talk about love's young dream. You're so lucky. I wish I had a bloke.'

'You'll meet someone soon, I'm sure,' Sadie said encouragingly. 'You're a good-looking girl and it could happen out of the blue like it did for me; your whole life changes almost in an instant.'

It was Sunday morning and the two friends were in Sadie's bedroom, which was wholeheartedly feminine with pink decor, a frilly bedcover and a collection of cheap perfume and make-up on the dressing table. Sadie was sitting on the bed with Pickles snoozing on her lap while Brenda relaxed in a white-painted wicker chair.

Having considered her friend's comments, Brenda said, 'As you say, it can happen when you're least expecting it. I still can't get over how quickly it happened for you. One day the two of us were out together all the time, having a laugh, the next you're courting strong and out of circulation. You've only known him a month and already you see him nearly every night.'

'And he comes to tea on Sundays,' Sadie added. 'We just can't stay away from each other. The only drawback is that we live at such a distance from each other, it's a long way for him to come. Even if I meet him halfway, he insists on bringing me home so he's having a lot of late nights, bless him.'

'Your family like him too.'

She nodded. 'Amazingly he gets on well with my brothers, even though he's not their type at all, him being a bit posh. But he's interested in motorbikes so that makes him acceptable, though they tease him about his scooter something awful; not manly enough for Derek and Don.' She paused, mulling things over. 'I'm pleased the family like him but don't think it would make any difference to my feelings for him if they didn't.'

'You have got it bad,' said Brenda. 'When are you going to meet his people?'

'This afternoon as it happens,' she replied. 'I'm going to his house for tea.'

'Ooh, that's a bit daunting.'

'You're telling me and I am a bit nervous but looking forward to it too, because it's the next step and shows he's serious about me,' she said. 'Anyway, if his parents are anything like him, they'll be lovely.'

'You seem very confident about him.'

'I don't mean to seem smug,' Sadie told her. 'It's just that . . . because of the way we are when we're together it's difficult not to feel positive about his feelings for me.'

'It must be fantastic to be that sure,' sighed Brenda wistfully.

'It doesn't pay to be overconfident so I'm trying to keep my feet on the ground.' Sadie pondered for moment. 'How about you and I go to the pictures one night next week,' she suggested in an effort to compensate for putting Paul first. She really was fond of Brenda and missed her even though she was so taken up with her love life.

'What about lover boy?'

'I'm sure we can survive for one night without seeing each other,' she said, adding with a grin, 'only just though.'

★ ★ ★

'Would you like another piece of fruitcake, dear?' offered Paul's mother, Harriet.

'Yes please, Mrs Weston,' said Sadie politely. 'It's delicious.'

'Thank you,' she said, sounding pompous. 'I've never had any complaints about my cakes so far.'

The last thing on Paul's mind was his mother's culinary expertise. 'You can have seconds without worrying about your waistline,' he said, looking at his girlfriend adoringly. 'Because you have the most fantastic figure.'

'Paul,' Sadie admonished, colouring up. 'You're embarrassing me.'

'I'm only saying what's true.' He glanced towards his parents. 'Mum and Dad will back me up on that, won't you? Isn't she the most gorgeous girl you've ever come across? Now that you've seen her in the flesh you know that I haven't been exaggerating.'

His father, Gerald, cleared his throat awkwardly. Such personal remarks were almost unheard of in this family. 'Yes indeed,' he said stiffly.

Harriet nodded but she was actually appalled at her son's choice of girlfriend. All that dreadful black eye make-up, the tight sweater that left little to the imagination and, worst of all, the hem of her skirt was indecently high. Her hair wasn't as nature intended either. No one could be that blonde without some chemical assistance. As for her ghastly diction, her speech was littered with dropped 'H's and glottal stops.

'I understand from Paul that your father is a carpenter,' she remarked conversationally.

'Yeah. That's right.'

'Specially commissioned finely carved furniture; that sort of thing?'

'No, he works on building sites mostly,' Sadie informed her breezily. 'The building trade is booming at the moment with so many new homes being built so he has plenty of work.'

This was getting worse by the moment. The

Bells were obviously not in the same league as the Westons, thought Harriet, whose husband was a partner in an old and respected accountancy practice.

'I love to watch a good tradesman at work,' remarked Gerald amiably. 'I can't even put up a picture myself without making a mess of it.'

'My dad can do anything,' said Sadie proudly. 'He's very good with his hands.'

Probably not much going on in the upper level, thought Harriet snobbishly, but said, 'Very admirable.'

'I think so too. Dad is a great believer in a man having a trade behind him,' Sadie said effusively. 'That's why he encouraged my brothers to do an apprenticeship. They're both car mechanics.'

Gerald gave a wry grin and said in a jokey manner, 'I know where to come when the car needs fixing then.'

While Sadie said politely that she was sure her brothers would be only too pleased to accommodate him, Harriet was busy imagining sweaty men in oily overalls with dirty hands sitting at the meal table. 'On the subject of occupations,' she said, looking at Sadie, 'I suppose Paul will have told you about the exams he has to do at the bank.'

'Er . . . I think he might have mentioned something about some exams,' she said vaguely.

'He obviously hasn't told you how important they are to his career.'

'Well no, I don't think he has, but I can guess how much they matter.'

Paul gave his mother a sharp glance then

36

turned to his girlfriend. 'It's all right, Sadie. Mum still hasn't grasped the idea that I have actually left school.'

'Don't be rude to your mother,' rebuked Gerald.

'Well, honestly . . . ' Paul began.

'Perhaps you and I can work together on it, Sadie,' suggested Harriet artfully. 'You can help me to encourage him to concentrate on his career.'

'Er, yes.' Sadie wasn't sure what this entailed. 'If I can, I'd be happy to.'

'Mum means that I should stay in every night to swot for the exams and go to bed early so that I'm fresh for work the next day,' put in Paul.

'Oh, I see.' Sadie's face fell at the idea of not being able to see him.

'Not every night,' corrected Harriet, 'just a bit more often than you do now. All these late nights must be affecting your performance at the bank.'

'I'm quite old enough to choose my own bedtime, Mum,' Paul pointed out, looking peeved.

'Just thinking of your future,' said his mother.

'I'll take care of my future,' he stated firmly, 'and in the present I intend to enjoy myself while I'm young.'

Sadie was beginning to feel most uncomfortable as the tension grew around her. Helping someone to stay at home to study of an evening was a new experience for her, as was worrying about her boyfriend's bedtime. People of her ilk were free to do as they pleased after work and didn't have bothersome careers to nurture. She and Paul were young and in love. When they were together, nothing else mattered. It was immaterial to Sadie that Paul lived in a big posh house in a tree-lined avenue with a gleaming car in the drive. Those things were of no consequence to her. He was her boyfriend and part of her life. But the nature of the conversation was beginning to make her realise just how different their backgrounds were.

'Anyway, shall we drop the subject?' suggested Paul's father tactfully.

'Good idea, Dad,' agreed Paul.

'I'll go and make some more tea,' said Harriet and left the room while Sadie concentrated on the new and delicate business of eating cake with a little fork.

★ ★ ★

Waiting for the kettle to boil in the kitchen, Harriet tried to calm herself. She had let her heart rule her head and antagonised her son, the last thing she intended. She needed to be clever; to go along with the way things were and let the romance run its course and fizzle out, which it undoubtedly would. Paul was her only child and her pride and joy and she wasn't going to let some common Cockney girl with no class steal him away from her. But she had to change her tactics or she would drive him even deeper into her arms. She'd managed not to lose him to university by persuading him to take the job at the bank in such a way that he thought it was all his own idea, so dealing with Sadie Bell should be a breeze, as long as she kept her head.

She made the tea and went back to the table.

'So, Sadie dear, did I tell you what pretty hair you have . . . such a lovely colour.'

'Thank you, Mrs Weston.'

Seeing the pleasure on her son's face as she complimented the awful creature, Harriet thought it was well worth a little play-acting to get back into his favour. Yes, that was the path she would take.

* * *

'It's really beautiful here, isn't it?' observed Sadie later that same day as she and Paul stood at Solomon's Memorial on Box Hill, looking out across the South Downs with the town of Dorking in the foreground. It was a gloriously verdant landscape dotted here and there with clusters of houses, a church spire in the distance, hills beyond sweeping and sloping in various shades of green. 'I've never been much of a country girl but I love it here. It's absolutely gorgeous. I came here once for a day out on a Sunday-school outing but it didn't register then in the same way as it does now.'

'Must be because you're with me,' he said teasingly.

'It is, most definitely,' she confirmed, being serious. 'I know there are a lot of people here but there is still so much open space. It feels like our special place.'

'I've been coming here all my life but it seems different to be here with you.'

'Ah, that's so sweet,' she responded. 'When we're old and grey, we'll remember how we loved to come up here when we were courting.'

'We're never going to be old and grey,' he laughed. 'I shall be nineteen forever.'

'Together we'll have eternal youth.' She paused, her brow furrowing. 'On a more serious note,' she began. 'Am I to send you home early from now on?'

'Don't you dare,' was his instant response.

'Seriously, Paul, you should have told me how important your exams are,' she admonished. 'I don't come from that sort of background and didn't realise that I was interfering with your career.'

'You're not.' He smiled at her, watching the spring breeze lift some loose wisps of hair from her face. 'When I'm with you, work is the last thing on my mind. Anyway, it's all under control.'

'How can it be? If you're out with me every night?'

'I get up early to do some study if I need to,' he explained. 'And at lunchtimes. Mum has the whole thing out of proportion.'

'What are the exams for?'

'Standard procedure to progress upwards in the bank,' he replied. 'I chose to do that rather than go to university. I'm very glad I did too. I might not have met you if I'd gone away.'

'University,' she said, awestruck. 'Oh Paul, you and I live in such different worlds.'

'University isn't just for the nobs nowadays, you know,' he said. 'Ordinary people can get in these days, which is why I could have gone.'

'You're not as ordinary as I am, in that sense,' she pointed out. 'I don't know one single person who even stayed on at school, let alone went to university.'

'So what?'

'So, our backgrounds are miles apart.'

'Not really. All right, so Dad's a professional but he isn't rich.'

'What about the posh house and the car in the drive?'

'He's got a mortgage.'

'We have a rent book and no drive, let alone a car to put in it.'

Paul took her in his arms and gave her a reassuring hug then led her away from the people who were gathering to look at the view.

'None of those things are important to me,' he assured her as they walked on. 'Tradesman or professional, rent book or mortgage; what does it matter?'

'It matters because I am dumb and you are clever,' she stated categorically.

'You are not dumb, Sadie,' he disagreed, frowning darkly. 'You shouldn't put yourself down.'

'I'm not putting myself down, honestly. I like being a dumb blonde. Clever is boring to me,' she told him. 'I don't want serious things in my life; just fun, enjoyment and glamour. So you'll be bored stiff with me when you get to know me better.'

'Sounds as though you're the one who'll be bored with me,' he responded. 'Anyway, I reckon

I know you pretty well now and bored is the last thing I am.'

'But I don't know you, that's the point I'm making,' Sadie said. 'I realised that as soon as I walked into your house and met your folks.'

'Well, you'll just have to get to know me better then, won't you?' he said. 'Because I'm not letting you go.'

'Thank goodness for that,' she said with a wry grin. 'But I can tell you here and now that I won't be signing up for self-improvement classes.'

'I should hope not,' he said. 'You're absolutely fine just the way you are.'

As they walked, arms entwined, along winding paths, through woodland burgeoning with fresh new leaves and then began to make their way back to the car park where they had left the scooter, it occurred to Paul that Sadie had no idea of her own worth or how much she meant to him. He loved her so much it was painful, and he wanted to be with her all of the time, which meant that he was in a permanent state of turmoil and exhaustion from all the late nights, though he would never tell her that. The geographical distance between them was a real drawback and he didn't know what to do about it.

'Beat you to the car park,' said Sadie and tore off down the hill with him in hot pursuit.

Because she had taken him by surprise, she was there before him and chatting to a young man when he arrived. Paul was quite unprepared for the violent feelings this evoked in him. He was beside himself with jealousy and rage.

'Oi,' he shouted to the stranger. 'Leave her alone.'

'Just passing the time of day, mate,' said the man, about to get on to his motorbike. 'So keep your hair on.'

'Clear off,' yelled Paul.

The man gave him a hard look, frowning. 'I've got as much right to be in this car park as you have so keep your mouth shut,' he warned.

'You've no right to be near my girlfriend.'

'Paul,' intervened Sadie, embarrassed. 'Calm down for goodness' sake. He hasn't done anything wrong. We were just talking.'

'He's all over you,' claimed Paul, grabbing the man by the arm. 'You just keep away from her.'

She dashed forward and seized Paul's arm, trying to pull him away. 'He was only being friendly,' she tried to explain, her voice rising, 'so stop this nonsense now, please.'

But he was deaf to her pleas and dragged the man away from his bike.

'It was me,' she screamed. 'I spoke to him first. It was just a few words.'

At last Paul seemed to come to his senses and let the man go.

'You wanna get your head looked at, mate,' he said, brushing himself down and pulling his jacket back into place. 'You need treatment.'

'I'm very sorry,' Sadie apologised. 'I don't know what came over him.'

'Yeah, I'm sorry too,' added Paul. 'It was a genuine misunderstanding.'

'All right,' muttered the man, though he didn't look happy. 'You wanna watch yourself though, mate. Not everyone will be as understanding as I am. You could get a right beating if you carry on like that.'

As soon as the man was out of earshot, Sadie turned on Paul. 'What on earth got into you, carrying on like a madman?' she demanded angrily. 'I've never been so embarrassed in my life.'

'Sorry, Sadie.' He seemed genuinely contrite.

'I should blinking well think so too. It was completely uncalled for.'

'All right, Sadie,' he said, his voice gruff with emotion, 'I have apologised. Can we let it go now?'

Realising that he really was upset, she linked her arm through his and said, 'Okay, let's forget all about it and enjoy the rest of the time we have together.'

'Yeah, let's do that,' he agreed but he was very subdued.

'Come on, don't let it spoil the day. Truth is, I quite enjoyed you being the he-man.' She paused and gave him a serious look. 'As long as you make that the last time.'

'I'll try but you bring out the caveman in me.'

She burst out laughing. 'As long as you don't try to drag me along by my hair.' She slipped her arms around him. 'We're friends again now. So give us a kiss.'

He didn't need a second bidding and by the time they got back to Sadie's that evening, the incident was put behind them, if not forgotten.

★ ★ ★

'Did you have a nice day, Sadie?' asked her mother that night after Paul had brought her home and left. Her brothers were still out and her father had gone to bed. Marge was in the kitchen in her dressing-gown.

'Yeah, it was good,' she replied.

'How did it go with his folks?'

'His mum and dad are quite posh,' she told her mother. 'A big house and all that.'

'Ooh, I say.'

'They're not at all like Paul, though,' she went on. 'He's not a bit stuck up.'

'They are then, I take it.'

'His dad was nice but his mum seemed a bit snooty,' Sadie said. 'I got the feeling she was looking down her nose at me the whole time, though she wasn't too obvious about it.'

'Blimin' cheek,' said Marge. 'You're as good as them any day of the week.'

'I know that, Mum.' It wouldn't even occur to Sadie to be put down by anyone of the older generation. Members of her own peer group could do it very easily but Mr and Mrs Weston couldn't touch her; their views were of no importance to her at this stage because her life was centred around youth. 'It didn't worry me in the least,' she said. 'I go out with Paul, not them. He is part of the same scene as me, even though he is a bit posh, and that's what matters to me.'

'He's just a boyfriend anyway,' her mother reminded her. 'It isn't as though you're going to marry him or anything, is it? You'll go out with

45

lots of boys before you need to worry about their parents.'

Sadie made allowances for her mother, who obviously knew nothing about love so couldn't possibly understand how she felt about Paul. But she didn't want to discuss it so she just said, 'Yeah, I suppose I will.'

'Would you like a cup of cocoa, love?'

'Not for me, thanks, Mum,' she said. 'I think I'll go straight up to bed.'

'All right then. See you in the morning.'

'Night, Mum.'

Marge was thoughtful as she put the cereal bowls out and set the table for breakfast in the morning. Sadie was seeing an awful lot of this boyfriend of hers and her enthusiasm for him didn't seem to be diminishing. Marge hoped to God she wasn't so keen on him she found herself in trouble. Daughters were a worry as regards that, given the power of passion in even the most sensible of girls. Still, Sadie might be a bit headstrong and irresponsible but she was a good girl at heart and young girls fell in and out of love all the time. Paul would probably be history this time next month.

★ ★ ★

Spring turned to summer, the leaves began to fall and Sadie and Paul's romance showed no sign of abating, much to the astonishment of both sets of parents. Paul's scooter still clocked up the miles from London to Surrey and the couple's feelings for each other grew even stronger. Longing to be alone together, they spent a lot of time in the leafy glades of Box Hill and Sadie grew to love the open air and the countryside as they walked through carpets of russet leaves and felt the weather turn, the scent of wood smoke filling the air.

She was a town girl at heart though, and still wanted to be part of the pop scene which — she was beginning to realise — didn't only exist in Central London. There was plenty of music and dancing on offer further out.

One autumn evening they decided to go to the dance hall that people were talking about on Eel Pie Island, a small island in the Thames at Twickenham.

'It's a whole lot different to the Palais anyway,' said Sadie after they left the scooter on the embankment and walked with crowds of other young people over a footbridge on to the island, and then headed through the trees where music could already be heard coming from the Eel Pie Hotel. Paul had told her that the hotel had once been the last word in elegance. It was a nineteenth-century building that had hosted genteel tea dances in the 1920s and '30s but was now a dilapidated nightspot that was a magnet to teenagers from all over London's suburbs. 'It seems a bit run down and there are a lot of arty types around.'

'It started as a jazz club but they have a lot of R and B bands playing here now. People come for the music as much as the dancing.'

'And the rest,' she said, observing couples snogging in the shadows even at this early stage of the evening.

'If we don't like it we'll leave.'

The dance hall was dimly lit and smoky. People were squashed together on the dance floor and the music was much grittier than they played at the Palais. This was loud, vibrant and sexy. There was a sleaziness about the place that created a kind of magic. Sadie thought it was the strangest place she had ever been to, completely unique.

'So this is rhythm and blues,' she remarked.

'Yeah,' replied Paul, shouting above the sound of electric guitars. 'Do you like it?'

'I'm not sure,' she said.

'We can leave if you want to,' said Paul, wondering if he should have brought his girlfriend to this place that was unashamedly louche.

'Oh no, I don't want to go,' said Sadie, who embraced new experiences and was enjoying herself. 'It's just that it's so different to what we're accustomed to and I have to get used to it. The band is brilliant but very informal and young.'

'By informal, you mean the longer hair?'

'And the casual clothes. No black jackets like the musicians at the Palais wear.'

'As they are an unknown group I suppose they think they can dress as they like. Good for them, I say. I like their look.'

'I think it's great too,' she said.

The music was beginning to appeal to Sadie.

'Come on, let's dance,' she said, 'if we can find any space.'

They joined the mass of couples in a dance somewhere between the twist and a slow jive but more seductive. Sadie and Paul just kept on going, the floor bouncing beneath the weight of so many dancing feet. The reason for this, someone told them, was because the sprung floor was rotting underneath.

'I'm having such a good time,' she told him in the interval when they got some drinks from the bar and sat outside gazing at the dark waters of the Thames in the moonlight.

'Me too,' he said.

'Funny how a band you've never heard of in some dusty, dilapidated venue can create such a fabulous atmosphere, isn't it?' she observed. 'We'll have to look out for them in the future. Find out where else they play around here. What are they called?'

'The Rolling Stones, I think someone said.'

'We must try to remember that,' she suggested. 'It's a pity they're not well-known. We could buy their records if they were. They are so good.'

'If they were famous they probably wouldn't play in a place like this.'

'There is that. But come on, the music has started again so finish your drink and let's get back to the dancing,' she said, flushed and full of energy.

'Anything you say, your ladyship,' he laughed.

★ ★ ★

49

As they came out into the night at the end of the evening, the air infused with the ambrosial scent of autumn, and headed across the bridge to where the scooter was parked, Sadie paused, looking at the reflection of the moon on the water, the trees swaying in the shadows. 'It was a smashing night, Paul,' she said. 'Thanks for taking me.'

'Thank you for coming.'

'We should be past all those polite formalities by now,' she told him. 'We love being together. End of story. I'm sorry you've got to take me all the way back to Hammersmith before you set off for home, though. It's a drag for you all the time. If you weren't such a gentleman you'd let me go on the train or bus.'

'There's a much better solution,' he said.

'For me to stay overnight at your place, you mean?'

'Better than that. Much better.'

'You stay at mine.'

'No.'

'What then?'

'I think we should get married,' he announced.

She laughed, not taking him seriously. 'To cut down on travelling? That's a bit drastic.'

'No. Because I love you and want to be with you all the time,' he stated solemnly.

'Oh Paul, that is so lovely,' she said, throwing her arms around him. 'So you want to get engaged.'

'Only briefly,' he whispered into her hair. 'I want to get married as soon as possible.'

She drew away slightly and looked into his

50

face in the moonlight. 'Me too. But there is a procedure to these things,' she reminded him. 'You get engaged and save up for a couple of years, then comes the wedding.'

'So we break with convention,' he suggested, enthusiasm growing with every word. 'The technicalities will have to be worked out, of course, but — if it's all right with you — I'd like us to be married by Christmas.'

'What! But it isn't much more than two months away.'

'Exactly.'

'It's a lovely idea but we've no money behind us; nowhere to live.'

'We'll find somewhere, a bedsit or something, and we'll build up from there. We'd spend a lot less money too if we were married because we wouldn't have to keep going out to places to be together,' he said. 'Just think, Sadie, no more long-distance courting. We'd be at home together.'

'It would be lovely,' she responded dreamily. 'But I don't see how we can do it.'

'All right, I know it seems a bit quick and unconventional. But I love you so much, if we can get it organised, will you do it, Sadie, will you be my wife?'

'Yes, Paul, I will,' she said excitedly.

They continued across the bridge, arms entwined.

★ ★ ★

'Married by Christmas,' gasped Marge, having heard the news the next morning at breakfast.

51

'Bloody hell,' added Cyril.

'Whoops, do we hear the patter of tiny feet?' joshed Derek.

'Ooh Sadie, you naughty girl,' put in Don.

'Don't be so disgusting, you two,' objected Sadie. 'It's nothing like that.'

'Why the hurry then?' asked her father.

'Exactly,' added her mother.

'We're in love and we want to be together,' she said simply. 'He's going to do things properly and ask Dad formally when he comes for me tonight.'

'That's something, I suppose,' said her father.

'Even apart from the fact that you have nowhere to live and nothing behind you,' put in her mother, 'we can't possibly get a wedding organised in such a short time.'

'We don't want anything fancy, Mum,' Sadie told her. 'Just a registry-office do and a few sandwiches back here.'

'No booze up,' said Derek disapprovingly. 'That's the best part of a wedding.'

'Trust you to lower the tone,' admonished his sister.

'Surely you wouldn't want to miss out on your white wedding with all the trimmings,' said Marge, full of concern. 'A girl's special big day.'

'If it means being able to get married quickly, I don't mind missing out on the trimmings,' she assured her. 'As it is now, we are both permanently exhausted because of all the travelling. We need to be together.'

'You're young with your life ahead of you,' her mother pointed out. 'This time next year you

52

might feel altogether differently about Paul.'

'I won't, Mum, honestly,' she said with complete confidence. 'He's the one for me.'

'He does seem a decent-enough bloke, I must admit,' put in Derek.

'She could do a lot worse,' added Don.

'I reckon he'd look after her,' was Cyril's opinion.

'She's far too young and immature to be thinking of getting married,' stated Marge, once again outnumbered by the men of the family.

'Paul and I are getting married, Mum, one way or the other,' declared Sadie meaningfully. 'Even if we have to elope.'

'Gretna Green here they come,' teased Don. 'Ooh, Sadie, you'll be in the local paper.'

'Don't threaten me, Sadie,' warned her mother firmly. 'I only want what's best for you.'

'I know you do and this is best for me, Mum. Honestly, I want this so much.'

'Like the clothes and the dance tickets that you *absolutely must* have and always get your own way about,' she said. 'Marriage is a serious commitment, Sadie. It isn't all fun and romance. It's about hard work and sacrifice, pulling your weight and putting someone else before yourself.'

'I'm talking about marriage, Mum, not joining the foreign legion,' said Sadie heatedly.

'That's enough of your lip,' said Marge.

'Let's all calm down, shall we?' suggested Cyril, finishing his tea and rising. 'We'll talk about it again tonight. I have to go to work now.'

There was a tense atmosphere after he left but

Sadie's brothers soon dispersed it.

'At least you won't have to worry about us getting hitched, Mum,' said Derek. 'We're steering well clear of that particular minefield.'

'Paul must be off his rocker,' agreed Don.

'If it was you two I wouldn't be arguing. I'd be helping you on your way,' said Marge. 'You're old enough to look after yourselves.'

'Your comments about commitment and sacrifice reminded me why we don't want to do it,' chortled Derek.

'We're far too selfish,' added Don.

'So is your sister.'

'Thanks very much, Mum,' said Sadie huffily.

'It's because you're young and you've always been a bit spoilt,' Marge explained. 'You need time to mature a bit before you should even think about getting married.'

'I'm getting married and that's all there is to it,' she snapped then got up from the table.

'Which just goes to prove my point,' said Marge as Sadie left the room in a sulk. 'If she doesn't get her own way she has a tantrum. She doesn't yet have the ability to give and take that she would need as a married woman.'

'Paul will put his foot down if she comes it too much,' said Derek. 'She'll soon get the hang of it.'

'It's all just a game to her,' pronounced Marge. 'Something exciting to tell her friends. She hasn't the first idea of the seriousness of marriage.'

'Maybe she hasn't but she's very determined, Mum,' Derek pointed out, 'and what Sadie wants, Sadie usually gets. One way or another!'

'We'll see,' said Marge, sighing. She couldn't deny the truth of what he said.

* * *

Paul received a similar reaction to the news.

'The whole idea is ludicrous,' said his mother, having been told of his plans and established that pregnancy wasn't the reason. 'You're much too young.'

'People get married younger than that,' he pointed out. 'I was hoping you'd be pleased for me.'

'It is a bit soon to take such a step, isn't it, my boy?' said his mild-mannered father. 'If you're really serious about the girl, why not get engaged and have the wedding in two or three years' time like most people do.'

'Because that isn't what I want,' Paul stated categorically. 'I love her and want to be with her.' He didn't add that he didn't just *want* to be married to her; he *needed* to be. He couldn't tell anyone how terrified he was of losing her. A beautiful girl like Sadie could have anyone, certainly someone more handsome and sexy than a skinny bank clerk with muscles like soft-boiled eggs. He needed the security of marriage because he honestly didn't think he could live without her.

'You should be concentrating on your career, not thinking about tying yourself down to a girl you've only known for five minutes,' his mother lectured.

'I've known her for more than six months and she's the girl for me,' he declared. 'Anyway, Sadie will support me in my career.'

'What about her job?'

'I don't know what will happen about that yet,' he said. 'It depends where we live.'

'You can't leave this area because of your career at the bank,' pronounced Harriet. 'She'll be the one who has to change if you do go through with this harebrained scheme.'

'Those sorts of details will be sorted out between the two of us,' he told her.

'You don't know the first thing about marriage,' his mother reminded him.

'I don't suppose anyone does until they experience it for themselves, do they?' he came back at her. 'I don't see how they can.'

'Someone more mature would be ready to settle down,' she pointed out. 'You certainly are not.'

'The thing is, Mum,' he began in a controlled tone, his gaze fixed firmly on her, 'Sadie and I are going to do this with or without our parents' blessing, somehow. I've never been more serious about anything in my life.'

His determined attitude suddenly registered with alarming clarity and frightened Harriet because she knew he meant it and she wasn't ready to lose her boy. In fact, she doubted if she ever would be. So she had to come up with a plan, and quickly.

'I suppose, if you're absolutely determined to get married, you could always live here, rather than paying the earth in rent,' she suggested artfully. 'Sadie would need to change her job to save all the travelling but you, Paul, could stay where you are. We've plenty of space; you could have two rooms upstairs. We could even have a sink and a cooker put into the box room so that you could be more self-contained.'

Two pairs of eyes stared at her in astonishment.

'That's a sudden change of heart, isn't it, dear?' suggested Gerald.

'Yeah,' added Paul, looking at her suspiciously. 'You were dead-set against it just now.'

'I still am very much against it — I think it's a ridiculous idea — but I can see that your mind is made up, so your father and I might as well get used to the idea and do what we can to help instead of opposing you,' she said.

'Do you mean it?' Paul asked, a hesitant smile beginning to light up his face.

'I wouldn't have said it if I didn't,' she confirmed, forcing a casual air. 'Obviously you'll have to speak to Sadie about it but the offer is there if you want it.'

'How would you feel about it, Dad?' Paul asked considerately. 'Would you mind having your home turned upside down to accommodate a couple of newly weds?'

'Whatever your mother decides is all right with me,' Gerald said predictably. It was common knowledge who was the boss in that marriage.

Paul smiled at them both. 'You're a couple of stars and I'm so glad to have you on our side,' he told them. 'It really means a lot to me.'

'Good, I'm pleased,' said his mother graciously.

'I hope we can win Sadie's parents over too. We want everyone to be happy about it.'

'Anything we can do to help the two of you, you only have to ask,' offered Harriet.

Paul went over and wrapped his arms around her. 'Thanks, Mum. What would I do without you?'

If I have my way you'll never have to, she thought, but said, 'You'd manage.'

Harriet was delighted with herself, having turned a potential disaster into a blessing. An early marriage wasn't such a bad thing after all. This way she kept her son close and would have control without him even knowing it. He and Sadie were young and vulnerable and would be grateful to her and Gerald for the accommodation. Had he waited until he was more mature his bride might have been more difficult to manipulate. As it was Harriet would be on hand to help whenever they needed it. Oh yes, this was going to work out better than ever.

Naturally, of course, she would appear to be the perfect mother-in-law . . .

3

One thing the Bell family excelled at was rising to the occasion and they did so magnificently for Sadie's wedding. Once they realised that it was a *fait accompli*, no effort was spared to make sure she had a day to remember, albeit not as grand as it would have been, had they had more time.

By arranging the nuptials for a Friday instead of the traditional Saturday, they managed to get a booking at the church and a function room at the local pub. Savings were drawn, resources pooled and Sadie, Brenda and Marge descended on Oxford Street in search of a wedding dress, bridesmaid's frock and an outfit for the mother of the bride. A pal of Derek and Don's organised a small band for the reception at special cheap rates.

Sadie had expected nothing less from her family; she had never doubted that she would get her own way about the wedding because the pattern of her life had given her certain expectations. But she was appreciative and became so overcome with gratitude and happiness, she broke with tradition and made a speech at the reception after the best man, bridegroom and father of the bride had spoken.

'I want to thank my lovely mum and dad and brothers for making this day so wonderful for us,' she began. 'Paul and I dropped a bombshell on them by wanting such a quick wedding. They weren't happy about it but they have come up trumps as usual. My family have organised all this for us and Paul's parents have very kindly offered us a place to live in their house. Both families have clubbed together and treated us to a posh hotel for our wedding night. Thanks, all of you, so much; for the presents and for being here today.'

There were cheers and whistles and the party carried on, the tables cleared and moved to the sides of the room, the small band ready to start their set. The happy couple swept on to the floor and led the dancing to the Elvis Presley hit 'Can't Help Falling in Love'.

'This is the happiest day of my life,' Sadie said to Paul, her arms around his neck, her face close to his.

'Mine too,' he whispered into her hair. 'No one could be as much in love as we are today.'

'They certainly couldn't.'

He kissed her and the onlookers emitted a communal 'Aaah'.

★　★　★

Quietly observing the scene from a table with other friends of the Bell family, Ray Smart was feeling emotional but in a different way to the other guests. He was pleased, of course, to see Sadie so happy; she was a lovely kid even though she was spoilt rotten. But that wasn't what had brought a lump to his throat.

Family occasions like this one always had a profound effect on him. Seeing the bond that

60

existed between his pals and their folks caused a dragging sensation in the pit of his stomach. He didn't begrudge them, it wasn't in his nature; anyway the Bells were the nearest thing he had to a family and they meant a lot to him. But in reality, he wasn't one of them. He wasn't a part of anything and he longed for that sense of belonging.

The loneliness he'd experienced when he had first come to Hammersmith from Essex had driven him almost to desperation at times. It got easier once he'd begun to make friends. But even then he had always felt different because everyone else went home to their families and he went back to his lodgings. He'd soon learned to create a protective shell so that no one would ever know when he had his dark times. His past life had made him very self-reliant and that had stood him in good stead as an adult.

He'd first met the Bell brothers at the garage where they all worked as apprentice car mechanics and they had soon become mates. After he'd finished his national service he'd decided that a lifetime in car repairs wasn't for him. He fancied something more entrepreneurial. So, after a spell working on the record counter in a music shop where he'd gained some useful experience, he'd set up on his own with one of the most popular commodities of the times: pop records, which he sold initially from a suitcase on the street and then from a market stall, where he added classical titles and second-hand musical instruments to his stock.

The stall didn't provide him with a fortune

but he earned enough to live decently, pay the rent on a flat of his own and run a car. Ambitiously driven, he was working towards moving his business into a shop before too long. So he had no complaints about life. He had good mates and girlfriends didn't seem too hard to come by, though there was no one special at the moment.

His reverie was interrupted by a female voice.

'Fancy a dance?' invited Brenda, flushed and emboldened by the wine they'd had with the meal and resplendent in her bridesmaid regalia, a blue satin dress and a matching headdress carefully arranged to fit around her bouffant.

He smiled at her. 'Isn't it customary for a man to do the asking?' he said.

'I've changed the rules,' she told him.

'You'll get yourself in trouble, approaching men,' he warned her jokingly.

'Good. I can't wait.'

He grinned. 'You've got some front, I'll say that much for you, and I think you've had a drink too many.'

'Maybe I have but my best friend is moving out to the sticks, so I'm trying to deaden the pain of having to live without her,' she explained, giggling drunkenly. 'Anyway, this is a party so let's have some fun.'

One of his pals, sitting next to him, said close to his ear, 'Go for it, mate; you're well in there.'

'She's just a kid,' Ray replied.

'I'm old enough to know who I want to dance with,' Brenda chipped in, having caught the gist. 'So are you coming with me or not? Come on.

Let your hair down and have a good time.'

'Yeah, why not,' he said, rising and taking her hand. 'You can show me how it's done.'

They went on to the dance floor as the band started playing 'Let's Twist Again' and got their hips swinging with the rest of the dancers. Brenda twisted so low at one point Ray was amazed that she managed to stay on her feet. But Brenda was an expert and could out-twist anyone without so much as a wobble. Now that the formalities were over and the booze flowing, people young and old were really beginning to lose their inhibitions and enjoy themselves. Everybody was singing along with the music.

★　★　★

'It's been very nice, Marjorie,' said Harriet, who insisted on using Marge's full name since the shortened version was a little common for her taste. 'You've done very well.'

'Thank you,' responded Marge pleasantly, though she couldn't bear Paul's mother with her exaggerated posh accent and superior attitude. Flushed from a good few port and lemons, Marge was looking smart in a pale blue dress and jacket, her hair having a salon shine from a rare visit to the hairdressers. She glanced towards the dance floor. 'They all seem to be enjoying themselves, anyway.'

Frankly, Harriet thought they looked like a herd of wild animals, shaking and gyrating in a disgusting manner, but she said, 'Yes, I'm sure they are.'

'Are you and Gerald going to take to the floor for a dance?' asked Marge wickedly, knowing that the other woman would rather die than do so.

'I don't call that dancing,' Harriet replied, looking staid but expensively dressed in a brown suit and matching fur-trimmed hat. 'The waltz and the foxtrot — that's proper dancing.'

'Maybe so but I think this modern stuff looks like fun,' said Marge, unable to resist the opposite view. Harriet brought out the very worst in her. 'But perhaps you'd rather wait for something slower and more formal. The band have been told to cater for all ages and tastes so something traditional will come up soon.'

'I think that will probably be better for us,' said Gerald, supportive of his wife as always.

'I might have a dance with you later on myself,' said Marge, looking at him with a gleam in her eye. 'Just to show the kids that their folks aren't quite past it.'

'I'll look forward to it,' responded Gerald politely.

'I can see I'm going to have to keep a beady eye on you two,' jested Cyril.

Being devoid of a sense of humour, the light-hearted nature of the conversation went over Harriet's head and she gave her husband an icy look. 'We'll have to be going soon,' she said.

'Oh. Why is that, dear?' he asked.

'It's December, Gerald, and a cold night,' she stated through gritted teeth. 'The roads will probably be slippery later and we have a long drive.'

He looked about to protest but caught the full blast of her eloquent stare. 'Yes, yes of course,' he agreed.

'Well, it might be the style of dancing for the young but Cyril and I are going to have a go,' said Marge, keen for a break from the tiresome presence of Harriet Weston whom she'd had far too much of today. 'Come on, Cyril, let's twist.'

'Right you are, love,' he said, rising and leading her towards the dancing where they copied what everyone else was doing, laughing and singing.

'Peasants,' scorned Harriet. 'Fancy carrying on like that at their age. It's positively uncivilised.'

'I think it looks rather enjoyable,' remarked Gerald bravely. 'Maybe you and I could give it a try.' Wincing from the force of her withering look, he said, 'Perhaps not then, dear.'

★ ★ ★

'Fabulous wedding, Sadie,' said Brenda when the two friends managed a few moments alone together in Sadie's room when they went back to the house to get changed. 'I'm having the time of my life.'

'Good, I'm glad,' said the bride, carefully taking off her dress and hanging it up.

'I wish you weren't moving away, though,' said Brenda sadly.

'Yeah, I wish I wasn't too,' sighed Sadie. 'That's the only downside.'

'As you don't want to go, is there no other way?'

'Not really. It's the best practical solution as Paul's parents have space for us and his job is in Kingston.'

'You've had to leave your job though.'

'Yeah, but his is a career; mine's just a job,' Sadie pointed out. 'Anyway, I've got another one in an insurance office in Kingston. It can't be any more boring than the last one. Filing is filing wherever you do it.'

'Even so . . . '

'His work is for life, mine is just until we start a family,' she went on.

'There is that, I suppose.'

'I'll be coming back regularly to see the family, so I'll still be seeing you and we'll talk on the phone.'

'I know.' Brenda was thoughtful as she hung up her bridal wear and slipped into a red shift dress with long sleeves and a short skirt. Not wanting to spoil Sadie's day, she decided to adopt a more positive attitude. 'Well, I do have something to look forward to that might help to take my mind off missing you.'

Sadie raised her eyes. 'Oh yeah, and what might that be?'

'A date with Ray Smart.'

'He asked you out?'

'No. I asked him,' Brenda said, laughing. 'If I waited for him to ask me I'd be too old to care. So I just came out with it.'

'And he agreed?'

'Not right away. He took a bit of persuading,' she admitted. 'He says he doesn't date children but I talked him into it by saying that it isn't really a date but just a one-off, and he's taking me to the pictures on Wednesday. So you've done me a favour by getting married because it's given me the chance I needed to get things going with him.'

'I thought you said it was just a one-off.'

'No, I said that I told him that, but I shall make sure it doesn't stop there,' she said wickedly. 'You'll be coming to my wedding before too long if I have anything to do with it.' She paused. 'Anyway, enough about me. Today is your day. Seriously, kid, you made a gorgeous bride and I know you'll be very happy with Paul. You two are made for each other.'

'Thanks, Bren.'

A sudden stillness came over them as they both felt the significant reality of an era ending. With one accord they wrapped their arms around each other, tears falling.

'Our mascara will be ruined,' said Brenda as they drew apart.

'And our hair,' added Sadie.

But they were both feeling so emotional their devotion to glamour deserted them.

★   ★   ★

Having never done more than help with the dishes before, the unromantic practicalities of married life came as something of a shock to Sadie. The cooking was quite fun, provided she remembered to shop for food in her lunch hour, but she wasn't too keen on the rest of it. The fact that if she didn't take care of the laundry they

67

had nothing in a fit state to wear, if she didn't shop and cook they had nothing to eat and the place didn't clean itself as if by magic as it had seemed to under her parents' roof was a definite drawback.

Paul's mother seemed keen to help and offered to do their washing for them in her twin-tub, but, although Sadie was none too keen on washing the clothes in the sink, she didn't like the idea of her mother-in-law taking over the job. Their laundry was private to her and Paul now.

Guessing that Mrs Weston needed to feel useful, however, she diplomatically suggested that she do the towels and bed linen in her sparkling new machine. When her mother-in-law invited the newly-weds to eat with her and Gerald every night to save Sadie the bother of cooking, Sadie suggested just once a week. As blinkered by love as she was in her married life, she knew that given the opportunity Harriet Weston would take over completely.

There was something very sinister about the woman somehow; something more than just her irritating supercilious attitude. Sadie could see it behind her eyes; feel it in her presence. She was never openly unkind to Sadie yet somehow she exuded malice. Sadie said nothing to Paul about this; she saw no point in upsetting him about something that was nothing more than just a feeling and could be just Sadie's imagination. Anyway, she was too deeply in love to let outside influences affect her unduly.

★ ★ ★

'It's nice to be out in the swing of things after the week at work, isn't it, Paul?' asked Sadie as they danced at Eel Pie Island.

'Even nicer to go home together at the end,' he said.

'Yeah, I like that part too,' she laughed.

The couple didn't go out much of an evening now that they were married and trying to save money. They preferred to snuggle up together on the sofa that Paul's parents had given them and watch the second-hand television set which was a wedding present from Sadie's brothers. But no one of their age or ilk stayed at home on a Saturday night, so that was when they went out dancing. Even the freezing weather of early 1963 — which had frozen the Thames in places and was officially the coldest winter in Surrey since 1740 — couldn't keep them in on a Saturday once the roads were clear.

The place was really rocking, the dance floor crowded. Sadie and Paul were near the stage where there was a young mod with high-heeled boots and a bouffant hairstyle filling in for the main vocalist. His voice had an unusual gravelly sound to it.

'He's good,' said Sadie.

'Yeah, not bad at all,' agreed Paul.

When the dance came to an end, they made their way off the floor and stood with Paul's pals who they had arranged to meet here. Among them was Brian, the boy who had taken Brenda home the night Sadie and Paul had first met. Sadie asked him if he knew what the singer's name was. He said he thought it was Rod

Stewart, which meant nothing to any of them but they all agreed that he was worth looking out for.

One of the other friends said something and both Paul and Brian turned towards him, leaving Sadie seeming to be unattached. As the band started playing again, she was invited to dance by a tall man with longish brown hair.

She was about to inform him that she was with someone when Paul turned round.

'Oi, you. She's with me,' he roared, giving the man a hefty shove. 'So keep away.'

''Ere, who do you think you're pushing?' objected the man.

'What does it look like,' said Paul, white with rage. 'Clear off and don't come anywhere near her again.'

'For goodness' sake, Paul, he wasn't to know I wasn't on my own,' Sadie began but her husband was far too immersed in his grievance to pay attention to her.

Paul grabbed her hand and thrust it into the man's face. 'See that,' he snarled. 'It's a wedding ring, my wedding ring, and she's married to me.'

'Sorry, mate,' said the stranger. 'No offence intended but maybe you should pay more attention to her. She was standing there on her own. How was I to know she was attached?'

'You've got eyes in your head, haven't you? You should have seen her wedding ring.'

'Don't make me laugh,' responded the man in a mocking tone. 'It isn't a woman's hands you look at when you come to a place like this.'

'That's it.' Paul lunged towards him with his

fists up while Sadie tried to drag him away.

'That's enough, Paul,' intervened Brian, grabbing him and pulling him back with the aid of another friend. 'I don't know what's got into you. Calm down.'

Incandescent with rage, Sadie announced, 'I'm leaving,' and stormed off.

* * *

He found her shivering at the bus stop, having walked past the scooter and headed for the town.

'Go away,' she said, moving out of the queue and earshot of the other people. 'You've turned into a thug and I want nothing to do with you.'

'You are just being overly dramatic,' he accused. 'There's nothing thuggish about me.'

'Ooh, not much. You should take a closer look at yourself.' She stared at him, her eyes blazing. 'How dare you treat me like a piece of merchandise, flashing my wedding ring around as if it's a badge of ownership?'

'That was out of order,' he admitted, looking sheepish. 'I'm sorry.'

'Sorry just isn't good enough, Paul. This isn't the first time you've lost your temper because of your unnecessary jealousy,' she ranted. 'I fell in love with someone I thought was kind and gentle. It turns out that you've got more than just a streak of violence in you. You're nothing more than a ruffian with a posh accent.'

'You know that isn't true,' he said.

'I thought I knew you but it turns out that I don't.'

71

'Yes, you do.' He raked his fingers through his hair in anguish. 'I'm still the same person you first met and I'm not violent by nature. I don't know what happens to me. I get this fire in my head and it takes over completely. I never had it in my life before I met you.'

'Oh, so I'm to blame.'

'No, of course not. I'm just saying that I'm not normally an aggressive person,' he tried to explain. 'It must be because I'm so scared of losing you.'

'Why would you lose me?'

'Because you're a very beautiful girl and you can have anyone you fancy.'

'I don't want anyone except you.' She was shouting now with frustration. 'But I'm not sure if I will still want you if you're going to carry on turning into a monster at the slightest provocation and showing me up in public. It hurts to know that you don't trust me.'

'I do trust you,' he assured her. 'It's the men I don't trust. I can't bear to see them looking at you.'

'Well, you're going to have to get used to it, mate, because I'm not going to become a recluse. Men look at women, and vice versa. It's normal and it's life. Girls eye you up all the time when we're out but I don't fly into a rage about it.'

The bus came into view and she moved back towards the queue.

'Come home with me on the scooter, Sadie,' Paul begged, his voice hoarse with emotion. 'Please.'

She wasn't one to bear a grudge and she knew things must be put right between them as they were married people. 'Come on then,' she said, linking arms with him, 'but you've got to stop this ridiculous jealousy. I mean it, Paul. Let's have no more scenes. I want you to promise me.'

'I promise,' he said, drawing her into his arms.

He knew he must do his best to keep his word for Sadie's sake but the intensity of his feelings for her frightened him because he didn't seem able to control them. It was as though he was possessed when any man paid her the slightest attention. He hated the way it made him feel. It spoilt everything! So it had to stop.

★ ★ ★

The bitter weather — nicknamed the Big Freeze — showed no sign of abating, with patches of frozen snow and ice still on the pavements and kerbsides in March. There were many bright, clear days though, which made the bleakly beautiful countryside register with intense clarity beneath the pale blue skies and often dazzling but heatless sunshine. Most Sunday afternoons Sadie and Paul could be found walking in some nearby woods or on the slopes of Box Hill, where the winter views were so stunning they made Sadie catch her breath.

Saturday nights they went off on the scooter in search of entertainment in such palaces for the young as the Orchid Ballroom in Purley or Wimbledon Palais. Eel Pie Island was still a favourite too.

It was late March before the temperatures finally began to creep up a little but whatever the weather Sadie was blissfully happy as she revelled in her life with Paul, who kept to his word and created no more angry scenes in public. Everything in Sadie's life was better because Paul was in it. Her boring job as a filing clerk, his mother's veiled hostility, even the fact that she missed her family could be borne because Paul was around.

One evening in the late spring Brenda telephoned Sadie for a natter.

'How about you and Paul and Ray and me make up a foursome some time soon,' she suggested after they had caught up with all the news, Sadie sitting on the stairs, hoping she was out of earshot of her inlaws. 'It would be good if you could come over our way as there's not much doing out there in the sticks.'

'Oi, watch it,' objected Sadie lightly. 'There's plenty going on out this way. In fact, you know that new group, the Beatles . . .'

'Yeah, I've heard of them. Quite new on the pop music scene but had a hit record, 'Love Me Do'.'

'They're the ones.'

'What about them?'

'They're doing a show in Guildford at the Odeon.'

'Wow. I'm glad to hear that there is life beyond Hammersmith Bridge.'

'Cheeky cow.'

'Just kidding. But, seriously, if you were to come over here we could go to the Palais, the

74

Lyceum or even just have a wander round the West End,' Brenda went on. 'Perhaps you and Paul could stay at your mum's to save going home late on that draughty scooter.'

'All right, don't rub it in just because Ray's got a car,' Sadie laughed. 'Paul's mum and dad are buying him a Mini for his twenty-first. So you won't be able to lord it over me then.'

'Sorry, kid, I still can't get over the fact that I've managed to nab the delectable Ray Smart, complete with wheels.'

'It seems to be lasting between the two of you.'

'I told you it would be more than a one-off.'

'You certainly did.'

'I can be very determined when I've a mind,' Brenda told her friend. 'I know I was a bit slow about it originally but once you provided me with an opportunity to get together with him by getting married, I didn't waste any more time.'

Harriet came out of the living room on her way to the kitchen and Sadie instinctively lowered her voice. 'I'll have to go in a minute,' she said, intimidated by the older woman even though she wasn't waiting to use the phone. 'So when do you want to do the foursome?'

'How about this weekend?'

'I'll have a chat with Paul about it and let you know later in the week.'

'Okay, bye for now then.'

'Bye.'

Sadie replaced the receiver, called out, 'Thank you, Mrs Weston', and hurried upstairs to tell Paul about the proposed outing.

The West End was vibrant and exciting on Saturday night as people filled the streets, determined to have a good time. There were queues for the cinemas and eateries, crowds outside the theatres and the pubs were overflowing. The foursome had a mooch through Piccadilly to capture the atmosphere and enjoy the lights then went into a pub just off Leicester Square for a drink before making their way to the Lyceum.

The pub was packed and smoky, all the seats taken. They managed to find a space in a corner and put their drinks on the edge of a table nearby. Nobody minded standing. They were all in good spirits and dressed up, the boys in suits with shirt and tie, the girls in mini-dresses, their eyes heavily made up and skin fashionably pale, lips a light shade of pink and luminous.

'I understand that Sadie and I are responsible for you two getting together, Ray,' said Paul lightly. 'As it all started at our wedding.'

'Yeah, you're the culprits,' grinned Ray. 'I was wondering if I could sue you for damages.'

'Oi, you,' said Brenda, slapping him playfully on the arm. 'You ought to be thanking them for changing your life.'

'I would if it was for the better,' teased Ray. 'Instead of that I've got no peace because I'm plagued by some slip of a kid wanting me to take her out all the time.'

'Slip of a kid, my Aunt Fanny,' she protested. 'There's only six years between us, and anyway, you love going out with me.'

He did actually. Once he'd got used to the idea that she was a grown woman and not just a kid whom he'd seen for years at the Bell house, he'd allowed her to grow on him. The initiative had been entirely hers for a while and he'd spent his time trying to shake her off. It had been a joke between them. Then one day he realised that he liked having her around. She was attractive, good company and made no secret of the fact that she was keen on him. So she had become his regular girlfriend.

'All right, I admit it,' he responded now. 'You're not so bad, I suppose.'

'Would you care to improve on that?' she asked, holding her glass of gin and orange close to him in a playfully threatening manner. 'Something along the lines of my being the best thing that's ever happened to you.'

'I wouldn't go that far,' he joshed.

'Are you sure about that?' she asked, raising the glass and tilting it in his direction.

'All right, you're gorgeous, lovely and the best thing that's ever happened to me,' he responded quickly to roars of laughter from the others.

'That's better,' smiled Brenda.

The atmosphere was light-hearted among the group. Typically, the men steered the conversation towards cars while the girls chatted among themselves, happy to be together again.

'That's a smashing set of wheels you've got, Ray,' said Paul, referring to the Ford Zephyr in which they'd travelled here tonight, Paul having left the scooter at Sadie's parents' house.

'Yeah, not bad, is it? She's got some power under the bonnet and that's a fact,' said Ray. 'Not much use in London with all the traffic jams but she really goes when I put my foot down on the open road.'

'I can't wait to get a car.'

Ray sipped his beer, looking at him studiously. 'My guess is that you'll go for a Mini.'

'Yeah, that's right. How did you know?'

'You're young and trendy, so is the Mini,' he replied. 'Too small for me with all the stock I have to carry around for the business. Besides, they seem like toys to me.'

'They're all the rage,' Paul pointed out. 'Especially with pop stars and other showbiz types. Very economical with petrol.'

'A popular car, I grant you, but not for me.'

'Each to his own,' said Paul.

'Exactly.'

Paul turned to get his beer that he'd put on a table to the side of them.

'So when do you reckon you'll be getting the car then?' enquired Ray, by way of conversation.

But Paul's attention had been attracted elsewhere and when he eventually turned back to Ray, his mood had changed completely.

'What's up with you, mate?' asked Ray, noticing his grim expression. 'Did someone drop fag ash in your beer or something?'

'No,' he said, taking a swig.

'You don't look too happy all of a sudden.'

'I'm okay really, so what were you saying . . . ?'

★ ★ ★

Brenda was telling Sadie about a 'fabulous' new hairdressers that had opened in Hammersmith.

'He does all the latest styles,' she said, 'and is absolutely brilliant at cutting. He's Italian, goes by the name of Carlo . . . what's the matter, Sadie, you're not listening.'

A group of young men had come in and were standing near to Sadie and the others. She had noticed one of them giving her a very obvious and lingering once-over. 'Sorry, Bren,' she said, 'can you change places with me? I'm getting a bit of unwanted attention from some bloke and if Paul spots it he'll go mad.'

'I didn't realise he was the jealous type,' said Brenda as they swapped places so that Sadie had her back to the man.

'He tries not to be but he can't seem to help himself and there's no point in asking for trouble,' replied Sadie.

★ ★ ★

'I've known Sadie since she was a little kid, so it seems a bit strange being on a grown-up night out with her,' said Ray, trying to keep the conversation going with Paul, despite the fact that he didn't seem to be listening and kept turning away.

'Mmm,' muttered Paul, looking to the side again. 'I suppose it would do.'

'A nice family, the Bells; you won't go far wrong being related to them . . . Paul, what's the matter with you? Has no one ever told you it's

79

rude to look away when someone is talking to you?'

'Sorry, Ray,' he apologised. 'What was it you were saying?'

'About having known Sadie a long time and being out with her on an adult outing . . . Paul . . . oh, I give up,' he said as the other man turned away again.

Paul was trying his best to ignore the man who had been ogling Sadie ever since he'd come in but he couldn't take his eyes off the situation. He watched her change places with Brenda but still the man persisted in looking in her direction even though she had her back to him. Almost ill with fury, he was unable to stand it any longer, and marched over to him.

'Oi, you! That's my wife you're eyeing up,' he said, having to tilt his head because the other man was a lot taller than he was. 'So pack it in, right now.'

'I don't know what you're talking about, mate,' said the man, who was well-built and muscular.

'Don't try and deny it,' persisted Paul, taking his arm roughly. 'I've been watching you.'

The man drew hard on his cigarette and blew smoke slowly into Paul's face. 'Don't you dare touch me, little boy,' he said, brushing Paul's hand away. 'This is a free country and I'll look at any woman I like and if one of them happens to be your wife, that's your hard luck. Now go away and play with your toys.'

Paul squared up to him. 'You arrogant bugger,' he said, pushing him, too fired up to notice that

80

Sadie was begging him to stop and Ray was trying to pull him away.

Looking furious and about to retaliate physically, the man said in a controlled manner, 'How many times must I tell you? Clear off and leave me to enjoy my night out with my mates.'

There was a sudden intervention as two male members of staff appeared on the scene. 'Outside,' they said to Paul, taking hold of him firmly. 'You want trouble, you have it outside. We don't allow fighting on these premises.' And they marched him to the door and pushed him out with such force he fell to the ground.

'Are you all right?' asked Sadie as Ray helped him to his feet.

'Yeah, I'm okay.'

'So much for your promise,' she said, her voice shrill with anger. 'What do you think you're doing, embarrassing us all like that? You've ruined the whole blinking evening. Not just for me this time, but for Brenda and Ray too. It really isn't on, Paul.'

'He was giving you the eye and don't deny it because I saw you change places with Brenda so that you had your back to him.'

'Which should have pleased you,' she said as they moved along with the crowds. 'But so what if he was looking in my direction. People have to look somewhere. There was no call for you to start a fight about it.'

'Calm down, the pair of you.' Ray tried to appease the situation. 'There's no harm done. It's just as well he didn't retaliate, Paul, as he's a whole lot bigger than you are.'

'You promised me that there would be no more scenes caused by your stupid jealousy,' said Sadie. 'It's so childish and completely uncalled for.'

'Sorry.'

'No you're not,' she snapped furiously. 'You're still fuming. I can see it in your eyes.'

As much as he hated to admit it, she was right. The red mist had come down again and he couldn't shake it off. 'I'm really sorry,' he apologised again.

'I hope you mean that because you're going to end up in real trouble one of these days if you don't give up,' she said, her voice now breaking with emotion. 'You scare me when you get like this because I feel as if I don't know you. It's upsetting all of us, not to mention the poor bloke you tried to beat up just for looking in my direction.'

'He wasn't just looking . . . '

'All right, Paul, pack it in because we don't want to hear any more about it,' Brenda intervened. 'Let's forget all about it and go to the dance. It's over with and there's no point in letting it spoil the rest of the evening.'

'She's right, Paul,' agreed Ray.

But Paul was out of control and he felt compelled to glance back towards the pub where he spotted the object of his jealousy and his mates in the neon lights as they came out and headed off in the direction of the Odeon cinema. Completely in thrall to his emotions, he left Sadie and the others without a word, and went after the man, dodging in and out of the crowds.

82

'Paul, no,' cried Sadie, looking across and seeing where her husband was aiming.

'You wait here,' Ray suggested, 'I'll go after him.'

'I'm coming too,' said Sadie but Ray was already being swallowed up by the crowds.

* * *

'Oh, no, not you again,' said the stranger when Paul caught up with him and gave him a hefty shove in the back. The man's mates were walking on ahead, talking and enjoying themselves, completely unaware of anything amiss behind them. 'Go away before I really lose my temper.'

Out of his mind with jealousy, Paul said, 'I don't like the way you were looking at my wife.'

'I don't like paying my income tax but I don't get into a fight about it,' the man said. 'Keep her locked up indoors, mate, if you don't want anyone to look at her. Now run along and leave me to enjoy myself. It's Saturday night and I've come out to have a laugh with the boys. So bugger off!'

As the man turned away and started to move on, Paul tried to pull him back by the bottom of his jacket. The man swung round — temper finally roused — and Paul took a hard swing at him, causing a torrent of blood from his nose.

'Right, that's it, you wouldn't be told, now I'm gonna have to teach you a lesson.'

Grabbing hold of Paul and dragging him through the masses, he pushed him towards a wall and pinned him against it.

'Welcome to the real world, Sonny Jim; the world where men look at women regardless of whether they're married or single. I work hard all week and look forward to Saturday night out with my mates. I don't expect to be pestered by some toffee-nosed upstart when I've done nothing wrong. You've done your best to ruin my night so now I'm gonna ruin yours and don't say you weren't warned. You shouldn't mess with someone like me; you shouldn't have made me lose my temper. That was a big mistake.'

He punched Paul on the jaw and even as Paul reeled he hit him in the stomach so hard that Paul cried out. But he wasn't ready to give up.

'You shouldn't have been after my wife,' gasped Paul, going for the man's face and landing a punch on his eye that made him groan and sent him staggering. As he recovered and came back towards Paul, his eye already swollen, Paul tried to wrestle him to the ground.

'When are you going to learn the facts of life?' said the man, landing a blow to Paul's jaw that sent him crashing to the ground, his head hitting the kerb. 'That'll teach you. Now get up and take your medicine like a man. Get up, you poncy little twerp. Come on; don't make a drama of it.'

But Paul didn't move a muscle.

* * *

Sadie and Brenda finally caught up with Ray but he had lost sight of Paul completely.

'There's something going on over there,' observed Brenda, looking across the square in

84

the direction of the Odeon cinema and seeing a commotion.

'Looks like a rumpus,' said Ray, spotting a policeman. 'The coppers are there too.'

'Oh no,' said Sadie and the three of them jostled their way towards the spot. 'I hope to God Paul isn't involved.'

★   ★   ★

There was chaos. One policeman was trying to keep the crowd under control, the other was talking to the man Paul had gone after who was holding a handkerchief to his bloody nose and insisting that he hadn't started the fight and had only been defending himself.

'He struck the first blow, the bloody lunatic,' he said. 'He came after me looking for trouble. He's probably broken my nose and blinded me as I can only see out of one eye. I was the one provoked. He just wouldn't leave me alone.'

'All right, sir,' said one of the policemen. 'You can tell us all about it at the station.'

'But I don't even know the bloke,' the man protested furiously. 'Never set eyes on him in my life before tonight.'

'Keep back,' one of the officers said to Sadie and the others as they pushed their way to the front of the crowd.

'It's her husband,' Ray explained as Sadie darted forward and went down on her knees to the silent figure on the ground.

'Don't move him, please,' said the officer.

'Someone has called an ambulance; they won't be long.'

But Sadie didn't hear a word. She was deaf and blind to everything except her beloved husband lying there so still with a stranger's coat over him.

4

Because of her seemingly blessed existence, Sadie had the idea that tragedy didn't happen to someone like her with a charmed life full of happy endings. So when her husband was declared dead on arrival at the hospital, she was in total denial.

'You've made a mistake,' she shrieked at the doctor. 'Paul wouldn't do that. He wouldn't leave me.'

'People can't choose . . . '

'He's young and strong so he can't be dead,' she insisted, her voice rising hysterically. 'You should be ashamed of yourself for saying such things.'

'I'm really very sorry, Mrs Weston . . . '

'Admit that you've made a mistake,' she interrupted, clinging to a hope she knew wasn't there. 'Go on; tell me you've got it wrong. For pity's sake, please tell me that.'

'I'm afraid I can't do that . . . '

'All right then, so he was injured,' she continued, changing tack and channelling her anguish into blame because she couldn't face the awful truth. 'You should have put him right. Not let him die.' She was completely beside herself and barely aware of what she was saying. 'He's twenty years old, for God's sake! Call yourself a doctor. I'd call you hopeless.'

'That's enough, Sadie,' said Ray firmly,

stepping forward, taking her arm and gently encouraging her to come away. 'There's no need to speak to the doctor like that. I'm sure the staff here did everything they could for Paul.'

'Your husband sustained a very severe blow to the head when he fell,' explained the doctor with a sigh of weary patience, obviously accustomed to this sort of thing. 'There was nothing more we could do. I really am very sorry.'

'Liar,' she shouted.

'Come on now,' intervened a nurse, making as though to take her other arm. 'Let's go and find you a cup of tea.'

'It's all right, nurse,' said Ray who, with Brenda, had followed the ambulance to the hospital. 'We're her friends; we'll look after her.'

'I don't need looking after,' Sadie objected, forcibly removing his hand from her arm and pushing a pale and tearful Brenda away. 'I want to see my husband.'

'I'm sure that can be arranged,' said the doctor, seeming keen to get away. 'The nurse will go with you.'

She was taken to a room where Paul was lying on a bed in a hospital smock. To Sadie he seemed to have a slight smile on his face. 'There you are,' she said to the nurse. 'He's smiling so he can't be dead.'

'It's the passing over,' she heard someone say and turned to see a man of the church.

'He's passed nowhere, mate,' she said insolently to the hospital chaplain, too distressed to realise how badly she was behaving. 'He's twenty years old and people don't pass over at that age.'

'Sadly some do, my dear,' he said kindly.

'Yeah, well, my husband hasn't.'

The nurse and the chaplain exchanged a look; they both knew she was speaking from grief and shock.

Bending over and kissing Paul's brow, Sadie silently willed him to speak to her. If she concentrated hard enough maybe he would sit up and everything would be back to normal.

'Perhaps you should go now, my dear,' suggested the nurse, perceiving the extent of Sadie's distress and trying to help. 'You can see him again in the chapel of rest.'

Standing up slowly, her eyes fixed on her beloved husband and the terrible stillness of him filling her with pain, she finally accepted that he wasn't there; only an empty shell remained. She walked numbly from the room, barely aware of her surroundings. For the first time in her life, things couldn't be put right for her. No amount of coaxing or conniving would bring Paul back.

Rage at his untimely and unnecessary death lashed through her, all consuming and uncontrollable. She could hear someone screaming and feel an ache in her throat but was unaware that the violent cries were hers.

'Sorry, Sadie,' she heard Ray say. 'I had to do it.' And she realised that he had slapped her face.

She wanted to punch the walls like a child in a tantrum to get her own way. But she said, 'That's all right. Was I making a fuss?'

'Just a bit,' he said tactfully.

'Come on, Sadie,' said Brenda, taking her arm. 'Let's go and get a cup of tea.'

'Someone will have to let Paul's parents know,' she said stiffly, dry-eyed and unable to shed a tear.

'I'll take care of that,' offered Ray. 'Anything you need, anything at all, Brenda and I will be here for you.'

★　★　★

'What does it matter now,' Sadie said wearily to the policemen who came to the hospital to question her and Brenda. Apparently it was routine procedure when someone died suddenly, especially as the result of a fight. They were in an empty visitors' room. Ray had gone to Surrey to break the news to Paul's parents, deciding it would be too cruel to tell them by telephone. 'My husband is dead and talking about the fight won't bring him back.'

'It matters very much to us because we need to know exactly what happened,' said one of the officers.

'I wasn't there so I don't know,' she replied dully.

'By the time we got there the fight was over and Paul was lying on the ground,' Brenda explained. 'Could have already been dead for all we know.'

'What about the events leading up to the fight?' enquired the policeman. 'Did your husband seem angry about anything, Mrs Weston?'

'He was absolutely furious,' replied Sadie. 'He caught the bloke looking at me and he saw red.'

'Jealous type, was he?'

'Yes,' admitted Sadie, being honest by nature and seeing no reason to hide the truth about Paul. 'I warned him about it. I told him he'd end up in big trouble if he didn't get it under control.' She cleared her parched throat, feeling utterly desolate. 'Of course, I didn't expect anything as dreadful as this to happen.'

'Would you say that he instigated the fight then?'

'As I have already told you, I don't know. But he started the fight in the pub,' she said, brushing a tired hand across her brow, unaware that her replies might be particularly significant. 'He got thrown out because of it, and still he wouldn't let it go. As soon as he saw the bloke again, off he went after him before any of us had a chance to stop him. So he could have started it. I can't say as I wasn't there. Anyway, even if Paul did start it, the man had no right to kill him. He wants hanging and I hope you throw the book at him.'

'Mmm, only time will tell about that,' said the detective, looking at his partner. 'But that will be all for now; we'll go away and leave you in peace.'

Peace! That was a joke! Sadie didn't think she would ever experience such a thing again. It was as though someone had physically tied her insides together, her legs were shaking, her head ached and she felt nauseous.

When Ray arrived with Paul's parents, she

could see his mother's pain but couldn't feel it, so deeply was she engrossed in her own agony. There was a brief, perfunctory embrace between the two women but no warmth or empathy on either side. This didn't seem in the least bit strange to Sadie. Nothing registered. Nothing seemed real.

★ ★ ★

'Oh, Mum,' said Sadie later after Ray had driven her to Fern Terrace and the family were told the news. 'Make it not be true. Please make it just be a bad dream.'

'Oh, love, if only I could,' responded Marge, holding her close. She thought of all the times in the past when she'd tried not to spoil her daughter, had wanted to prepare her for a time when things might not go her way. She hadn't expected tragedy to strike this early and so shockingly. Her darling daughter was about to be tested like never before. Marge would do everything she could to help her but — as much as she might wish to — she couldn't go through it for her. That hurt; that really hurt. 'I'm so sorry, darlin'.'

★ ★ ★

So, here I am again, thought Sadie, lying on her bed with Pickles beside her. Back home in her old bedroom alone, almost as though she'd never got married. But she wasn't the same. She stroked the cat, seeking comfort in the silky touch of his fur and the evidence of life in the sound of his purring. 'Poor Paul,' she said aloud before lapsing into thought. All of his life ahead of him and now there was nothing. It wasn't even as though he'd died for his country or anything useful and honourable like the war heroes. At least there was some purpose to that. He'd died because of needless jealousy. 'Oh, Pickles,' she said, putting her face against him. 'What am I going to do without him?'

The cat just continued to purr, enjoying the attention.

★   ★   ★

Sadie decided to stay with her family until after the funeral, at least, and then she would decide where her future lay. The next day her brothers drove her to Surrey to collect some of her things. She also astonished herself by wanting to find out how her in-laws were coping and feeling sorry for them. Her conscience was troubling her because of her lack of compassion for them yesterday.

'My wife has taken it very hard, as you can imagine,' said Gerald, after he'd greeted them and she'd told him of her plans. He was very pale and heavy-eyed. 'She adored him. He was her life.'

'Yes, I know they were very close,' said Sadie.

'But how about you, my dear?' asked Gerald, seeming genuinely concerned. 'It must be very difficult for you.'

She nodded, not able to trust herself to speak

because of the choking sensation in her throat.

'She's gutted, o' course,' brother Derek answered for her.

'Absolutely,' added Don. 'We all are.'

'Is Mrs Weston around?' enquired Sadie.

Gerald shook his head. 'She's taken to her bed and doesn't want to see anyone.'

'Oh, I see. I'll just go upstairs and get some of my things then, if that's all right with you,' she said, as though she needed to ask now, even though the rooms she would be visiting were still officially her home. She felt like a stranger here without Paul.

'Of course,' he nodded, waving his hand towards the stairs.

Wanting to be alone, she asked her brothers to wait downstairs, and made her way up.

In their little home, everything was as they'd left it when they'd gone out to enjoy themselves. The clothes they'd been wearing before they'd got ready to go out were thrown on the bedside chairs because they'd left in a hurry. She picked up Paul's sweater and buried her face in it, breathing in the combined scent of sweat and Old Spice. She went into the living room and looked round at the shabby brown second-hand sofa where they'd cuddled up together, the sleek contemporary coffee table they'd bought one Saturday afternoon in Kingston. It was the only thing they'd purchased themselves; everything else was hand-me-downs, mostly from the Westons.

There was an eerie silence about the place; as though the life had been sucked out of it by

Paul's death. It had only ever been a stepping stone until they could get a place of their own but it had been a home, full of love and hope for the future. Without Paul it was just two rooms in his parents' house. She knew instantly that she didn't want to live here without him. There was no point since he had been the only reason she was here. Everything in their rooms except their clothes belonged to the Westons so she would take no baggage. She didn't even want Paul's beloved scooter because it would make her too sad.

She found a suitcase in the wardrobe and began to pack, tears finally flowing.

★   ★   ★

'Obviously we'll take care of the funeral arrangements so you won't have to worry about that,' said Gerald when she was back downstairs. 'We can't get anything organised until after the post mortem and as you're his next of kin now they'll give the result of that to you. If you could let us know when we can start things moving, I'd appreciate that.'

Sadie winced; she couldn't bear to think of the ghastliness of what they were going to do to Paul but it had to be done because his was a sudden death and they needed to know the actual cause. 'Of course.'

'Thank you, my dear.'

He looked so achingly forlorn, her heart went out to him and she went over and put her arms around him in a gesture of compassion. 'I'm so sorry, Mr Weston,' she said. 'I know how much you must be hurting.'

Unaccustomed to such impulsive and tactile behaviour, Gerald cleared his throat and she felt him tense.

'Thank you, Sadie,' he said hoarsely, drawing back. 'You take care of yourself now.'

'We'll look after her, don't worry,' said Derek, walking to the front door with her suitcase.

If only it was that simple, thought Sadie, as they went out to the car her brothers had borrowed from a mate. The days when her family could soothe and protect her had ended with Paul's death. She was on her own with this one, no matter how many people were around her.

*   *   *

It was a fine sunny day for the funeral, the stained-glass windows of Paley village church resplendent with colour, every pew filled and people standing at the back. Paul had been well-liked in the area and his dying so young caused an outpouring of sympathy, even from strangers. Sadie managed to get through the service but her legs were trembling as they left the church and headed for the cemetery, the cars moving slowly around the village green and past the duck pond, over the stone bridge where weeping willows swept down towards the stream.

She was dreading the actual burial but at the same time wanted it over. Her brothers were at her side, as though ready to catch her if she collapsed under the strain. She did feel very lightheaded but somehow stayed vertical and serene, mainly because she didn't feel as though any of this was happening to her. When the coffin was lowered, however, the feelings that had been subdued by shock raged through her body and she wanted to climb down into the ground with Paul. But ostensibly she was composed, every muscle strained with the effort of it.

There was a sudden disturbance as the formal proceedings came to an end. Harriet's voice resounded through the graveyard.

'She killed my son,' she yelled at Sadie. 'That trollop he married. He died because of her.'

'Now, now, dear,' her husband chided. 'There's no call for that sort of talk.'

'Yes, there is; it needs to be said,' she burst out, her voice distorted by grief as she marched over to Sadie and stared at her with undiluted hatred. 'My son died because of you. If you hadn't been flirting with another man there would have been no fight and he would have been alive now.'

'This isn't the time or place, Harriet,' admonished Gerald sternly. 'Please show some respect for the occasion.'

But Harriet was out of control. 'She's to blame,' she ranted. 'She was never good enough for him. Always a flighty type with her short skirts and thick make-up.'

Sadie couldn't be hurt any more than she was already so her mother-in-law's cruel words made virtually no impact. But her family weren't

97

prepared to stand back and let Harriet get away with it.

'How dare you say such things to my daughter,' warned Marge, pushing in between Harriet and Sadie, 'You wicked old cow.'

'Bloody cheek,' added Cyril, moving to his wife's side. 'You should be giving her support, not telling lies about her.'

'My daughter is one of the loveliest girls in West London and your son was lucky that she even gave him a second glance,' declared Marge. 'Paul was very much aware of that too. He told me so himself on several occasions.'

'Not much up here, though,' said Harriet, pointing to her head. 'She's far too dull to have been an asset to him, especially in his career.'

That was too much for Marge and she stepped forward and brought her hand hard across Harriet's face.

'That's enough now, Mum,' said Derek, pulling her away while Harriet stood there looking shocked. 'Don't lower yourself.'

'Perhaps I could remind you all of the solemnity of the occasion,' intervened the vicar nervously.

'Quite so,' agreed Gerald, taking his wife's arm in an effort to stop her retaliating.

'Don't worry, we're going,' said Marge, glaring at Harriet who was being led away by her husband and one of the mourners on the Weston side. 'Come on, you lot. It's all over anyway, so let's give the ham sandwiches a miss and go home. They're bound to be stale anyway. Come on, Sadie.'

'I'd like to stay for a while, Mum.'

Marge looked concerned. 'I don't want to go off and leave you,' she said.

'She can come home with Brenda and me when she's ready,' offered Ray, stepping forward as the gathering dispersed. 'We'll wait for her, don't worry.'

'All right. We'll see you later then,' said Marge, and the Bell clan went on their way, speaking in loud tones of disgust of the events at the graveside.

* * *

'Leave her be, Brenda,' said Ray as she went towards her friend who was standing by the grave.

'She needs some support,' Brenda said tearfully, 'especially after that awful woman saying those terrible things to her. She'll be feeling awful.'

'Support her but give her the time she needs alone as well,' he advised. 'She wants to be private right now.'

'How do you know?'

'Just a hunch.'

Ray had had more than his share of sadness; he'd seen misery of the sort that his present-day friends couldn't even imagine. But few incidents had moved him as intensely as the sight of that young figure standing alone at her husband's grave. His instinct was to go to her and offer solace but his insight held him back. At some point later on maybe but not now.

* * *

'Thanks for waiting for me,' said Sadie when she finally joined them. 'I just needed a few more minutes.'

'Let's get you home,' said Brenda with a purposeful air of protectiveness.

It surprised Sadie to find she was recoiling from her friend's rather cloying compassion, even though it was well-meant. Excessive sympathy seemed to weaken her even more. Grief by its very nature made you an object of pity and set you apart. That was the last thing Sadie wanted.

'I don't want to go home just yet, Brenda,' she told her. 'I have something I must do first.'

'Oh really,' said Brenda in surprise, 'and what might that be?'

'We're going to a party,' she replied and her voice had a resolute ring to it.

* * *

'Hello, my dear,' said Gerald, opening the door to them and behaving as though the incident at the graveside hadn't happened. 'Come on in. I'm glad you decided to come to the house after all. It's only right that you should be here. I'll get you something to drink and there's plenty of food, so help yourself.'

'Thank you but we're not stopping,' Sadie told him while her friends trailed after her, wondering what was going to happen next. 'We've come because I'd like a few words with

100

Mrs Weston, please.'

He looked extremely cautious but said, 'Er . . . yes, of course,' and ushered them into the large bay-windowed sitting room where the mourners were gathered, mostly middle-aged people, but some of Paul's young friends were there too.

Harriet was holding court and her jaw dropped when she saw Sadie. 'Oh, it's you,' she said dully. She was looking very gaunt today, Sadie noticed, in a black dress, her face ashen, eyes red and shadowed. Normally a woman of generous proportions, she had become noticeably less so even in the short time since the actual death. 'What do you want?'

A hush fell over the room as the two women faced each other.

'I'd like the opportunity to reply to the remarks you made to me at the cemetery,' announced Sadie, who was now in no doubt as to the depth of the other woman's grief but felt compelled to speak out even so. 'I feel I owe it to Paul. He would expect me, as his wife, to defend myself.'

'We're all upset,' began Gerald in the hope of averting the confrontation.

'Yes, we are, and I understand how terrible Mrs Weston must be feeling,' said Sadie, 'but I must be given the chance to give my side of the story.'

There was a communal intake of breath.

'First of all, I was not encouraging any other man on the night of the fight. It was all in Paul's mind. He was very jealous. It was almost an illness with him. That's why he went after the man, not because of anything I had done.'

'How dare you,' retorted Harriet.

'It's wicked to speak ill of the dead,' said one of Harriet's cronies, putting a comforting arm around her.

'I'm not speaking ill of him in any malicious way. I am merely telling you how it was because it's important for you to know,' Sadie made clear. 'Paul knew he had this failing and he lost his life because he wasn't able to control it.'

'She's right,' said Ray supportively. 'We were there; we saw what a state he got himself into, the poor lad, and it was all over nothing at all.'

'Yes, you could say he died because of me but he had free will,' Sadie continued. 'I tried to stop him fighting, as I had done on several previous occasions, but Paul was an adult and he did what he felt compelled to do.' Her voice was beginning to break with emotion. She cleared her dry throat. 'It's a tragic waste of a young life and no one is more devastated than I am. But — do you know what — I'm angry with him too for bringing it on himself and causing us all such pain. The man who struck the fatal blow will probably go down for murder so maybe that will give you some sense of satisfaction, as you're so full of malice and blame.'

'Stop,' screeched Harriet. 'Get out.'

'I shall go when I've finished what I have to say,' Sadie went on, her nerves raw with tension. 'As regards your remarks about my intellect, it's true that I'm not as well-educated as Paul was but intelligence isn't all about education. I admit

102

I've never been a serious-minded sort of person. I've always preferred fun to learning but, as stupid as you think I am, I would have been an asset to him in his career because I loved Paul and he would always have been my first priority. Your son chose me because he loved me. It didn't matter to him that I'm not much of a scholar. Anyway, I may not be well-educated but I have plenty of savvy. Probably more than you'll ever have!'

There were cries of outrage from the gathering while Harriet seemed lost for words. Her husband moved towards her to demonstrate his allegiance.

'We're going now so you can all put your eyeballs back in their sockets,' said Sadie, the words seeming to tumble out almost of their own volition. 'But know this, Mrs Weston, I would have given my life for your son and I shall love him until the day I die.'

With that she turned and swept from the room with Brenda and Ray following.

'Magnificent,' said Ray as they walked to the car. 'You really told her. Your family will be proud of you.'

'Yeah, well done,' added Brenda. 'You can't let people like her walk all over you.'

But Sadie had no sense of satisfaction or victory. There was a feeling of tightness in her stomach and she felt as though everything about her life with Paul had been stripped away from her, almost as though it had never existed.

Brenda sat in the back of the car with Sadie on the drive home but she felt only slightly comforted by her presence because her pain was still so intense.

'Thanks, you two,' she said when they pulled up outside her house. 'You're good friends to me.'

She got out of the car and walked towards the house, her mother already at the front door to greet her. Neither Brenda nor Ray attempted to follow her. They both knew that there were times when being a good friend meant standing back.

★ ★ ★

While the rest of the country was enthralled by the Profumo sex scandal, which involved a senior member of the government and filled the newspapers day after day, Sadie was too busy adjusting to life without Paul to take much of an interest.

She got a job as a clerk in the offices of a local engineering factory. It was the routine, unchallenging clerical work she was used to and entailed filing, sorting the post and delivering it to various offices around the building. To this end she was often required to walk through the factory, which produced a chorus of wolf whistles; par for the course for any office girl and she usually enjoyed that sort of thing, but now it went unnoticed. Even the loud, cheerful music they had on in the workshops barely registered.

The trauma of Paul's death had taken its toll on her physically as well as mentally and she felt exhausted and sickly. It was only natural, people said. Her nervous system had taken a battering and it was bound to have an effect on her health. It would pass in time.

It wasn't until she gathered her wits sufficiently to realise that she had been too preoccupied with her grief to pay proper attention to the ordinary events of life, that she realised there was more to her parlous state of health than bereavement. Oh no! Not now, she wailed inwardly. Not without Paul.

★ ★ ★

'So congratulations aren't in order then,' said Brenda, who was Sadie's first confidante.

'No they're flippin' well not,' confirmed Sadie adamantly. 'I can barely look after myself, let alone a baby.'

'Your mum will help you,' encouraged Brenda, 'and you've got me.'

'But it'll be mine, my responsibility, and I just can't do it without Paul.' Sadie looked into space. 'Just once we took a chance. Once, Bren, honestly. Other people could be careless for years and not get caught.'

'Are you sure it is pregnancy?'

'I've missed two periods, my breasts feel like bruised melons and I'm nauseous.'

'It does seem pretty conclusive then.'

'Mmm. I wish I'd gone on the contraceptive pill that everyone's talking about,' Sadie went on. 'That's what comes of being too scared to try something new.'

'Things could be worse though. I mean, you are a widow so it's all very respectable. And it means that Paul will live on in his son or daughter so he'll always be in your life.'

But Sadie couldn't see beyond the problems. 'I have nothing to offer a child. I don't even have my own home. I'm dreading telling Mum and Dad. Their life is going to be disrupted as well as mine with a screaming baby about the place.'

'Your mum will be great about it,' suggested Brenda encouragingly. 'You know what a good sort she is.'

'Yes, she is. But even so, it's a bit much inflicting a baby on the family. Keeping everyone awake at night.'

'Babies don't scream all the time and they only cry a lot when they are very little, I think,' said Brenda. 'They settle down after a while. You'll soon get the hang of it.'

'Oh Bren, you know how selfish I am. I could never put a baby before myself like you're supposed to do.'

'Perhaps that comes naturally once the baby is actually here,' said Brenda.

'It won't come to me,' Sadie stated categorically. 'I know what I'm like. We are what we are and I don't see how a baby will change that.'

'So are you saying that you don't want to have it?' asked her friend.

'Yes, I am saying that,' she confirmed miserably. 'But since I don't have a choice I shall just have to blinking well get on with it. I'm not happy though; not happy at all.'

'There is an alternative.'

'Oh no, I'm not doing that, Bren.' She was adamant. 'Not to Paul's child.'

'In that case you'll just have to do your best,' said Brenda. 'Personally, I think you're really lucky. I'd love to be pregnant with Ray's baby.'

'What, now?'

'Any time.'

'But wouldn't it be a good idea to get married first?'

'In a perfect world, yeah, it would, of course. But Ray isn't keen on the idea of marriage,' she explained. 'If I got pregnant, he'd marry me because he's a decent bloke and he'd want to do right by me.'

'You've only been going out with him just over six months,' Sadie reminded her. 'Give it time.'

'Like you and Paul did, you mean,' Brenda quipped.

Sadie managed a watery smile. 'Okay! Point taken,' she conceded. 'Paul and I were crazy but I'm very glad we were, as things turned out. At least we had some married time together and I'll always have that to look back on.'

'Marriage isn't on Ray's agenda at all,' Brenda went on to say. 'He's mentioned his feelings on the subject several times during general conversation, as though his remarks aren't directed personally to us. But I think he wants to make sure that I don't get any ideas in that direction.'

'Why is he going out with you then, if he has no long-term intentions?' enquired Sadie.

'Because he enjoys being with me, I suppose,' she replied. 'But he's got a hang-up about marriage. He says you don't need a piece of paper to show your commitment to someone.'

107

'So he isn't against commitment; just marriage.'

'That's the impression I get,' Brenda agreed. 'He's very cagey though. Doesn't like to talk about himself or his feelings.'

'He's always been a bit deep, now you come to mention it. I remember Mum saying something about it once,' remarked Sadie. 'Probably because his parents died when he was just a kid. I think they got killed in the war.'

'Yeah, that's what he told me.'

'His grandparents brought him up and I think they are dead too now.'

'That's right, they are,' Brenda confirmed.

'That's probably why he doesn't open up to you, because he's got so used to keeping things to himself,' suggested Sadie. 'It's only since you've been going out with him I've got to know him better as a person. Before then he was just a pal of my brothers; sort of always around.'

'He's much more than that to me.'

'Yes, so I gather,' said Sadie. 'So what are your plans then, if he doesn't want to get married?'

'I don't have any; except to keep on going out with him and hope he changes his mind about marriage with plenty of subtle persuasion from me.'

'If anyone can make him see things differently, it's you,' encouraged her friend.

'I do hope I can,' said Brenda dreamily. 'Anyway, what's your next move?'

'Breaking the news to the family.'

'Oh dear.' She mulled it over. 'They'll be fine about it, I'm sure.'

'We'll see,' said Sadie worriedly.

★ ★ ★

'It's the best thing that could have happened,' approved Marge, beaming. 'A baby will be the making of you.'

'The breaking of me, more like,' wailed her daughter. 'I'm not ready for a baby, Mum.'

'You'll have to make yourself ready then, won't you, love?' said her plain-speaking mother. 'There's a kiddie on the way and it'll need loving and looking after.'

'I don't think I can do it, Mum.'

'You've no choice in the matter, I'm afraid,' her mother declared. 'It's happened and you'll have to accept it.'

'I'm sure your mother will help you,' stated her father eagerly.

Marge threw him a look for speaking on her behalf in a manner to suggest that she absolve their daughter from all maternal responsibility. 'Yes, of course I will help you; that goes without saying. But I will not bring the baby up for you. You're a grown-up and a married woman. You're going to be a mother and you are going to face up to the reality of it.'

'That's a bit hard, Mum,' said Derek. 'She's just a kid.'

'No she isn't,' Marge reminded him. 'She'll soon be a mother. As a family we will do all we can to help her but we won't do the job for her.

109

It wouldn't be right for her or the baby in the long run. Though I realise that you, your brother and your father would be happy to let Sadie be a child indefinitely. You really must let her grow up and now is the time.'

'What am I going to do?' cried Sadie. 'I won't be able to work if I've got a kid to look after.'

'We'll cross that bridge when we come to it,' said Marge with a comforting use of the word 'we'. 'Meanwhile you can carry on working for a good while yet. I think you get maternity benefit if you work until you're about seven months.'

'It'll be a bit of fun, having a nipper around the house,' remarked Don cheerfully. 'I hope it's a boy. We can teach him how to play football.'

'Not for a long time,' Derek pointed out. 'Babies don't do anything at first except scream their heads off. It will definitely be your baby when it's hollering, Sadie.'

'Now look what you've done,' said Marge as Sadie dissolved into tears. 'Come here, love.' She wrapped her arms around her daughter. 'You'll be the best mum ever. I know you will.'

'You're going to desert me,' she wept feebly.

'No I'm not. I said I won't bring the baby up for you,' she pointed out. 'I didn't say I wouldn't be there for you, helping out and giving you moral support. What sort of a mother would I be if I didn't do that?'

'Thanks, Mum,' said Sadie, relieved.

'That's all right, love.'

Marge was delighted at the prospect of being a grandparent but she was worried about how her daughter was going to face up to the frustrations

110

and worry of raising a child. Or, indeed, if she would face up to them at all and not try and delegate all responsibility. After she'd got married she'd seemed to mature but as soon as she came back home to live she fell back slightly into her old ways.

For Sadie's own sake Marge was determined that this baby was going to be its mother's child first and foremost and not its grandmother's with Sadie watching from the sidelines. Otherwise Sadie would miss out on life's greatest gift. So her daughter was going to need to do some serious growing up.

★ ★ ★

'So Sadie isn't overjoyed about the pregnancy then,' remarked Ray when Brenda told him the news over a drink in a local pub a few days later.

'She certainly isn't,' she replied.

'Is that because she doesn't have Paul to support her?'

'Partly that, I suppose, but I think it's also because it wasn't planned and she doesn't feel ready for motherhood.'

'It'll be good for her, though, in that she'll have a new purpose in life and a part of Paul to live on,' he suggested.

'Exactly. That's what I told her but it didn't seem to help much,' she said. 'I was amazed by her attitude. I thought she would be delighted. But Sadie, bless her, is just a big kid really. It's the way she's been brought up. The youngest usually gets spoilt and she has been. She doesn't like responsibility and, by her own admission, she is a bit selfish. She thinks that will make her a bad mother.'

'She doesn't seem much more than a kid herself to me; neither of you do,' he pointed out.

'We are both more than old enough to tackle motherhood. I am anyway.'

Ray ran his eyes over her slim body clad in a summer blouse and short skirt, her brown hair worn high on top and falling to her shoulders, eyes panda-like as was the fashion, and he said, 'You mean you would give up being a dolly bird to become a mum.'

'I wouldn't stop dressing in fashion just because I'd become a mum. You don't have to be frumpy because you have a kid you know, not these days,' she said. 'But I would love to have a baby . . . ' She paused, adding quickly for fear he might think she was taking things too fast, 'When the time is right, of course.'

'Naturally.' He looked at her glass. 'Another gin and lime?'

'Yes please.'

He got up and went over to the bar. Waiting to be served, he mulled over his relationship with Brenda. She was a great girl: goodlooking, good fun and warm-hearted, and he thought a lot of her. But she had just complicated the situation by making it clear what she had in mind. Marriage and babies. It wasn't a total surprise since it was the natural outcome of a relationship. But he hadn't expected it this soon. Marriage was absolutely out of the question for him, whether he wanted it or not. But at the same time, he didn't want to end it with Brenda because she meant too much to him. Maybe later on he could persuade her that marriage wasn't the only way to live in a committed way. Forward-thinking bohemian types lived together unashamedly these days without a legal document. But, if he was truly honest, he knew that a girl like Brenda — for all her modernity — wouldn't be prepared to do that.

Was it selfish of him to go on seeing her, knowing that she wouldn't be getting a marriage proposal? Maybe he should be straight with her right away and risk losing her. On the other hand he'd given her plenty of hints, told her that marriage wasn't for him in a casual sort of way and she'd still wanted to go on seeing him. She seemed very keen as it happened. So there was no need to do anything drastic for the moment. They were very happy together as things were, so why not let it continue?

★ ★ ★

One Saturday a few weeks later, Sadie took a long journey on public transport — the train, two buses and a lengthy walk — to the beautiful Surrey village of Paley and rang the doorbell of an elegant house in a leafy avenue on the outskirts.

Gerald answered the door. 'Oh . . . Sadie, hello.' She saw a mixture of surprise and panic in his eyes as this visit was unannounced and would doubtless upset his wife. Ever the gentleman, however, he managed a smile and said, 'Come on in.'

'Thank you.'

He led her into the sitting room where his wife was sitting in an armchair reading the *Lady* magazine.

'You,' she said, looking up and starting to rise. 'You dare to show your face here.'

'Yes, I do as it happens,' agreed Sadie. 'I'm sorry to have come without letting you know but I felt I had to see you because I have something very important to tell you. I thought if you knew I was coming you'd make sure you were out.'

'We would indeed,' confirmed the older woman. 'But if you've come to tell us about the date for the trial of Paul's murderer you could have sent a letter or telephoned.'

'It isn't about that,' she told her. 'We still don't have a date for the trial.'

'That's the only thing that could be important enough to allow you inside this house,' Harriet said. 'I want that murderer to pay the price for what he's done.'

'We all do,' said Sadie, 'but there is something more important even than that.'

'I can't think what it can be,' said Harriet.

Sadie hesitated, looking from one to the other, then said, 'I've come to tell you that you are going to be grandparents.'

Gerald beamed instinctively. 'Oh, how lovely. That's wonderful news,' he said. 'Congratulations, my dear.'

Harriet peered at Sadie over the top of her glasses. 'How many months pregnant are you?' she asked.

Sadie recognised the accusation in the

question. 'Four months,' she informed her. 'So you need have no doubt about it being your son's child.'

'I'm sure Harriet wasn't suggesting . . . ' began Gerald.

'Yes, she was,' said Sadie while Harriet remained silent. 'But it's no more than I would expect from Mrs Weston.' Sadie had not come here lightly or with any notion of pleasure. She had given the matter a great deal of consideration and decided it was the least she could do for Paul, who would have wanted her to offer an olive branch to his parents and news of a baby was surely the perfect opportunity. 'I thought it was only right that you should know about the baby, that's all. Yes, I could have saved myself a long journey and written to you but it's such a personal thing, I wanted to tell you face to face. I expected you to be pleased.'

'You did the right thing in coming here and we are very grateful to you,' Gerald told her with obvious sincerity. 'Now please sit down and have a cup of tea with us. Harriet was just going to make one, weren't you, dear?'

'It's kind of you to offer, Mr Weston, but I don't think that's a good idea,' said Sadie before Harriet had a chance to react. 'I want to go to the grave while I'm here then I shall go to Box Hill. That's where I feel closest to Paul. We spent a lot of time there together.'

'It's quite a long way for you,' Gerald pointed out.

'I'll get the bus a part of the way and the walk will do me good,' she said.

There was a painful silence. Gerald was obviously hoping for some sort of softening from his wife that wasn't forthcoming.

'Well, cheerio then,' said Sadie and turned and left the room with Gerald following her.

'Don't forget to let us know the date of the trial,' Harriet called from the sitting room.

Sadie didn't bother to reply. Her disappointment at Harriet's response to her big news was too much of a blow. She was surprised at her own reaction. After all, Paul's evil witch of a mother meant nothing to her. But it was as though she had snubbed Sadie's unborn child and that was painful. Her emotions were all over the place with this damned pregnancy. She hardly knew who she was any more.

* * *

'There are times when I don't understand my wife, even now after all these years of marriage. It's as though there's a part of her that is out of my reach,' Gerald confessed as he and Sadie sat together on a bench on one of the grassy slopes of Box Hill with a glorious view spread out in front of them. Despite his wife's unveiled disapproval, he had insisted on driving Sadie to the places she wanted to visit and was going to take her to the station when she was ready. He'd seemed to want to join her on the hill rather than wait in the car. 'She really isn't as heartless as she sometimes seems.'

'She's still grieving, I understand that,' Sadie responded. 'But she didn't like me from the very

116

first moment she saw me. She never thought I was good enough for Paul.'

'No woman ever would have been,' he told her. 'It's nothing to do with you personally and everything to do with the intensity of her feelings for Paul. She worshipped the ground he walked on and didn't want to let him go.'

'Yes, that was the impression I got,' she said. 'They say some mothers are like that about their sons, though my mum isn't with my brothers. She's always telling them it's time they were married and off her hands. But I suppose it's different when you only have one child.'

'Yes, that must make a difference. But I have always thought there was something more than that in Harriet's feelings for Paul,' he confided, looking ahead of him, almost as though he was thinking aloud. 'I don't know what it is but there is something that troubles her deeply at times. I am convinced that whatever it is made her possessive of Paul and caused her to shut me out. There is a dark part of my wife's nature that makes her wicked sometimes. I suspect it is out of her control.' He turned to Sadie, looking worried. 'Oh dear, I think I have said things I shouldn't. It's just that I don't want you to judge my wife too harshly. I know she can be very malicious but she does have a heart and has always been a very good wife and mother.'

'Don't worry. This conversation will go no further,' Sadie assured him, sensing that he had needed to talk and guessing that he was a very lonely man within his marriage.

'Thank you.'

'I honestly thought it would please her to know that there is to be a child; her own flesh and blood, her first grandchild who she can watch grow up; something of Paul to remind her of him. I think Paul would have wanted his parents to be involved with his child. So I was disappointed by her reaction.'

'It is only natural that you would feel that way,' Gerald said. 'I'm hoping that in time she will be pleased about the baby. Perhaps when the pain of Paul's death has faded. Maybe after the trial, when justice has been done, it might help her.'

'She does seem very eager about the trial,' Sadie remarked. 'I must admit, I haven't given it a great deal of thought; probably because I've been too busy trying to survive without Paul, and then getting used to the pregnancy and everything. Anyway, nothing is going to bring Paul back. Of course justice must be done but it won't make me miss Paul any the less or change things for any of us, whatever the outcome of the trial.'

'That's true,' he agreed. 'But Harriet is full of revenge so once the man is sentenced I'm hoping it will give her some peace of mind.'

'What about you?' she asked, turning to him. 'How are you coping with your grief?'

'Me?' Gerald seemed surprised that she, or anyone, would ask. 'I'm all right. It's my job to help my wife through it.'

'You have feelings too.'

He shrugged his shoulders, looking sad. 'I

miss him dreadfully, of course, but he was always primarily his mother's son,' he said hoarsely, and she could sense his pain and regret that he hadn't been closer to Paul.

She placed her hand on his briefly in a gesture of friendship. Neither of them spoke for a while then he said, 'When you're ready, I'll drive you to the station.'

'Thank you,' she said.

Sadie knew that his loyalty would always be to his wife, and rightly so. But here on this beautiful sun-drenched hillside, the beginnings of a bond had been forged between them and she sensed that a tiny part of him would be on her side too in the future.

5

It was January 1964 and the trial of Jack Trump for the murder of Paul Weston was underway. Sadie was in the witness box and the atmosphere in the courtroom was breathless with expectation, the questioning intimidating and relentless. Her mouth was so dry she could barely utter a coherent word. This was the first time she had ever been inside a court and she'd had no idea it would be so harrowing for an innocent party. Being eight months pregnant added to the strain too. The room was crowded, every eye upon her. Her family, Ray and Brenda and the Westons, were here but she paid them no heed, being focused entirely on the questions that were being fired at her.

'Would you say that your late husband was a violent man, Mrs Weston?' asked the barrister for the defence.

She considered her answer carefully, mindful of the fact that she was under oath. 'Not usually, no,' she replied nervously.

'When you say 'not usually', are you implying that he could be violent?'

'Occasionally he lost his temper.'

'And then he would become violent?'

'Well . . . not always.'

'Answer the question please,' he ordered brusquely. 'Was your husband capable of violence?'

120

She cleared her throat, nerves giving way to anger at the man's pompous attitude towards her. 'Yes, he could behave out of character if he was angry enough but he wasn't normally like that,' she explained, sounding more confident.

'He was violent on the night of his death in April of last year, wasn't he, Mrs Weston?' His daunting stare never left her face.

'He was in a temper, yes,' she replied, matching his steady gaze with one of her own.

'And this caused him to instigate a fight with the accused, earlier on in the evening before the incident that cost him his life; a fight that was stopped. Is this correct?'

'Yes.'

'Why did he start the fight?'

She paused momentarily then looked the man straight in the eye and said, 'He didn't like the way that Mr Trump was looking at me.'

Her questioner's mouth curled into a sneer. 'Didn't like the way Mr Trump was looking at you,' he repeated with exaggerated incredulity.

Steeling herself against his contemptuous manner she said, 'Yes, that's right.'

He emitted a scornful sigh. 'And did the defendant behave in any other way improperly towards you?' he asked. 'Did he approach you, for instance?'

'No, he just looked . . . er, in the way a man does when he fancies someone,' she said.

'So your husband wanted to fight with the defendant just because of the way he was looking at you?' His voice boomed out in a mocking tone. 'Is that correct?'

An echoing silence descended on the court-room as they waited for her reply. 'Yes,' she said at last.

'The fight which cost your husband his life, was that started by him too?'

Having to go over the terrible events again was very upsetting. 'I don't know because I didn't see what had happened or who struck the first blow,' she told him, forcing herself to go on despite her distress. 'It was all over by the time we got there.' Her voice broke with emotion. 'My husband was already lying on the ground.'

'But prior to this, your husband did pursue the defendant who was going about his business peacefully with his friends at this time with, presumably, no thought of you or your husband.'

'Paul did go after him, yes.'

'What frame of mind was your husband in?' he asked.

'Angry.'

'Was that because he was jealous?'

There was a brief hiatus before she replied defensively. 'Yes. But I don't think he could help it when it came to me.'

'Thank you, Mrs Weston.' The barrister turned to the bench. 'No more questions, m'lord.'

Sadie stepped down and went back to her seat feeling shaky and traumatised. She knew that her evidence would go some way to sealing the fate of the defendant and that was a huge responsibility. But she couldn't lie. It just wasn't in her nature.

★ ★ ★

122

When the murder charge was reduced to one of manslaughter and the defendant found guilty for which he was handed a prison sentence of ten years, Sadie thought it was rather severe, given that he almost certainly hadn't started the fight. She'd been vengeful in the immediate aftermath of Paul's death and wanted the worst for Jack Trump; now all she could think was that one man was dead and another had to go to prison, and all because of Paul's insane jealousy.

She said as much to her mother as they made their way out of the court. 'Yeah, it does seem a terrible waste,' agreed Marge. 'I bet you're glad it's over.'

'It was nerve-wracking to say the least,' she said.

'I think the sentence was probably about right,' remarked her father. 'Admittedly Jack Trump was goaded but he was too heavy-handed and a man died so he has to be punished. You can't kill someone and get away with it, no matter what the provocation.'

'He probably won't serve the full sentence anyway,' opined Don. 'He could get a few years knocked off for good behaviour.'

'You reckon?' said Sadie.

'Definitely,' Don replied. 'You hear about that sort of thing all the time.'

This news made Sadie feel better. Anyone could see that Jack Trump was no murderer. He'd simply inflicted an unlucky blow under pressure.

Outside in the corridor people were milling about. Ray and Brenda, who had also had to give

123

evidence, both gave her a hug and said she'd done well, then joined in the general conversation. Excusing herself, Sadie headed for the ladies, a slave to her bladder at this late stage of the pregnancy.

Deeply immersed in her thoughts, she didn't notice anyone else around as she washed her hands at the basin so it was a shock to find herself being attacked from behind as she dried her hands on the roller towel. Someone was hitting her across the back and shoulders. She swung round.

'You filthy liar,' roared Harriet Weston, her face contorted with fury. 'Because of your lies my son's murderer has got away with it. You're a traitor. How dare you tell them that Paul was violent?'

'Mrs Weston, please,' gasped Sadie, managing to keep the woman at arm's length. 'I was under oath. I had to tell the truth about what happened that night. Anyway, Jack Trump hasn't got away with it. He's going to prison.'

'Ten years, that's nothing to what he deserves, especially as he'll probably be released early,' she ranted. 'He should be hanged. Or sent to prison for the rest of his life.'

'It was a fight, Mrs Weston . . . not a premeditated murder. There is a very big difference.'

'My son was not violent,' she shrieked. 'He wouldn't have hurt a fly. You shouldn't have said those things.'

Sadie could see how genuinely distressed the other woman was. They were both grieving so

124

she could understand her pain, even though she was angered by her behaviour. 'Calm down,' she urged her. 'Let's go for a cup of tea and talk about it.'

'I'd sooner die than discuss anything with you,' the other woman shouted, her voice trembling, cheeks bright and feverish. 'You're nothing but a common little liar.'

Exhausted from her ordeal in court and pained by these vile accusations, Sadie felt sick and lightheaded. 'Just leave me alone, will you,' she said, tears welling up. 'Get out of here and give me some peace.'

'Don't you dare tell me what to do,' the older woman ranted, clearly beside herself. 'I'll go when I'm ready.'

Before Sadie had a chance to put up any kind of defence, Harriet laid into her again, hitting her around the head, then pushed her so hard that she fell against the sink, lost her balance and bumped to the floor, landing on her bottom with a thud that sent a jarring sensation right through her.

'I never want to set eyes on you again,' was Mrs Weston's parting shot before she left.

Slumped on the floor, leaning against the wall, Sadie was trembling all over, her skin suffused with cold sweat. As she tried to get to her feet a pain shot through her lower abdomen and she went back down, crying out.

'Oh, my good Gawd,' said her mother who had come to find out what was keeping her daughter. 'What's happened to you, darlin'? Have you had a funny turn? Let me help you up.'

'I slipped, Mum,' Sadie said, knowing that the family would be incensed if they knew the real reason she was sitting on the floor. 'I've got a nasty pain though. I think it might be the baby starting.'

'It can't be,' declared Marge, taking her hand and helping her up. 'You're not due yet.'

'It must just be wind or something then,' she said so as not to worry her mother. 'I'll be all right.'

But even as they reached the corridor and she felt another pain bearing down, she knew something was dreadfully wrong. She was absolutely terrified but somehow, and she surprised herself in this, she managed to stay strong. She just said calmly, 'I think I need to go to hospital, Mum.'

'Ray,' bellowed Marge, pale-faced and worried. 'We need a lift to the hospital pronto. It's the baby. We think it's coming early.'

'Bloody 'ell,' exclaimed Sadie's father as the others looked on in horror.

'We'll have you there in no time, don't worry,' said Ray calmly, striding up to Sadie and talking her arm. 'Leave it to me.'

★ ★ ★

It was obvious to Sadie that the medical team delivering her baby at Hammersmith Hospital were worried, even though she could barely think straight against the agony of the labour pains. There was a doctor in attendance throughout for one thing, instead of just the midwife and nurses, and they kept speaking in low voices and using medical terms that meant nothing to her.

'What's the matter?' she asked at one point. 'Is there something wrong with my baby? Why do you keep whispering?'

'Just doing our job,' replied the midwife. 'You do yours by following our instructions please.'

'Is it because it's coming early?' persisted Sadie.

'Obviously it would have been better if you'd gone the full term,' said the midwife. 'But you concentrate on getting it born and leave the rest to us.'

Sadie did as she was told, pushing and panting, yelling and screaming. Then, after one final almighty shove that felt as though it would split her in two, she heard a cry and the midwife said, 'Well done, Mrs Weston, you have a beautiful little girl.'

She held the child for Sadie to see then cut the cord and said, 'She has to go in an incubator for a while.'

'An incubator,' said Sadie worriedly. 'Why? What's the matter with her?'

'She didn't stay quite long enough on the inside so she needs a little help out here,' the midwife explained.

'Can I hold her?'

'No, not yet,' said the midwife, handing the baby to a nurse who took her away.

'She will be all right, won't she?' probed Sadie when a nurse handed her a much-wanted cup of tea.

'There is always a risk with a premature baby,

of course,' explained the other woman, putting the fear of God into Sadie. 'But she's in good hands. We'll do everything we can and we have a very high success rate here at this hospital.'

'Thank God for small mercies then,' said Sadie.

'I'll leave you alone to drink your tea then someone will take you to the ward,' she said and hurried away, her rubber-soled shoes squeaking against the polished floor.

Sadie drank her tea, tears streaming down her face. Something — other than the physical side of childbirth — had happened to her and she was bewildered by it. She felt as though she wasn't the same person who had been driven to the hospital by Ray. During the months of pregnancy, a situation she hadn't wanted, she had dreaded the idea of motherhood; had worried about it incessantly, fretting about her ability to face up to the responsibility of raising a child. She had even been resentful at times of having her life turned upside down for the second time.

But the instant she'd seen that fragment of humanity, she'd felt both strong and vulnerable almost simultaneously and had experienced a surge of love so strong it had brought tears to her eyes. She knew instinctively that she would give her life for her if it was ever necessary. As it was with her baby's father, it had been love at first sight and now she might lose her because of that witch Harriet Weston. No one had told Sadie the reason she had gone into labour early but she was certain it was because of the force with which she had hit the floor after Harriet's assault. She'd felt something happen as the shock waves jarred through her body. God help that bitch if my baby dies, she thought.

'If someone has to die let it be me, not her,' she said to the nurse who came to take her to the ward.

'Now you're just being dramatic,' said the nurse chirpily. 'You're not the first mother to have a premature baby you know, some much earlier than yours, and lots of them come through it without any permanent ill effects. It isn't the olden days when there was no modern equipment, remember. This is the 1960s. Your daughter will be fine, I'm sure.'

'I hope so, I really do.' And Sadie had never meant anything more sincerely in her life.

* * *

'Oh Harriet, how could you have done such a terrible thing?' exclaimed Gerald a week or so later when he finally persuaded his wife to tell him what had been upsetting her so much ever since the trial. He'd known she was rattled by the verdict but she'd been especially agitated and he'd been married to her for long enough to know when her rarely used guilty conscience was bothering her. 'I can hardly believe that you would physically attack Sadie, especially when she's heavily pregnant. How was she when you left?'

'Sitting on the floor, looking dazed.'

'Oh my God! Didn't you even try to help her

up? Or stay to see if she was all right?'

'No. I was in such a rage, I stormed off and then came home with you, so I don't even know the outcome and I've been worrying about it ever since.'

'I should damned well hope you have been too. You are the giddy limit Harriet, you really are,' he admonished angrily. 'Something like that could have seriously damaged the baby and heaven only knows what it's done to Sadie.'

'I know and that's why I'm so worried,' she confessed. 'I mean, if it really is Paul's baby it's our own flesh and blood.'

'It *is* Paul's baby. There's no *if* about it,' he declared, his voice rising. 'You had no right to doubt Sadie. She wouldn't lie about a thing like that. Even apart from the fact that it isn't in her nature, why would she since she wants nothing from us? Honestly, Harriet, I sometimes wonder why I put up with you when you do such wicked things.'

'I'm sorry, Gerald. I don't know what makes me do them,' she said, looking downcast. 'Losing Paul has been such a blow. I'm not thinking straight.'

'Yes, I know you've been traumatised,' he said, observing how emaciated she was now. She'd lost more than just her appetite over Paul's death; she seemed to have been robbed of every last vestige of her limited supply of good will. She was so full of spite, it hurt him to see her like it. 'But you can't go around attacking people, especially Sadie who has lost the man

130

she loved too. There really is no excuse for that sort of behaviour.'

'She didn't love him like I did.'

He doubted if any normal person could have been as obsessed with her son as Harriet had been but he said, 'Of course not. A mother's love is quite different to that of a wife. But let's not waste time discussing that; we need to find out if she's all right.'

'Do you think she's told her family about what I did to her?' she asked.

'If she had done they'd have been after you with fury in their hearts,' he said. 'And I wouldn't blame them either. So I think you can safely assume that she hasn't. She knew it would cause trouble so she kept it to herself. That's the way she is.'

'I'm sorry, Gerald.'

'It isn't me you need to say that to,' he pointed out coldly. 'It's Sadie.'

She made a face. 'I suppose so. But we need to find out how she is first,' she suggested.

'I'll phone them.' He perceived her genuine anxiety. 'It's all right, Harriet. You don't deserve it but I won't mention what happened between you and Sadie after the trial. I'll make it a casual grandparent to grandparent call. She's near to her time so it won't seem odd. Don't stand over me in the hall telling me what to say while I make the call though. You wait in here out of the way.'

'All right, Gerald,' she said meekly, her power substantially reduced by the enormity of her transgression.

When he came back into the room, looking pale and anxious, she said, 'Whatever is the matter?'

'Sadie went into labour immediately after the trial. The baby was premature.'

Her hand flew to her throat. 'Oh no,' she cried.

'You may well look worried, as the premature birth is obviously a result of your attack,' he said gruffly. 'But fortunately the baby, a little girl, is doing well. She's still in an incubator but expected to come out of it any day now.'

'Thank God,' she said.

'You'll apologise to Sadie at some point soon if I have to drag you there and stand over you while you do it,' he said grimly. 'That's the very least you can do.'

Harriet ruled the roost in their marriage but she knew she could only push her husband so far and then the tide turned. 'Yes, you're right, Gerald; it is,' she agreed without argument.

★ ★ ★

Sadie's confidence grew as day followed day and little Rosie Weston continued to survive. Sadie's joy knew no bounds when she was allowed to hold her for the first time and feed her. She had been expressing milk for the nurses to do it up until now.

'She's like a delicate little rosebud,' she said to the nurse. 'So pretty and sweet. Her name really suits, don't you think? I'm really glad that I chose it.'

'I think it's a lovely name.'

Sadie was suddenly imbued with a wave of sorrow as she thought of Paul and how they should have chosen the name together like couples did, arguing about it and taking time to agree. Paul hadn't even known she was pregnant but she would make sure Rosie knew all about her dad and what a terrific person he had been.

Even when Rosie came out of the incubator she and Sadie had to stay in hospital until the baby regained her birth weight. The medical team were taking no chances and insisted that she wait until they were absolutely certain that Rosie was strong enough for Sadie to take her home. Naturally the new mother was eager to leave the hospital but she didn't want to take any risks with her precious daughter. Anyway, there was always visiting time to give her contact with the outside world. It was a somewhat sad time of day for her as all the other young mums had their husbands to visit, but Sadie was so full of gratitude to have her baby alive and thriving there was no room left for envy.

Every day the family plus Brenda and Ray trooped into the ward and took their turn at the bedside to conform to the only-two-at-a-time rule. One day Marge said to Sadie, 'Your in-laws are outside. I said I'd ask you if you want to see them. I wasn't sure.'

Sadie's mother had already told her that the Westons had been in touch by telephone and she had guessed that Gerald would want to see the baby. But she was amazed that Harriet had the temerity to come anywhere near her after what she'd done. Still, even Harriet Weston's evil nature couldn't touch her now that her baby was thriving. Motherhood had brought with it a feeling of fearlessness against outside influences. 'Yeah, you can tell them to come in please, Mum.'

'Only for a few minutes,' warned Marge. 'Visiting time isn't long, and your brothers want to come in too.'

'A few minutes will be quite long enough, believe me, Mum,' said Sadie with a wry grin.

* * *

Sadie didn't know what to expect, other than that Gerald would be his usual amiable self. The last thing she was anticipating was an apology from his wife, and an exaggerated one at that.

'Can you ever forgive me for what I did to you?' she asked, and Sadie couldn't help but notice how haggard she looked.

'Forgive you? Are you mad?' was Sadie's honest response. 'I could have lost my daughter because of your wickedness and I very nearly did.'

'I know, and I can't tell you how sorry I am,' she said, seeming genuinely contrite. 'I don't know what came over me. I wasn't in my right mind after the trial.'

Oddly enough, Sadie believed her. She'd seen how demented Harriet was when she'd attacked her. But she still didn't trust her. 'You can't come in here all sweetness and light expecting me to behave as though nothing has happened. I

134

accept that you were very distressed on the day of the trial but that doesn't excuse your behaviour.'

'I know,' she said feebly.

'You've never liked me, and vice versa. So we aren't going to become bosom pals just because you are grandmother to my daughter. Too much has gone before.'

'I think a lot of what I said and did was caused by grief,' Harriet tried to excuse herself. 'But, anyway, I only came here to apologise. I'm not expecting anything more.'

'Thank you for not saying anything to anyone else about what Harriet did to you,' said Gerald and Sadie guessed that he was behind this visit. He must have insisted his wife come to make amends. 'It was very good of you.'

'I didn't keep quiet to protect her,' she told him. 'I didn't want my family upset, that's why I didn't say anything. They would have been beside themselves and there was no point in causing uproar if there was no need. All's well that ends well as it happens.' She looked at Harriet with a grim expression. 'Though I can't begin to imagine what I would have done to you if Rosie hadn't come through it so well.'

At least the other woman had the grace to look sheepish. 'I can see your point,' she said and with a swift change of subject added, 'We haven't brought a present for her; we thought it would be better to find out what you need before we do that. Anything at all and don't worry about the expense. It isn't every day you become grandparents.'

'Thank you,' said Sadie. 'I'll give it some thought.'

'May we have a look at the baby?' asked the older woman.

'Yes, of course.'

'She's beautiful,' said Harriet, gazing into the cot.

'Hear hear,' added Gerald.

'Yes, she is,' agreed Sadie.

'Not surprising when you think who her parents are,' said Gerald lightly.

He was such a thoroughly good sort Sadie found herself wanting him to be involved in her daughter's life, if only in a small way. But he came as part of a package with his ghastly wife, that was the snag. However, her own joy in life made her feel generous towards others and she made a sudden decision.

'Look, it won't be easy after everything that's happened and it may take a long time but I think you and I should try to get along, Mrs Weston, for Rosie's sake. She is your granddaughter, after all, and I think Paul would want you to get to know her as she grows up. I'm not saying you will see a lot of her but I'm prepared to bring her to see you every now and again, if you would like.'

'We'd like that very much, wouldn't we, dear?' said Gerald, looking pleased.

Harriet was too busy inspecting her grand-child for any noticeable likeness to her son to answer, even though she had heard what was said. She desperately wanted to see something of him in this child. But the baby's eyes were closed

136

and she was wrapped in a shawl so it wasn't easy to tell. However there was something about the shape of her face that reminded her of Paul at that age. The more she peered at her and willed it to happen, the more certain she made herself become. Oh yes, this child was the image of her father. Paul would live on through her.

'What do you say then, Harriet?' asked Gerald.

At last she looked up. 'That would be very nice indeed. Thank you, Sadie,' she said, and smiled for the first time since the death of her son. In fact she was beaming. It did Gerald's heart good to see it. Harriet was a very difficult woman, there was no denying that. But she was his wife and, for all her many faults, he cared deeply for her.

★   ★   ★

Back at home, Sadie fell into the routine of motherhood as though born to it. As Rosie grew and her features began to develop, her likeness to her father was wonderfully conspicuous. She had Paul's dark eyes and hair and Sadie was delighted.

When Rosie was two months old, Sadie found it necessary to take an evening shift in a factory three nights a week, and her mother looked after the baby with Dad and the boys as back-up. Even by living rent-free and only having to pay for her keep she could still barely manage so a part-time job wasn't a permanent solution. She needed full-time work but couldn't bear the thought of putting Rosie into a nursery or leaving her with a child minder who would be a stranger.

A few hours babysitting in the evening was one thing to ask of her mother but it wasn't fair to burden her by asking her to have Rosie all day. Mum had raised three children and was entitled to some time to herself now. Anyway, she'd made it clear when Sadie first became pregnant that she wouldn't bring the baby up for her, and neither would Sadie want that. She wanted to raise her own child and hated the idea of going back to work full-time, but without a husband to support her and Rosie she needed to earn a proper wage.

By breast-feeding and using the clothes Rosie had been given as gifts, she managed to keep her daughter's upkeep to a minimum. Paul's parents had given her money as a birth present so she had that put by for clothes for the baby as she grew out of the ones she already had. She would get the christening over with and then seriously look for a job and a child minder.

* * *

'That mother-in-law of yours seems to have turned over a new leaf,' observed Marge on the evening after the christening party when the guests had gone except for Brenda and Ray and they were all relaxing at the house, the baby asleep in her cot upstairs. 'She was as nice as pie to me and seems very fond of the baby.'

Leopards and spots came into Sadie's mind

but she said, 'Yes, she's changed her attitude to me altogether.'

'There's nothing like a baby to bring out the best in people,' said the good-hearted Marge.

'Her husband Gerald is a nice bloke,' remarked Cyril. 'He says the little one has bucked up his missus no end. He was very pleased you invited them to the christening, Sadie.'

'I thought it was only right they should be asked,' she said, though she was very glad to see the back of them because she still didn't feel comfortable with Harriet Weston around. 'I want them to be involved with Rosie . . . only in a small way.'

Laughter erupted.

'Little and not too often, eh,' grinned Ray. 'Is that the way to get along with in-laws?'

'Depends on the in-laws,' smiled Sadie.

'There you are, Ray,' said Derek jokingly. 'Now you know how to stay friends with Brenda's folks.'

Brenda coloured up. 'You're being a bit previous, Derek,' she said. 'We aren't even engaged.'

'As good as,' put in Don devilishly, glancing at the couple who were sitting in the same armchair, Brenda on Ray's lap. 'You're always together and all over each other. I'm sure it won't be long before he makes an honest woman of you, Brenda.'

'Shut up, Don,' admonished Sadie, seeing her friend squirm. 'You're embarrassing them.'

'Sorry, folks,' he said. 'No offence meant.'

'None taken,' said Ray.

'Let's have some music to liven things up,' suggested Marge to gloss over an awkward moment. 'Let's put on the latest Beatles record that Ray brought over for us.'

'Yeah, let's do that,' agreed Sadie, picking up the disc from the top of the radiogram and looking at the title. ''Can't Buy Me Love'. Are you all ready for it?'

There was a cheer of approval.

'Fetch some drinks, Cyril,' said Marge, getting in the party mood. 'We've got some booze left from earlier. It won't wake the baby, will it, Sadie?'

'No, she's used to noise, living in this house, and that's the way I like it. She'll sleep through anything.'

As they all joined in with the lads from Liverpool, Ray wasn't singing along. He was thinking about Derek's remarks. Everyone, especially Brenda, was expecting their relationship to lead to marriage and now that the hints about an engagement had started there would be no stopping them. Everyone would be at it. Why did people always assume that everybody wanted to get married?

The irony was that Ray was beginning to warm to the idea himself, especially since Sadie had had the baby. He adored little Rosie and found himself lingering on the idea of fatherhood. A family of his own; he wanted that more than anything. The baby had certainly transformed Sadie. She had changed from a spoilt, empty-headed brat into a caring and responsible woman whilst retaining her sense of fun.

The only way he could have a family of his own was if he could persuade Brenda to set up home with him without a marriage certificate. It would be a serious commitment on his part — he would love her and look after her, protect and provide for her; all of those things — but there would be no legal document. Although 'living together' wasn't entirely unheard-of in these modern times it was still considered shocking by the greater part of society. Brenda was a traditional girl and there was no way she would consider such an arrangement. No matter how much she loved him. It was ingrained in working-class girls like Brenda almost from birth. They didn't have academic qualifications or career aspirations so marriage was their aim in life. And there was nothing wrong with that at all. But it made it difficult for someone like him, for whom marriage wasn't an option.

Sooner or later things were going to come to a head and he would probably lose Brenda. He couldn't bear to think of that because she had become a very important part of his life and he wanted it to stay that way. His conscience told him he couldn't have it both ways and therefore his only option was to end it with her so that she could find someone else who could give her what she wanted. He would do anything in the world for her; except marry her!

He was startled out of his reverie by the sound of the Beatles and Sadie's cheery tones.

'Come on, Bren,' she said, pulling her friend to her feet. 'Let's have a dance. I don't get to go out dancing nowadays so let's have some rock'n'roll here at home.'

★ ★ ★

Watching Sadie jigging around with Brenda, both singing their heads off, Marge's pride in her daughter was renewed. She'd lost none of her youthful exuberance to motherhood but she had matured hugely since she'd had Rosie. Frankly Marge was amazed. She had expected all the laborious tasks to land in her lap; changing the baby, washing the nappies and getting up to go to her in the night.

But Sadie, who had previously been known to lie in bed until dinnertime on a Sunday, now rose early every morning and had the nappies on the line straight after breakfast. Appreciative of being able to live here as she never had been before she'd left, she helped with the shopping and cleaning, took the baby almost everywhere with her and never once asked for help. She did so much that Marge wished she would. Now that Sadie had proved herself and didn't take everything for granted as she had in the past, Marge was only too willing to lend a hand with her granddaughter.

Her worries about Sadie being selfish and spoilt had ended with Rosie's birth. In putting her baby first by instinct Sadie seemed to have learned to be more thoughtful towards other people too. In a process that had begun with Paul's death, Sadie had grown up. She still had her off moments, the same as everyone else, but she was a much nicer human being now.

★ ★ ★

'Sorry I dropped you in it with Brenda on Sunday with all that talk about in-laws,' said Derek Bell to Ray one evening in the pub a few days later. 'I'd had a few drinks and my mouth had a life of its own.'

'You could do a lot worse than Brenda if you're thinking of settling down,' added Don, deliberately provoking him.

'Don't encourage him,' joshed Derek. 'Once he goes up that aisle he'll be lost to us. No more coming out for a drink with his mates, not without the wife's permission anyway.'

'I wouldn't bet on it,' said Ray, joining in the joke even though the issue hit a raw nerve. 'There are pubs all over the country full of married men any night of the week.'

'All escaping,' said Don.

'Just taking a break, I should think,' said Ray, keeping it light to hide his feelings.

'Don and I know when we're well off,' Derek went on. 'We've got a smashing mum to look after us and we come and go as we please. Why would we throw that away?'

Ray didn't continue along those lines and the conversation moved to other things.

'How's business, Ray?' Derek enquired casually.

'I've no complaints,' he replied.

'Everyone's dipping into their pockets and buying records then?'

'A lot are, fortunately for me.'

'Are the Beatles your top seller?' asked Don.

'Oh yes,' he confirmed without reservation. 'Young girls want to sleep with them and the boys want to be them so they're all buying their records.'

'I wouldn't mind their money,' Don remarked. 'They must be making an absolute packet, especially now that they've cracked America. They've gone down a storm over there.'

'It would be nice for you if you earned as much selling their records as they do for making them.'

'Wouldn't it just,' agreed Ray lightly. 'But I'm doing all right so I'm happy. Every young bloke wants a guitar these days. So they go out as fast as I buy them in.'

'You'll be able to retire to Spain soon,' suggested Derek with a hearty laugh.

'You're being a bit overly ambitious there, mate,' Ray smiled. 'But I am thinking of expanding and moving the business inside.'

Both brothers waited with interest for him to go on.

'There's an empty shop for rent near the Broadway that I'm interested in,' he explained. 'It's in a side street off the main shopping area, so the rent is affordable, but it isn't too far off the beaten track as to make it unviable as a good business opportunity.'

'What's brought this on?' asked Derek because Ray, typically, hadn't previously discussed his plans.

'It just seems like the next step for me. The

144

stall isn't big enough now that I'm selling more musical instruments,' he told them. 'The storage is a problem too with just the stall and keeping the stock in a lock-up. The overheads of a shop will be more but, with a bit of luck and plenty of effort on my part, the turnover should be too.'

'Seems as though you've got it all worked out,' said Derek. 'So you must be serious about it.'

'Serious enough to put an offer in for the shop,' he told him.

'That's really good news and I hope you do well,' said Derek.

'Me too,' added his brother.

'Thanks, boys,' said Ray, warmed by their support. Their friendship was as important to him now as it had been when he'd been a lonely teenager new to the area. As brothers they were complete in themselves but seemed to like having him around too. He enjoyed their company and had done since the first time they'd met. Some people you bonded with instantly and he had with them. 'Let's drink to it. What are you having?'

As Ray ordered the drinks, Derek found himself thinking about his pal. He'd done well for himself since coming out of the car trade, and obviously had a flair for business. He was a genuine bloke and Derek trusted him implicitly. But, although he was sociable and just like one of their own, he was a bit of a loner in some respects and never liked to talk about himself; maybe because his upbringing had been different, having been raised by his grandparents. But it was odd that he rarely spoke about them and always changed the subject if it strayed anywhere near to his life before he'd come to Hammersmith.

It must be hard for him, not having any folks of his own, thought Derek. Hardly imaginable for someone as deeply rooted in family as he himself was. Still his pal was with Brenda now and she seemed to think a lot of him. She was a decent girl and would give him plenty of support. He really did wish him well with his business expansion. No one deserved success more than Ray.

'Cheers, mate,' he said as Ray handed him a pint.

6

Until she'd got pregnant Sadie almost never visited a doctor's surgery. Since she'd had Rosie she seemed to spend half of her life there. As well as the series of infant essentials such as vaccinations and weight checks there were also sudden and inexplicable symptoms that sent Sadie scurrying in search of medical advice for her baby.

'You'll be charging me rent soon,' she said lightly to the receptionist when she went to the surgery one morning in June. 'The amount of times I'm here lately.' She looked at Rosie and placed her hand gently on to her brow. 'It's madam again. She's been fretful on and off all night. She keeps coming over very feverish so I'd like the doctor to have a look at her, please.'

'She looks perfectly all right to me,' said the receptionist curtly.

'It comes and goes but there is obviously something the matter so I'd like her to see the doctor.'

'Babies' temperatures vary and don't need to be constantly monitored,' responded the woman critically.

'I'm aware of that which is why I don't do it,' retorted Sadie. 'So now that we have established that, can you fix me up with an appointment, please?'

Thin-faced and fortyish, the receptionist had a

superior manner and a distinct lack of interest. She looked at the appointments book. 'The doctor is fully booked so you'll have to wait until after surgery and take a chance that he can see you then, though there are already a few patients waiting so you might not be lucky. It will probably be better to make an appointment for another day.'

'As it's today and not another day that my daughter is poorly, I'll wait, thank you,' said Sadie coolly.

'Give me your details then and take your turn,' the woman said with an irritable sigh.

The waiting room was crowded but Sadie managed to find somewhere to sit with Rosie on her lap.

'You wouldn't think so many people would be ill in the summer, would you?' remarked the woman sitting next to her.

Finding it rather an odd observation, Sadie said, 'People get ill at any time of the year, don't they?'

'Yeah, I suppose they do,' she replied. 'But I always think of winter as the sickly season because of all the colds and flu that do the rounds.'

'I see what you mean,' said Sadie.

'I've had a belly ache for a couple of days so I need something to shift it.' She lowered her voice and assumed a confidential air. 'Mind you, you'd think we weren't entitled to see the doctor at all the way that bitch of a receptionist carries on. It's the National Health Service and available to us all by law and I've had to remind her of that a good few times, the stuck-up mare. She makes me feel like a time waster just because I want to see the doctor. She's even turned me away before now because I didn't have an appointment. Blimin' cheek. Anyone would think she had medical qualifications herself. Mind you the doc is a real sweetheart, don't you think?'

'Yes, he is very nice,' agreed Sadie.

'Deserves better than the likes of her working for him.'

'She isn't very pleasant, I must admit,' said Sadie.

'Still, we won't have to put up with her for much longer, thank goodness,' the woman remarked.

'Is she leaving then?'

'Yeah, as soon as they find a replacement for her, apparently,' the woman informed her. 'Good riddance too. A sourpuss like her shouldn't be in a job dealing with people who are feeling off-colour. The doc needs someone with some understanding. It's all very well being able to move a few files about and answer the phone with a bit of savvy but you've got to have a way with people too in the medical game.'

'Yes, you're quite right,' said Sadie thoughtfully.

★ ★ ★

'It's a mild virus,' diagnosed Dr Russell after examining Rosie.

'A virus,' said Sadie. 'Does it have a name?'

'Take your pick.' He was a hearty, middle-aged

149

man with vivid blue eyes, white hair and a jovial manner. 'There are so many bugs about these days it's often impossible to tell.'

'Oh,' said Sadie, not liking the sound of this at all. 'Isn't a virus serious?'

'Some are. This one isn't. There's nothing for you to worry about at all, my dear. She might be a bit off-colour for a few days but it will pass. Make sure she has plenty of liquids. Keep your eye on her and come and see me again if she seems worse or it doesn't clear up.'

'Thank you.'

'Everything else all right?' he asked in a friendly manner. He was a local man and knew about her circumstances.

'Yes. Everything is fine.' She stood up to leave, holding the baby against her shoulder. 'May I ask you something please, doctor? I'll be very quick because I know you have to go out on your rounds.'

'Ask away, my dear,' he said, looking at his watch.

★ ★ ★

'So what did the doctor have to say?' asked Marge when Sadie got home. 'What's the matter with our beautiful baby girl?'

Sadie told her.

'Oh, thank God it's nothing serious.' She studied her daughter who seemed worried, and jumped to conclusions. 'She'll be all right, love. Babies do get these little upsets. You did the right thing in taking her to the doctor to stop you

150

from worrying. We know it's nothing serious. That's the important thing.'

'It isn't that, Mum,' Sadie said. 'Something else has come up that needs sorting.'

'Oh?'

'There's a receptionist's job going at the surgery because the woman who works there is leaving. I've got clerical experience and I'm sure I could handle it,' she told her. 'Four days a week and it's only a few minutes' walk from here. Monday, Tuesday, Thursday and Friday, so it's almost full-time. The doctor's mother looks after the reception on Wednesdays.'

'Did you tell him you were interested?'

She nodded. 'But I said I have to arrange suitable childcare before I can take it any further. He told me to go and see him after surgery this evening for a proper chat about the job.'

'So why the long face?'

Sadie looked at her daughter who was now being cuddled by her grandmother. 'It's the thought of leaving Rosie. I need a job and I really fancy this one.' She made a face. 'But I hate the idea of her being with a stranger all day. A woman who does child minding is advertising in the newsagents' window. I'll have to give her a ring to find out more about her, I suppose. Or I could ask at that nursery near the Broadway to see if there are any vacancies.'

'You'll do no such thing,' said her mother.

'But I have to work, Mum.'

'I know but you don't have to leave Rosie with a stranger when you have me.'

Sadie looked astonished. 'I thought, I mean,

151

you said from the start that you wouldn't . . . '

'I said I wouldn't bring the baby up for you, I didn't say I wouldn't look after her while you face up to your responsibilities and go out to work to provide for your child. You've proved what a good and caring mother you are, now I'm going to step in and help out. If you'd asked me before Rosie was born I would probably have said no, but I'm proud of the way you've coped since losing Paul. It can't be easy for you but you get on with it and don't complain.'

'Are you sure you don't mind having her?'

'Positive,' Marge confirmed. 'It's the obvious solution. It isn't as if I have a job to go to. So you go and see the doctor later on and snap up the job if he offers it to you.'

'It's so good of you, Mum,' Sadie said, tears of gratitude welling up. 'At least this way I can go to work with an easy mind knowing that my baby is being well looked after.'

'It will be nice for me too,' Marge remarked. 'It will give me a chance to do things for my granddaughter. You're so damned independent these days, I don't get much of a look-in.'

'I didn't want to impose on you after what you said.'

'The girl I said that to no longer exists,' she pointed out. 'So forget all about it. I'll soon tell you if you start taking liberties again. You know me, I speak my mind.'

'You certainly do,' said Sadie, smiling. 'But all three of your kids have turned out all right.'

Marge smiled back and Sadie felt a powerful surge of love for her. Having a child of her own

152

had aroused strong filial feelings in her. After taking everything for granted all her life, she now realised just how much her parents had done for her over the years.

★ ★ ★

The job at the surgery was rather daunting initially, mostly due to the fact that the phone rang relentlessly and the number of patients wanting to see the doctor by far outweighed the number of appointments available. Being the other side of the counter certainly gave Sadie an understanding of why her predecessor had been so grumpy. When someone was ill they wanted to be made better pronto and took it out on the receptionist if she couldn't magic up an appointment.

But from day one Sadie knew that this was the right job for her. For the first time ever she enjoyed going to work. Instead of filing meaningless documents all day, her routine tasks were much more personal. She found pleasure in the interaction with the patients and took a pride in the clerical work. Her duties were varied. Among other things she had to find and re-file patients' notes, book surgery appointments and home visits, deal with people on the phone, judge whether a situation was serious enough to interrupt the doctor during a consultation, and remind him of phone calls and letters he had to do regarding the patients who were being referred for further investigation. This was a whole lot more satisfying than any of her previous positions. Until now she hadn't realised that employment could be so fulfilling.

'How are you settling into the job, Sadie?' asked Dr John Russell one day when she'd been there about a month, as she was taking his coffee in to him.

'Very well, thank you,' she said. 'I enjoy it actually.'

'Good.' He had been the Bells' family doctor for as long Sadie could remember and she liked him. In his late fifties, he was married to a doctor and they had grown-up children. He had a warm smile which he didn't use sparingly, no matter how busy he was. 'I must say I'm pleased with you. The patients seem to have taken to you. I've had several positive comments.'

'Oh, that's nice,' she beamed.

'Everything all right at home?' he asked. 'Is your mother coping with the baby?'

She smiled. 'More than coping; she's in her element. Rosie is getting so interesting now. She's doing something new every day. Mum seems reborn, especially since she's been looking after her while I'm at work.'

He leaned back slightly and tapped his chin with a pen, looking at her meditatively. 'I'm pleased to hear that because I was telling a colleague of mine — a lady doctor — about you,' he said.

'Oh really,' she responded, wondering why he might have done that.

'She needs a receptionist for her family planning clinic on Wednesday mornings and she wondered if you might be interested. I know you

154

value your day off but it would only be for a couple of hours a week. Not nearly as hectic as this job, I promise you, and it would be a bit of extra money for you.'

Sadie was flattered that he thought highly enough of her to recommend her to another doctor. She also thought the job might be interesting and the money would be very useful indeed. But her time off was precious and she also had her mother to consider.

'Where is the job?'

'At the town clinic,' he replied. 'So it's very local.'

She was extremely tempted. 'Can I think about it?' she asked.

'Of course. My colleague would expect that. She knows that you have responsibilities.' He sipped his coffee and changed the subject. 'Now do you have my list of home visits ready for me?'

'Yes, it's all ready. I'll go and get it,' she said with mixed feelings as she left the room. She wanted to do the second job but it would be more time away from her baby. Anyway, before she could make any sort of decision she needed to speak to her mother.

★ ★ ★

Marge was happy to look after Rosie for a couple more hours a week and Sadie was in no position to turn down the opportunity to earn extra cash so she started at the family planning clinic the following week. As Dr Russell had predicted it was a much less frantic atmosphere. Compared to the surgery it was peaceful.

Sadie sat at a table outside the room the doctor was using and checked the patients in and made further appointments for them after their consultations. As she did at the surgery she found and refiled their notes and gave new patients an attendance card with their number on it. Some of the women were to be fitted with the coil or a cap but most were either on the Pill or considering it, a few feeling apprehensive because it was still relatively new.

Some patients assumed that because Sadie worked there she had specialised knowledge so she quickly and politely disabused them of that assumption. She also made coffee for the doctor and the nurse who was always in attendance. The job required good communication skills, which her position at the surgery had taught her she had plenty of. It was a nice little earner and she was home by lunchtime and able to spend the rest of the day with her daughter.

Life fell into a busy but pleasant routine. She spent every moment of her time off with Rosie and made sure that her mother wasn't burdened with any jobs just because she happened to be around. Marge was offended at the idea of any financial reward for childcare — 'Charge you for looking after my own granddaughter? Don't be so ridiculous' — so Sadie made sure she treated her on a regular basis, very much aware of how lucky she was to have her.

Disapproval from the anti-working mothers contingent came in bucket loads and her most

156

ardent critic on the subject was her mother-in-law. Sadie had kept her word and visited the Westons occasionally.

'A mother's place is at home with her baby,' Harriet stated categorically when Sadie mentioned her job to the Westons as she visited them one Sunday.

'In an ideal world, maybe it is,' Sadie came back at her. 'But I don't have any choice in the matter because I need the money. Anyway, it isn't as if Rosie is in a strange place with someone she doesn't know. She's at home with my mother and perfectly content.'

'Even so . . . '

'Harriet . . . ' interrupted Gerald in a cautionary manner.

'You should have come to us if you needed money,' she went on, ignoring him completely.

And have you rule my life and tell me how to raise my child, not likely, Sadie thought but said, 'It's my job to provide for Rosie, not anyone else's.'

'She's our son's child,' Harriet reminded her unnecessarily. 'Surely you must know that we are willing to help.'

'That's very kind of you,' began Sadie, determined to stand her ground though hoping to avoid a major altercation, 'and in a small way that would be lovely. But I need regular money coming in so I prefer to go out to earn it and I am not thinking of changing anything.'

'Paul must be turning in his grave.' Harriet was relentless. 'I'm sorry if you don't like hearing it, Sadie, but it has to be said.'

157

Keen to avoid an argument as she'd been trying to get on better with Harriet since her grand apology in the maternity ward, Sadie stifled her irritation and just said, 'Look, I can understand why you might feel the way you do, and I know there are plenty of others who share your opinion, but needs must, I'm afraid, and I'm sure Paul would understand.'

'Humph,' Harriet snorted.

'Anyway, how have you both been since I last saw you?' Sadie asked as a diversionary tactic.

'All right, dear, thank you,' replied Gerald. 'No need to ask about you and the little one. You both look very well.'

Now turned six months old, Rosie was sitting on her mother's lap. Her dark hair was brushed up into a tuft, her cheeks pink and her round brown eyes sparkling.

'Yes, we are indeed.'

Gerald made a series of clucking noises with his mouth and flapped his hands at Rosie, who put her arms out and leaned towards him.

'Would you like to hold her?' asked Sadie. 'She obviously wants you to.'

Beaming, he took her, sat her down on his lap and bounced her on his knee for which he was rewarded with a huge gappy smile. 'She is gorgeous, isn't she, Harriet?'

'Yes, she is,' agreed his wife. 'The absolute image of her father at that age.'

'I think she looks like Paul too,' commented Sadie, 'and I'm so pleased because I'm reminded of him every day. None of us will ever forget him while Rosie is around.'

'I should hope you'd never forget him anyway,' responded Harriet, only just managing not to succumb to the violent bad temper Sadie guessed was hovering.

'I wouldn't, of course,' she said quickly, feeling an unexpected pang for Harriet even though she was driven almost to distraction by her attitude. It must be truly devastating to outlive your child. 'I just meant that I see him in her all the time.'

'I'll put the kettle on for tea,' the older woman said suddenly and hurried from the room.

'So,' began Gerald, looking at Sadie whilst Rosie settled happily on his lap, 'you managed to get a lift over here today.'

'Yes, Brenda and Ray fancied a run out into the country so they dropped me off here and are going exploring. They'll pick me up later.'

'I'm glad about that because it's quite a jaunt for you on public transport, isn't it?' he remarked.

'Yes, it is a bit of a drag, especially with a baby,' she said, so much more relaxed in his company than his wife's. 'But I want you and Mrs Weston to see something of your granddaughter so I'm happy to do it every now and again.'

'We could come to London and take you both out one Sunday perhaps, to save you travelling,' he suggested. 'If you wouldn't think of it as an imposition.'

She wasn't keen on seeing too much of his wife but he was an absolute joy and increasingly she wanted Rosie to grow up with him in her life. 'Of course not. That would be lovely,' she said, hoping it would only be occasionally.

Harriet came back into the room with a tray of tea and a large sponge cake.

'That looks nice,' remarked Sadie politely. 'Have you been baking?'

'Oh yes, I always make my own. I wouldn't touch shop-bought cakes.'

As if Sadie hadn't already been told a dozen or more times, but she just said, 'It looks absolutely delicious.'

'What time are your friends picking you up?' asked the older woman, seeming to have calmed down after her somewhat heated views on working mothers.

'About four o'clock,' Sadie replied. 'I mustn't be home too late because of getting the little one to bed.'

'Perhaps you could come for lunch next time then we can have you both for longer,' suggested Harriet.

Almost a whole day in Harriet's company would probably have Sadie heading for the nearest psychiatric ward but she said, 'We'll see. But don't worry. I'll make sure you get to see Rosie regularly, I promise.'

'You could always move back in upstairs if you wanted to, you know. It must be rather crowded at your parents' place,' offered Harriet. 'It's all just as you and Paul left it.'

Sadie tried not to show just how horrifying the suggestion was or how worrying that the flat hadn't been returned to its prior state as part of their house. 'Thank you. It's kind of you but Rosie and I are very settled at Mum's. And I

160

have my job close at hand and my friends. It wouldn't be sensible for me to move away.'

'If you lived here you wouldn't have to go out to work,' persisted Harriet. 'We'd take care of all your needs as our son isn't here to do it.'

Gerald's eyes widened in surprise, so he obviously hadn't been expecting this, and Sadie really was worried now. Harriet would go to any lengths to control her and take over Rosie's life. If she didn't know Harriet better Sadie would see this as an altruistic gesture but she guessed that Harriet was being manipulative. She was prepared to pay to get a large slice of her granddaughter's life, probably because she was looking for a replacement for the son she had lost.

'That really is generous of you,' Sadie said in a polite but firm manner. 'But, as I have said, I am very happy where I am and money isn't too much of a problem for me now that I have a job.'

'It would be a much better environment for Rosie to grow up in.' Harriet just wouldn't let go. 'It's a very refined area round here.'

Sadie bristled about the slur on her home neighbourhood but was determined not to get into a quarrel. 'I think she'll do all right where she is, thank you,' she said.

'Oh, well, if you change your mind you only have to let us know and we'll get the rooms aired for you,' said the determined Harriet. 'I know that you and I have had our differences in the past but that's all behind us now. And it would be just like your own place upstairs.'

No it wouldn't. I'd never be allowed to forget

that I was in your debt and my life wouldn't be my own, Sadie thought, but said in a more resolute manner, hoping that Harriet would finally catch on, 'Yes I'm sure it would but, as I've said, I'm very settled where I am and I've no plans to move.'

'We quite understand,' said Gerald, giving his wife a warning look. 'You're doing very well where you are by the sound of it and young Rosie is a credit to you. Isn't that right, Harriet?'

Harriet looked at her granddaughter and studied her. 'Yes, that is right, Gerald,' she agreed.

Roll on four o'clock, thought Sadie, feeling stifled by Harriet and on the verge of an argument the whole time. It was as though the older woman was about to lose control and explode at any moment.

* * *

'Well, what do you think of that, Gerald?' asked Harriet as soon as the door closed behind Sadie. 'Her going out to work and leaving that poor child.'

'She doesn't abandon her, dear,' he reminded her. 'She leaves her with her mother.'

'That's as good as abandoning her.'

'No, Harriet, it's nothing like it and you know that perfectly well,' he said in a tone of admonition. 'You really aren't being fair.'

'Well, all right, maybe it isn't quite the same thing,' she conceded grudgingly, 'but a child needs to be with its mother.'

'Yes, I agree with you but Sadie's circumstances are such that she can't be with Rosie all the time like you were with Paul,' he pointed out. 'Surely you must admire her spirit in going out to work to support her child. Anyway, things are different to what they were in our day. The status quo is beginning to change.'

'But it's all so unnecessary because she doesn't have to go to work, Gerald,' Harriet insisted. 'She could come and live here and we would support her.'

He sighed wearily. His wife could be such hard work at times. 'Surely you can see that it's only natural she would want to stay in her own neck of the woods,' he said, 'and I don't blame her either. She's lost her husband; she needs her family and friends around.'

'She'd have us?'

'You're not her friend, Harriet,' he reminded her. 'And she knows that.'

'I've apologised for what happened in the past.'

'An apology doesn't make a friendship,' he told her. 'That takes time and a great deal of effort, especially after what's gone before. Anyway, be honest, it isn't really Sadie you want to come and live here. It's Rosie. I notice you didn't offer our support if she stays where she is.'

'She doesn't need it if she stays there because she has her precious job.'

'But it's Rosie you're after, isn't it?'

She knew she couldn't lie to him. 'All right, so what if it is,' she admitted. 'There's nothing so terrible about a grandmother wanting to be close

163

to her grandchild, is there? And if it means having her mother as well, then so be it. It isn't a crime, Gerald.'

'No, but it is devious. Sadie is a bright girl; she will have guessed what's going on in your mind. Anyway, regardless of anything else, she isn't the kind of girl who would want to rely on us for support. She's far too independent.'

'You can't blame me for wanting to have my granddaughter in my life,' she said.

He thought carefully about his next words because he knew how hard she had taken Paul's death and he didn't want to be cruel. But certain things had to be said. 'No, I don't blame you, dear, but I think you may have the wrong idea about our role. We are grandparents and as such our place is in the background; there if we are needed. Important but not at the forefront. Sadie is doing her best to make sure we see something of Rosie and we must be grateful for that. If you're not careful, we'll see nothing of her at all.'

'Why, what do you mean?'

'Well, your reaction to her going out to work for instance,' he explained. 'I know you disagree with it but it would be wiser to use a little discretion and keep your feelings on the subject to yourself or talk to me about it to get it off your chest. Not have a go at her about it. If you disapprove of everything she does she will stop coming over, then we won't see Rosie at all.'

'I had to tell her what I thought about it, Gerald.'

'I don't see why.'

'Because I wanted to be honest.'

'You didn't have to do so in such definite terms though, did you? She's doing her best to bring a child up without the support of a husband,' he reminded her. 'The last thing she needs is criticism. And then there was the dig about us living in a better area than her. That probably put her back up.'

'But we do live in a more refined area.'

'Maybe, but you don't need to come out and say that sort of thing. She likes it where she lives. It's where she comes from and is her patch. She's a Londoner through and through. She would never have agreed to live here in Surrey at all if it wasn't for Paul.'

'So, what are you saying exactly?'

'I'm suggesting that you watch your tongue or risk losing your granddaughter altogether and that would hurt me as well as you,' he told her firmly. 'Rosie is the only grandchild we're ever going to have so please don't jeopardise our chances of being a part of her life, however small.'

'Am I that bad, Gerald?' Harriet asked feebly, seeming surprised by his comments.

He didn't want to be too hard on her when she was still hurting so badly from their loss. But neither did he want to risk losing all contact with Sadie and Rosie because of his wife's sharp tongue and lack of tact.

'It isn't a question of being bad exactly,' he said. 'It's more a matter of diplomacy. Try to think before you speak and take it easy on Sadie or we will lose contact with Rosie.'

'I'll do my best, Gerald,' she said solemnly.

'That's good,' he said, 'and I shall be on hand to remind you if you slip back.'

★ ★ ★

'So your ma-in-law wants you to move in with them, out here in Surrey,' said Brenda, frowning.

Sadie nodded. 'And they'll support me financially so that I don't have to go out to work.'

'And?' asked Brenda.

'I didn't even consider it for a second,' she replied.

'Phew, that's a relief,' was Brenda's hearty response. 'We lost you to Surrey once before and we don't want to do so again, do we, Ray?'

'Not likely,' confirmed Ray, looking around, 'but I must say that this is a truly beautiful part of the world, especially on a day like this.'

Enchanted by their surroundings after they left the Westons, they had stopped at Paley Village Green, where a cricket match was in progress. They were out of the car and sitting on a bench enjoying the late-afternoon sunshine, the soft crack of leather on willow pleasant and relaxing. It was a glorious summer's day; the sky endlessly blue, the mowed grass carpet-smooth and a light breeze rustling through the trees surrounding the green, where birds chirped and twittered among the foliage. The church presided over everything including the thatched-roofed pub and the village shop which had tearooms attached. The river that meandered through this picturesque settlement was to the side of the green and ducks

166

wandered on to grass as though they owned it.

'Yes, it is lovely, all seasons of the year, and stunning in autumn when all the trees change colour. It's a very leafy county,' agreed Sadie. 'And a good environment for Rosie, but I don't want to live here, not without Paul, and especially not with the Westons. He's a sweetheart but it would be hell on earth with his wife around because she would try to take over my life and my baby's. That's why she wants me to go there. So that she can take Rosie over. She lost her only child and she wants mine.'

'From what I've heard, I think you're probably right,' agreed Brenda.

'I don't actually blame her; it's a terrible thing to outlive your child, and it's understandable that she sees a replacement in her grandchild but from my point of view it just isn't on,' she told them. 'Anyway, I don't want to move. I want to be near to my family and friends.'

'Good,' said Brenda.

Sadie looked from one to the other. 'Thanks for bringing me over here today,' she said.

'A pleasure,' smiled Ray. 'We've enjoyed ourselves, haven't we, Bren?'

'Yeah, we went to Box Hill while you were with your in-laws. It was lovely. We thought of you and Paul. We know you used to go there a lot together.'

Sadie nodded.

'Mind you,' said Ray, slipping an affectionate arm around Brenda's shoulders. 'This girlfriend of mine doesn't have much stamina when it comes to walking.'

167

'Ooh, don't listen to him, Sadie,' she said with mock outrage, giving him a playful slap. 'He was the one who couldn't keep up with me.'

Seeing them so engrossed in each other, and in a place that wasn't accessible to anyone else, Sadie remembered experiencing that same thing with Paul and ached with missing him.

As though sensing her friend's feelings, Brenda put her hand on hers. 'Perhaps you and I could have a girls' night out sometime soon,' she suggested. 'We could go to the flicks or something, if your mum will babysit.'

'She has Rosie all day, I wouldn't want to burden her at night too,' Sadie said, kissing the top of Rosie's head. 'But thanks for the idea anyway.'

'I'll look after her for you if you like,' offered Ray, 'if you two want to go out.'

Sadie was moved almost to tears by the warmth of their friendship. 'When she's a bit older maybe we can arrange something, Ray,' she said. 'But thanks anyway.'

'Anytime,' said Ray, 'and meanwhile let's take Rosie to see the ducks.'

'She'll love that,' she agreed.

The three of them walked across the green with Ray carrying Rosie on his shoulders. Anyone painting a picture of the scene would probably see perfection; the weather, the beauty of the environment and the young people ambling across the green, happy in each other's company. But they couldn't know that there was someone missing from the picture which made it unbearably incomplete.

It started like any other morning at the surgery; the telephone ringing endlessly, people arriving for their appointments and others turning up on the off-chance of getting one.

Then, suddenly, the place was filled with a foul and overpowering smell and the source of it, a man of about fifty, said across the counter to Sadie, 'My name is William Steel and I want to see Dr Russell at once, please.'

'I'm afraid he's fully booked for morning surgery and there is already a full quota of patients hoping to see him afterwards, Mr Steel,' she said politely, almost gagging from the noxious odour as she looked at the book. 'I could fit you in at four o'clock this afternoon. Is that any good to you?'

'No, none at all. I want to see him now,' he demanded.

Something about the man's manner made her pay closer attention and she noticed his unnatural pallor and a kind of intensity in his eyes that didn't seem quite normal. Although he was wearing a well-cut suit, he was very dirty and unkempt with stubble on his chin and a matted look about his hair.

'Is it something urgent you need to see him about?' she asked, mindful of the fact that she mustn't overbook the doctor. It was part of her job to organise the appointments so that this didn't happen. She knew his schedule and had to work things around it for the sake of the patients as well as the doctor. There were only so many people he could see in any given time.

'Yes. It is very urgent to me.'

'Mmm, I see.' She looked at the book again, the man's uncompromising attitude making her feel uneasy. She wished she could find a space for him. 'As I said there's nothing until the afternoon surgery but it could be that someone doesn't turn up this morning so if you'd like to wait.'

Turning her insides to water suddenly, the man pulled a knife out of his pocket and brandished it at her. 'Dr Russell killed my wife and he's going to pay for it. So I don't need a bloody appointment to do what I have to do,' he said, moving towards the doctor's room.

Despite the fact that she was trembling all over, Sadie rushed out of the door of the office and went after him. People in the waiting room were screaming as the man waved the knife around, the chilling gleam of the blade sending panic through the place. Some patients got up and ran from the building, others looked too frightened to move. What was Sadie to do? She needed to get them all out of here but would too much movement end in someone getting hurt?

However William Steel wasn't interested in the patients, only the doctor, and he marched into the room with his name on the door. Asking the patients to leave until the situation was resolved, Sadie followed the man.

'You're not fit to practise medicine,' he was saying, waving the knife across the desk at the doctor who'd been in mid-consultation, while the patient fled. 'Because of you my wife is dead.'

Dr Russell was obviously unnerved and the colour drained from his face but he managed to stay calm enough to reason with the man. 'Your wife died because she was ill, Mr Steel,' he said in a reasoning tone. 'I know it must be very hard for you but I'm afraid you'll have to accept that.'

'You should have diagnosed it earlier then she would have had a chance.'

'Unfortunately I wasn't able to because she didn't come to see me earlier,' explained the doctor, keeping his eyes fixed on the man and the knife. 'By the time she did consult me the tumour was too far advanced for curative treatment. You know all of this, old boy. We discussed it at the time.'

'Yeah, maybe we did but I've been giving it some more thought and I've come to the conclusion that you could have got something done for her quicker.'

'I got her into hospital as soon as I could.'

'It wasn't soon enough, though, was it,' said the man, going round to the other side of the desk and grabbing Dr Russell from behind and holding the knife close to his face. 'You're all right. You're very cosy indeed. You've got your wife fit and healthy. What have I got without my Mary?'

'You do have your life,' suggested the doctor, his voice shaking slightly.

'It's worth nothing without her,' said the other man, hopeless rage exuding from every pore. 'You don't know what it's like to lose the person you love.'

'I do though,' put in Sadie, moving right into

171

the room and standing near the desk. 'My husband was killed when he was only twenty. So I know exactly what it feels like.'

'Sadie dear, you go and leave me to deal with this,' said the doctor, concerned for her safety yet clearly terrified.

'She's going nowhere,' said the man, putting the knife against the doctor's throat.

'Let her go,' urged the doctor. 'Your grievance is with me, not her, so there is no reason to make her stay.'

'I want her here, that's a good enough reason,' he said, looking directly at Sadie. 'You set one foot out of here and the doctor gets it good and proper. Then his wife can grieve for him like I'm grieving for Mary.'

'And you think you'll feel better, do you?' asked Sadie. 'Knowing that other people are suffering because of you?'

'Yeah, I think I will get some satisfaction from that,' he replied. 'I certainly can't feel worse than I do now.'

'Yes, you can, and you will if you harm the doctor,' she told him. 'You won't ever feel better if you do that but if you get through this crisis with no harm done, with a little help you stand a chance.'

'How do you know?'

'Because I have been through the same experience as you, am still going through it to a lesser degree.' She looked at him with compassion. 'It was as if I'd been turned upside down and shaken until everything good in my life had been taken from me and all that was left was pain and emptiness. So I know exactly how you must be feeling because I have felt it too.'

'You're having me on,' the man said, his face now beaded with sweat. 'Your husband didn't really die; you're much too young to be a widow. You're just saying it to humour me.'

'I wouldn't lie about a thing like that, and I think you know that,' Sadie said.

'How come he died then?' he asked, as though interested despite himself.

'He picked a fight with a man who was a lot stronger than him,' she explained. 'He died in a street brawl. He didn't even make it to the hospital. And I didn't have anyone to blame because my husband brought it on himself.'

'So how did you get through it?'

'I just kept going. I felt absolutely terrible. Couldn't eat or sleep for a while. Then I discovered that I was pregnant so I didn't have a choice. I couldn't give up then. I expect you have people who care about you.'

'My kids are grown up.'

'That doesn't mean they don't care about you,' she suggested. 'They must be missing their mother and having you so full of rage and blame can't be helping them.'

'They've got their own lives.'

'I bet they still want to know that you're all right though,' she said. 'How long is it since you lost your wife?'

'About a month, I think, though I've lost track of time,' he said. 'One awful, endless day rolls into another.'

'What about your job?'

'I haven't been back to work,' he replied. 'I just haven't felt up to it.'

'I know the feeling. I was like that for a while but I couldn't afford to stay home in the long term. I moved house so I had to find a new job.'

'This one?'

'No, I didn't get this job until after I'd had my daughter, as it happens,' she said.

Dr Russell looked on in astonishment as the drama changed from a life-threatening incident into a conversation.

'Oh I see.' The man shook himself as though remembering why he was here. 'None of this alters the fact that this man is to blame for my wife's death.'

'I'm sure you know in your heart that that isn't true, Mr Steel,' Sadie said in a gentle manner.

'I wouldn't be here if I did, would I?' he said.

'No, I suppose not. But why not give me the knife and let the doctor get on with his surgery and you and I can have a chat about it. If you would like to come down to my room, I'll make you a cup of tea or coffee.'

'Don't patronise me,' he objected, anger flaring again, the knife placed closer to the doctor's throat.

'That was the last thing I intended.' Her heart was beating against her ribs because she knew they were a whisper away from catastrophe.

'Losing my wife doesn't mean I have lost my mind too, you know,' he pointed out.

The situation indicated otherwise but she just said, 'Of course not, Mr Steel. No offence meant. I'd be making coffee for us around this time anyway and thought you might like one.'

He looked at her and her gaze never left his face as she willed him to give up this dangerous course. His lips trembled and his face crumpled, the knife falling to the floor. He started to cry and it broke Sadie's heart to see him.

'How about you and me let the doctor get on with his surgery,' she suggested as Dr Russell gave him a handkerchief. 'He does have patients waiting.'

'I'll have a chat with you later on, old boy, when I've dealt with the people who are waiting to see me,' said Dr Russell, giving Sadie a grateful look.

'They'll be getting fed up with waiting, I expect,' added Sadie.

'They will indeed,' agreed the doctor. 'So you go with Sadie and I'll get things moving. See you later.'

The man wiped his eyes, blew his nose and followed Sadie from the room.

7

Sadie's heroics at the surgery didn't pass without censure.

'That was downright irresponsible; you could have got yourself seriously hurt or even killed,' admonished her mother, having heard the story from Dr Russell when he called in briefly at the house in Sadie's lunch break to make sure that she had sustained no serious ill-effects from her ordeal.

'Oh Mum, you don't half exaggerate.'

'There was a man waving a knife about with intent to harm Dr Russell and you intervened, so of course you could have got hurt. He could very well have turned on you,' she lectured. 'You should have stayed well away, not gone after him into the doctor's room.'

'I don't think Mr Steel would have hurt anyone when it came down to it, even if I hadn't got involved.'

'Even so, you shouldn't put yourself at risk now that you have a baby to consider.' Marge looked at Rosie, who was in her high chair. 'What would happen to this little one if you got yourself killed?'

'I didn't tackle a gang of hooligans, I only talked to a poor soul who was at breaking point,' she reminded her. 'Am I supposed to turn a blind eye because I have a child? Is that what you're saying?'

'Yes, I suppose I am.'

'And, of course, you'd stand back and do nothing in a similar situation because you have me and the boys, wouldn't you?' she said with irony.

'That's different, you're all grown up and able to fend for yourselves.'

'But you used to do it when we were children. I remember once when I was little being at a bus stop with you when a brawl broke out between two men and you went and stood between them. You stopped the fight too.'

'That's a figment of your imagination,' she denied sheepishly.

'It isn't,' Sadie argued. 'I distinctly remember it. There were other times too when you've got involved in trouble when we've been out.'

'Well maybe I have,' Marge was finally forced to admit, 'but never when someone was armed.'

'He wasn't a gangster with a gun,' she pointed out. 'He was a grieving widower with a kitchen knife.'

'A lethal weapon none the less.'

'Maybe,' she conceded. 'But when something like that happens you act on instinct. You don't stop to think about it as you very well know. Anyway, the poor man was harmless really.'

'Sounds like it if he was holding a knife to Dr Russell's throat,' Marge came back at her scathingly.

'Only because he was out of his mind with grief,' her daughter said. 'He'll get better now that he's got some of it out of his system. It must have been building up inside him for ages, the poor thing. Dr Russell has given him something to calm him down and has referred him to a psychiatrist to be seen quickly.'

'I should think the man needs locking up,' said Marge heatedly.

Sadie stared at her mother in amazement because she was behaving completely out of character. 'Mum, why are you being like this?' she asked. 'It isn't like you to be so uncaring of other people.'

'The man had a knife,' she said, then her voice broke and she burst into tears.

'Come here,' said Sadie, putting her arms around her. 'This isn't just about the baby, is it?'

'Course it isn't,' she sobbed. 'It's about you putting yourself in danger.' She mopped her eyes with a handkerchief and blew her nose. 'I don't know what I'd do if anything happened to you, and it could have done today whatever you say.'

Sadie was crying now too. 'I will be more careful in future, I promise,' she said emotionally. 'I won't be able to stand back if someone needs help though, and I don't think you would want me to if the truth be told. It isn't in our nature.'

'Probably not,' Marge conceded. 'But what you did today has scared the pants off me.'

'I expect I'll be the same with Rosie when she gets big enough to go out on her own,' Sadie said, looking at her daughter who was creating a modern artwork on the tray of her high chair and her face with a spoon and a dish of custard. 'Come on then, sweetheart, let's see if we can get some of this food into your mouth instead of all over the rest of you and your chair.'

Rosie looked up and chuckled, banging the spoon on the tray and revealing a couple of newly arrived teeth, her dark eyes shining through a sea of custard. Oh yes, thought Sadie, I will definitely suffer later on if she ever does anything like I did today.

★   ★   ★

That same evening, Sadie was sitting in an armchair watching 'Z-Cars' on the television with Pickles on her lap. Her mother had gone to Bingo, Dad was at the pub, her brothers had gone to the billiard hall and Rosie was upstairs asleep in her cot.

It had been one heck of a day, what with the occurrence at the surgery, then her mother going all emotional on her. She couldn't get poor Mr Steel off her mind, probably because she herself had felt that low sometimes after Paul died. Maybe the pregnancy had been her salvation, though she hadn't been pleased about it at the time.

This morning's happening had put her in mind of Harriet Weston and the way the woman had attacked her after the trial, reminding Sadie of what terrible things grief can do to people. Although she couldn't find it in her heart to like Harriet Weston, now that she was a mother herself she did have a new understanding of the intensity of her feelings for Paul. Though she did hope she wasn't as obsessive about Rosie when she grew up as Harriet had been about her son.

'Oh well. We're all just people, Pickles,' she said, fondling his head and feeling his life force in the gentle rattle of his purr. 'Except you, you're just a lazy cat with no worries.'

In response he looked up and rested his yellow-green eyes on her expressively.

'All right, you spoilt moggy,' she said, rubbing him under his chin. 'I know you want more fuss.'

★　★　★

Oxshott Woods were stunning in the autumn with the dazzling array of colours, the shards of light, the softness underfoot of the fallen leaves and the earthy scent of incipient winter. Harriet and Gerald Weston liked to walk here at a weekend and were doing so one Sunday afternoon in October.

'The good thing about walking here is that although there are people about you don't have to speak to any of them,' remarked Harriet.

'That isn't necessarily a good thing for you, dear,' he said. 'You're getting much too anti-social lately. You hardly see anyone except me. It would do you good to talk to a few more people. Take you out of yourself.'

'I don't want taking out of myself, thank you very much, Gerald,' she said, sounding peeved. 'I see the people I want to see and I have you. That's enough for me. So no more lectures, please.'

'As you wish, dear.'

'Good.'

These woods were a magnet to dog owners

and there were plenty of them here today, strolling along, lead in hand, after their pets that were bounding through the falling leaves, sniffing around the trees and barking at the slightest movement in the undergrowth.

'Maybe it would be a good idea for us to get a dog,' Gerald suggested unexpectedly.

'A dog,' she said in a tone not dissimilar to that of Oscar Wilde's Lady Bracknell when she famously referred to the 'handbag'.

'Yes, that's right.'

'What in heaven's name would we want a dog for?' she demanded.

'It would be company for you while I'm at work,' he replied.

'Are you mad?' was her appalled reaction. 'You know I can't bear dogs.'

'A cat then,' he proposed gingerly.

'I do not want an animal of any kind in my house,' she stated categorically. 'They are messy and full of horrid things like fleas and worms. Ugh, just the thought of it makes me feel sick. I don't know how people can bear to have them.'

'From the look of the dog owners in these woods they bear it very well,' Gerald said. 'In fact they seem to get a great deal of pleasure from them.'

'All a pet would do for me is to drive me insane,' she said. 'So let's not hear any more about it.'

'Fair enough. It was just a suggestion.' They fell silent as they trudged on, both in the formal clothes they wore for every occasion, she in an expensive but frumpish grey coat and hat, he in an overcoat and golfing-style cap. 'But I do think you need to open up your life again in some way, dear. You spend too much time alone and have done since Paul died. It must be lonely for you when I'm out at work.'

'I thought we agreed there would be no more lectures.'

'Just expressing an opinion.'

'Do you really think some smelly cocker spaniel is going to cure me of missing Paul?'

'Of course not. Anyway, I was thinking more of a poodle.'

'Ugh, ghastly things.'

'What about a West Highland terrier then?' he proposed. 'Little white dogs. They are really cute.'

'Gerald,' she began with an eloquent sigh, 'if you want a dog why not say so instead of pretending that I need one?'

'It's for you mainly that I suggested it,' he said. 'But, actually, I think it would be good for us both.'

'You think a dog will replace Paul.'

'Now you're just being ridiculous,' he said brusquely. 'All right, I admit I've always thought it would be nice to have a pet of some kind, especially when Paul was little. But you would never consider the idea so I gave up.'

'And you can give up again now because nothing has changed,' Harriet said firmly. 'You know I'm not an animal sort of a person, Gerald, so I can't understand why we are having this conversation.'

'I thought it would be a good idea at this stage

182

in our lives as we are on our own now,' he told her. 'It would get you out because it would have to be taken for walks.'

'Exactly! You'd be at work so I'd be the one who would have to clear up after it and take it out.'

'I could walk it in the evening,' he suggested. 'In fact, I probably would do anyway. A man and his dog out for a stroll of an evening; what could be nicer?' He spotted something white go scampering by. 'Look, there's a little Westie. Isn't it sweet?'

'It might look pretty from a distance but it will be as messy as any other dog around the house.'

'We could have it trimmed and shampooed professionally on a regular basis.'

'*We are not having a dog,*' she shrieked, causing people to look in their direction. 'So will you please just shut up about it.'

'All right, all right, don't get yourself into a state,' he said. 'I won't say another word about it.'

'Thank heavens for that.'

They walked on in silence for a while.

'A dog would be nice for Rosie when she comes to see us, especially as she gets a bit older,' Gerald persisted.

'Will you stop going on about it,' she snapped. 'You said you'd drop the subject.'

'Yes, I know I did but I was just thinking that children usually love animals and a dog would be something for her to take an interest in when Sadie brings her over to see us. Otherwise she might find Grandma and Granddad a bit boring,

183

especially as there aren't any other children for her to play with.'

'Visiting grandparents isn't supposed to be fun,' Harriet pointed out. 'It's a thing of respect. A duty.'

'I used to hate going to visit mine,' he confessed reflectively. 'My grandmother was a real disciplinarian. I was terrified of her, and there was never anything for me to do at her house. I was always bored stiff.'

'As I said, it isn't meant to be playtime.'

'I don't see why it can't be fun,' he went on. 'Times are changing, Harriet. The rules of our youth no longer apply and grannies don't wear long black dresses and have their hair dragged back into a bun any more. I think we should make our time with Rosie, such as it is, something for her to look forward to, not dread.'

She didn't respond at once. Then she said, 'No dog, Gerald. Absolutely not! How many more times must I tell you?'

'All right,' he sighed. 'You win.'

Knowing that she would do almost anything to see more of their granddaughter, he'd thought that his last ploy might have worked but as it hadn't, he would have to think of something else, for her sake. He was convinced that she needed something else in her life apart from him, something to care for. They both did if the truth be told. It was a strain living with a depressed and bitter person and his wife was becoming increasingly withdrawn, seeming to live only for Rosie's visits. Understandably Sadie couldn't come all that often; neither would she want her in-laws visiting her and Rosie too regularly because of Harriet's tendency to criticise, especially on the subject of Sadie going out to work.

Of course, a pet wouldn't be the answer to the problem but at least it might have helped in giving Harriet and himself a shared interest and made the house seem less empty and sad. It had been a long shot because she had never been an animal lover, but something had to be done. He couldn't just stand by and do nothing while his wife sank ever deeper into a trough, so he would have to think of something else.

'Shall we head back to the car, dear?' he suggested. 'It's getting a bit chilly now.'

'Yes, I think it's time we went home,' she agreed and they made their way back to their car parked on the edge of the woods.

★ ★ ★

They were watching a documentary on the television that same evening when the seemingly impossible happened.

'How would we go about getting to look at some of those little white dogs, Gerald?' asked Harriet.

He lowered his newspaper, brows rising. 'Oh, so you've changed your mind then, have you?' he said hopefully.

'No, not necessarily,' she said. 'I just thought I might like to look at some.'

'I suppose the first step would be to make some enquiries at the local kennels. They might

185

know of a breeder who has some puppies.' If it was up to him he'd get an abandoned dog from Battersea Dogs' Home; a poor thing that needed to be loved. But he knew Harriet wouldn't even consider such a thing. Any animal that came into this house would have to have a pedigree. 'Of course, if we have it as a puppy it would have to be housetrained and I'd be at work during the day so that would fall to you. Puppies can be quite a handful, I understand.' He decided to push his luck. 'Of course, we could get an older dog that's already been trained from a dog's home.'

'Don't be ridiculous. We are not having one of those. In fact, I haven't said we're having one at all, Gerald,' she pointed out. 'I think we might make some enquiries about the little white dogs, that's all; just as a matter of interest.'

In actual fact, as soon as her husband had pointed out the benefits of a dog with regard to Rosie, Harriet had known she wanted them to have one, though her pride wouldn't allow her to admit it to Gerald at that stage. She would do anything to see more of her granddaughter and if the child had something to make her visits attractive it could only help matters. She couldn't say the idea of a dog *per se* appealed to her — appalled was nearer the mark, and she could hardly bear to think of the housetraining — but anything that might bring Rosie closer to them was worth doing, no matter what the inconvenience.

'I'll talk to a few people about it tomorrow,' he said, trying not to smile.

186

Ray decided to open his record shop on a Saturday when there were plenty of punters out on the streets of Hammersmith. It also meant that friends could call in to wish him well.

'Well, this is really great, Ray,' complimented Sadie when she called in during the afternoon with Rosie in the pram, the little one having fallen asleep. She looked around the newly decorated shop to see several people browsing the record displays, the youngsters crowding round the latest Hit Parade releases, older people searching through the classical section and Collector's Corner. The listening booths were all occupied, and a crowd of teenagers were leaving, proudly clutching bags printed with 'Smart Records'. A young man was looking longingly at an electric guitar. 'It seems nice and busy; are you having a good first day for business?'

'Yeah, it's been very encouraging so far, hasn't it, Brenda?' he said to his girlfriend, who was standing alongside him behind the counter.

'It's been brilliant,' replied Brenda, looking flushed and happy. She pointed to a tray of drinks on a table beside the counter. 'Help yourself to a glass of bubbly. It isn't actually champagne but it tastes vaguely like it.'

'An opening-day sweetener,' explained Ray, moving out from behind the counter and handing her a glass.

Sadie raised it. 'Congratulations, Ray,' she said. 'I hope your business goes from strength to strength, which I'm sure it will.'

'Thanks, Sadie. I couldn't have done without your friend today,' he said, looking at Brenda affectionately. 'She's worked her little socks off; she's been here since early this morning helping me.'

Brenda was positively glowing. 'I'm enjoying being part of things,' she said.

'I am taking her to the West End for a slap-up meal tonight as a thank you.'

'I've told him there's no need,' she said, but it was only a token protest. She was obviously delighted.

Sadie was very impressed with what Ray had achieved. He had progressed from a barrow in a street market to a smart shop with a flat over the top in which he now lived. The shop wasn't huge but he had plenty of stock on display and posters of the latest titles attractively placed around. 'Honestly, Ray,' she said, sipping her fizzy wine, 'I think you've done wonders.'

'It's only the first day,' he reminded her. 'I hope you'll come back and say the same thing this time next year.'

'It's an achievement to have got this far, all on your own,' she complimented him. 'Your people would have been so proud of you.'

'A pity they didn't live to see it,' added Brenda.

Ray cleared his throat, looking uncomfortable, probably because blokes were never happy with flattery, Sadie guessed.

'Yeah,' he said vaguely. He looked towards the pram. 'I can't say I'm happy that my special girl is having some shut-eye. Shall I wake her up to show her my shop?'

'Don't you dare,' warned Sadie lightly. 'If she wakes up before she's had her sleep out, she'll be grumpy.'

'Don't believe you,' he said jokingly. 'She's never grumpy when I'm around.'

'Mmm, that's true.' Ray always made a great fuss of Rosie and the little girl loved him to bits; he lifted her in the air and she chuckled like mad. He would make a wonderful father one day, Sadie thought. 'But you're not chucking her up in the air now.' She looked towards the counter where a queue was forming. 'Anyway, you're needed.'

He went back to his position and Sadie finished her drink and left with a cheery 'Ta-ta, both. Have a good time tonight!'

'We'll try,' said Brenda.

'See you,' added Ray.

* * *

Ray took Brenda to the Cumberland Hotel and they had a three-course meal of prawn cocktail, mixed grill and blackcurrant tart. Even swankier, they had a bottle of wine.

'I don't know what people see in wine,' remarked Ray as they lingered over coffee. 'I'd sooner have a pint of beer any day of the week.'

'It's the latest trend and people have got the taste for it,' Brenda suggested. 'It isn't just for the toasts at wedding receptions any more. I really enjoyed mine.'

'Perhaps you have more sophisticated tastes

than me,' he said, smiling.

'Oh definitely.' She looked at him. 'Seriously though. This is all really nice and I'm having a wonderful time.'

'Good,' he said softly.

'But you needn't go to all this expense for me.'

'Nonsense, you deserve it. You've been behind me all the way with my new venture and helped me no end today,' he said. 'Anyway we should go to nice places more often. It's easy to get into a rut.'

'You won't build up your fortune if you spend all your dosh on me,' she responded.

'You let me be the judge of that.'

'All right, moneybags,' she said lightly.

There was a strong sense of occasion in the air. It was a special day for Ray, of course, having opened his shop, but Brenda had been very much a part of it. A more personal celebratory feeling was evident too and he decided that it was time to put things on to a proper footing with Brenda. He hadn't originally planned this dinner with that in mind but it felt right.

He looked at her with a serious expression. 'Actually I've been meaning to have a chat with you for a while.'

'Oh yes,' she said expectantly.

He knew what she was hoping for and he hated himself for what he was about to say.

'Get on with it then,' she said with an encouraging smile.

He reached over and took her hand across the table. 'I love you, Brenda,' he said with deep

190

sincerity, 'and I want to spend the rest of my life with you.'

'Oh Ray . . . ' she began.

'I haven't finished yet.' He broke off, mustering his courage. 'This is the bit you won't like.' He hesitated again, feeling like Satan himself. 'I don't want to get married.'

She pulled her hand away sharply, her eyes heavy with disappointment, cheeks burning with embarrassment. 'So what are you on about then? Is this some sort of a sick joke or a roundabout way of chucking me?'

'Of course not,' he assured her. 'I have just told you how I feel about you.'

'But what do you have in mind then, if you don't want marriage?'

He made a face. 'Well . . . '

'Oh no,' she cut in. 'Surely you're not suggesting that we live together without getting married.'

'It isn't unknown these days.'

'It is in my circles, mate,' she snapped. 'That's an insult, Ray Smart. A blinking great insult. What sort of a girl do you think I am?'

'A beautiful one,' he said.

'Don't start all that old codswallop because I won't fall for it,' she warned, tears welling up. 'All this time we've been seeing each other, you've just been leading me on.'

'No I have not, Brenda, and you know that in your heart. I have never hidden my feelings about marriage from you,' he reminded her, deadly serious. 'I told you from the start that it wasn't for me. You could have walked away but

191

you still wanted to carry on seeing me, knowing where I stood on the subject.'

She couldn't deny it. 'People say things like that; they don't always mean them,' she said. 'Anyway, I thought you would grow to love me and change your mind.'

'I have grown to love you, as I've told you. But I haven't changed my mind about marriage,' he said, his voice gruff with emotion. 'It's nothing personal to you, honestly. It's just that I don't believe that marriage is the be-all and end-all. Not everyone can be in favour of the way things are done traditionally.'

'If you love me you'd want to marry me.'

'That works both ways,' he came back at her. 'If you loved me you'd be willing to take me on other terms.'

'It's a disgusting idea,' she blasted. 'I can't begin to think what my mum and dad would say if I was to do a thing like that. They'd disown me for sure.'

'Oh, I see.' Her reaction was as he'd expected but disappointing none the less, because he'd hoped she might at least consider what he'd had to say. 'We could always just stay as we are then, if you don't want to move in with me.'

'I don't know which is more of an insult,' she ranted. 'The first or the second part of that sentence.' Leaden with disappointment, she picked up her handbag from the floor. 'Will you ask the waiter to bring my coat, please? I'm leaving right now!'

'Wait for me to pay the bill and I'll come with

you,' he said. 'We are not leaving things unresolved like this.'

'The subject is closed as far as I'm concerned.'

He called the waiter who brought the bill and the coats at the same time so they left together.

'Look, Brenda,' Ray began as they walked to the tube, having left the car at home because of the increasing parking problem in the West End. 'I want to be with you more than anything. I want to share my life with you. I would love you and look after you.'

'And make me have bastard children?'

'Oh!' That was like a blow to the chest. 'Do you have to use that awful word?'

'That's what any kids we had would be.'

'Only technically. They would be loved and wanted.'

'Tell that to the rest of society. Tell it to your children when the other kids are calling them names and making their lives a misery.' She halted and turned to him as the crowds milled around them. 'What are you, anyway? Some sort of a Bohemian?'

'No, not at all,' he said. 'But I do have ideas of my own which aren't always in tune with the conventional way of doing things.'

'Well go and try your batty ideas on some other girl because I want nothing more to do with you.'

He grabbed her arm as she went to walk away. 'You don't mean that,' he said.

'What choice do I have?' she asked, sobbing now. 'You don't want us to have a proper future together and I do, so there's no point in us seeing each other.'

'It would be a proper future,' he insisted. 'It would be a marriage in every way except a legal one. A serious commitment on my part, forsaking all others, till death us do part, all of that.'

'Go away and leave me alone.'

Brenda marched off with her head in the air and he went after her. Fortunately she had to wait because he had the return tickets and he stayed by her side on the platform and on the train and then walked to her front gate with her, despite her verbal objections.

'I really don't want to lose you, Brenda,' he said ardently.

'Then do the decent thing,' she responded, and walked up the path, turned the key in the lock and closed the door after her.

As soon as he saw the light go on in her bedroom, he found some small pebbles and threw them up at the window. Nothing happened at first but he persisted until she finally opened the casement.

'What are you trying to do?' she hissed furiously. 'Wake up the whole neighbourhood and ruin my reputation even more than you are already by courting me with no serious intentions?'

'Come down please, Bren, just for a few minutes,' he begged. 'I must talk to you.'

'About a marriage proposal?'

'Well . . . no.'

'Then bugger off,' she said and closed the

window. He stood there for a while, then turned and made his way home, hands in pockets, shoulders down.

★ ★ ★

When Brenda finally managed to stop crying that night in bed, she began to think about the situation and get it into some sort of perspective. He hadn't said he wanted to stop seeing her. Or that he wasn't serious about her. Just that he didn't want to get married. Did she really want not to have Ray in her life at all because she couldn't have him as a husband? He did love her; he'd been definite about that and she believed him. She was equally sure that she wouldn't move in with him. She was far too conventional to fly in the face of society so blatantly.

There was a new breed of adventurous people who wouldn't give it a second thought. Part of her wished she could be more outrageous and not worry about other people. But she was a slave to the principles she had been brought up with, so marriage was the natural outcome of a serious romance. Not having Ray in her life at all though. Did she want that, knowing that he loved her and still wanted her? She thought about all the fun they had together; all the laughs and the loving. Did she give up the man she loved because of his quirky views? Might it not be better to carry on as things were; to give it a try and see if it would work now that she knew for certain that there would be no wedding?

Throughout their relationship there had always been the hope of a marriage proposal on her part and aching disappointment as time passed and it didn't happen. At least she knew exactly where she stood now, so the agony of expectation would be gone. She lay there in the dark, mulling it over and wondering what to do for the best.

★ ★ ★

'Maybe he'll change his mind in time,' suggested Sadie the next morning as she and Brenda walked through the park with Rosie sitting up in the pram. 'He wouldn't be the first confirmed bachelor to do that, would he?'

'It's more than his being a confirmed bachelor like your brothers,' said Brenda, who had gone to Sadie's in search of solace quite early, after a sleepless night. 'I mean the boys just don't want to be tied down. But Ray wants to settle down with me, for us to live together, but not as husband and wife legally.'

'If this was anyone else but Ray and I hadn't known him since he wasn't much more than a boy, I might begin to wonder if he was already married,' said Sadie. 'At least we can rule that out.'

'Yeah, that's true. The problem is, I can't bear the thought of not having him in my life at all,' Brenda confessed.

'Stay with him then and see how it goes,' suggested Sadie. 'As I said, he might change his mind over time.'

'I shall have to rule that out altogether,' said Brenda. 'If I stay with him it must be with a different attitude. I must be adult about it and accept that there isn't going to be a wedding. Otherwise my life will be one big disappointment and I'll be resentful.'

'I can see your point. But one thing I do know for sure,' began Sadie with conviction. 'He won't ever let you down.'

'You call refusing to marry me not letting me down?'

'He was straight with you about it so he didn't break any promises,' Sadie reminded her.

'Eventually he was, I suppose.'

'But you've known from the very beginning that he didn't want to get married,' Sadie reminded her. 'You told me so yourself. He didn't ever try to hide it.'

'Mmm, well, I didn't think he really meant it,' she said. 'Blokes say that sort of thing all the time, don't they?'

'Some do because they think it's clever,' Sadie agreed. 'But Ray doesn't strike me as the type to do that.'

'Oh no. His announcement was much more serious than that,' she said. 'Oh, what shall I do, Sadie?'

'You're going to have to make your own mind up about this,' Sadie told her friend. 'Only you know how you feel.'

'Trust me to fall in love with an anti-marriage freak,' she wailed. 'Flamin' man. I wish I'd never met him.'

They had reached the duck pond and Rosie

was making squealing noises and pointing.

'Come on then, sweetheart,' said Sadie, taking her out of her pram along with a bag of stale bread from the carrier. 'Let's give the ducks some dinner.'

Brenda felt a stab of envy seeing Sadie enjoying her daughter so thoroughly. Her friend had experienced tragedy that made Brenda's own problems seem trivial, and raising a child on her own couldn't be easy, but at that moment she seemed to have everything.

*　*　*

That evening Brenda walked through the town to Smart Records and rang the bell on the door at the side of the shop which led to the flat upstairs.

'Brenda,' said Ray, opening the door and looking delighted to see her.

'No need to look so pleased with yourself,' she told him in a tone of admonition. 'I'm not moving in with you.'

'Oh. That's a pity.'

'But for some idiotic reason I want to carry on seeing you, so I'll give it a try, your way, and see how it goes.'

'Come on up,' he said, wishing he had been able to give her what she really wanted.

*　*　*

Harriet was at her wits' end and wishing they had never taken on the puppy, who had turned

198

her life into hell itself.

'You'll have to take it back, Gerald,' she wailed when he got home from work on her first day on her own with the dog. 'I can't have it in the house. It's driving me mad. I feel quite ill with the worry. It has to go immediately.'

'He isn't an 'it', he's a 'he', his name is Fergus and I'm not taking him back,' declared Gerald. 'You made the decision to have him and he's here to stay. He's an animal, not a toy.'

'Why are you being like this?' she demanded because her husband usually did what she asked without argument.

'Because he's a living thing, not an artefact that can be discarded at will. Anyway, you haven't given him a chance,' he told her. 'I warned you that he would be difficult and time-consuming in the early days and you still wanted him. So he's staying.'

'But he's chewing everything in sight and keeps making a mess on the floor,' she pointed out. 'You know how squeamish I am.'

'You'll just have to toughen up, old girl, because he's not going back,' her husband told her.

'You don't seem to understand, Gerald,' she persisted. 'I have spent most of the day outside in the cold in the garden trying to get him to do his business out there but he comes inside and does it indoors. Please take him back to the breeder, Gerald. I really can't cope. It was you who suggested we get a dog, so now you can get rid of it. Just do it and stop arguing!'

None of this was any surprise to him. He had

been expecting just such a scene as soon as the reality of having a puppy registered with her. But he was still convinced that a dog would bring a much-needed new element to their lives once she got used to it. So somehow he had to win her over as his hard line didn't seem to have worked.

'Look, I really would like us to keep him, Harriet,' he said, watching the exuberant little bundle scampering around the kitchen floor. 'I'm fond of him.'

'In that case you'll have to stay home from work to look after him because I'm not going to,' she said miserably. 'It just isn't in me. I'm sorry if it upsets you but it's the way it is.'

'He won't be a puppy forever, dear,' he pointed out. 'Once he's a bit bigger and settled into a routine, he'll be a companion for you, for us both.'

'Oh no,' she said as another puddle appeared on the floor. 'That does it, he has to go. I mean it, Gerald, take him away. I want him out of here this instant.'

Gerald picked up the puppy who licked his face, his black eyes looking at him adoringly, tail wagging. 'How can you not love this little thing?'

'Very easily.'

'But he's so gorgeous.'

'Handsome is as handsome does,' she snorted, 'and the things he does are not in the least bit pretty.'

The phone began ringing but Harriet was far too preoccupied with their incontinent guest to pay any attention, so Gerald put the dog down on the floor and went to the hall to answer it.

'It's Sadie,' he said a minute or so later, peering round the door with the receiver in his hand. 'She wants to know if she and Rosie can come over on Sunday afternoon.'

Her eyes lit up. 'Of course they can,' she said without hesitation. 'Tell her we'll look forward to seeing them.'

'Will do.'

When he came back into the room, she said, 'I think I will persevere for a while longer with the puppy.'

'His name is Fergus,' he reminded her. 'If you get used to using his name instead of calling him 'it' or 'the puppy' it might help you to bond with him.'

'I know what his name is, thank you very much, and I will try to observe it,' she said.

'Until after Sunday anyway,' he said silently.

★ ★ ★

Sadie had never seen anyone so out of their element as Harriet was with Fergus. She had a cloth and a bottle of Dettol on hand the whole time and had Gerald taking the dog outside at the slightest sign that nature might be about to take its course. Sadie had difficulty keeping a straight face a few times at the look of horror on the other woman's face when the puppy was found chewing her knitting bag.

It was love at first sight for Rosie though. Now able to crawl quite speedily, she was having a lovely time going after him. She was even allowed to stroke him under supervision. At least

201

it livened things up and made the normally stilted atmosphere slightly less difficult. The house felt more cheerful too.

'How is the job going, Sadie?' asked Gerald over tea.

'Good,' she replied. 'It's the first job I've ever had where I've actually enjoyed the work.'

'I thought you only went out to work because you had to,' said Harriet.

'I do,' she confirmed. 'But since I don't have a choice, I might as well make the best of it.' She looked at Rosie, who was on her lap. 'This little one came to work with me the other day, didn't you, pet,' she said, kissing the top of her head.

'Went with you,' said Harriet with obvious disapproval.

'Yeah. My mother went down with an upset tummy so I had to take Rosie with me to work.'

Harriet looked appalled. 'You put her at risk of all those germs; being among people with all sorts of illnesses.'

'She was in my room with me,' Sadie explained. 'Well away from the patients.'

'Germs breed in that sort of environment,' said Harriet.

'There are germs everywhere, Mrs Weston,' Sadie reminded her. 'Children have to build up immunity.'

'She could have caught goodness knows what.'

'But she didn't, and Mum was feeling better by the afternoon so she was able to stay at home with her after lunch,' she said.

'That's something, I suppose.'

'One of the many problems of being a working

mum is that you're completely reliant on other people.'

'You don't have to be a working mother,' Harriet blurted out. 'Our offer still stands.'

Sadie looked directly at her. 'It's much appreciated but I'd sooner keep things as they are.'

'If you enjoy the job I suppose you would. Never mind about your daughter.'

'Harriet,' reproved Gerald, warning her with his eyes.

'I'm entitled to my opinion, Gerald,' she snapped.

Sadie wanted to throttle her but she said, 'It isn't exactly a party at work, you know.'

'Of course not,' said Gerald, ever the peace maker.

'You've just said you enjoy it,' Harriet reminded her.

'Yes, but I earn every penny of my wages, and there is a certain amount of stress involved,' Sadie went on.

'I thought you were the receptionist, not the nurse,' said Harriet sarcastically.

Gerald held his head, despairing of his wife.

'Obviously I am just the receptionist but it doesn't come without responsibility. Patients can get very upset when they can't see the doctor right away and I have to try and do my best for them as well as the doctor,' Sadie told her, managing to hang on to her severely tried patience. 'Since I do have to work it's better I have a job that I enjoy rather than one where I hate every moment. As for your insinuation that

I don't bother about Rosie, I can assure you that she is the love of my life, my first priority and I know she is well cared for when I'm not there.'

'Of course she is,' said Gerald and moved on swiftly. 'How are the family? Are they well?'

'Yes, they're all fit and thriving, thank you,' she said, throwing him a grateful look.

★ ★ ★

'The baby seemed to love the dog, didn't she?' Harriet said to Gerald later.

'His name is Fergus.'

'Why do you keep reminding me of his name?'

'Because I want you to use it,' he explained. 'I want you to think of him as one of the family rather than 'it' or 'the dog'.'

'How can an animal be one of the family?'

'Millions of people think they can.'

'You'll be taking the damned thing to bed with us soon,' she said. 'You're completely besotted with the animal.'

'Is there anything wrong with that?'

'All things within reason.'

He gave a dry laugh. 'You should remember that when you're having a go at Sadie about her going out to work and putting her down about the nature of her job. She knows you disapprove; she doesn't need reminding every single time she comes. You just have to have a dig at her, don't you?'

'Because it isn't the best thing for Rosie,' she protested. 'Can't you see that?'

'Not having a father isn't the best thing for

Rosie but it's the way things are,' Gerald said.

'That can't be altered, Sadie's going out to work can.'

'You won't persuade her to give up the job by going on at her about it but she might get fed up with hearing your views on the subject and stop bringing Rosie to see us.'

Harriet shot him a look. She had her faults and plenty of them but she did love her only grandchild in her own unhealthy way. 'You don't really think she would do that, do you?'

He sighed, shaking his head. 'No, not really. Not at this stage anyway. She obviously wants Rosie to grow up knowing her paternal grandparents.'

'So why worry me by saying it then?'

'Because Sadie is only human and she will only take so much. You give her such a hard time I'm surprised she comes to see us at all. She probably feels bad about leaving Rosie while she goes to work anyway, so why keep on about it?'

'She doesn't seem to feel bad.'

'That's just her way,' he said. 'She doesn't make a fuss about things. She gets on with what has to be done and makes the best of it. But it's bound to be an emotional struggle for her.'

Harriet sighed. 'I can't seem to do right for doing wrong with you lately,' she said miserably.

Looking at her, Gerald noticed again how much she had aged since Paul's death and he had no doubt as to the extent of her suffering. She wasn't an easy woman by any means but he did believe that she cared for her only grandchild.

'Take it easy on yourself as well as others, dear,' he said in a softer tone. 'Sadie will make a good job of bringing Rosie up, I'm sure. So let her get on with it and enjoy the little one when Sadie brings her to see us. Be happy to stay in the background and try to be pleasant when they are here.'

'I'll try.'

The puppy came scuttling across to Gerald, looking for some attention.

'What about Fergus? Is he staying or going?' he asked.

Harriet reflected on how much Rosie had enjoyed the dog. 'Staying, I suppose,' she said with a sigh of resignation. 'So I shall have to get used to calling him Fergus, won't I?'

'You certainly will,' he said, smiling down at their pet.

8

Several months had passed since Ray opened his shop and business was booming. He'd had to become a lot more professional in his management since moving inside in order to keep up with the competition. Rather than just buying stock cash in hand from small suppliers who didn't always have a huge range — as he had done on the stall — he now had accounts with the major record distributors so that he could be sure of getting the latest releases immediately they came out. It was an absolute necessity for any serious record retailer but meant that he was subject to the distributors' release dates and choice of title for promotion, for which they sometimes supplied advertising material such as posters and, occasionally, a few free records to give away.

Everything had to be done by the book now, though not all dealers were quite as scrupulous as he was about release dates. Eager punters would sometimes come in asking for a new record. On being told that it hadn't been released yet the customer would inform Ray that the shop in the main street had had it in and already sold out.

Pop music was Ray's biggest seller but, determined to be a good all-rounder, he kept his classical section well stocked as well as easy-listening numbers such as songs from the

West End musicals. He was building up his Collector's Corner by buying in used records in good condition. He still stocked both new and used guitars and a few drum kits as well as sheet music.

The expansion of the business had increased the workload considerably and he struggled to keep on top of stock control, special orders and the normal weekly paperwork, which he usually tackled in the afternoons on Wednesday, which was half-day closing. His only employee was a Saturday boy but he knew it was time to consider taking on a full-time assistant.

Although all was well with the business, the same couldn't be said for his private life. His relationship with Brenda had deteriorated significantly since he'd told her that marriage wasn't on his agenda. She seemed to be in a state of stifled fury the whole time and snapped his head off at the slightest thing. It saddened him to see her unhappy because he really did love her but they were at an impasse. She wanted something he couldn't give her and, although the subject of marriage wasn't mentioned, it was always there between them.

When she had made her decision to stay with him she'd told him that the only way forward for them was for her to accept the way things were, but it clearly hadn't been possible for her to do that. As a result, arguments were constantly flaring up and the fun times seemed to have disappeared. Obviously the situation couldn't continue as it was but he couldn't bear to contemplate the alternative. Something would have to be done but right now his dinner hour was over so he had to turn the closed sign to open and start on the afternoon's business.

* * *

Sadie's twenty-first birthday was celebrated at home in usual Bell style with plenty of booze and a buffet spread to feed an army. The little house in Fern Terrace was packed to the doors and music from the radiogram could be heard the length of the street. But as most of the neighbours were there as usual, it wasn't a problem. People were bopping, jiving and jigging to all the latest favourites. Things got a bit more sentimental as the booze kicked in and they played the Beatles 'Do you Want to Know a Secret'.

The Westons had recognised Sadie's coming of age with a very different sort of celebration the last time she was there with Rosie: a birthday cake and special tea, all very sedate and much appreciated by Sadie but it was a million miles from this jolly, riotous affair. Sadie recalled with a smile Harriet's *volte face* over their little dog now that she was used to him. Having initially been horrified to have Fergus anywhere near her, now she doted on him and, apparently, even took him out for his daily walk. Sadie found it rather encouraging to know that her adversary did have it in her to show a softer side.

Here at the party it was time to cut the cake; her mother had had a traditional one made in the shape of a key. They all drank Sadie's health, she thanked everyone for coming and for the lovely presents and there was a lively rendition of 'Twenty-one Today'.

Sadie welled up, partly because of the warmth and sincerity of her friends and family but mainly because she was missing Paul so much. He should have been beside her at an occasion like this and she wanted to weep with the sadness of his absence. But she swallowed hard, arranged her features into a smile and went to mingle with the gathering.

'I haven't seen you dancing much tonight,' she said to her brother Derek, who was in the kitchen pouring drinks for the guests.

'I'm busy looking after the bar, aren't I?'

Something about his demeanour made her say, 'Are you all right, Derek?'

'Yeah. Course I am, sis. Why wouldn't I be?'

'You don't seem yourself somehow,' she replied. 'Not as lively as you usually are at a party.'

'I can't see to the drinks and join in the dancing at the same time, can I?'

'You usually manage to cope with the two.'

'You wait until later,' he said, pouring some lime cordial into a healthy measure of gin. 'I'll be dancing on the table then.'

'Good, that's the spirit,' she said, but she was still convinced that all wasn't well with him.

Living in a small house, so close together, you were able to sense the mood and feelings of the other family members without them even uttering a word. Something was definitely bothering Derek and, after giving the matter more thought, she realised that it had been for a while. But he wasn't likely to tell his sister what it was, especially not in the middle of a party, so she moved on, enjoying the party and dancing along with the others.

Noticing that she hadn't seen Brenda for a while, she went in search of her and found her and Ray in the back garden having a blazing row.

'You are so bloody selfish,' Brenda was saying. 'Only your opinion matters.'

'Ooh, hark who's talking,' he retorted. 'You refuse to even consider my views.'

'They don't deserve consideration because they are not genuine,' she shouted at him. 'It's all just an excuse to be selfish. All you care about is yourself.'

'That isn't fair.'

'Hey, calm down, you two,' Sadie interrupted, seeing how upset they both were. Brenda was on the verge of tears; Ray was pale and tense. 'Come on inside and join in the dancing. It's a party. Not the right occasion for a barney.'

'Sorry, birthday girl,' Ray apologised. His tone was light but his voice trembled slightly and he looked very sad. 'Come on, Brenda. Let's not spoil things for Sadie.'

'Sorry, kid,' added Brenda.

They trooped back into the house and joined in the celebrations. It seemed to Sadie at that moment as if the whole world was made up of couples and she was the odd one out. Oh Paul, she cried silently, why did you have to go and die?

Monday morning was always the busiest time of the week at the surgery. All the ailments of the weekend culminated in a rush of patients desperate to see the doctor. The phone rang nonstop and the appointment slots were disappearing faster than tickets for a Beatles concert.

'I can fit you in this afternoon at three o'clock,' Sadie was saying to a woman who had almost lost her voice. 'The next available appointment after that is tomorrow morning.'

'I'll come this afternoon,' said the patient hoarsely.

Taking the woman's details and entering the appointment in the book, Sadie looked up and her eyes widened in surprise as she saw both her brothers standing there.

'What are you two doing here?' she asked, thinking there must be trouble at home as they were never ill.

'It's him,' said Don, looking at Derek. 'He's been taken ill at work so I drove him straight round here.'

'Oh my God. You must be feeling bad for you to be here,' she said anxiously. 'I've never known either of you to go to the doctor's.'

'We don't usually have cause to,' said Derek, ashen-faced and frightened. 'But there's something not right now. I've got shocking pains in my chest. I've been having them on and off for a while.' He took a laboured breath. 'The pain came on real bad while I was working under a car.'

'I knew there was something the matter with you at the party.'

'Never mind that now,' he said quickly, 'just ask the doc if he can see me, will you please, Sadie. I wouldn't be here if it wasn't absolutely necessary.'

'Not a word of this to Mum,' added Don. 'We don't want her worrying before she has to.'

'I'll see what I can do. Have a seat in the waiting room,' she said and slipped out of the reception office and hurried towards the doctor's door.

★   ★   ★

'Well?' she asked nervously when her brothers emerged from the consulting room, Don having gone in with his brother.

'The pain has gone off now, thankfully, but he's arranging for me to see a specialist. He reckons it's my heart,' Derek informed her, looking shaken.

Sadie's legs almost folded beneath her. It sounded so frighteningly serious. 'Your heart,' she echoed, trying not to look too alarmed. 'But you're a young man.'

'Exactly. But he examined me thoroughly and that was his diagnosis. The specialist is only a formality to confirm his opinion, I think. It was a terrible shock, I can tell you. I mean, there's no history of that sort of thing in our family that I know of.'

'So what has he told you to do?' she asked.

'He's given me a prescription for tablets and

213

told me to rest up for a week or two, pack up smoking immediately, cut down on the beer and give up my job,' he said.

'Give up work,' she gasped in astonishment. 'Blimey. That seems a bit extreme.'

'No, not give up work,' he corrected, 'just give up the job I'm doing at the moment and get some sort of light work. He said I shouldn't be doing heavy work with a heart condition. Gawd only knows how I'm supposed to earn my living. Mending motors is all I know. It's what I'm trained for. It's all very well for a doctor to sit there spouting advice but there's a real world out there.'

'He's only doing his job and you don't have to take his advice,' Don told him. 'But these doctors know what they're talking about and you'd be very silly not to do as he suggests. Anyway, there are jobs around much less strenuous than ours.'

'Light work. What's that? Working in an office or something I suppose. I'd be no good at anything like that. I'm a tradesman. My skill is in my hands.'

'Don't worry about that now,' advised Sadie. 'Get your prescription made up and go home and rest.'

'Mum will have to know now,' he pointed out.

'We'll have to make sure we don't make too much of it,' suggested Sadie, adding with false levity, 'Anyway, if you do as the doctor tells you, you'll outlive us all.'

She was scared though. She had learned from painful experience of the fine line between life and death, and Derek's news had made her feel fragile all over again.

★ ★ ★

'Your great-grandfather on my side suffered with his heart, I seem to remember someone saying,' said Marge, when she'd got over the shock of the news and realised that it wasn't the end of the world. 'It must have missed a couple of generations.'

'Now you tell me,' said Derek.

'I haven't given it a thought until now,' she responded. 'I've had no reason to. Anyway, it wouldn't have made any difference.'

'How old was he when he died?' asked Derek.

'I don't know,' she said truthfully. 'They died younger in those days anyway so there could be no comparison even if we did know. Don't start getting morbid.'

'I feel like an old man all of a sudden,' Derek confessed.

'Give over,' said his father. 'You're the same age as you were this morning before you found out about this.'

'Exactly,' agreed Sadie, determinedly staying positive. 'If you do what the doctor suggests there's no reason at all why you can't have a normal life span.'

'Light work though,' Derek said in disgust. 'It's what old men do.'

'Of course it isn't,' his mother disagreed. 'Lots of young men do jobs that don't involve heavy lifting and crawling around under cars in a

215

draughty workshop.'

'Yeah, white-collar workers,' he groaned, 'and you need academic qualifications to be one of those.'

'You don't know what opportunities there are until you look into it,' his mother pointed out. 'You only found out about it today so give yourself a chance.'

'Did the doc tell you to give up beer as well as cigarettes?' asked Don. 'I can't remember.'

'He told me to cut right down but I don't have to give beer up altogether,' said Derek.

'There is some light at the end of the tunnel then.'

'Just about,' said Derek gloomily.

'What about sex? Is that banned as well?'

'That wasn't mentioned.'

'Thank God for that,' laughed Don.

'Enough of that sort of talk,' admonished their mother. 'I don't want to hear what you two boys get up to when you're out.'

They all laughed but it wasn't heartfelt. It was as though a shiver of fear had descended upon the family.

★　★　★

After a period when marriage wasn't mentioned at all, now it didn't matter what else Brenda and Ray talked about, somehow the forbidden M word always seemed to creep in and cause an argument between them. Even a subject as unrelated as the recent news about Derek Bell's heart condition developed into a row.

'Shame about Derek, isn't it?' Ray remarked when he and Brenda were walking home from the cinema. 'It must have been one hell of a shock for him to find out his ticker isn't quite what it should be.'

'I'll say. I'd probably die of fright if something like that happened to me.'

'Me too. He's all right though. It isn't as if he's desperately ill or anything,' he said.

'So long as he changes his lifestyle he should be okay.'

'It must be hard for him, though, to have to come out of his trade,' Ray went on. 'All that training gone to waste.'

'Yeah, it's frustrating for him, and it must be a worry, having to start again doing something completely different for a living.'

'Still, at least he's single and doesn't have a wife and kids depending on him.'

Despite all her good intentions Brenda was niggled. 'Oh, thank the lord for that,' she burst out with withering sarcasm. 'As long as he isn't lumbered with some drag of a wife tying him down and relying on him for money, everything in the garden is rosy.'

'I only meant that he can probably manage financially until he gets another job with only himself to support.'

'I know exactly what you meant,' she said, hearing her own nagging voice and powerless to do anything about it. 'The slightest chance to remind me of your feelings on the subject of marriage and you're in there with a dig. Well, you don't need to bother because you've already

217

spelled it out loud and clear.'

'Brenda, love . . . ' he began.

'Don't 'Brenda love' me,' she snapped, dangerously close to tears. 'I know you don't want to marry me, so stop rubbing it in for goodness' sake.'

'I wasn't, I just meant that . . . '

'I know what you meant.'

'I was talking about Derek.'

'But it was another chance to make sure I've got the message. Well, I have, so you can stop going on about it. I am not thick and I know exactly where I stand.'

'I didn't . . . I wasn't . . . '

As the anger drained away leaving her embarrassed and depressed, she deeply regretted her outburst, which could only work against her. The scenes she'd been causing lately were enough to send any man running in the other direction but the words came out as though of their own volition. 'No, I don't suppose you were. It's me getting the wrong end of the stick again. I'm sorry, Ray. I was well out of order.'

'That's all right, love,' he said, putting his arm around her. 'Are we friends again?'

'Friends again,' she said.

But they both knew that the issue wasn't going to go away, even though neither could bear to admit it.

*　*　*

'So how's the job hunting going, Derek?' asked Ray a few weeks later when he and the Bell brothers were having a drink together at the local pub.

'A bit grim,' he replied. 'I've been hoping for a job on the counter at a motor spares outlet for the trade but there's nothing doing at the moment. At least I know about car parts.' He sighed. 'I can see myself ending up as a petrol-pump attendant, which is a bit of a comedown after all those years of training.'

'Why not broaden your horizons and consider something outside of the motor trade?' suggested Ray.

'He doesn't have any faith in himself,' Don answered for him.

'The motor trade is what I know,' explained Derek, 'and my confidence has taken a hell of a battering. I mean, who would want to employ someone with a dicky heart?'

'Plenty of people, I should think, but if you're worried about it don't tell them,' advised Ray. 'It won't be the sort of job where you have to give your life history.'

'There is that,' agreed Derek. 'I'll go down the labour exchange again tomorrow and see what they've got outside of the motor trade, though Gawd knows how I'll be able to do anything else as I know bugger all about anything except cars.'

'Talking about the labour exchange, reminds me that I've got to get in touch with them to ask them to find me an assistant for the shop.' Ray paused thoughtfully. 'Not unless you'd be interested, Derek.'

The brothers stared at him.

'Your friendship doesn't have to stretch to charity, you know,' said Derek stiffly.

'It isn't charity, mate,' Ray assured him. 'I need someone. There's too much work for me now. I've been thinking about getting someone for a while and I haven't got round to it. I was telling Brenda about it the other night. Ask her if you don't believe me.'

'It just seemed a bit convenient.'

'Not at all,' denied Ray. 'Your mentioning the labour exchange reminded me, that's all. I haven't offered you the job before because you've been intent on staying in the motor trade. Now that you're prepared to consider something else, maybe we could do each other a favour.' He paused. 'Though perhaps it isn't the sort of thing you fancy.'

'I don't know anything about selling records.'

'That applies to anything new,' suggested Ray. 'You'd soon pick it up.'

'What would it entail, exactly?' asked Derek.

'Serving behind the counter mostly, keeping an eye on the stock for re-ordering and general shop duties. No heavy lifting involved. On the odd occasion something might need shifting, I'd do it. I have to spend quite a lot of time on paperwork and general admin so I could concentrate on that with an easy mind with you on the counter, though very often I need two serving. You'd have to work on Saturdays, our busiest day, but you'd get a day off in the week to make up for it, and Wednesday is early closing, so you'd get a half-day off.'

'Sounds fair enough to me,' said Don.

Derek didn't look too keen, Ray noticed. 'I didn't think you'd be interested,' he said. 'It couldn't be more different to mending cars and I speak as someone who has done both and I know which I prefer. It was just a thought. But don't worry. I'll get the labour exchange to find me someone. If they don't come up with anyone suitable I'll put an ad in the local paper next week.'

'It isn't that I'm not interested,' began Derek, 'it's just that I don't know if I could do it.'

'I'd tell you what to do every step of the way,' Ray explained. 'You never know, you might like it once you get used to it.'

'I'm not sure.'

'I tell you what,' suggested Ray. 'Let's give it a couple of weeks' trial on both sides. If you don't like the job after two weeks you leave, and if I'm not happy with you, I don't take you on permanently. Does that sound fair?'

'Very,' said Don, looking at his brother.

'I'll give it a go,' agreed Derek, still doubtful of his ability.

'Start next Monday then, does that suit you?' He nodded. 'Thanks, mate.'

'Thanks aren't necessary. I'm not doing you any favours,' Ray told him again. 'I was going to take someone on anyway, and you'll have to work for your money, but not in the same way as you did at the garage.' He thrust forward his hand. 'Deal?'

'Deal,' said Derek, shaking his hand.

★ ★ ★

Marge called at Smart Music the next morning with Rosie in the push chair.

'It isn't often we see you in here, Marge,' said Ray after he'd picked Rosie up and got her chuckling by lifting her in the air. 'What do you fancy, something out of the Hit Parade? The Beatles, Freddie and the Dreamers? Or maybe Petula Clark is more to your taste.'

'I've just called in to thank you for giving my boy a job,' she told him. 'It's given him a real boost to his confidence.'

'There's no need to thank me . . . ' he began.

'He's taken this heart-trouble business real hard,' she cut in as though Ray hadn't spoken. 'It's scared the living daylights out of him, though he would never admit it, of course.'

'It would frighten anyone,' said Ray.

'I know. Fancy a young man in his prime having to worry about his health,' she went on. 'He loved his work at the garage with his brother. And if that isn't enough he's had to give up his fags too, and cut right down on the beer.'

'Don and I will keep him on the straight and narrow as far as that's concerned,' he told her. 'Once he gets used to his new way of living and feels better in himself, things will look up. It's just getting used to it that's so hard. Give it a couple of months and it will all seem very different, I'm sure.'

'I hope so, Ray, I can't bear to think of anything happening to him so I daren't dwell on it or I'll make things worse by fussing over him,' she said. 'Anyway, love, Cyril and I want you to know how very grateful we are to you.'

'I didn't do it as a favour,' he tried to explain. 'I really do need someone to help me.'

'Yeah, yeah, course you do.' She obviously didn't believe a word. 'But thanks again.' She leaned forward and spoke in a confidential manner though there was no one else around. 'Couldn't thank you when you come round the house, with the boys there.' She pointed to her nose. 'Didn't want Derek to think I was sticking this in.'

'Thanks aren't necessary, honestly.'

'I know that but there's no harm in a little word of appreciation, is there?' She looked around the shop, which was without customers at this early hour. 'Everything still going well?'

He nodded.

'You and Brenda still going strong?'

'Yeah.'

'You make a lovely couple,' she said.

'Thank you.'

'Well, I must leave you to get on,' she said, putting Rosie back into her push chair. 'See you round the house before long, I expect.'

'You will.'

'Ta-ta, love.'

'See you, Marge.'

★ ★ ★

No sooner had he recovered from the hero treatment from Marge than her daughter appeared in the shop with another huge helping.

'I'm on my way home from my shift at the family planning clinic and I just had to call in to say thank you for giving Derek a job,' she said brightly.

'Sadie, I didn't do it . . . '

'We've all been so worried about him,' she interrupted. 'I know you've only offered him a trial but it's a chance for him to learn something new. We're ever so grateful, honestly. It's a hell of a thing having to come out of your trade and start something else. Heart trouble at his age, blimey! It makes you think.'

'Sadie,' he said, his voice rising to a shout. 'I didn't do it as a favour. I need an assistant.'

'Oh, well, it's good that you chose Derek.'

'Look, I'm not a do-gooder and I don't want to be treated as one,' he said with ardour. 'Your brother wants a job and I need someone to help me with this place; an arrangement that suits us both. It's as simple as that.'

'All right, Ray. Don't get narked about it.'

'I'm not. I'm just trying to make sure you know the truth of it, that's all.'

'Embarrassed about doing a favour, are we?' she said lightly. 'That follows. You've always been a modest sort of a bloke. It's better than being a bighead.'

He spread his hands helplessly. 'I'm not in the least bit embarrassed. I'm just telling it like it is.'

'Okay, Ray, don't panic, no one is going to think you're a plaster saint or anything like that but we are all very grateful,' she said.

'I give up.'

'I should,' she said breezily. 'Anyway, I must go. Got to get home to my darling little daughter, bless her little cotton socks. Cheerio and thanks again.'

'Cheerio,' he said.

What a family they were, he thought. Talk about unity. They had it in spades. He didn't feel comfortable with the idea of them thinking he'd come to the rescue because it hadn't felt like that at the time and had just seemed to be the obvious solution. But the Bell family judged everyone by their own standards and there was nothing he could do about that. He found himself hoping ardently that Derek made a success of the job. He himself would do everything he could to help him along the way.

* * *

'I'm looking for a record by an American singer,' said a middle-aged woman to Derek, who was behind the counter.

'What's his name?' asked Derek in a pleasant manner, as directed by Ray.

'I'm not sure,' she confessed. 'His name has slipped my mind. Isn't that the silliest thing?'

'Elvis Presley,' suggested Derek. 'He's American.'

'No, not Elvis, I wouldn't forget his name.'

'And you don't happen to know the name of the song,' assumed Derek.

'Not exactly, but I'd know it if I heard it. My son's always singing this song around the house, so I thought I'd buy him the record for his birthday.'

'Very nice too,' said Derek patiently, having

been told by Ray the importance of customer relations. 'Could you tell me what the song is about?'

'It goes like this, la la la la la la la la la cigarettes,' she sang tunelessly.

' 'King of the Road' by Roger Miller,' said Ray, appearing beside Derek.

'That's the one,' said the woman, looking delighted.

'Would you like us to play it for you, madam, to make sure?' offered Ray.

'No. I know it's the right one now that you've said it.'

'On display over there, Derek,' said Ray. 'It's not long been out of the charts.'

'Anything else for you today?' asked Derek, having taken her money, successfully used the cash register and put the record and her receipt in a Smart Music bag.

'That's all for today but thanks for your help,' said the customer. 'You certainly know your stuff.'

'And so we should. That's what we're here for,' said Ray and the customer left, smiling.

Derek looked at Ray. 'How did you know which song she meant?' he asked.

'Experience, mate,' he replied. 'You'll soon get to know song shorthand. People can very often only remember a word or a few notes of a song.'

'But her few notes sounded nothing like the song,' Derek said. 'Even I know that one.'

'Cigarettes was the clue, as in 'aint got no'.'

'Amazing,' said Derek.

'You'll learn,' said Ray. 'When they say the

Welsh fella with the swivel hips they mean Tom Jones and Pelvis is Elvis Presley.'

'Right.'

Ray handed him a sheet of paper. 'This is a list of dates of forthcoming new releases. It's a good idea to keep familiar with what's coming up because people will always be asking, especially the youngsters who follow the Hit Parade. And another golden rule, anything we don't have in stock we can order as long as it isn't a really old number, and in that case we try and find it second-hand. Never lose a sale just because we don't have it on the shelves.'

'I'll remember that,' said Derek.

Another customer came in and had a look at the displays.

'Do you need any help?' asked Derek, after the man had been browsing for a while.

'Got anything by the Seekers?' he asked. 'I can't see anything of theirs here. My missus loves that group so I thought I'd give her a bit of a treat.'

'We can order it for you,' suggested Derek.

'Oh, good. Will you do that for me then?'

'Sure,' said Derek.

After the customer left, having been asked to call in at the end of the week, Derek said to Ray, 'So how do I go about placing an order?'

'I'll show you,' said Ray.

'There's so much to learn in this job, I feel as though I'll never get the hang of it.'

'Give yourself time, mate,' said Ray. 'It's only your first week. And you're doing okay.'

'Really?'

227

'Yes, really,' Ray assured him and he meant it. He had great hopes for Derek. Once he knew his way around the job, having him here would take a lot of pressure off Ray. He himself could spend more time on the administration and stop being so hopelessly behind with the reams of paperwork. So things at work were really good. If only they were going half as well with Brenda!

9

Brenda decided to kill two birds with one stone. Firstly she thought it was time Sadie had a fun night out and secondly she herself needed a respite from Ray's company alone because of her tendency to quarrel with him. The marriage issue continued to rankle with her no matter how hard she tried to accept the situation. This meant she invariably had a stab at him when they were on their own together, which led to them going at each other hammer and tongs. For how much longer they could continue with this charade of a romance she didn't know but she couldn't pluck up the courage to face the alternative. It was just too painful.

'How can I go out dancing with you and Ray when I have a child to look after?' asked Sadie, having had Brenda's suggestion put to her one sunny Sunday afternoon when they were in the park with Rosie.

'Your mum and dad wouldn't mind looking after her, would they?'

'Probably not but Mum has Rosie while I work, I don't want to take liberties with her,' Sadie told her, pushing the swing gently for her daughter, who was now a year and a half and able to enjoy the playground.

'It isn't as though you ever go out of an evening and ask them to have her,' Brenda persisted. 'It's only a one-off and you must miss the fun of going out at night.'

'That part of my life has passed, Brenda,' she said. 'So I don't really think about it.'

'Blimey, Sadie, you're only twenty-one,' Brenda exclaimed. 'It's a bit young to settle into carpet slippers.'

'That isn't what I'm doing at all but my circumstances are such, at the moment, that I have to stay at home of an evening. Surely you can understand that.'

'But it's a special pop night at the Palais,' Brenda continued persuasively. 'They'll be playing all the latest tunes. We could go for a few drinks first to get us in the mood.'

'I'm not looking for a new partner, Brenda,' Sadie stressed. 'And that's what most single people go to the Palais for, as you very well know. I don't want to stand there in the ranks like a desperate widow on the prowl while you and Ray go off dancing.'

'It's more than two years since Paul died, and high time you started living again.'

'I am living,' Sadie told her with emphasis. 'I work and I'm bringing up my daughter. I'm doing all right as I am.'

'I'm suggesting a night out, not a change of lifestyle,' Brenda pointed out.

'I appreciate your concern for me but I don't want to do it,' said Sadie with an air of finality.

'All right, so it isn't only for your sake I'm suggesting it,' her friend finally admitted. 'I just fancy a night out with some laughs for a change. If someone else is with us it might stop me getting at Ray and us rowing all evening.'

'Oh, I see,' Sadie said. 'Wouldn't it be more sensible to get things sorted out between the two of you rather than involving other people?'

'Of course it would,' Brenda replied. 'But I don't want to be sensible. For one night I don't want to be fretting about marriage. I just want to have some fun, like we used to.'

'We were young and single then.'

'We still are.'

'No we're not; well, I suppose I am technically. But you and Ray are courting.'

'If you can call it that,' she scoffed. 'Anyway, he would be coming with us. It isn't as though I'm going out on the razz without him.' She paused thoughtfully. 'How about we ask your brothers to come along too? You could dance with them and eliminate any suggestion of your being on the prowl. Oh, come on, Sade. It will be a laugh with a group of us.'

'Well . . . ' Sadie was beginning to feel tempted. 'If we can get it arranged, and I can't promise that we will because my brothers are more into darts than dancing. But if Mum and Dad are okay with babysitting and the boys can have their arms twisted into agreeing to come, okay, I'll do it.'

'Fabulous,' said Brenda jubilantly.

★ ★ ★

On Saturday evening Marge and Cyril were enjoying a supper of egg and chips on a tray in front of the television when the telephone interrupted them. Marge went into the hall to answer it.

'Oh hello, Harriet,' she said. 'How are you?'

'I'm well, thank you. Yourself?'

'Can't grumble.'

'Can I speak to Sadie please?'

'She isn't in this evening.'

'Not in?' Harriet said incredulously.

'That's right.'

'Where has she gone?'

'Out dancing with her friends and brothers,' Marge explained. 'Cyril and I are babysitting. Rosie is in bed fast asleep, bless her.'

A silence echoed down the line. 'Sadie has gone out dancing?' repeated Harriet, as though she'd just been told that Sadie had been taken into custody for drug-dealing.

'Yeah, there's some special night on at the Hammersmith Palais apparently,' Marge informed her.

'Shall I call again later?' asked Harriet.

'Ooh, I should leave it until tomorrow if I were you,' Marge advised helpfully. 'She'll be late in, I should think. We're not expecting them back until long after Cyril and I have gone to bed.'

'Really?'

'That's right. You know what young people are like when they're out enjoying themselves. We told her not to rush back. She doesn't often get a night out.'

'What about Rosie?'

'She's fast asleep, as I've just told you,' said Marge. 'She gets worn out, running about all day.'

'Mmm.'

'Anyway, would you like me to give Sadie a message?' offered Marge, keen to get off the line and back to her armchair.

'No, that's quite all right,' said Harriet frostily. 'I'll call again another time.'

'All right then. Ta-ta.'

'Cheerio.'

Stuck-up cow, thought Marge as she replaced the receiver and hurried back to the living room where her husband's eyes were glued to the screen. 'What's happened, Cyril? Have I missed anything important?' she asked.

'You'll soon catch up,' he said. 'But eat your supper before it gets cold.'

★　★　★

Gerald Weston was watching the television, too, with Fergus settled contentedly at his feet. Then Harriet came off the phone, thrust herself into the room, marched across to the cabinet in the corner and switched off the set.

'Hey, I was watching that,' he objected.

'You shouldn't watch so much television because it'll cripple your intellect and make you mentally lazy,' she pronounced. 'That's common knowledge. Anyway, I have something important to say to you and I want your full attention.'

Gerald wasn't happy about having his entertainment curtailed but he knew better than to argue. 'What is it? What's happened?' he asked dutifully.

'Sadie has gone out for the evening and left

Rosie,' she announced with intense disapproval.

He frowned. 'Not on her own, surely?'

'Of course she hasn't left her on her own; even someone as irresponsible as Sadie wouldn't stoop that low,' she snapped. 'Marjorie and Cyril are looking after Rosie.'

'That's all right then,' he said, relieved. 'So can we have the television back on now, please?'

'No, you can't,' she announced, 'and it isn't all right at all. Sadie already leaves that child for hours on end while she goes to work. Now she's leaving her to go out enjoying herself too.'

'I'm sure she doesn't make a habit of it,' he suggested, 'and Rosie won't come to any harm with Marge and Cyril.'

'That isn't the point,' she ranted on. 'Sadie shouldn't be going out and leaving her if she doesn't absolutely have to.'

'I'm not sure I agree with you about that, Harriet,' said Gerald. 'Sadie is young; and young people like to go out.'

'And you haven't heard the worst part,' she went on as though he hadn't spoken.

'Which is?'

'She's gone out dancing.'

'Oh . . . well, that will be nice for her?'

'*Nice for her,*' she repeated scathingly. 'Is that all you have to say about it?'

'What else am I supposed to say? There's no harm in dancing. It'll do her good to have a break,' was his response. 'She must miss having a social life.'

'She's got her family, and those friends of hers that she sees.'

'That isn't the same thing as an occasional night out though, is it?' he said. 'You know very well what I mean so don't pretend you don't.'

'Will you stop taking her side against me,' she said in such a loud tone the dog growled.

Gerald calmed Fergus by stroking his head and speaking to him gently. 'I'm not taking anyone's side, Harriet,' he told his wife. 'I just want to be fair about it and can't see why you're making such a fuss about Sadie having a night out.'

'She's a mother; she should be at home with her child,' Harriet declared.

'Everyone is entitled to some fun now and again,' he said. 'Anyway, what Sadie does is none of our business.'

'I disagree. She is the mother of our grandchild. It's our duty to protect Rosie.'

'From what?'

'A mother who neglects her.'

'Oh, come on, Harriet, that's a wicked thing to say,' he said in a tone of strong admonition. 'You can't really believe that; you must know in your heart that it isn't true.'

'I know nothing of the sort,' she retorted, her voice rising emotionally. 'All I know is what I hear and I have just heard that she has gone out dancing and left her child.'

Realising that his wife had worked herself up into one of her states and was out of control and genuinely upset, Gerald said, 'Harriet, dear, calm down. She's gone out for a few hours, that's all. It's nothing for us to worry about.'

'She's gone out dancing to find a man,' she

said, tears of frustration gathering. 'And you know what will happen if she finds someone to replace Paul. We'll never get to see Rosie.'

'You've got this whole thing out of proportion.' He tried to reason with her. 'One day Sadie probably will meet someone else. She's far too young to be alone for the rest of her life. But she wouldn't shut us out. Anyway Rosie will always be our granddaughter, whatever else happens.'

'A new man in her life will take over as Rosie's father and he won't want us in the picture, reminding Sadie of Paul.'

Giving up the idea of any relaxation this evening, Gerald stood up purposefully. 'You're upsetting yourself over nothing again, dear,' he told her patiently, 'so let's take Fergus out for his walk. It might help to calm you down so that you can see things more clearly.'

'Yes, all right,' she said miserably. Why did no one understand how worried she was?

★ ★ ★

The band was playing the Petula Clark hit 'Downtown' and the place was like a fairground of excitement, coloured lights from the ceiling shining through a pall of cigarette smoke on to the swaying mass of dancers, an atmosphere of fun and exuberance pulsating through the entire dancehall.

Wearing a sleeveless mini-dress in blue that enhanced the colour of her eyes, Sadie was dancing with brother Don near the band. Her blonde hair was worn less bouffant and simpler

236

these days in a similar style to the pop singer
Sandie Shaw, whose look she admired. She was
singing along with the music and having a great
time. Don wasn't much of a dancer but he could
move in time to the music and catch Sadie when
she twirled.

'I hope they have the twist,' he said as the
music ended and they left the floor. 'That's one
dance I can do. I learned it one night at a party
when I'd had a few to drink.'

'They're bound to have it at some point
during the evening.'

'I'll show you how it's done,' he told her.
'Then you'll have absolutely no cause to call me
a square.'

There was a lot of joking when they joined the
others because Derek had been dancing with the
same girl all evening and seemed very pleased
with himself.

'You're supposed to be here to dance with
me,' said Sadie, teasing him.

'You don't mind, do you, sis?' he asked
hopefully. 'Only she does seem very nice.'

'Course I don't mind,' she assured him. 'I'll let
you know when Don needs a break.'

'You look as though you're well in there,' said
Don, glancing towards the attractive brunette his
brother had been giving so much attention to.
'She's looking over this way. Very nice too.'

'It's only a few dances,' Derek reacted,
brushing their comments aside.

'Don't you go overdoing things,' advised Don
jokingly. 'A man in your condition . . . '

'It's heavy work, fags and booze I'm supposed

to avoid, not women,' he laughed. 'Anyway, we're not all like you with a one-track mind.'

Brenda and Ray appeared from the dance floor.

'Everybody enjoying themselves?' asked Brenda, who was wearing a sleeveless top and a mini-skirt, her hair heavily backcombed and very high on top, her make-up more exaggerated than usual.

There was a general affirmative reply.

'How about you?' enquired Sadie.

'We're having a wonderful time, aren't we, Ray?' she said, sliding her arms around his neck and holding him close.

'Yeah, it's a really good night,' Ray agreed.

'You'd better watch yourself with her tonight, mate,' said Don in a jokey manner, looking at Brenda. 'She could lead an innocent young bloke like you into bad ways.'

There was a roar of laughter but Sadie didn't join in too heartily because she was concerned about her friend. Brenda was in a peculiar mood tonight. She'd had much more to drink than anyone else when they'd called at the pub on the way here, and her behaviour was very extreme. Sadie had never seen her like this before and, had she not known her better, she might have wondered if she'd had something more potent than alcohol.

'No one could lead him anywhere,' said Brenda, her mood changing suddenly and becoming aggressive. 'He's his own man. He does exactly what he wants regardless of other people. What I want is the last thing on his mind. He couldn't care less about me.'

238

'Now, Brenda,' said Ray, looking edgy. 'Don't start. We're here to enjoy ourselves.'

'Which is exactly what I'm doing,' she told him. 'Or I will be when I've powdered my nose. See you in a minute, boys. Are you coming with me, Sadie?'

Sadie nodded and followed her.

'What's the matter with you, Brenda?' she asked when they were washing their hands.

'Nothing. Why? Should there be?'

'You seem to be in a peculiar mood,' Sadie said. 'Have you had purple hearts or something?'

'Blinking cheek. Of course I haven't. Can't a girl enjoy herself without getting questioned?'

'I don't think you are enjoying yourself,' said Sadie.

'I'm doing my best.' Brenda got her lipstick out of her handbag and applied it in front of the mirror. 'I'm absolutely determined to have a good time.'

'Maybe you're trying too hard,' suggested Sadie. 'There's no point in forcing it and showing yourself up.'

'I don't care,' she said. 'For one night I want to pretend everything is all right. I don't want to have a go at Ray.'

'You've already had a swipe at him.'

'Have I?' Brenda looked as though she didn't remember. 'Oh well, I'll just have to try harder.'

'All this sniping is doing neither of you any good,' said Sadie. 'So either accept him on his terms or give him up.'

'I know what I have to do and I'm going to do it.' She rubbed her lips together to even out the

239

fresh layer of lipstick, which was very pale and shimmery. 'Until then I want to enjoy myself, so do me a favour and do the same. This night out was partly for your benefit, so have fun and stop worrying about me. Let it be like the old days when the two of us used to go out having a good time, before men came into our lives in any serious way.'

'Okay,' said Sadie. 'So stop titivating and let's get out there and on to the dance floor.'

★ ★ ★

They did the twist to 'Twist and Shout', did a slow jive to a Rolling Stones' number and wiggled their hips to the Beatles' 'She Loves You'.

'I didn't think I'd ever sink so low as to do the last waltz with my brother,' Sadie said to Don as the lights were dimmed and they danced together.

'Likewise,' he grinned.

'I just don't feel ready to get back into circulation yet,' she told him. 'So thanks for coming along and rescuing me. Sorry to have cramped your style.'

'That's all right,' he assured her. 'I came to be with you.' He saw his brother over her shoulder, smooching with the brunette. 'That was the idea for both of us but Derek's got lucky and deserted us. I doubt if he'll be coming home with us.'

'Good luck to him,' she said. 'It was all looking so gloomy for him for a while with the shock of the heart trouble and the change of job but he seems to be getting on really well at Ray's shop, and if he had a girlfriend that would make it even better.'

'Stop trying to marry him off, you're as bad as Mum,' he admonished lightly. 'He only met the girl tonight.'

'Everything has to start somewhere,' she said.

The music came to an end, the bandleader wished them all goodnight and a safe journey home, and Sadie and her brother walked back across the dance floor.

★　★　★

Brenda ended the dance with Ray in a much more dramatic way. She already had her arms around him and she reached up and kissed him passionately.

'Wow. What was that for?' he asked.

'Something for you to remember me by.'

He looked puzzled. 'What are you talking about?'

'We've had a good time and now it's over,' she told him.

'All dances come to an end.'

'I mean us,' she said. 'It's over, Ray. Finished! That really was our last waltz together. I don't want to see you again.'

'Brenda, don't be daft.'

'I've never been more serious.'

'This is the marriage thing again, isn't it?' he said. 'Another way of trying to get me to change my mind.'

'Oh no, I've given up on that completely,' she

answered. 'I've tried to accept things your way and I just can't do it. It niggles and niggles away inside of me and makes me feel angry and bitter and I take it out on you. I don't want to feel like that any more, Ray, so, for both our sakes, I'm calling it a day. I'd sooner be on my own than miserable and tormented in this way.'

'Oh Brenda, you can't half be melodramatic.'

'Maybe I can but it makes it none the less serious.' She looked around to see the dance floor empty except for them. 'Everyone is going and so must we. I'll get the train home. No point in prolonging the agony, is there?'

'Brenda, stop this right now.'

'I already have stopped it,' she said, and turned and ran across the floor.

'Brenda, what is it?' asked Sadie, seeing her friend in tears.

'Nothing for you to worry about,' she replied, her voice thick with anguish. 'But I won't be coming home with you lot in Ray's car. I'll get the train.'

'What's going on?' asked Sadie.

'I'll tell you tomorrow,' she said and fled, elbowing her way through the crowds towards the foyer.

★ ★ ★

Ray was in a state of shock as he stood on the dance floor, a lone figure; even the band had packed up and gone. Initially, he'd thought Brenda was just harping on about the same old issue. But there had been something different

242

about her all evening. She'd been more demonstrative; all over him, in fact.

But on reflection and in the light of her final bombshell, her mood could have been valedictory. They hadn't been getting on lately but she had never spoken of ending it, or walked away from him as she had tonight. He'd known things would come to a head eventually but he hadn't expected this. Shaking himself out of his reverie, he hurried across the dance floor towards the foyer, looking for her.

★　★　★

Not wishing to interfere but far too worried about her friend to do nothing, Sadie went in search of the distressed Brenda. She was about to go through the glass foyer doors into the street when she and Ray almost collided.

'You're looking for Brenda too, then?' he assumed.

'She seemed so upset, I can't just leave her.'

'She's just given me my marching orders,' he told her.

'What!'

'At the end of the dance she told me it's over between us, and she meant it.'

'Oh dear . . . I'm so sorry, Ray.'

'I'm not leaving it at that,' he declared. 'I'm going to find her and put things right, whatever it takes.'

Crowds were surging out of the dancehall on to the pavement and the traffic on the road heading towards the Broadway was fast-flowing and heavy.

'Don't mess her around, Ray,' said Sadie, looking at him in the Palais' neon lights. 'If she can't accept things your way, let her go so that she can find someone who does want the same as she does.'

'I'm not going to mess her around, I promise you, but how am I going to find her in this crowd?' he demanded.

'I'll help you,' she offered. 'We know she's heading for the station so that's where we'll go. Not unless you want me to keep away. It is a private matter between the two of you.'

'Two pairs of eyes are better than one,' he said.

'You could always leave it until she's calmed down,' she suggested. 'Go and see her at home tomorrow.'

'I can't leave it. It's too important. I can't bear to think of her on her own feeling so upset.'

'There she is,' Sadie said, having spotted Brenda's distinctive hair in the street lights. 'She's trying to cross the road.'

Ray was off into the crowds with Sadie following. When she caught him up Brenda was halfway across the road, dodging in and out of the traffic.

'Brenda,' he shouted with such force his voice rose above the street noise.

There was no acknowledgement. She just hurried onwards until she reached the other side.

Standing on the kerb, unable to go forward because of the oncoming traffic, he called out again. 'Brenda, I love you and I want to marry you. *I want to marry you.* Can you hear me? I love you. Will you marry me?'

At last he's come to his senses, thought Sadie. About blinking time too! She was so pleased for Brenda because she knew how much her friend wanted this. Tears pricked at the back of her eyes.

Then she watched as Brenda turned and put up her arms to him in a gesture of absolute joy and shouted back, 'Yes, I will marry you. Course I will. Wait there, I'm coming over.'

Even in the dim light Sadie could see how happy and eager to be with him she was. So eager she stepped forward without looking to either side; right into the path of an oncoming car!

* * *

Sadie lay in bed, listening to her daughter's even breathing and watching the dawn light creep through a gap in the curtains. She'd been awake for most of the night and when she had dozed off from sheer exhaustion she had come to with a jolt and remembered the awful truth.

In a strange sort of way, losing Brenda was worse than losing Paul. When he'd died, there had been Brenda. There had always been Brenda for as far back as she could remember. Now she'd gone in the second it had taken to step off the kerb.

Last night was a blur; the chaos, the ambulance, the look on the doctor's face at the hospital when he'd told them that Brenda had never regained consciousness. It was a look Sadie had seen before on another doctor's face when Paul had died: a kind of guarded seriousness tinged with acceptance. The doctor had already moved on mentally. It was all in a day's work to him.

As well as the pain there was anger; hot flashing fury at the sheer waste of a young life and a death that needn't have happened. She wanted to scream with rage. But she knew she must control herself for Rosie's sake.

★　★　★

The rest of the family were deeply shocked too and everyone was very quiet over breakfast. No one bothered with the usual Sunday lie-in. Relaxation wasn't possible at a time like this.

'It's her parents I feel for most,' said Marge, who had been given the news by Sadie who had telephoned from the hospital to explain why she and her brothers were so late home. 'How do you get over something like that?'

'You don't,' said Cyril. 'I should think you just keep going as best as you can. Paul's parents haven't got over losing Paul, have they? You can see it in their eyes.'

'It'll be hard for Ray too,' added Don. 'He and Brenda have been together a long time.'

There was a murmur of agreement and a silence fell over the room, everyone lost in their own thoughts. Then Rosie said 'Wings', which meant swings, and it lifted the atmosphere.

'I'll take you to the park this afternoon,

sweetheart,' said Sadie. 'But you finish your toast now.'

'Dolly wings,' the little girl said with a melting smile.

'Yes, all right, we'll take your dolly when we go to the swings,' agreed Sadie.

'If you're a good girl and finish your toast,' added Marge and they all concentrated on Rosie. She was the ray of light on this darkest of days.

Later on, when Sadie and her mother had been to pay their respects to Brenda's distraught parents and Rosie was having her afternoon nap after lunch, Sadie asked Marge if she would keep an eye on Rosie for a short time and she left the house.

★　★　★

As soon as Ray opened the door Sadie laid into him.

'You killed her,' she shouted, aiming blows at his chest. 'You killed her as sure as if you strangled her. She wouldn't have died if it wasn't for you. Because of you I've lost my best friend and her parents have lost their daughter.'

'Come inside before you disturb the whole neighbourhood,' he said commandingly.

'No thanks,' she said, completely beside herself. 'I don't want anything to do with you, ever again. You murderer. You rotten bloody murderer!'

'Oh come in, woman, for God's sake,' he said, and pulled her inside and shut the door so that they were in a narrow hall with stairs leading up to the flat. 'Come on upstairs and you can continue your assault on me there; at least it will be private rather than letting the whole of Hammersmith see you in such a temper.'

Reluctantly she followed him up and into a smart, unfussy lounge with contemporary furnishings in dark blue with spindly legs, a television set in the corner and a fashionably slender coffee table.

'Would you like a cup of tea?' he offered dully.

'No thanks.'

'You might as well sit down.'

'No.'

'As you wish,' he said in an even tone. 'So you were saying . . . '

'That you're to blame for Brenda's death.'

'Yes, I know.'

She was astonished. 'You admit it then.'

'Of course I do,' he replied. 'How can I deny it? If I'd agreed to marry her a while ago as she wanted, she wouldn't have given me the elbow and gone rushing off and if I hadn't shouted my proposal across the road she wouldn't have stepped out.'

'Oh, I didn't realise . . . '

'What do you think I am, thick or something?' he cut in and she noticed his pallor and the grim line of his mouth. 'Too dense to realise the result of my actions?'

'You seemed so calm last night.'

'We don't all get hysterical and go around attacking people at their front door because we're upset,' he told her. 'It doesn't mean we don't have feelings. I thought you'd left behind that spoilt, selfish brat you used to be but you haven't changed. You still can't see beyond yourself and the way you feel.'

'That's got nothing to do with this.' Sadie raked her hair back from her brow with her fingers. She was in a very distressed state. 'Why couldn't you have done as she wished and married her when she wanted it?'

'I have my reasons.'

'You soon cast your reasons aside when you thought you were going to lose her, though, didn't you, so why couldn't you have done it before? She'd still be alive if you had.'

'Yes, very probably.'

'Pure selfishness.'

'If you say so.'

'She's been miserable for ages about the situation between you and her,' Sadie informed him. 'I told her to either accept things your way, or get rid.'

'So she took your advice last night.'

'Yes, maybe she did,' she conceded. 'We'll never know, will we? I don't know how much influence I had on her decision. All I know is that I've lost my best friend. You only had her in your life for a couple of years. She'd been in mine forever. First Paul, then Brenda. When will it end? Everything seems so fragile and temporary.'

'I'm sorry,' he said in a gentler tone, but he looked ill with misery. 'It must be awful for you.'

'Yes, worse than awful,' she said. 'Anyway, I've

said my piece so I'll go now.'

Ray didn't argue about it. 'I'll see you out.' He walked to the stairs and went down. She followed him. 'See you around,' he said, opening the door.

'Not if I see you first,' she said and marched off down the street.

*   *   *

Why did everything always happen at once, Marge asked herself, as Rosie woke up and started to cry at the same time as the phone trilled through the house. There was no one else around to answer it — the boys were out and Cyril was working in the garden — so she rushed into the hall and picked up the receiver.

'Hello, Marjorie, this is Harriet Weston again. Is Sadie there please?' she asked.

'No, I'm afraid she isn't. She's gone out.' Marge was preoccupied because Rosie was crying and she needed to go upstairs and see to her.

'Oh,' Harriet said in surprise. 'Will she be long?'

'I shouldn't think so but I don't really know. I shall have to go, Harriet,' she said. 'The baby is crying.'

'You're looking after the baby *again*?'

'That's right. I can't stop. I'll tell Sadie that you called. Bye for now.' She replaced the receiver and rushed up the stairs.

*   *   *

Harriet hurried into the garden where her husband was on his knees weeding the flower bed with the dog by his side, the garden still in colour in the incipient autumn, though the glorious scarlet geraniums were beginning to look a bit tired.

'Gerald, she's gone out again.'

'Who?' he asked, looking up, trowel in hand.

'Sadie, of course.'

He got to his feet, frowning. 'Harriet dear, you must stop checking up on her. It isn't right.'

'I'm not checking up on her,' she denied hotly. 'I merely telephoned today for the same reason that I called yesterday, to invite her and Rosie over. But she isn't there and her mother was looking after the baby again and Rosie was crying.'

'It really isn't our business, how many more times must I tell you?' he said.

'As I've told you before, *it is our business*,' she stated categorically. 'Saturday night, Sunday afternoon, out both times. Where could she have gone on a Sunday afternoon without her daughter?'

'I've no idea and you'd do well not to ask when you do get to speak to her.'

'As Rosie's grandmother I've every right to know.'

'And she's every right not to tell you,' he came back at her. 'She's got her own life and it's nothing to do with us.'

'You're entitled to your opinion but I completely disagree with you,' Harriet declared.

Sighing heavily, he went back to his gardening.

He could see real trouble ahead if his wife didn't moderate her behaviour towards Sadie. But she would do what she wanted whatever he said about it. His opinion counted for nothing with Harriet.

★ ★ ★

It was very strange, thought Sadie, on the way home from Ray's place, that she felt even worse after her altercation with him. She'd got it off her chest so she should be feeling better, but the rage that had driven her to go there had drained away leaving her more miserable than ever. All her mind would allow her to see was the agony in his eyes as he'd admitted responsibility for Brenda's death. Sadness overwhelmed her. It filled every part of her body to the point where she ached with it.

When she got in Rosie ran towards her with her arms raised and Sadie wanted to weep with love for her. She picked her up and smothered her with kisses. Her daughter was the reason she must keep going, despite her own feelings.

'Shall we go to the swings now, sweetheart?' she suggested.

The child beamed, dark eyes sparkling, cheeks dimpled. 'Dolly, wings?' she asked again.

'Yes, we'll go and get your dolly,' Sadie told her.

Marge suddenly remembered something. 'Oh Sadie, Harriet Weston has phoned a couple of times for you,' she told her.

'What did she want?'

'She didn't say. Probably just phoned to see how you are. You'd better ring her back though. It might be important.'

'Mummy will be just two minutes, Rosie,' she said, putting her daughter down on to the floor. 'I have to make a very quick phone call then we'll go.'

★ ★ ★

'Hello, Mrs Weston. It's Sadie. You've been trying to get hold of me, I believe.'

'Yes, that's right.'

'Is it anything in particular you wanted me for?'

'I was wondering when you and Rosie will be coming over to see us,' Harriet said.

'I'm not sure,' Sadie said dully, too full of grief to see beyond Brenda's funeral.

'Oh.' She sounded disappointed and Sadie sensed criticism in her tone. 'Well, don't leave it too long, will you. It's quite a while since we've seen you and Rosie.'

'Is it?' Why was the woman pestering her to visit them at a time like this?

'Did you enjoy the dance last night?'

The dramatic events following the dance had almost erased the earlier part of the evening from her memory altogether. 'It was all right,' she said vaguely.

'Was Rosie fine with your mother?'

'Of course she was. Why wouldn't she be?'

'I thought she might miss you.'

'No, she's used to being with Mum. Anyway

253

she was in bed and asleep before I went out.'

'I should think she is used to your not being there, the amount of times you leave the child,' Harriet blurted out with overt criticism. 'You were out when I phoned earlier today as well.'

That severed the remaining vestiges of Sadie's patience. 'My best friend was killed last night in a road accident, so I am not in the mood for the third degree on my activities, and I thought you would have the sensitivity to realise that.' Her voice rose to a shriek. 'So get off the phone, you interfering old cow, and leave me alone.' She slammed down the receiver.

Her mother appeared at her side. 'Oh Sadie, there was no need for that. I know Harriet isn't an easy person to get on with but she didn't deserve that.'

'But she was questioning and criticising me, Mum,' she said, trembling in the aftermath of her outburst. 'Fancy having a go at me at a time like this? You'd have thought she could have left it at least until after the funeral.'

Marge considered this for a few moments then bit her lip. 'She doesn't know about Brenda,' she told her worriedly. 'I didn't have a chance to tell her when she phoned earlier because Rosie was crying and I needed to see to her.'

'Oh.' Sadie sighed, brushing her brow with the back of her hand. 'I didn't realise that. Now I feel awful. But even so, she shouldn't be poking her nose into my business. You've said so yourself before now.'

'Yes I have, and I know that she's demanding over Rosie and I agree that she shouldn't interfere in your life. But that isn't the way to speak to her, or anyone,' she lectured. 'You know better than that, Sadie. I know how much you must be hurting, love, and my heart goes out to you. But don't take it out on other people.'

'But she was so rude to me, Mum.'

'You weren't exactly polite yourself.'

'Well, this possessive attitude she has towards Rosie drives me mad,' Sadie said. 'She's always pestering me to take her over there.'

'Rosie is all Harriet has left of Paul,' said Marge, 'so it's only natural she would want to see as much of her as possible. Remember that we have Rosie all the time; she doesn't. I don't like the woman any more than you do but I do have a certain amount of sympathy for her, having lost her son so young.'

'Okay,' agreed Sadie with a sigh of resignation. 'I'll call her back to apologise when Rosie and I get back from the park.'

'Good girl,' said her mother.

10

Some childhood memories have a lasting effect, and Ray's hatred of Sunday afternoons had stayed with him as an adult. But when Brenda had come into his life and they had spent them together, the scars of the past had lessened their hold on him. Now he loathed Sunday afternoons all over again, especially this particular one: the day after her death.

It wasn't as if there was anything much you could do to take your mind off things and relieve the tedium and the sense that time had almost come to a halt. Everything was closed except the cinemas and they were full of teenagers and courting couples in the afternoon. The pubs didn't open until the evening so he couldn't even go in search of liquid refreshment to take the edge off the pain.

Sitting in the armchair with the unread newspaper on his lap he reflected on how he and Brenda used to go for a walk in the park or along by the river. Sometimes they might even go to the West End for a mooch round and a bite to eat. At least there was some life there. Neither of them had been keen on the peculiar quietness of Sunday afternoon in the suburbs.

Like many things in life that are around all the time, the joy of his relationship with Brenda was taken for granted. On reflection, it was surprising that she had stayed with him for so long when, because of an issue she knew nothing about, he hadn't been willing to let the relationship take its natural course into marriage. Not until it was too late anyway.

Brenda had been a beautiful girl with an outgoing personality. She could easily have found someone else. But it was him she had wanted. Only him! And he had let her down by not giving her what she desired so much.

For as long as he lived he knew he would never forgive himself. She'd been an only child too. Her poor parents had been inconsolable at the hospital last night. He missed her already and it was less than twenty-four hours since they'd been out together enjoying themselves. He would never forget the image of her in the street lights, after his proposal. She'd had her arms raised in joy and a beaming smile on her face. Then she was gone — forever. In the midst of life . . . how true that saying was!

At the beginning of their romance she had forced herself on him. Up until then he had seen her as a kid, just a friend of Sadie's who was always round the Bells' house, giggling and whispering with their youngest child. He remembered Sadie's wedding and how Brenda had strutted up to him, asked him to dance and wouldn't take no for an answer. She'd had plenty of front; one of the many things he'd grown to love about her.

Feeling a choking sensation rising in his throat, he knew he must occupy himself or he would sink into helpless weeping, unacceptable in a grown man. Work; perhaps that might help.

There was always plenty to be done in the shop so he made his way down the stairs.

He was looking through the stock on display with a view to doing some filling up when there was a tapping on the shop window.

'Sadie,' he said warily, opening the door to her and out of politeness adding, 'Come in.'

'No I won't, thanks, this time,' she said, looking down at Rosie in the push chair. 'I have to get her ladyship home for her tea. We've been to the park. She loves it so much I have a battle with her when it's time to come away.'

'What can I do for you?' He looked at her questioningly, moving back slightly and adding with a wry grin, 'Do I need to protect myself?'

Despite everything, she managed a watery smile though there were tears in her eyes. 'No, you'll be quite safe. I've come to apologise actually.'

'Really?'

'Yeah, I had no right to say those things to you this morning,' she told him.

'Don't worry about it.'

'I've been upsetting people right, left and centre all day. I have to phone Paul's mum as soon as I get home to apologise.' She paused, looking sheepish. 'Truth is, I'm hurting so much and feeling so damned helpless to do anything about it, I've just been hitting out at all and sundry. I didn't really mean it.'

'In my case there's no need to apologise because, as I said earlier, I agree with everything you said. If I'd behaved like any normal bloke the accident wouldn't have happened. No one

258

could feel worse about it than I do.'

'That's like saying that I'm to blame for Paul's death because he loved me so much he was jealous,' she said. 'And there have been times when I have thought along those lines. But there's no point in going down that road because we can't know for sure and it doesn't change anything anyway. It could have been what I said that persuaded Brenda to give you the elbow and set the whole thing in motion, we just don't know. Besides, we all have free will. Brenda stepped off that kerb without looking. No one pushed her. It was a mistake, an accident. No one is to blame.'

'I know but . . . '

'You obviously had your reasons for not wanting to get married and that's your business,' she went on. 'But guilt is no good for you, Ray. It's going to be hard enough getting along without her. Don't make it worse by blaming yourself.'

'Easier said than done.'

'Well, you know my thoughts on the matter now.'

'Thanks for that. I didn't like the idea of having you as an enemy.' He paused. 'Are you sure you won't come in? I'm told I make a lovely cup of tea.'

'Another time, perhaps.'

Rosie was straining to get out of her push chair. 'Oh all right,' Sadie said to her. 'You can get out for a minute to have a cuddle with Uncle Ray. But you're not walking home. We won't get there till Wednesday if I let you do that.'

Ray lifted the little girl up in the air as he usually did, the fact that his heart wasn't really in it going unnoticed by the child as she chuckled and yelled for more.

'Enough,' said Sadie after a while, taking her and putting her back in her buggy, at which point she protested noisily. 'She'll stop crying once we get going, Ray. Bye for now.'

'See you, Sadie.'

Watching her go, Rosie's shrieks lessening, he realised that for a few minutes his grief had eased, such was the power of a child who was unaware of the drama going on around her. He found himself thinking what a blessing it was that Sadie had her. Two people she had loved deeply had been taken from her and she was only twenty-one. Because of how he himself was feeling, he knew a little of what it must be like for her. A few years ago, she would have collapsed under the strain and had everyone running around after her. Now, give or take the odd outburst, she was able to accept what came and be strong for the sake of little Rosie.

He turned and went inside, a knot of despair and loneliness descending as he went back into the shop. The business and his ambitions for it didn't seem important any more. But he had to soldier on, despite his personal feelings.

★ ★ ★

'So, how did the funeral go?' asked Harriet when Sadie took Rosie to visit a few weeks later.

'Very sad, as you'd expect,' replied Sadie. 'It's

260

not natural burying someone of twenty-one.'

'It brought back memories, I dare say,' suggested Gerald.

'Yes.' Actually the whole thing had been almost unbearable for Sadie, the awful sense of *déjà vu* and the desperate sorrow of that final goodbye to her dearest friend. But she didn't want to bring it all back by going into detail so she just said, 'Brenda's parents were very brave. It must have been hard for them, as you know only too well.'

They both nodded and the conversation moved on, thanks to Rosie, who was full of fun and energy and currently trying to catch the dog who had taken cover behind the sofa.

'I think he'll be safer staying where he is,' remarked Sadie lightly as Gerald tried to persuade him to come out.

'Fergus is very gentle,' said Harriet.

'I can't say the same for Rosie,' laughed Sadie. 'She can be a bit too boisterous with her cuddles. He'll wonder what's hit him if she gets hold of him. Our cat usually hides somewhere when she's around. She adores him and wants to hug him but he can only take so much. She isn't old enough to realise her own strength.'

'She seems to like Fergus,' observed Harriet.

'Yes, she does,' agreed Sadie. 'She loves animals, and he is a dear little thing.'

'We think so,' said Harriet proudly. 'And as for Rosie, she gets prettier every time we see her.'

Sadie smiled. A compliment to her daughter was worth far more than any directed to herself and Harriet wasn't generous with them towards

261

anyone. At almost two Rosie was a picture with dark wavy hair, velvety near-black eyes and a round face with dimples in her cheeks when she smiled. Sadie didn't have a great deal to spend on clothes for her but by using market stalls and other inexpensive outlets she managed to keep her looking nice.

'Yes, if I say so myself, she is beautiful.'

'Very much like her father,' said Harriet.

Sadie couldn't disagree because every day she saw Paul in her. 'Yes, she's her daddy's girl all right.'

'I saw a little dress I thought she would look nice in,' said Harriet, making Sadie's heart sink because she and Harriet had very different ideas on kiddies' clothes. 'So I got it for her. I'll give it to you before you go.'

'That's very kind of you, thank you.'

'I've never seen her in the last outfit I gave you for her.'

'Haven't you?' said Sadie innocently. 'It must be because she didn't happen to be wearing it when I've been over here. She's grown out of it now. Her clothes hardly last any time at all.'

This was very awkward; especially as anything Harriet bought for Rosie probably cost more than three outfits in Sadie's price range. But she didn't have the heart to tell the older woman because she knew she would be offended, unlike her own mother who never bought anything for Rosie unless Sadie was with her. Perhaps this latest offering wouldn't be quite so hideous.

Harriet did seem to be genuinely fond of Rosie, though she didn't take any nonsense and was quite liberal with the phrases 'No, Rosie' and 'Don't touch'. The visits were still an ordeal for Sadie, mainly because Rosie was their only common interest and Sadie was always on edge in the expectation of criticism from Harriet. The dog helped. At least he created a diversion and made everyone smile.

The minutes dragged by but at last Sadie felt she could leave without causing offence. Surprisingly the item of clothing for Rosie was a cute pinafore dress with a jumper to wear underneath, which would be very useful with the winter approaching. Maybe Harriet had taken note of the way Sadie dressed her daughter because this outfit was a definite improvement.

'We'll see you again soon,' she said at the door.

'Sooner rather than later,' responded Harriet meaningfully.

'When you can,' added Gerald tactfully.

Bless him, thought Sadie. He was such a dear. 'Yes, will do,' she said non-committally and hurried away with Rosie in the push chair.

★ ★ ★

'Phew, what a blinking palaver,' groaned Sadie when she finally arrived home, having missed the bus, had to wait ages for another and then encountered a delay on the train service. 'Honestly it's a nightmare travelling on public transport with a young child. Some of the bus conductors aren't a bit helpful and won't let you on at all with a push chair. Honestly I thought I'd never get home.'

'It's time you learned to drive,' suggested Don casually. 'A modern young woman like yourself should be at the wheel.'

She gave him a questioning look. 'Oh yeah, and what good would that do me since I don't have a car and am never likely to?'

'You could borrow mine for these jaunts out to Surrey.' Her brothers had moved on from their shared motorbike and now each had a second-hand car. 'As long as we worked it out for a time when I don't need it myself, of course.'

'Really?' she said, touched by his offer. Driving a car had been so far out of reach for her, she had never even considered it.

'Yeah, why not? As long as you don't take liberties and start taking the car off me too often.'

'As if I would.'

He narrowed his eyes at her. 'The sister I used to know would have,' he said, 'but I think maybe she's improved a bit since then.'

'Me driving a car. Blimey, I never thought I'd see the day.'

'Women drivers are no novelty these days,' her father put in. 'You see them at the wheel everywhere.'

'You're telling me,' added Derek disapprovingly. 'All over London and all over the road.'

'Oi,' admonished Sadie. 'That's enough of those kinds of comments. You'd better not say that about me when I'm a driver.'

'Don't bank on it, sis.'

'Driving lessons are expensive, though,' she

264

pointed out, thinking about it realistically.

'I'll teach you,' offered Don. 'So it wouldn't cost you a penny.'

'That's good of you. Thank you.'

'I would offer to help,' added Derek. 'But I don't have the patience for that sort of thing so it would be a disaster with me beside you.'

'A new challenge is just what she needs,' approved Marge heartily. 'Something to take her mind off things. What with losing Brenda and everything.'

'It would be very handy to be able to drive out to Surrey, I must admit,' said Sadie, enthusiasm rising.

'You'll have to pass your driving test first,' Derek reminded her. 'So don't get too carried away.'

'It will take a while to get you ready for the test as we'll only have the time for a lesson at the weekends with the nights drawing in,' Don pointed out. 'But you could start the ball rolling by applying for a provisional licence.'

'Oh, how exciting.' She picked her daughter up and danced around with her. 'How about that, Rosie. You and I going out to the country in a car. Won't that be fun?'

Picking up on the jolly atmosphere Rosie gave a great big toothy grin, then spotted Pickles on the window sill and struggled to get down to go after him. 'Off you go then,' said Sadie, putting her down, knowing she would be quite safe because the cat was well out of reach. 'But it will soon be time for bed.'

Rosie took no notice at all.

Watching the way her daughter handled Rosie, Marge's pride in her was strengthened. Brenda's death had been a shocking blow for her but since that first terrible day when she'd barely known what she was doing, she'd kept her sadness out of sight of Rosie. She'd shed copious tears but very much in private. Sadie seemed to grow in maturity with every day that passed whilst retaining her sense of fun. She'd had more than her share of grief for a person of that age but she coped and seemed to grow stronger in the process. She had exceeded all Marge's expectations of her.

★ ★ ★

'So you're seeing that woman you met at the Palais on a regular basis now, then,' said Ray to Derek in a quiet moment at the shop in between the rush of Christmas shoppers.

'Her name is Christine and yeah, I am, as it happens,' replied Derek. 'She's lovely and we get on great together.'

'Serious?'

'Oh, I don't know about that,' said Derek with a wry grin. 'It's still early days. You know me. I don't like to be tied down.'

'You've got to grab your happiness while you can, mate, you never know when it's going to end.'

'I'm beginning to realise that,' said Derek. 'You go along for years taking everything for granted then out of the blue something unexpected happens. That heart scare really

266

brought that home to me.' He paused, as though uncertain whether to utter his next words. 'Then Brenda . . . I still can't believe it.'

'It does take some getting used to.'

'I expect you're still feeling raw?'

'Very.'

'Sadie took it hard too,' her brother said. 'She keeps it to herself though, 'cos of the nipper.'

'I can imagine.'

'She's amazing the way she carries on,' Derek continued. 'Her and Brenda had been friends forever so it's bound to leave a huge hole in her life. And, of course, she'd already had to cope with losing Paul, the poor kid. She used to be a right little madam — probably our fault for spoiling her — but she seemed to grow up overnight after she had Rosie.'

Their conversation was interrupted by a sudden surge of customers, a group of noisy young girls.

'Have you got the new Beatles record, 'Day Tripper'?' asked one of them eagerly.

'Sorry. We've sold out, I'm afraid,' replied Ray.

'Oh no,' said the girl dramatically, almost as though she'd just been told that her mother had died.

There was a wailing chorus of disappointment from her friends.

'We just have to have it,' said one of them ardently.

'We're serious Beatles fans,' said another. 'We adore them. Anyway, everybody else has got the record so we have to have it or we'll be freaks.'

'Have you tried Woolworths?'

'They're sold out too,' the first girl said. 'That's why we're here.'

'We're expecting a delivery at any time.'

'Can you save us one, please?' she asked.

'Yeah, and for us,' echoed some of the others.

'We can't, I'm afraid. There's too much of a demand. It's strictly first come, first served,' Ray said.

'But that isn't fair,' objected the girl, pouting. 'We won't know when they're coming in so we'll miss them.'

'Why not give us a ring to find out if they've come in yet,' suggested Derek.

'We're at work all the week,' she said, still disappointed.

'We're open in the lunch hour until after Christmas, if that's any help,' he informed her.

'Not really,' she said and the girls left the shop, complaining bitterly about their lot.

'The new Beatles record will be the Christmas number one if our sales are anything to go by,' said Ray.

'Looks like it,' agreed Derek. 'It can be quite exciting, this business, can't it?'

'It has its moments,' Ray agreed. 'It still gives me a buzz when we have a really massive seller.'

'Never in a million years would I have thought that I would say this but I really enjoy working here,' Derek confided. 'In fact I'd go so far as to say that my heart trouble has done me a favour. I'd never have come out of the motor trade otherwise. I'd have been a grease monkey for the rest of my life.'

'It's an ill wind that blows nobody any good,

so they say,' said Ray, though he couldn't think of anything positive that could possibly come out of Brenda's untimely death.

* * *

Christmas had been an emotional time for Sadie since she lost Paul, and this year it was even more wretched without Brenda. But life had to go on, especially when you had a child, so she put a brave face on it and celebrated with the family in the usual way, though Rosie was the saving grace for everyone. Still at an age when she was more interested in the wrappings than the presents, she was none the less an absolute joy and kept them all entertained.

'How do you keep up with her, Sadie?' asked Ray, who had been invited for Christmas Day and happened to be sitting next to Sadie in the afternoon when they were all lazing around eating sweets and watching Rosie play. 'She's got more energy than an E-Type Jag.'

'She keeps me on my toes and that's a fact,' she told him. 'But she keeps me going too. Without her I'd probably fall apart.' She looked at him, seeing the strain in his eyes and the tense set of his mouth. 'How about you? Are you coping?'

'Yeah, I'm fine.'

She knew that he wasn't but Ray was a man who didn't take kindly to sympathy or enquiry into his private life so she just said, 'Good for you. Christmas can be hell when you're grieving. I won't be sorry to see the back of it this year.'

'Me neither.' He looked at Rosie, who was on the floor surrounded by Santa's many offerings. 'Meanwhile we have your daughter to help us through the day.'

'Yes, thank goodness,' she said.

'I understand that Don is going to teach you to drive in the New Year,' he continued.

'Yes, once my provisional licence comes through, we'll make a start,' she said.

'So if I value my life I must remember to stay off the road on the days you're having a lesson,' he said.

'That's enough male cracks like that,' she admonished, taking the joke in the manner it was intended, as a diversionary tactic to avoid speaking about what was really on their minds. 'I'll soon show you what I can do behind the wheel. You just wait and see.'

★ ★ ★

The driving lessons were a complete disaster.

'That's it, Sadie, I'm finished. I'm not prepared to go through that nightmare ever again,' declared Don one Sunday morning in March 1966 when he and his sister got home. 'You've taken years off of my life with these driving lessons and today was too much. My nerves are completely shattered.'

'I wasn't that bad, surely,' she said.

'You were worse than bad,' he informed her. 'You were a life-threatening menace to me and other drivers.'

'What exactly did she do that was so awful?'

their mother wanted to know.

'Speeding round Hammersmith Broadway to mention just one thing,' he replied. 'I thought my end had come, I tell you. We were a fraction of an inch away from hitting another car.'

'It wasn't that close.'

'Yes it was,' he insisted.

'If you say so I suppose it must have been,' she conceded. 'Sorry, Don, but I didn't realise I was going too fast.'

'You should keep an eye on the speedometer.'

'How could I when I was keeping my eyes on the road like you told me?'

'You're supposed to be able to do that as well. Anyway you should have known by the feel that you were going too fast. It's a built-up area, not a race track.'

'Why were you taking her around the Broadway in the first place?' enquired Derek. 'It can be tricky for an experienced driver round there, let alone a learner. You should be taking her round the back streets where there isn't much traffic.'

'We do all that as well,' Don informed him irritably. 'Three-point turns or, in her case, thirty-three point turns. Hill starts that make your blood run cold. She's been learning for two months. She needs to practise among traffic in places like the Broadway. But not with me. No more. I've had it, mate. She's ruining my gearbox as well as my nerves. You can hear it complaining every time she changes gear. It'll give up the ghost altogether if she carries on.'

'I'll go out with her next time,' offered Derek.

'Oh no, you don't.' Don was adamant. 'That will finish you off altogether. You heart won't be able to take it. Mine will be on the way out if I carry on with this lark.'

'You shouldn't shout at me so much,' Sadie told her brother. 'It unnerves me and causes me to make mistakes.' She looked at her mother. 'He keeps screaming at me and throwing his arms in the air. It's no wonder I do it all wrong.'

'Of course I shout when you're veering towards the wrong side of the road and about to hit something.' He looked at the others. 'She's a lunatic when she gets behind a wheel. Don't be fooled by those innocent blue eyes.'

'I'm sure I can't be as bad as you say,' she objected. 'Anyway, I do my best.'

'You don't do as I tell you, that's at the root of the trouble,' Don carried on. 'You just sail along doing your own thing and causing havoc all around. I've never heard so many motorists honking in all my life as when we went round the Broadway today. It's a wonder they didn't hear it at home here. Gordon Bennett, Sadie, we're lucky to be alive. There could have been a major pile-up.'

'I'm sorry I've been such a dead loss,' she said miserably. 'So are you definitely giving up on me?'

'Too true I am.'

'That doesn't seem very nice, deserting your sister like that,' Marge intervened. 'She's been enjoying the lessons.'

'She's not been sitting where I am in the car, has she?' Don retaliated.

'Honestly, he doesn't half exaggerate,' Sadie protested.

'Are you sure the problem isn't partly yours, Don? Maybe you're being impatient because she's your sister?' suggested Cyril.

'I've nothing to compare it with because I've never taught anyone else, and I won't be either,' he declared. 'My days as a driving instructor are well and truly over.'

'Everyone knows that driving lessons can wreck a marriage when a husband tries to teach his wife. Same thing with sister and brother, I suppose,' his father commented. 'If a stranger was giving you lessons, Sadie, you'd do as they said and they wouldn't have cause to shout at you.'

'I try to do what Don tells me, but I get so nervous,' she said.

'No you don't,' claimed Don. 'You're overconfident and it's dangerous.'

'Please don't give up on me, Don,' she urged. 'This is so important for me because of the Surrey trips. It's only practice I need.'

'Just give her one more chance?' begged Marge.

'Please, Don?' coaxed Sadie. 'I promise I'll do better next time. I'll be very careful and I'll do everything you say.'

'You offered to teach her,' Derek reminded him. 'You ought to stick it out.'

'Exactly,' agreed Marge. 'She had no thoughts of learning to drive before you put the idea into her head. The least you can do is see it through to the end.'

273

Don gave an eloquent sigh. 'It'll probably be my end but all right, I'll carry on, but only if you promise to do exactly as I tell you, Sadie.'

'I promise.'

'Nothing's changed,' said Don. 'You can still worm your way around me.'

'Thanks, Don,' she said. 'You're such a sweetheart.'

He raised his eyes in an affectionate manner. 'I must be flamin' barmy,' he said.

* * *

The Bell brothers usually met Ray for a pint or two at the local at Sunday lunchtime. One of the rules since Ray and Derek had been working together was no shop talk.

One Sunday in April, Don was detained because of Sadie's driving lesson so Ray and Derek were deeply involved in business chat when Don came in looking extremely harassed.

'Ooh, get me a pint, someone,' he said. 'Never did a man need one more.'

'It didn't go well then,' assumed Derek.

'Course it didn't,' his brother confirmed. 'It never does. It's always hell on earth being in the passenger seat with Sadie at the wheel.'

'I can't understand it,' said Derek. 'I mean, Sadie is a bright girl, so why is she having such a problem learning to drive?'

'You tell me, mate,' Don said. 'It's beyond me.'

'She must have learned something over all this time, surely,' said Derek. 'You've been teaching her for months.'

'She's been taught all the basics but it's getting it right that's the problem. It's practice she needs.' Don paused thoughtfully. 'It could be that some people just don't have the co-ordination or somethin', though I'm beginning to wonder if Dad might be right and part of it might be my fault. Sadie and I are an explosive combination in the car now. She's nervous because I lose my temper with her and I'm on edge because I'm trying hard to keep calm and she makes mistakes and I yell at her and then she does it all wrong and so it goes on. I'm getting to the end of my tether with it.'

'It's a shame because she's so keen and wants to drive,' remarked Derek, 'and it would be so much easier for her when she takes Rosie out to Surrey.'

Don nodded. 'I think I'll have to buy her some lessons from a professional because she's getting nowhere with me and it always ends up in an argument because we are both so frustrated.'

'Lessons will be pricey if she needs a lot,' Derek pointed out. 'I'll chip in with you though.'

'Thanks, but no. I took the job so it's my call,' Don said. 'She probably won't hear of it anyway. You know Sadie. She likes to pay her way and she can't afford lessons herself, not with the nipper to support.'

'I could try and teach her in my car, if she would agree to it,' suggested Ray. 'It just might work with me as we're not close. It would save a lot of money in lessons.'

The brothers looked at him in surprise.

'It's very good of you to offer,' said Don. 'But

you might live to regret it and I really do mean that.'

'If it doesn't work out, you'll have to revert to the lessons idea,' said Ray. 'But surely it's worth a try.'

'I'll put the idea to Sadie,' Don decided. 'And thanks very much, Ray. It's much appreciated.'

'What are friends for,' said Ray.

★   ★   ★

It was a beautiful Sunday morning in spring and Surrey was green and fragrant with blossom, the trees and bushes burgeoning with new leaves, flowers in bud, the sun beaming down from a clear blue sky.

Gerald was in the back garden checking things over and enjoying the gentle sunshine when, inspired by the weather, he had a sudden idea so he went indoors to tell his wife about it.

'Drive into London for an outing, just like that, out of the blue?' was Harriet's predictable reaction. 'You know we don't do things on the spur of the moment, Gerald.'

'Then it's high time we did,' he pointed out. 'And why not. We don't have any ties here. It's a lovely day.'

'I've got a lamb joint to cook for lunch,' she told him.

'We can have it tonight,' he suggested.

'It's Sunday, Gerald,' she reminded him. 'We always have lunch at lunchtime on a Sunday.'

'All the more reason for a change,' he replied. 'Maybe we could be even more daring and have something to eat out, and keep the joint for tomorrow.'

'What did you have in mind on this outing exactly?' she asked.

'Whatever takes our fancy,' he said. 'A walk in Hyde Park or Regent's Park, maybe, or a stroll by the Thames at the South Bank. Just a day out to capture the atmosphere. It will be a nice change for us.'

Not being a spontaneous person, Harriet was worried about upsetting their routine. 'Oh, I don't know, Gerald,' she said. 'It's all a bit sudden.'

'It's only a day out, dear,' he pointed out.

'Even so . . . '

'Perhaps we could stop off on the way to see Rosie if there is time,' he proposed craftily.

Now she *was* interested. 'Oh, what a good idea,' she said, all objections cast aside. 'I'll get on the phone to Sadie to tell her that we're coming.'

'No, don't do that, in case we're held up in traffic and we don't manage it,' he said. 'We'll play it by ear and surprise them.'

'I'll get ready then,' she said eagerly.

* * *

'I can't say I'm thrilled at the idea of your being roped in because my brother has given up on me,' said Sadie, in the driving seat of Ray's estate car with the L-plates firmly in place. 'In fact I feel terrible about it. I'm sure you've got better things to do with your time on a Sunday morning.'

'No, not really,' he assured her.

'If you shout at me I shall go to pieces and do it all wrong,' she warned him. 'I'm at the stage now where I think perhaps I'm not meant to drive a car.'

'Rubbish,' he stated categorically. 'You are a very bright and confident girl in all other aspects of your life so there is no reason why you can't drive a car and between us we are going to prove that you can. Don has taught you the basics and by the time we've had a good few practice sessions you'll sail through your test and be driving out to Surrey to see those in-laws of yours without a second thought.'

'Do you really think so?'

'I certainly do.'

'In that case, let's get started,' she said, imbued with new hope and confidence. 'So let's get it right ... turn the engine on, check rear-view mirror, put indicator on then go into first gear.'

'Off you go then, let's see what you can really do.'

★ ★ ★

Things went so well, Sadie was smiling when she drew up outside the house after the lesson.

'It was a completely different experience to when I go out with Don,' she confided to Ray. 'I can't believe how much better it was. In fact I'd go so far as to say that I enjoyed it.'

'All you needed was confidence,' said Ray. 'I

278

shall have a word or two to say to Don; all this business about you being such a nightmare behind the wheel. It isn't true at all.'

'I was when I was with him,' she freely admitted. 'I could feel his tension even before he yelled at me and then I made a complete pig's ear of everything.'

'It must be something to do with being related, I suppose,' he said. 'As far as I can see, all you need is some more practice then you can apply for your test.'

'My test,' she said. 'Blimey.'

'It won't be for a while yet, though,' he said. 'You'll have to wait ages for a slot anyway. The waiting time for driving tests is terrible in London at the moment, so don't panic.'

She smiled at him. 'Thanks ever so much, Ray,' she said. 'I'm very grateful to you.'

'A pleasure,' he said. 'Same time next week?'

'If you're sure you don't mind, yes please,' she enthused. 'Meanwhile, let's go indoors and have a cup of tea. They'll all be waiting to know how it went.'

They were both smiling as they went into the house.

'We're back,' Sadie called out as they headed for the living room. 'And whoever said I could never drive a car will have to eat their words now. I am officially learner of the year.'

Entering the room, they were all there. Mum, Dad, her brothers and Rosie, who ran to meet her and was immediately picked up and cuddled. Then Sadie saw the visitors sitting stiffly on the sofa.

'Mrs Weston,' she said, aghast. 'And Mr Weston. What are you doing here?'

★ ★ ★

'So it's happened, Gerald,' said Harriet as they continued their journey into Central London after leaving Fern Terrace. 'Sadie has got another man.'

'You know he's a friend of her brothers, dear, the chap who came to tell us when Paul died,' he pointed out. 'He's teaching her to drive, that's all.'

'Are you blind, Gerald?' she blasted at him. 'Didn't you notice the way they were together? All smiles and friendly looks.'

'Wasn't that because she had done well with her driving?' he suggested.

'That was what we were meant to believe but there was more to it than that and it was written all over them.'

'I could see that they get on well,' he admitted. 'But they've known each other for years so they are sure to be comfortable in each other's company.'

'You can be so naive at times.'

'Look, the chap was going out with her best friend, the one who died, so they are bound to have lots in common. I don't think they are anything more than friends and if they are, so what? She's entitled to see whoever she wants and there is no reason for her to hide it from us. As far as I'm concerned, the more support she has, the better, after losing her friend. And he is

280

very good with Rosie; she seems to be very fond of him.'

'Which indicates that she sees a lot of him, which proves my point, don't you think?'

'Not at all. He would see Rosie when he goes to see Sadie's brothers, I imagine,' Gerald said. 'He's a family friend and it's the sort of household where people drop in unannounced, I should think. Of course, as he's teaching her to drive, Sadie would be seeing more of him at the moment. Don't forget she's only learning to drive to make it easier to bring Rosie out to Surrey to see us. You should be pleased.'

'I am, of course,' Harriet conceded. 'I was only saying that she seems very friendly with the chap.'

'No, Harriet, that isn't what you were saying. You were suggesting that there is something going on between them,' he corrected her. 'I'm sure there isn't but whether there is or not is none of our business because Sadie is a free agent, so let's forget about it and enjoy the rest of our day out, shall we?'

'Yes, of course,' she said, but the outing was completely ruined for her. The thought of Rosie having a stepfather filled her with dread because she couldn't bear to lose her only link with Paul. When she looked at Rosie, the years rolled away and her son was back with her. She could touch him; breathe in his scent; feel the connection she'd had with him at that age. It meant the world to her and now she was in danger of having it taken away.

11

Sadie's driving lessons were put to the back of her mind a few days later by news of important changes at work.

'I'm going into partnership with two other doctors,' announced Dr Russell, having invited her into his consulting room one morning after surgery. 'The idea is to offer patients a more efficient service and make life easier for us all. Patients will be able to see one of the other doctors if their own isn't available, which means they'll get medical advice quicker and it will take some of the pressure off us GPs.'

'I see.' Naturally she was wondering how all of this was going to affect her. Changes of this sort usually meant jobs were lost.

'It will be a huge upheaval but worth it in the long run, if all goes to plan,' he went on. 'So there are going to be significant alterations to the practice.'

'Oh.' Tension grew as she waited for him to tell her what this would mean to her personally.

'Obviously this surgery won't be big enough, so we shall be moving out of here into larger premises,' he explained, 'and we're thinking of taking ground-floor rooms in a large house just a few minutes' walk from here.'

She nodded.

'One of the doctors is an established GP of long standing and he will be bringing his receptionist with him. She's been with him for many years.'

That was the blow Sadie had been dreading but she nodded politely, even though she was leaden with disappointment. This was the only job she had ever enjoyed and she was about to lose it. 'So you won't need me then,' she assumed, trying to take it with good grace.

'On the contrary,' he told her. 'The third doctor in the partnership is just starting out in general practice so has no staff to accommodate. With three doctors and their patients to look after there will be plenty of work for you both. With the increasing advances in medical science, which allow us to offer more services such as cervical smear tests and so on and all the extra administration that sort of thing entails, you'll be kept busy.'

'I see,' she muttered, almost weak with relief. 'So when is all this going to happen?'

'We hope to be ready to do the change-over in the autumn,' he replied.

She nodded.

'It's going to be a new experience for me as well as you, my dear; both of us are used to working alone, so we shall have to adapt to a new environment. But I'm sure we'll soon get used to it.' He smiled. 'I know that you young people like to move with the times so you'll have no trouble in rising to the challenge. This is the way forward for a new and better medical practice.'

'Yes, of course,' she said, able to smile now that her job was safe.

*   *   *

'It might be fun having female company in the reception office,' she remarked to the family that night over the evening meal, having told them about the forthcoming plans at work. 'The nurse is nice but she has her own room so we don't have much chance of a chat.'

'You go to work to do your job, not to socialise,' said Don, teasing her. 'That's the trouble with you women. You must spend half your life nattering.'

'Oh yeah,' Sadie retorted, 'and I bet you blokes at the garage don't talk while you're working. Not much. I went there once to bring your lunch when you'd forgotten it and the place was noisier than Saturday night at the local. The men were singing and shouting across to each other.'

Don couldn't deny it so he just gave a wry grin.

'I think it will be rather nice for you to have a woman to work with, Sadie,' her mother chipped in.

'I was so relieved when I realised that I wasn't going to be sacked I would have agreed to work with Jack the Ripper if that's what the doctor wanted,' Sadie said.

They were all laughing when the telephone rang and Derek went to answer it. 'It's Ray on the phone,' he called out. 'He wants to know if you fancy some extra driving practice, Sadie, as it's still light.'

She looked at her mother questioningly. 'I

could do with the experience and I'll be out for less than an hour. And she is fast asleep in bed.'

'Go on,' said Marge. 'I'll listen for Rosie.'

'Tell him yes, please,' she said to Derek.

* * *

'So how did I do, Ray?' Sadie asked when she had successfully parked the car outside the house after the lesson.

'I don't want you to get big-headed and over-confident,' he said. 'But you were excellent.'

'Oh, isn't that amazing? How can I be so bad then suddenly get to be good, I wonder?' she said.

'It must all be down to the teacher,' he laughed.

'I think it must be,' she agreed, her tone more serious than his. 'And I'm not joking around either, Ray. I feel much more confident with you by my side. I was all knotted up before I even started with Don.'

'Only because he's your brother and thinks nothing of yelling at you.'

'You would too if I needed it, wouldn't you?'

'I'd tell you and I do when you make mistakes, as you know, but you would have to do something really bad before I'd shout at you.' He grinned. 'I'm far too scared of you.'

'I don't believe that for a minute,' she said, smiling, and then added more seriously, 'Look, I feel guilty for taking up so much of your time but I can't afford . . . '

'Don't you dare mention payment,' he

interrupted sharply. 'I've been a friend of your family for years and I want to help. I want to see you through the driving test.'

'Well, you just say if you get fed up.'

'I will, don't worry,' he told her. 'But with the evenings getting lighter we could do some practice during the week on a regular basis as well as Sunday mornings, if you would like.'

'I would like that very much, but I'll have to check with Mum about it because of Rosie.'

'Of course. It was just an idea,' he said casually. 'Anyway, I'm coming into the house with you to see if those brothers of yours fancy a game of darts down the pub later on.'

'Okay,' she said and they walked to the house together.

Assisting Sadie with her driving was helping him every bit as much as it was helping her, Ray admitted to himself. It was much more enjoyable than sitting in the flat alone or going out to the pub in an effort to forget how much he was missing Brenda and the guilt that burdened him about her death. Sadie's company refreshed and cheered him, maybe because she was so similar to Brenda in age and outlook.

'So when is our very own Stirling Moss putting in for her driving test?' asked Don as they went into the living room.

'Very soon, if she continues as she is,' replied Ray.

'Well, well,' said Don. 'It must be a different Sadie to the one I tried to teach.'

'No. Only a different teacher,' joshed Ray. 'You just don't have the knack, mate.'

'All right, bighead, don't push it.'

'Anyone coming for a game of darts?' asked Ray.

'Yeah, I'll come,' said Don. 'But I expect lover boy here will have a date.'

'You are absolutely right,' confirmed Derek lightly. 'I've better things to do with my time nowadays than hang around with you two.'

'It's time your young lady came to Sunday tea with us,' suggested Marge.

'Whoops,' laughed Don. 'You'd better start saving for a ring if you're going to bring her to Sunday tea.'

'Give over,' countered Derek.

Standing back from the banter, Sadie turned to Ray. 'Thanks again,' she said with a warm smile. 'I have to go and check on Rosie now. So I'll say goodnight.'

'See you, Sadie,' said Ray, smiling after her.

★ ★ ★

'So how's the driving coming along?' asked Gerald a month or so later, when Sadie took Rosie to visit.

'It's going really well now,' she replied enthusiastically. 'In fact, I've got a date in October for my test.'

'Oh really, I didn't realise you were that far advanced,' he said.

'I've come on in leaps and bounds since Ray took over from Don,' she explained. 'He's so calm, he gives me confidence. It's quite amazing the difference.'

287

I bet it is, you little slut, thought Harriet but said, 'I think it's very brave of you to learn to drive a car. I would never have the nerve. I'd much rather leave that sort of thing to the men.'

'I was a bit nervous at first,' Sadie admitted, ignoring Harriet's outdated point of view, 'and I shall probably be a bag of nerves when I take the test, but I enjoy the actual feeling of driving now that I'm improving. It's the sense of freedom and power, I suppose, which is why men like cars so much.' She looked at her daughter, who was sitting on her lap. 'We'll be able to come and see Grandma and Granddad in Uncle Don's car. That will be fun, won't it?'

Rosie nodded, seeming shy.

'Would you like to come in the garden with me, Rosie, while Grandma makes the tea?' invited Gerald.

She cuddled into her mother.

'You're not shy, are you?' he said.

'Of course she isn't,' replied Sadie, because Rosie was normally the most outgoing of children.

But it took quite a bit of persuasion, the promise of a visit to the village duck pond later and the lure of the dog for her to get off her mother's knee and go into the garden with her grandfather.

'You and this Ray fellow seem very friendly,' Harriet remarked as she and Sadie waited for the kettle to boil.

'Yes, we do get on very well,' said Sadie unashamedly. 'He's a really nice bloke.'

'Oh, I see.'

Something about the tone of her voice made Sadie realise what Harriet was getting at. The idea of herself and Ray in any role other than friends was so ludicrous she wanted to laugh out loud and put the other woman's mind at rest. But there was something so cloying about her unhealthy interest in Sadie's private life she decided to let it go. It might do Harriet good to accept that Sadie wasn't just Paul's widow. She was a person in her own right too.

How Ray would laugh if she told him about Harriet's ridiculous assumption but, somehow, she suspected that she wasn't going to mention it.

★ ★ ★

As it happened the next time she saw Ray on the following Saturday afternoon there was something else on all their minds. The streets around Fern Terrace were empty and silent. Everyone was indoors, gathered around their television sets, all other concerns cast aside while they watched Bobby Moore's England team battle it out with Germany on the football field in the final of the World Cup. When in the dying moments of the game the ball was placed in the back of the net by Geoff Hurst, sealing victory for England, the Bell family plus Ray, who had closed the shop in honour of the event, rushed into the street along with all the neighbours. There was much jubilation. Even Rosie picked up on the atmosphere and danced around excitedly with her mother.

Everyone was happy, the cares of the world set aside in a huge surge of national pride. It occurred to Sadie fleetingly that Harriet Weston's ludicrous insinuations seemed a million miles away.

★ ★ ★

Sadie's hopes for a good companion at work were shattered when she met her new colleague, who was bossy, belligerent and keen to point out that she had been in the job for over twenty years so was senior in every respect to Sadie.

Her name was Edith Brown, a married but childless beanpole of a woman in her mid-forties with opinions about almost everything, in particular the way the reception office should be run and the degenerate youth culture of today. Also, she was violently opposed to mothers of young children going out to work.

'It's really a matter of opinion,' Sadie commented when Edith was holding forth on the subject with vigour. 'Anyway, some of us don't have a choice.'

'There are exceptions of course,' the older woman admitted grudgingly. 'Now come along, let's get this office ready for work tomorrow. Then we need to get the waiting room tidy; magazines in neat piles and everything ship-shape.'

'We've already done it,' Sadie pointed out.

'I know that but there's no harm in us checking it over again. I like everything to be immaculate in my waiting room.'

The move had taken place over a weekend in early September and Sadie and Edith, along with the doctors, had had to work extra hours to get everything ready for surgery on Monday morning. It hadn't been very convenient for Sadie because of Rosie but it was only a one-off and she liked to be involved. She found the prospect of the new, enlarged practice rather exciting, despite her domineering new colleague and her proprietary air.

★ ★ ★

If Sadie had thought Edith was strident towards herself, she was appalled by her behaviour towards the patients the next day during morning surgery. So bad was her attitude she even made Sadie's dreadful predecessor seem amiable.

'The doctors will only do a home visit if it's very serious, so you must bring your child to the surgery,' Sadie heard her say to a patient on the phone. 'Well, how ill is she? . . . You don't know. In that case your best bet is to bring her along to the surgery . . . she feels terrible, you say. Yes, well, children are up and down as you know. Junior Disprins should do the trick. The doctors are very busy people; they can't go out to see everybody who's feeling a bit off-colour. Someone can see your child at four o'clock this afternoon here at the surgery. Name and address please.'

Sadie felt compelled to say a few words when her colleague had finished on the phone. 'If someone feels really ill Dr Russell will go out to see them; that's the whole idea of doctors doing their rounds,' she pointed out.

Edith's cold grey eyes rested on Sadie with overt hostility. 'I hope you are not trying to tell me how to do my job,' she snarled. 'Because I have been doing surgery work for a lot longer than you have. Really ill warrants a home visit. Not just trivial aches and pains.'

'I doubt if they feel trivial to the person who has them,' Sadie suggested. 'Dr Russell has told me to use my judgement.'

'Which is exactly what I was doing,' Edith retorted. 'And I don't like my judgement being questioned, especially by a slip of a kid like you who's only been in the job five minutes.'

The phone rang simultaneous to a flurry of patients appearing at the reception window so the conversation ended, and the surgery was busy right through the shift so there was no time for Sadie to raise the subject again. But at the afternoon surgery a woman brought in a child who was found to have suspected meningitis and an ambulance was sent for as a matter of an emergency. The patient was the one to whom Edith had refused a home visit and told to come to the surgery.

'It was serious after all,' Sadie said to her meaningfully.

'The child has only been taken to hospital as a precaution,' her colleague pointed out, not seeming in the least defensive.

'Let's hope she'll be all right then,' said Sadie. 'Meningitis can be lethal. I'd be worried sick if my daughter had so much as a suspicion of it.'

'My conscience is clear, if that is what you're trying to suggest,' Edith said crossly. 'I was doing my job as I see fit. I'm a receptionist, not a nurse.'

You could try to remember that when using your judgement on the patients' symptoms, thought Sadie, but held her tongue for the moment. She could see troubled times ahead and would keep a close eye on Edith Brown.

★   ★   ★

Sadie's driving test was on a Thursday afternoon, so she arranged to have a couple of hours off work. She was doing the test in Ray's car as she was used to it and they had an hour's practice beforehand, which was a complete disaster. Her reversing was awful, three-point turns a joke and she couldn't even seem to get into gear properly.

'I don't see any point in my going through with it,' she said when they parked at the test centre, 'seeing that I'm so hopeless. Don was right. I'm a rubbish driver.'

'No you are not,' Ray emphasised. 'A bad last practice means a good test.'

'Does it?'

'So they say about any big event, an exam, a show, so why not a driving test? Stop being so negative. You know how to drive,' he reminded her. 'All you need is confidence. Put everything else out of your mind except what the examiner is saying to you, which might help to keep the

293

nerves at bay.' He saw a man with a clipboard walking towards them. 'Here he comes now. I'll be waiting for you when you come back.' He went round from the passenger side and opened the car door for her. 'Good luck.'

'Thanks,' she said through dry lips.

★ ★ ★

Ray was so nervous for her he hardly knew how to contain himself. He walked around, had a cup of tea in a café and walked some more. When he saw her drive the car back to the finishing point his heart was in his mouth. Come on, he thought, as she stayed in the car with the instructor. What was he saying to her and why was it taking so long? At last the car doors opened. The man said something to Sadie then walked away. Sadie came towards Ray. She was looking very subdued. Oh no!

'Well?' he asked nervously.

She lowered her eyes.

'Never mind,' he said. 'You can always try again.'

Then her face was lit with smiles. 'Just teasing,' she told him. 'I passed.'

'Oh, that's wonderful,' he said, hugging her. 'Well done. Congratulations.'

'Thank you,' she said, 'and thanks for teaching me. You've been brilliant.'

'I've enjoyed it,' he told her.

'Me too,' she said. 'You made what was an ordeal with my brother into a pleasure.'

His emotions were out of all proportion to the

event, he told himself. She had passed her driving test, not just come round from a life-threatening operation or swum the English Channel. But he was extraordinarily happy for her.

'Get in, then, and I'll drive you home,' she said.

'So you're the boss now, are you?'

'Absolutely,' she confirmed, smiling at him.

* * *

Sadie's personal triumph was pushed aside when she got back to work to find a heated argument in progress between a patient and Edith.

'I definitely made an appointment,' the woman was saying. 'I did it on the phone. Mrs Joan Daker, number 2 Reed Street.'

'Well, there's nothing here for you,' said Edith, looking at the book. 'So you couldn't have done.'

'Are you calling me a liar?'

'No. I'm just saying that there isn't an appointment for you. Would you like to re-book?'

'Certainly not. I want to see the doctor as I arranged.' The woman was seething now. 'I had a long walk to get here and I'm not feeling well so I'm not going home until I've seen Dr Russell.'

'Why don't we have a word with the doctor, Edith?' suggested Sadie. 'He might be able to fit her in.'

'He shouldn't have to fit me in as I made an appointment,' said the patient.

Sadie had a look at the book and there was no appointment for Mrs Daker. She turned the page and saw an entry for the patient for the same time tomorrow in Edith's writing but she kept quiet about it so as not to embarrass her colleague.

'Don't worry, Mrs Daker,' she said. 'One of us will pop in and see Dr Russell when he's finished with his current patient and explain what's happened. If you'd like to have a seat in the waiting room.'

'Thank you, dear,' said Mrs Daker.

'How dare you go against what I say and make me look like a fool in front of a patient,' blasted Edith when Mrs Daker was safely out of earshot.

'I had to intervene because Mrs Daker is clearly not well,' was Sadie's reaction, 'and she did make an appointment but you put it in the book for tomorrow instead of today, so that solves the mystery.'

Edith frowned darkly. 'I wouldn't have made a mistake like that,' she declared. 'I've been in the job too long.'

'We are all only human,' Sadie pointed out. 'But as long as we can get Dr Russell to see her there will be no harm done.'

Edith turned the page in the book and rubbed out the erroneous entry. 'It isn't like me to make a mistake,' she said irritably. 'I'm far too efficient.'

'Don't worry about it. Dr Russell is free now so one of us needs to go and have a word,' said Sadie.

'I'll go,' said Edith.

Sadie heaved a sigh of relief. The last thing she

wanted to do was report a colleague's mistake to the boss. Even if that colleague was hateful.

★   ★   ★

After the excitement of passing the test and all the resulting congratulations, Sadie felt a sense that something wasn't quite right. It was more than just an anti-climax. It was as though something was missing in her life. During her driving lessons she had felt the tiniest stirrings of something she had never thought she would ever feel again. It was so faint she'd barely noticed it until it wasn't there any more.

But she wanted it back so decided to do something about it, which meant being unconventional bordering on to outrageous. On her way home to lunch one day, when she knew it was half-day closing for the shops, she made a detour and rang the bell to the flat above Smart Records.

'Sadie,' said Ray, looking delighted. 'What are you doing here?'

'I've come to say that I shall miss going out driving with you on Sundays,' she said candidly.

'Oh, really . . . I shall miss it too.'

'That's what I thought, so I wonder if you might like to come out with Rosie and me on Sunday afternoon, provided Don will lend me his car. If it's a nice day we could go out of London, to Richmond Park or Hampton Court.'

'Well, yes . . . but don't you have to drive out to Surrey to see your in-laws?' he asked.

'Not every week,' she said.

'Would it be better for you if we went in my car?' he suggested. 'As you're used to it.'

'That would be lovely.'

'See you Sunday then,' he said, and she could tell that he was pleased.

There were times when you had to take your courage in your hands if you wanted something, even if you risked rejection. She knew from bitter experience that you didn't always get a second chance.

★ ★ ★

'I knew that you'd never ask me out,' Sadie explained to Ray as they walked in Richmond Park, Rosie skipping along between them. 'So I had to take the bull by the horns and ask you.'

'Is that what you've done then; asked me out, as in, you know, er, out?'

'Yes, I think it is, but I can't do evenings and I don't often come alone. Rosie comes too,' she admitted. 'So I don't have a lot going for me. But if you might fancy my company at any time under those conditions, I'm your girl.'

'I never know when you're being serious or mucking about,' he said. 'So what is this really all about?'

She halted in her step and turned to him. 'Look, there is nothing sinister in my motives at all,' she said seriously. 'I enjoyed being with you when you were teaching me to drive and I want to enjoy it some more. I think you liked my company too so why don't we spend some time together? No strings, no plans for the future, just a bit of light relief for us both now and again. I know you must miss Brenda as much as I do and my brothers' company probably gets a bit boring if you have too much of it. It's over a year since Brenda passed on and I've been a widow for more than three years so I'd enjoy some male company again, apart from what I get at home. I'd like us to go out now and again, that's all. I might even be able to manage a very occasional evening out on my own if I talk nicely to them at home. But please feel free to say no if you'd rather not.'

'It isn't that . . . it's just . . . '

'That you're a friend of the family and my brothers' mate, I know all about that, and you and me is the last thing anyone would expect. It's the last thing I expected, to tell you the truth. But spending time with you recently made me see you in a completely different light and I liked what I saw. There's a lot more to you for me now than just my brothers' mate. You'll have to forgive me for being so forward but I think you feel the same way about me and I know you would never ask because I am your mates' sister. We've known each other forever, Ray, but we don't really know each other at all. It might be rather fun to rectify that, don't you think?'

'Talk about you and Brenda being two of a kind,' he said. 'She asked me out first too.'

'I know, and it must be a terrific boost to your ego having women asking you out, but the difference between Brenda and me is, I'm not hankering after marriage as she was. As I said, no plans, no strings, let's just see what happens.'

299

'How can I refuse?' he said, smiling at her.

When Rosie ran on ahead, Ray took Sadie's hand. It was the most unexpected thing he could ever have imagined but it felt so right. Who would have thought that a few driving lessons could lead to the promise of such happiness?

* * *

'Ray and Sadie,' said Don in astonishment a few days later when Sadie was upstairs putting Rosie to bed. 'I don't believe it.'

'I was surprised too but I can see nothing wrong with it. They are both free agents, both on their own and missing Brenda,' said Marge, in whom Sadie had confided. 'Anyway, it isn't serious. They're going to keep it casual for the moment and I think it'll be good for them to get together. Why not keep each other company?'

'I think it's a good thing too,' added Derek.

'It probably is but it feels a bit peculiar when it's your mate and your sister, because you know the things your mates get up to,' said Don. 'Still, he's never been a rascal where women are concerned so that's okay. But they've known each other years and there's never been anything like that between them before.'

'It blossomed when he was teaching her to drive apparently,' Marge explained.

'So that's both my brother and my best mate out of circulation,' said Don gloomily.

'I don't think Ray is out of circulation as such,' observed Marge. 'It's only a casual thing between him and Sadie, and she won't be able to go out with him very often because of Rosie, so he'll still be around to keep you company of an evening.'

'You should get yourself a job as a driving instructor,' joshed Derek. 'It might work for you too.'

'We all know I'm not cut out for that after what happened with Sadie,' Don reminded him. 'Anyway, I'm quite happy as I am, thank you, single and glad of it.'

'We must invite Ray to Sunday tea sometime,' suggested Marge predictably.

'He'll run a mile if you do that,' said Don. 'You know Ray doesn't want to get married.'

'She's going to ask him to tea, not ask him about his intentions,' chuckled Cyril.

'Same thing, round here,' said Don jokingly, 'once they come to Sunday tea it's halfway to the altar, which is probably why Derek hasn't bought his lady friend home yet.'

'I haven't brought her home because I don't want you lot interrogating her,' said Derek.

'As if we would,' protested Marge.

'You can't help yourselves. You must be the nosiest family in the whole of West London,' Derek accused them lightly. 'When I'm ready, she'll come to Sunday tea. But not until then.'

Sadie came into the room. 'Who's coming to Sunday tea?' she asked.

'Ray, if your mother has her way,' said Cyril.

'So what,' said Sadie, casual and unconcerned. 'He's been here to Sunday tea plenty of times before.'

'But this time he's being invited because he's

301

going out with you,' explained Don.

'Oh, I see,' she said. 'It isn't serious between us but I'd like him to come to tea anyway sometime. It must be miserable for him in that flat on his own.'

★ ★ ★

As they had agreed, Sadie and Ray kept things casual but there was an underlying affection growing between them beneath the kidding around and teasing each other. For the first time since she'd lost Paul, Sadie felt special again. There were no romantic dinners or formal outings. In fact they were rarely alone. Sadie's maternal responsibilities meant that sort of thing wasn't possible very often. But somehow it worked and Ray seemed happy to have Rosie along. Sundays were always hard when you'd lost a loved one but they were transformed for them both because this was the day they saw each other.

They took Rosie to the zoo, the park and down by the river. The days were cold and the nights drawing in as winter took hold, so sometimes they stayed in his flat and played snakes and ladders or snap with her.

Then came the invitation to Sunday tea at the Bells'.

'Don't panic,' Sadie said to Ray. 'They know we're not serious.'

'I wasn't panicking,' he said. 'It won't be the first time I've been to your house to Sunday tea.'

'No but it's the first time as my guest,' she

302

pointed out. 'But as our place is a home from home to you, it'll be fine except for the kidding from my brothers, of course.'

'I can handle them, don't worry,' he assured her. 'I've been doing it for long enough.'

In actual fact Ray was in something of a dilemma. Despite all their talk about keeping it casual, he was beginning to fall in love with her and that meant problems. It was unthinkable that he would do to Sadie what he'd done to Brenda so if things between him and Sadie developed, he was either going to have to tell her the truth about himself or give her up. And the thought of the latter was too painful to contemplate. The feelings he had for Sadie were growing stronger and more intense by the day. It was a different and more powerful thing altogether than the way he'd felt for Brenda, whom he had loved but never with the same intensity as she'd loved him. Only when faced with losing her had he been prepared to confide in her and marry her if she'd still wanted that when she knew the truth. But would he have actually gone through with it if she'd lived? He hoped he'd have kept to his word but it was something he could never be really sure of.

The way things were developing with Sadie he was going to want to marry her, which meant he must risk losing her. Experiencing a shiver of fear he reminded himself that it was still early days, and she might not feel the same as he did. She'd made it clear from the start that she didn't want anything serious. So he could leave well alone for the moment.

303

Sunday tea at the Bells was always a pleasant interlude but Marge had made a special effort today with a choice of sandwiches, scones, a selection of cakes and a lemon meringue pie.

'This looks lovely, Marge,' Ray complimented her.

'Thank you, love.'

'It's only because you're here,' joshed Don. 'We only get something decent when we have company.'

'Rubbish,' smiled Ray, completely at home with this family. 'I don't believe a word of it.'

'That's right. You tell 'em, Ray,' said Marge, enjoying the joke.

'Will you give me a piggy back, Uncle Ray?' Rosie chipped in, childishly ignoring the current topic.

'Ooh, let me see,' he said, smiling at her. 'I think that depends on whether or not you eat your tea.'

'Crawler,' teased Derek. 'You're just trying to impress her mother.'

'No he isn't,' defended Sadie. 'He's always very considerate of the right thing for her, and tries not to spoil her.'

'Unlike me and Derek who spoil her rotten,' said Don.

'Like you spoilt me,' added Sadie.

'You haven't turned out too bad though, have you, after a few wild teenage years,' said Don.

'A compliment from my brother. Wow! I must be hearing things,' she said with a chuckle.

'Wow,' mimicked Rosie, who was nearly three.

'So how are things going at the shop?' asked Cyril. 'Is Derek pulling his weight?'

'He wouldn't still be working for me if he wasn't,' replied Ray. 'We make a good team.'

'Records are all the rage these days with young people, aren't they?' remarked Cyril.

'They certainly are but we cater for all tastes and all age groups,' he explained.

'I bet pop songs are your best sellers.'

'Oh yes, by far. But I like to stock as broad a range as possible and what we don't have we order when the title is still available.' Ray sipped his tea. 'The musical instrument side of the business is where my interest really lies. I love to see someone buy a guitar and sign up for lessons because that's doing instead of just listening.'

'I suppose you can put people in touch with teachers,' said Marge in an enquiring manner.

'Oh yeah, we do that all the time. We have teaching adverts on the notice board and posters for gigs by local bands up in the window. Unknown musicians. People who have ordinary jobs by day and at nights they're in a band.'

'Amateur musicians are always in and out of the shop,' added Derek, 'wanting sheet music, plectrums and so on.'

'Sometimes they just call in for a chat,' said Ray. 'It makes for a good atmosphere.'

'You should let one of these unknown bands do a gig at the shop,' suggested Sadie. 'It would give them a chance to play in a public place and encourage people to use your shop instead of going to Woollies for their records.'

'There wouldn't be room in a little shop like ours, would there?' questioned Ray.

'It isn't all that small and you could make space for an hour or so by moving things around,' she suggested. 'These pop bands aren't the size of a full-scale orchestra, are they? Probably three or four musicians. You could give them a few bob and you'd make that up in extra record sales. At least it would give your shop a special interest.'

'Do you know, Sadie, that isn't a bad idea,' said Ray, warming to the thought.

'If you had it on a Saturday we'd all come to make up the numbers,' she offered.

Derek and Ray exchanged a look. 'We'll have a chat about it tomorrow at work,' said Ray.

The conversation moved on; they discussed the recent tragedy in South Wales when a coal tip had slipped down the mountain and buried a school, wiping out a generation of children. The whole nation was still mourning them and their families. Having a child of her own, Sadie was very upset by it.

Moving on to a more cheerful subject, Marge said to Sadie and Ray, 'Look, you two, I know you don't get any time on your own without Rosie and I think it would be nice if you had a night out together. So if you would like to go out one evening, Cyril and I will look after Rosie.'

'M-u-m,' said Sadie, embarrassed. She didn't want Ray to feel pressured into anything.

But he said, 'Thanks, Marge. That would be lovely. I'll fix a date with Sadie and book a table somewhere nice.'

'Only the best for our sister,' joked Don. 'Don't think you can get away with cod and chips down the local chippie, especially as you're one of these entrepreneurs with plenty of dough.'

As much as Sadie loved her family there were times when she could cheerfully throttle the lot of them and now was one of those moments. Why did they find it necessary to interfere? She and Ray were perfectly capable of organising their own social life. Now he'd been practically forced into taking her out somewhere. Of course it was very kind of her mother to offer to babysit but if only she had mentioned it to Sadie on the quiet she could have borne it in mind and maybe suggested it when the situation seemed appropriate. Now the poor bloke felt obligated.

'As if I would,' Ray was saying.

Oh, how toe-curling, thought Sadie.

★ ★ ★

'Take no notice of Mum and the others,' Sadie said to Ray when she saw him off at the front gate later that evening. 'We don't need to have a night out.'

'I think it's a really good idea,' he told her. 'Don't you fancy it then? Afraid I might not behave myself if Rosie isn't around?'

'Of course it isn't that,' she assured him in a definite tone. 'I just didn't want you to get lumbered, that's all.'

Ray couldn't believe his ears. Did she not see herself in the mirror or hear herself laugh? How could she think that any man wouldn't be

307

honoured to go out with her? But their relationship was young and fragile and any drastic admissions at this stage might do it harm.

'Lumbered is the last thing I would be, I can promise you that,' he assured her.

'In that case . . . '

'How about next Saturday,' he cut in quickly.

'Lovely. But nothing posh.'

'I want to do the thing properly. Maybe I could book a table at the Talk of the Town.'

'Far too expensive and dressy,' she said. 'We agreed to keep things casual and going posh would spoil the fun. A film in the West End and a bite to eat at the Wimpy or the Golden Egg will do for me.'

'All right then but don't dare to suggest that we go Dutch,' he warned.

'Actually, I was going to . . . '

'Absolutely not,' he stated categorically, 'and it has nothing to do with you being beholden or my making things serious. It's a question of economics. You have a child to support and I don't, which means that I have more money to spare.'

'All right then, if you insist. Thank you.'

* * *

They went to the West End to the cinema to see Michael Caine in 'Alfie' then to the Golden Egg afterwards. They both had sausage, egg and chips and frothy cappuccinos out of the Gaggia machine.

Sadie was enjoying herself immensely. It

reminded her that she was still a young woman, something that could easily be overlooked when you were immersed in motherhood and lacking in a social life.

'It's so good to be out of an evening again and feeling part of the scene,' she confided. 'The lights and the people and everything.'

'I'm glad you're enjoying yourself,' he said.

'Don't get me wrong. I'm quite content to be at home with Rosie at night but just now and again it's nice to be out having fun. Seeing all the scooters lined up outside reminded me of the old days and Paul. We used to go everywhere on his Lambretta.'

'It didn't upset you then, seeing them,' he said.

'Oh no. People are afraid to talk about him in case they offend me and I can't understand that, because why wouldn't anyone want to be reminded of a loved one they've lost? Just because they're dead, you don't stop remembering them, as you will know because of Brenda,' she said. 'I talk and think about Paul a lot because he was a reality, not just a figment of my imagination. He was a large part of my life and he's still in my heart even though he's no longer with us.' She paused thoughtfully. 'It wasn't far from here where it happened. I'm not saying I would like to go back to the actual street where he died but it hasn't stopped me enjoying the West End. For a while I thought I would never enjoy anything again but somehow life goes on, doesn't it?'

He nodded. 'It does if you make it, and you certainly have,' he told her.

'It's odd really,' Sadie went on. 'It was as though one minute I was this up-to-the-minute sixties girl in love and having the time of my life, the next I was on my own and a mother weighed down with responsibility. The fun times ended before I'd had the chance to grow out of them, I suppose that's why I miss them, even though Rosie is the love of my life.' She looked around the crowded restaurant, boys in Beatle suits, and girls in mini-skirts. 'You see, Ray, places like this are the sort of thing I enjoy. It's my world, or it was up until a few years ago. It's young and cheap and modern and to me it's just as glamorous as the Talk of the Town, although they say that is fabulous.' She gave him a wry grin and looked at his cup. 'Though I suspect that you'd rather have something a bit stronger than coffee at this time on a Saturday night.'

'I'm quite happy,' he assured her. 'Anyway, we might manage a quick one somewhere when we've finished here. So carry on with what you were saying.'

'I can't afford all the modern clothes now,' she continued. 'In fact I very rarely buy anything for myself these days because I have Rosie to clothe and I like her to look nice. But I still enjoy fashion, and as hemlines get higher so do mine, by means of a pair of scissors and a needle and thread.'

'You're quite a girl, do you know that? he said, looking into her eyes.

'Don't look at me like that.'

'Why not?'

'Because it makes me think you are going to go all soppy on me and neither of us wants that.'

'Am I allowed to say that you are very beautiful?' he asked in a soft tone.

She gave him the most gorgeous smile. 'I think I can accept that,' she said.

'What about if I were to ask you if we can do this sort of thing again?'

'Yes, that's within the rules,' she said. 'But I don't know when, because of Rosie.'

'I'll wait as long as it takes.'

'Oh.' Her eyes met his and she couldn't look away. 'Enough about me,' she said, shaking herself back to the present. 'What about you? Do you still think about Brenda a lot?'

'Yes, of course.'

'Me too,' she said. 'I still miss her like mad.' She looked at him again. 'And here I am, out with her boyfriend. She'd probably be livid if she knew. She was so mad about you, God help anyone who stole you away from her.'

'Yes. I don't think I really appreciated how strong her feelings were for me and I shall regret that until my dying day.'

'Would you have married her if she'd lived?' Sadie asked. 'I know you proposed to her very publicly but would you actually have gone through with it?'

'I like to think I would,' Ray told her. 'But who knows what would have happened?'

They stayed a while longer talking then went for a drink at a pub round the corner before making their way back to the car.

'It's been a lovely evening, Ray,' she said when

they drew up outside her house. 'Thanks ever so much.'

'You're welcome,' he said. 'I enjoyed it too.'

'We'd better make the most of it because heaven only knows when we'll get out on our own again.'

'We'll take it as it comes,' he said, slipping his arms around her. 'No pressure.'

As they drew closer together they both knew that they had found something very special in each other.

12

To Sadie and her colleagues at the joint practice, it seemed as if every patient on their books had fallen victim to some emergency ailment or other in the run-up to Christmas. The waiting room resounded with coughs, sneezes and complaints of aches and pains. The much-vaunted qualities of antibiotics were in great demand by patients seeking a miracle cure before the holiday.

The telephone rang continuously and the queue of hopefuls in the surgery seemed never-ending. Appointments ran out, the patients got cross and Edith was beside herself.

'The doctors are all booked up, as I have just told you,' she snapped at one poor woman who was whey-faced and shivering violently. 'I'm very sorry but I can't work miracles and it's doubtful if you'll be seen by a doctor this side of the holiday.'

'What am I supposed to do then?' asked the patient.

'How would I know?' barked Edith, her neck mottled with anxiety blotches. 'I only work here, I don't make the rules.'

'You do surprise me,' said the patient sarcastically. 'The way you carry on anyone would think you were in charge of the place, lock, stock and barrel.'

'Yeah, that's right, you sour-faced old bitch,' added another.

'So you're saying that we can only get ill when it's convenient for the doctors,' one woman piped up. 'I could be dead by Christmas Eve if I don't get proper medicine. I thought a joint practice was supposed to be better for the patients, yet we still can't get to see a doctor when we need to.'

Anarchy was becoming a distinct possibility as other patients in the queue began to make supportive comments among themselves, whilst making absolutely sure they were loud enough to be heard by the receptionists.

'Disgraceful,' muttered someone.

'If you ask me, these doctors work to suit themselves,' put in someone else. 'The receptionists think they're God Almighty too. They get behind that counter and go all high and mighty. I don't know who they think they are.'

'The doctors make plenty of dough so the least they could do is offer a decent service,' grumbled a man.

'You can't stop getting sick just because it's going to be Christmas, can you?'

'Course you can't.'

And so it went on, the patients united by their grievances. Deciding it was time for an intervention, Sadie came out of the reception office and addressed the queue.

'Look, I really am very sorry, folks, but we've got a bit of a panic on our hands at the moment because so many people are poorly and there are no more appointments left. The joint practice is better for everybody usually; today really is an exception so we'd be ever so grateful if we could

314

have your co-operation.'

'By buggering off out of here, is that what you mean?' suggested a man.

'No, not at all,' replied Sadie. 'Anyone who feels they have an urgent need to see the doctor this morning, please wait in the queue and we'll take your details and do all we possibly can to get you seen by a doctor after surgery. Anyone who thinks they can manage until tomorrow, please come back then. There might be cancellations by then and open surgery appointments are allocated on a daily basis anyway so there's no need to panic with the holiday coming up. We all know how miserable it is when you're not feeling well but it would really help if you could bear with us on this occasion.'

Her careful way of handling the situation seemed to defuse the rising storm. Some left, others stayed on in hope.

'Phew,' sighed Sadie after surgery when she and Edith were clearing up the last of the filing. 'What a morning.'

'Hmph,' snapped Edith.

Sadie looked at her, noticing that her eyes were bright with anger, her cheeks suffused with pink. 'What is it, Edith? Is something the matter?' she asked.

'You are what's the matter,' her colleague informed her curtly.

Sadie was astonished. 'Why? What have I done?' she wanted to know.

'You undermine my authority at every opportunity,' she accused her. 'You had no business to step in earlier on when I was dealing with the patients. It's embarrassing and insulting, the way you show me up in front of everyone.'

'But I'm a surgery receptionist as well as you are,' Sadie reminded her. 'It's our joint responsibility to keep things running smoothly. And you practically had a riot on your hands.'

'I had everything under control.'

'That wasn't how I saw it.'

'Well, that's how it was,' Edith said, her voice rising. 'You've no right to put your interpretation on everything.'

'I'm sorry to have put you out but I was doing my job as I see fit. A spot of diplomacy certainly works better than your way,' Sadie told her. 'Being downright rude to the patients only makes things worse.'

'I wasn't being rude.'

'Oh Edith, you were very rude,' she disagreed. 'Maybe it's just your way and you didn't mean it but if I'd been the patient and you spoke to me like that I would have reported you to the doctor. People don't pay their national health subscriptions to be talked down to, especially when they are feeling ill.'

Much to Sadie's amazement, Edith burst into tears.

'Oh Edith,' said Sadie in a gentler tone, feeling terrible and not sure how to make amends. 'Look, I really am sorry to have upset you so much. I don't want us to fight and for you to be reduced to tears. Honestly I don't. But all's well that ends well. Morning surgery is over and there were no fatalities.'

'It's all so easy for you, isn't it?' the older woman said thickly. 'You can get a job anywhere. You're young and that's all employers seem to want these days. The doctors will probably get rid of me. And I really do need this job.'

'And you think I don't, with a child to support on my own,' Sadie retorted.

'Jobs are ten a penny for someone like you.'

'But I happen to like this one,' she responded.

'At least you have a husband for support.'

There was a brief hiatus before Edith said, 'Yes, I realise that. But I still need this job.'

'The practice needs two receptionists so there's no call for either of us to feel threatened.'

'How can I help but feel threatened when you keep criticising the way I do the job?'

Sadie was in a quandary. Had she really been too hard on the other woman, who seemed genuinely distressed? She hoped not but if Edith continued to treat the patients so badly, sooner or later there would be complaints which, if there were enough of them, could put her job at risk. On the other hand Edith had been in the job for many more years than Sadie so she must have done something right.

'Look, I'm sorry if I've been unfair towards you,' she said to appease her. 'Perhaps it was wrong of me to intervene. But you were very uptight with the patients. Maybe if you were to calm down a little . . . '

'You're doing it again.' Edith cut her short in a shrill tone. 'Telling me how to do my job. You're just a slip of a girl and you know nothing, so stop telling me how to behave.'

317

Suddenly Sadie had a flash of insight and sensed a terrible sadness beneath the other woman's brusque persona. Edith was obviously very unhappy. She wasn't just bad-tempered and rude, she was deeply miserable, Sadie now realised, and wondered why. She didn't know much about her private life but she did seem to be happily married. Something more than the job wasn't right in her life, though, that much she was sure of.

'All right, Edith,' Sadie conceded with mixed feelings because her colleague would be in trouble with the doctors if she didn't make an effort to be more pleasant in her manner. 'I'll try to be more sensitive in the future. I promise.'

'Good.' Edith blew her nose then gave Sadie a hard look. 'I want no one to know about my pathetic outburst just now,' she said aggressively. 'Do you understand me? There was no upset and no tears. It didn't happen.'

'Okay, I won't say anything,' agreed Sadie, very puzzled indeed by her colleague's strange behaviour.

★　★　★

Christmas was transformed this year for Sadie by Ray's increasing presence in her life. He came to the house for Christmas Day and in the afternoon he and Sadie went for a walk by the river on their own as Rosie wanted to stay and play with her new toys. It was cold, damp and practically deserted on the riverside, the rolling grey clouds lying low over the muddy brown waters. But it was good to be out in the fresh air and there was always a kind of beauty about the Thames, whatever the mood of the weather.

'I'm enjoying the day enormously,' she confided, as they walked briskly along the towpath near Hammersmith Bridge. 'It's the first time I haven't felt miserable at Christmas since before Paul died.'

'I know the feeling. I hated the whole thing last year because it was so soon after Brenda's death but this one has been a whole lot better, thanks to you,' he admitted. 'Does that seem callous?'

'Not at all,' she assured him. 'You mustn't feel guilty for enjoying yourself. People used to tell me that all the time. I know how you feel though because I felt awful if I had so much as a glimpse of happiness for quite a long time after Paul died. You can't be miserable for the rest of your life and neither would they want that.'

'Strange how the two of us have got together, after being under one another's noses for so many years, isn't it?'

'Yes. It's a pity it took such tragic circumstances to bring it about, though it wouldn't have happened without them.'

'No, I don't suppose it would.' Ray paused for a moment. 'Anyway, since we have found each other, what are you doing tomorrow?' he asked. 'I wondered if the three of us could go out somewhere if you're free.'

'Duty calls for me tomorrow, I'm afraid,' she informed him. 'I'm taking Rosie to see her other grandparents. It's only right that they should see something of her over the holiday. They gave her some lovely presents.'

'Sounds as though you have to talk yourself into going.'

'It's never easy for either Rosie or me because Harriet is so formidable,' Sadie explained. 'You know Rosie; she's not a shy child but it takes ages to persuade her to leave my side when we're there and then it's only to go with her granddad. Harriet thinks my daughter is clinically shy and bangs on about it as though it's something I've done wrong in bringing her up and I should get something done about it but Rosie is only ever like that with her. So I don't enjoy the visits but they are her grandparents, so I feel I must continue with them. Besides Gerald is a sweetheart and Rosie likes him.'

'What about if I come with you for company on the drive over, in my car instead of Don's,' he suggested. 'Obviously I wouldn't come in. I'd just drop you off and pick you up later.'

'It's very kind of you to offer but wouldn't it be a bit boring for you?' she queried. 'Wandering around Surrey on your own for a few hours. On Boxing Day there won't be much open except the pubs but they are closed in the afternoon.'

'I'll find a way to pass the time, don't worry,' he assured her. 'I might even go to your beloved Box Hill.'

'In that case how can I refuse?'

★ ★ ★

As it happened Ray wasn't able to slip off after he'd dropped Sadie at the Westons'. Gerald must have been looking out for Sadie because he opened the front door as soon as they drew up outside the house and came out to greet them with the dog woofing at his feet. Being a courteous type and this being Christmas, he insisted that Ray come inside and have a festive drink with them.

'Ray is here, Harriet,' said Gerald as they went into the sitting room. 'He's been kind enough to keep Sadie company on the drive over here.'

'Hello.' Her face was a picture, thought Sadie, as she struggled to look pleased, failed miserably and then arranged her features into an attempt at a smile that didn't quite work. Sadie saw something that resembled fear in her eyes. 'Happy Christmas to you both.'

As always at the Westons', Rosie became clingy and wouldn't leave her mother's side as they all sat round eating cheese straws with a Christmas tipple and struggling to keep the stilted conversation going.

'Your decorations look pretty,' remarked Sadie dutifully.

'Thank you,' said Harriet. 'We weren't going to bother to decorate as we were on our own yesterday but Gerald thought we should make an effort as you were coming today.'

'That's nice of you,' said Sadie. 'Aren't they pretty, Rosie?'

'Not as good as ours,' she replied embarrassingly. 'Where's the Christmas tree?'

'We haven't got one, dear,' her grandfather told her.

'Oh.' She looked disappointed. 'I thought

everybody had a Christmas tree.'

'I think you've had more than enough presents off the tree at home to last you the whole year,' said Ray quickly before she had a chance to say something that might offend. 'You're one of the luckiest little girls in London.'

The conversation took a turn for the better, thanks to Gerald. 'How is your business coming along, Ray?' he enquired with interest. 'A record shop, isn't it?'

Ray nodded. 'Business has been very good actually, especially in the run-up to Christmas.'

'It might not be so busy in January though,' Gerald remarked. 'A lot of our clients are retailers and they expect things to be a bit slack after Christmas for a month or two.'

'I've got a plan to liven things up,' said Ray.

'Really?'

'Yes, I'm having a local pop group come in to play for an hour on a Saturday in the middle of the month. We're going to make a bit of an event of it,' he explained. 'We're not in the main shopping street so I'm hoping it will put us more firmly on the record buyers' map once they know where we are.'

'That's a good idea,' approved Gerald.

'Sadie came up with it,' Ray said, looking in her direction. 'Isn't she a genius?'

'Wait until after the event before you decide on that,' she smiled. 'If it's a disaster you can blame me.'

'I don't see how it can be a disaster,' he opined. 'The worst than can happen is that nobody comes and all we'll have lost is the cost of a few posters, a couple of bottles of cheap plonk and a few shillings we pay to the band. The posters will be good publicity anyway if we get them up all around the town. At least more people will get to know about us.'

'It's all part of the overheads,' agreed Gerald and went on to ask him more about the business, seeming genuinely keen.

'I'll go and get some more nibbles,' said Harriet as the men became engrossed.

As Sadie got up to go with her she saw Rosie go over to Ray and ask him if she could stroke the dog, whereupon he got up and did it with her. The way they were so easy with each other warmed her heart.

★   ★   ★

'You still seem to be very friendly with Ray,' remarked Harriet in the kitchen.

'Yes, we are getting on well.' Sadie pondered for a moment on her next words. 'In fact, things have moved up a notch since you and I last spoke about it.'

Harriet stood quite still, a packet of crisps in her hand. 'Oh really,' she said. 'I thought he was just a family friend.'

'He was and still is,' Sadie confirmed. 'But he's become more than just a friend to me.'

Sadie saw the other woman's hand tremble slightly as she emptied the crisps into a bowl. Clearly shocked, her face was flushed. 'Oh I see,' she said in a tight voice.

'Please don't be upset,' Sadie urged her with

323

feeling. 'It will be four years in the spring since we lost Paul.'

'I know exactly how long it is.'

'Surely you must have known . . . I mean, I'm young. Paul wouldn't have wanted me to . . . '

'So when are you planning to get married?' she interrupted sharply.

'Hey, slow down. There's nothing like that in the offing at the moment.'

'So what are your plans for the future then?'

'We don't have any,' Sadie replied. 'We're just enjoying each other's company.'

'But it must be leading somewhere.'

'Not necessarily,' she said. 'I lost Paul and both Ray and I lost Brenda, so we were on our own and lonely. Now we are not. It's as simple as that. We're taking it day by day to see how it goes.'

'Rosie seems very fond of him.'

'Yeah. He's been around since she was born, long before he and I got together, so she is used to him,' she explained. 'But he is very good with her.'

'An ideal stepfather then?'

'He would be, yes, if we were thinking along those lines but there is nothing like that on the agenda at the moment, as I have said,' she emphasised. 'Neither of us wants that, not for the time being anyway. We might get fed up with each other in a month or two then we will part with no hard feelings. That's how casual it is.'

Harriet visibly brightened. 'It's just that I . . . we . . . '

'You're afraid of losing Rosie, I know,' Sadie

finished for her, feeling a strong sense of empathy. 'And I promise you that I won't let that happen if I ever were to re-marry. I don't know if I have a future with Ray or any other man I might meet but you and Gerald will always be her grandparents and I will respect that. When she's older and more independent, you can form your own bond with her, regardless of me.'

'Yes. Of course.'

Sadie didn't have the heart to say that Harriet would have to be a lot less severe if she wanted to make a friend of Rosie. Maybe Gerald had enough good will for the two of them.

★   ★   ★

Ray found a traditional country pub with oak beams, a log fire and some very nice turkey sandwiches. It hadn't been easy to get away from the Westons, who had tried to insist that he stay for lunch. But he'd felt that he would be intruding, despite their claims to the contrary. This was their time with Sadie and their grandchild and they needed that.

Gerald was a nice-enough bloke and Rosie seemed to like him. But his wife was stern to the point of scary. It was no wonder that Rosie went into her shell the minute she set eyes on her grandma. Yet he'd sensed that Mrs Weston was genuinely fond of the little girl. It was a pity she couldn't loosen up a little and show it.

Thinking along these lines, it occurred to him how involved he had become in every aspect of Sadie's life. In a relatively short time his feelings for her had changed from a kind of casual affection for his pals' sister to something deep and passionate. This could mean trouble ahead, especially because of his close links with her family. What her brothers would do to him if he hurt her didn't bear thinking about. And the last thing he wanted to do was cause her pain of any sort. But there were things the Bell family knew nothing about. So if his relationship with Sadie became serious he would have to pluck up the courage to come clean. What would happen then he dreaded to think.

★   ★   ★

'So how did it go?' Ray asked Sadie on the way home as Rosie slept in the back of the car and Sadie was driving, still keen to use her new-found skills.

'It's always an uphill struggle,' she replied. 'Mostly because the only thing Harriet wants is her boy back. All I can do is make sure she sees Rosie on a regular basis. But you've seen what she's like; she isn't the sort of person a child would take to, so Rosie always goes for her granddad. Still, as long as I take Rosie over there regularly, at least Harriet gets to see her. Rosie is so much like her father Harriet must feel the connection, though I want her to love Rosie because she's Rosie, not just because she reminds her of Paul.'

'I think she probably is fond of her,' he remarked. 'You can sense it somehow, even though she isn't a warm person.'

'Yes, I expect she does care for her in her own way.'

'It's good of you to keep the visits up, especially the way she's treated you in the past.'

'She isn't an easy woman to get on with but I try to see it from her point of view,' she told him. 'I can't begin to imagine what I'd be like if I lost my daughter as she lost her son. I'd probably be even more bitter and twisted than she is, if that is possible. I mean, to her way of thinking, I must seem to have everything. Yes, I lost my husband, but I'm young enough to make a new life and, of course, I have Rosie. What does she have to look forward to?'

'Gerald seems like a good sort, so she has him to turn to,' he pointed out.

'Yeah, she's very lucky to have such a patient and loyal husband but it isn't the same thing as having a child,' she said. 'I can't explain it, Ray. It's something you can't fully understand unless you are a parent. It's only since I've had Rosie that I've begun to understand why Harriet behaved as she did after Paul's death.'

'Mmm.'

'Anyway, it was nice to have your company on the journey,' Sadie said. 'How did you fill the time when you went off?'

'I had a pint and a sandwich at the pub and then went to Box Hill and walked for a long time,' he told her. 'So now I'm the healthiest man in Hammersmith.'

She chuckled. 'It'll take more than one walk in the country to get you fit, though I do envy you. It was dark when we finally got away or I would have suggested that all of us went.'

'There will be other times,' he said.

'Good,' she said, picking up on the warmth in his tone. 'I'm glad about that.'

★ ★ ★

Harriet and Gerald were relaxing with a cup of tea now that the clearing up had been done after the visitors. The dog was asleep on the rug in front of the fire.

'Ray seems like a nice-enough chap, doesn't he, Harriet?' Gerald remarked.

'Do you mean as a stepfather to Rosie?' was her response.

'No. I mean as a man and a companion for Sadie,' he replied. 'I think they are a well-matched couple.'

'I don't know how you can say that.' She scowled at him. 'I'm not sure you realise the seriousness of what their being together means to us. It's the beginning of the end. They'll get married and have other children and we will be forgotten.'

'Hey, not so fast,' he urged. 'They've only been together a short time. I don't think there is anything serious between them at the moment. And anyway Sadie will always bring Rosie to see us, until she's old enough to come by herself.'

'That's what she says now but how can you trust people? When their circumstances change, so do they.'

'Not necessarily,' he disagreed.

'You always have been an optimist, Gerald,'

she said, making it sound like an accusation.

'You could do with being a bit more positive,' he advised. 'You'd find life much more enjoyable.'

'Enjoyable! I haven't enjoyed so much as one single second of my life since we lost Paul.'

'Then you should try a bit harder, for your own sake,' he told her. 'Find some new interest. Make a few friends. Get involved in the village affairs. They always want volunteers for various events.'

'You know very well that isn't my sort of thing.'

He stroked his chin meditatively, wondering if he dare mention something he'd had on his mind for a while. He decided to go ahead, as it really needed saying.

'I was wondering, Harriet,' he began, bracing himself for an eruption, 'if you might try being a bit friendlier towards Rosie when she comes to see us.'

His wife shot him a look. 'What on earth are you talking about?' she demanded. 'I am friendly. I always make sure there are sweets here for her. I give them nice food.'

Gerald made a face because he felt so awful about criticising her since she was clearly unaware of her manner. 'I know you do and I'm sure they enjoy it,' he said warily, 'but you are a little bit stern with Rosie. Couldn't you be a bit warmer towards her? Give her a cuddle, for instance, and smile at her more often.'

'You know I'm not a tactile person; that sort of thing doesn't come easily to me,' Harriet reminded him. 'I could do it when Paul was little because he was my own child but I feel as though I don't know Rosie, so I'm not able to be like that . . . ' Her voice tailed off. 'Am I really cold towards her then?'

'Not cold but a little remote, perhaps,' he told her. 'Nothing that can't be put right with a bit of effort.'

'Grandmothers are supposed to be stern, aren't they?' she said. 'Mine always was.'

'Not so much these days. Anyway, it's up to the individual to make their own rules as to what sort of relationship they want with their grandchild,' he said. 'I think you would enjoy Rosie more if you were to let yourself go a little; not only with Rosie but with life in general.' He looked at her, shoulders stiff and hands clasped together as though her life depended on it. 'You're much too tense and I'm worried about you, because stress isn't good for your health.'

'I am perfectly fine,' she said haughtily. 'So there's no need for you to worry.'

This conversation was pointless, as he'd suspected it would be, so he said, 'It's cold and dark out but the dog needs a walk. Do you fancy coming with me?'

'Yes, I'll get my coat.'

The one thing in her life that Harriet did seem able to enjoy was the dog. She would never admit it but she adored the little thing.

'Come on, Fergus,' Gerald said, getting the lead, and the dog bounced after him wagging his tail.

The Bell family turned out in force to support the event at Smart Music, which was on the second Saturday in January 1967. The afternoon was chosen because that was the time people were out on the streets with money to spend on luxury items.

It was a bit of a squeeze to make room for the musicians but with a little re-arranging of display units, they managed it. The band — which was made up of four boys who had modelled themselves on the Beatles and had mop-top haircuts and Beatles suits — arrived early to set up their equipment. Sadie and her mother set out the glasses, and wine bottles were on a table with crisps in little dishes. The group kicked off with 'She Loves You'. For an amateur group they weren't bad.

'Exciting, isn't it,' said Sadie, who was standing near the counter with her parents, Don and Rosie while Ray and Derek were behind the counter, expectations high.

'It will be when the people come,' remarked her mother.

'I hope we get some action soon,' observed Cyril, who had committed himself only for the beginning of the event. 'I don't want to miss all of the football.'

'Dad,' admonished Sadie. 'Surely it's worth it to support Ray and Derek.'

'Yeah, yeah, of course,' he said. 'But you know I like to go to watch Fulham play on a Saturday afternoon.'

331

'If no one comes I'll go out and drag some punters in off the streets,' offered Don. 'The amount of trouble Ray and Derek have gone to, to get this thing organised.'

The shop door opened and a man of about thirty came in, said, 'Oh this is very jolly,' then went straight to the classical section and politely refused the offer of a drink because he had just had lunch.

Rosie was bored so kept pestering for crisps and Sadie was just beginning to think the whole thing was going to be a washout when a trickle of people arrived, took advantage of the free refreshments, seemed to enjoy the music and went over to the record displays. A flood of people followed and suddenly the place was buzzing, the cash register making sweet music and people chatting together in a friendly manner. Some of the girls even began to dance near the band, despite the small amount of space. There was a really festive atmosphere. Even Marge and Rosie were jigging to the music.

'It's quite a party,' said Sadie to Ray as she went round to the other side of the counter to get the queue moving by putting purchases into bags for customers. Derek was away from the counter, showing someone an electric guitar.

'It does seem to be going rather well,' he agreed.

'I'm really enjoying myself,' she enthused.

New customers left saying they would visit the shop again now that they knew about it, pleased that they had all the latest releases in stock. With the music playing and the wine flowing it felt like a real party. As people left to finish their shopping so new arrivals came.

It was difficult to pinpoint the actual moment when Sadie noticed a change in the atmosphere but she judged it to be soon after a crowd of student types in duffle coats joined the party. At first she thought they had had too much wine as their laughter got noisier and their behaviour more relaxed and silly. But that wasn't likely, considering the weak strength of the cheap plonk. Anyway, they were rationing it to one glass per person and all the bottles were empty now and everyone except the family and the student types had departed. Then she noticed a strange and distinctive smell and saw the duffle-coat crowd passing what looked like a cigarette amongst them.

Sadie had no personal experience of this sort of thing but she had heard enough about it to say to Ray, 'I think that group over by the band are smoking pot.'

'Bloody hell,' he exclaimed. 'Can you take over here while I get rid of them? I'll get Derek and Don to give me a hand.'

But someone must have noticed something illegal in the air before Sadie did because even as Ray and her brothers started easing the transgressors towards the door, it burst open and a group of policemen walked in.

'Stay where you are, everyone,' said one of the officers as people tried to get out. 'You're all coming with us.'

'It's only this crowd here,' said Ray, looking towards the youngsters, who were too relaxed to be bothered about anything. 'We've only just realised what they were up to and I was about to throw them out.'

'Are you the owner of this business?'

'Yes.'

'Then we'd like you to come along with us, sir,' the policeman said. 'As the proprietor you are responsible for what goes on here.'

'But it isn't any of us.'

'There are drugs being used on your premises, so you are all coming down to the station.' He spotted Rosie. 'Who does the child belong to?'

'She's mine,' said Sadie. 'I'm her mother.'

He raised his eyebrows in disapproval. 'Not the healthiest environment for a child, is it?'

'It's a sales promotion,' she told him. 'We didn't know anyone was going to use cannabis. We just offered the punters a glass of wine, that's all. They brought the stuff in with them.'

'Even so,' he said suspiciously. 'We'll need you all down at the station.'

'You've got it all wrong, officer,' Ray appealed to him, waving his hand towards Sadie and her family, Cyril having already departed for the football match earlier. 'These people were here helping me and offering me their support.'

'You'll have every opportunity to tell us that down at the nick.'

Ray pointed to Marge. 'Surely you're not suggesting that she is involved in drugs.'

'No. All right. You take the child and leave,' ordered the policeman. 'Everyone else is coming with us.'

And the next thing she knew Sadie was being

escorted forcefully with all the others into a Black Maria.

★ ★ ★

Ray was almost ill with remorse that evening back at the Bells' house when the police had finally charged the transgressors and let everyone else go.

'I feel so bad about having got you all involved in something like that,' he said. 'It was the last thing I expected. I mean, I know that sort of thing goes on these days but no one in my world does it so such a thing never occurred to me. I thought it was just showbiz types and people like that. And subjecting you to it, I'm so ashamed.'

'It wasn't your fault,' Marge pointed out. 'You didn't know what they were going to do.'

'The door was open to anyone. It's my shop so my responsibility,' he told her. 'And having Rosie exposed to something like that is unforgivable.'

'She's not quite three years old,' Sadie reminded him. 'She didn't have a clue what was going on.'

'I thought they were going to take me away for a minute,' said Marge, finding it amusing suddenly. 'Me a pot smoker. What a scream! You wait till I tell my friends at the Bingo.'

'So much for our idea of putting the shop on the map, eh, Derek,' Ray went on.

'If the local paper gets hold of the story we'll be on the map all right,' Derek said. 'But as a dope den rather than a respectable record shop.'

'If you want to blame someone, blame me,'

said Sadie. 'It was my idea after all.'

'Look, nobody is to blame except the druggies,' declared Cyril. 'It's over and done with so why not forget all about it. There's no harm done. The coppers got the right people in the end and none of you were charged. So why worry?'

'One of the punters must have tipped off the Old Bill,' said Ray, mulling it over. 'I was too busy taking people's money to notice anything untoward.'

'There you are then,' said Cyril. 'You made some dough so it isn't all bad.'

'That makes me feel even worse.'

'Then it shouldn't do,' said Cyril. 'You've got a business to run and that's what you were doing.'

'It was the intrusion that upset me,' said Ray. 'You know me. Live and let live is my motto. What people do in private is their own business, but to come into my shop and do it, that's what is making me so mad. How dare they?'

'They must have been out in the town and heard there was something lively going on and thought they would come along and join the party,' suggested Don. 'And I suppose smoking dope is what they would do at a party if it's their way of relaxing, so they didn't see anything wrong in it.'

'A shop is a public place,' added Cyril. 'It isn't as though they came into your home, Ray. So they weren't trespassing.'

'There is that, I suppose,' he agreed, 'but it is my right to deny people access and if I'd noticed what they were up to I'd have had them out of there long before the police got involved.'

'You can't notice everything in a busy shop,' said Marge.

'If I ever see them again they'll wonder what hit them, I can promise you that,' said Ray.

'I doubt if you will so forget all about it,' advised Cyril and, moving on, swiftly added, 'Anyway, it's Saturday night and I'm going down the pub. Anyone coming?'

'I've got a date,' said Derek.

'I'll come for one with you, Dad, then I'll go and find my mates,' said Don. 'Coming, Ray?'

Ray looked at Sadie.

'You go,' she said. 'And what about you, Mum, why don't you go with Dad?'

'You can go with them if you like, love,' offered Marge. 'I don't mind sitting with Rosie.'

'No, you go,' Sadie insisted. 'You enjoy a night out so get your lippy on and get out of here. You've had your kids and done your share of staying in to look after them. Now it's my turn.'

'You always were a bossy little madam,' laughed Marge. 'But all right then, if you insist I'll go and get ready.'

'Off you go then, all of you,' said Sadie. 'Have a good time and don't forget to bring back some fish and chips.'

'On a Saturday night, as if we would,' said Marge.

'I'm staying with you, Sadie,' declared Ray.

She laughed. 'I appreciate the gesture. But I know you're dying for a pint so go and enjoy yourself.'

'I'd rather stay and keep you company.'

'Blimey, Ray,' said Don. 'You're going soft in your old age. Come out and have a laugh with the lads.'

'Not tonight,' he said.

'Oh well, there goes another good man heading for the slippery slope towards female domination,' joshed Don. 'I'll see you down there, Dad.'

★ ★ ★

'You should have gone with them, Ray,' said Sadie when they had all finally left. 'You mustn't feel that you have to stay in because I have to. That's the last thing I expect of you. You're a free man and you don't owe me anything.'

'Do you think I'm going to miss the chance of an evening alone with you for the sake of a pint down the pub?' Ray grinned. 'I'm not that much of a fool.'

'In that case,' she said with a wicked grin, 'we've had quite enough of an inquest about the goings-on at the shop for one day. It's fun time now.' She patted the space beside her on the sofa. 'So come over here.'

13

It didn't prove easy to put the 'incident' behind them as it was splashed all over the local paper the following week. *DRUGS BUST AT RECORD SHOP* shouted the headlines, followed by text informing the readership that several people had been arrested on drugs charges during a party at Smart Music.

'There's no mention of who was actually involved in the drug using,' Ray observed. 'Anyone reading this could be forgiven for thinking that all of us were in on it.'

'It's true what they say about today's newspapers being tomorrow's chip paper,' remarked Sadie, who had called in on her lunch break to commiserate with Ray and Derek. 'So let it pass and don't worry about it.'

'They also say that mud sticks,' Ray reminded her. 'I'm not bothered about what people think of me personally but I don't want the reputation of the business to suffer.'

'It'll be a five-minute wonder,' she opined. 'I doubt if you'll hear any more about it.'

But a customer who came in after she'd gone soon destroyed that theory. 'Oh good, you're still open,' said the man, who wanted sheet music. 'I thought they might have closed you down after what I read in the paper.'

'No, we're still here,' responded Ray without offering further comment.

Later that same day a group of teenage boys came in full of wisecracks about having some 'stuff' with no questions asked. They also had a visit from a girl who told Ray that she thought he was the coolest man ever to use drugs and all the trendy people smoked pot. No amount of denial could convince her that the shop wasn't a drug palace.

'We'll just have to rise above it,' Ray said to Derek, 'and see if our sales suffer. One thing we will do if we ever have a band to play here again is have someone on the door.'

'Our biggest market, the teenagers, will probably be forbidden by their parents to buy their records here,' suggested Derek. 'And what do youngsters do when their parents disapprove of something?'

'Do it all the more.'

'Exactly,' said Derek.

'Mmm, there is that, I suppose,' agreed Ray but he wasn't happy. He was no saint but he did have a high regard for the law and hated the idea that it had been broken on his premises.

★   ★   ★

The Saturday after the ill-fated gathering at the shop there was a party of a very different kind at the Bells' house. It was Rosie's third birthday and the house was invaded by infants whose collective energy could have fuelled the National Grid. The men of the family made a hasty exit when the entire membership of Rosie's nursery school, which she attended only in the mornings, arrived in an exuberant torrent.

Up until now her birthday had been celebrated in a small way with just the family so this was the first proper party she'd had and at several points during the procedure Sadie found herself inwardly vowing that it would be her last. The little boys tore around play-fighting with anyone in sight and the girls dissolved into tears as they got caught up in it. So between the lot of them it was chaos.

During tea, lovingly prepared by Sadie and her mother, there was all-out war. This one didn't like fish-paste sandwiches, that one didn't like cheese, another didn't like the colour of the lemon jelly because jelly was supposed to be red and someone else said that the crisps smelt funny. When one of the boys started throwing iced fairy cakes around, Sadie knew it was time to take a firm stand.

'Stop,' she shouted. 'Stop throwing food about and eat your tea.'

Silence reigned for a while then a precocious little girl in a frilly pink party frock, which made her look like a raspberry meringue, announced boastfully, 'We had chocolate cakes at *my* party.'

'Ooh, I like those. Have you got any chocolate cakes, Mrs Weston?' asked a boy, picking up on the girl's gripe.

Sadie knew she was going to have to resort to bribery since her stern tactics had been completely ineffective. 'No, we don't have any of those. But if you don't get on and eat what's there there'll be no lovely sweets to take home.

All those who want sweets later on put up their hands.'

Hands waved like flags at the Coronation.

'So be good children and get on and eat your tea then, please.'

This restored order but only temporarily. Musical chairs later ended in disaster because no one wanted to be out so it turned into a complete free-for-all.

'It seems as though they've been here for three weeks instead of less than two hours,' Sadie confided to her mother, 'and there is still half an hour to go until they go home.'

'Let's put some music on and let them go mad to that,' suggested Marge.

'Good thinking, Mum,' Sadie said, going over to the radiogram and calling out, 'Who wants to dance?'

At last a positive response, she thought, as they all shouted in the affirmative.

'Right, here we go then,' she said and put 'Yellow Submarine' by the Beatles on the turntable and started to jig around, singing along with the music. The kids joined in, jumping and jogging and having a wonderful time. Hearing the doorbell, Sadie thanked God that the parents had started arriving to take their offspring home.

But her hopes were dashed because it was Harriet and Gerald to whom she had casually mentioned the party, never dreaming they would take her up on her offer to drop in if they fancied it.

'Sorry we're late,' said Gerald, having to shout

above the noise. 'The traffic into London was terrible.'

'That's all right,' said Sadie, inwardly groaning because the last thing she wanted was Harriet's critical eye cast over everything. 'You've come at the best time; the end. It'll all be over in a minute.'

'We've got something for Rosie,' said Harriet. 'It's in the car.'

'How lovely; thank you,' said Sadie. 'Would you like to wait until the guests have gone home before you give it to her? It's rather noisy and chaotic at the moment, as you can see.'

The record finished and the kids screamed for more. So more they had until the blissful sound of the doorbell really did herald the arrival of parents to collect their little darlings.

'Phew, I thought it would never end,' said Sadie when they had all filed out, clutching a paper bag filled with sweets.

Sadie, Marge and the Westons were sitting drinking tea in the living room where all the furniture had been pushed to the edges to accommodate the children.

'It did seem rather boisterous,' Harriet commented.

'You should have heard them earlier,' Sadie said with a wry grin. 'It was bedlam, I tell you. I'd like to say never again but I doubt if I'll get away with that. I suppose it was because they are all so little. They'll be a bit older next year so maybe easier to amuse.'

'We used to hire a professional entertainer for Paul's parties when he was small,' Harriet said in that way she had of sounding superior.

'My budget doesn't run to that sort of thing,' came Sadie's honest response.

'We could help . . . '

'No, no,' Sadie cut in quickly, not wishing to be beholden in any way. 'We're fine doing it ourselves. The party was okay really. Just a bit hectic, that's all. I was only kidding when I said never again.' She paused then moved on. 'Anyway, are you both well?'

'Yes, thank you,' said Gerald. 'Is it time we gave the birthday girl her present?'

Sadie had known it would be something extravagant and it was indeed: a large and beautiful dolls' house, complete with furniture.

'Oh Rosie,' said Sadie with feeling. 'You are such a lucky little girl. What do you say?'

'Thank you,' she said with a shy smile and seeming a little overawed by the magnitude of the gift.

'Don't Grandma and Granddad get a kiss?'

The little girl padded dutifully to Gerald and did as she was bid but approached Harriet warily then ran back to her mother without doing the deed. Sadie saw the hurt in Harriet's eyes and felt a pang. This was something that couldn't normally be forced but she would have a damned good try in this instance.

When coaxing didn't do the trick Sadie got firm with Rosie until eventually the child trotted over to her grandmother, splashed a wet kiss on her cheek and ran back to her mother as though she would never let her go.

'She's still very shy then,' observed Harriet.

'No, not normally,' Sadie informed her.

'She's just a bit overwhelmed by her lovely present, I expect,' suggested Marge helpfully.

'Yes,' added Gerald supportively. 'That will be what it is.'

Sadie said no more on the subject. Thankfully Rosie adored the dolls' house and played with it for the rest of the time the Westons were there. But Sadie was relieved when they left because the visit was even more of a strain than usual. A child couldn't be made to bond with someone they had taken against. All you could do was encourage them and hope it was just a phase, though she suspected that the answer lay with Harriet, who didn't seem to have any natural aptitude towards children, even one she obviously loved.

'Come on, Sadie,' her mother was saying now, 'let's get cracking on the clearing up.'

'Okay,' she said, concentrating on the job in hand.

* * *

'Don't take it to heart, Harriet,' said Gerald as his wife sat scowling in the car on the way home. 'You know what kiddies are like for having funny little ways. She'll probably be all over you the next time we see her.'

'There is something seriously wrong with that child,' Harriet stated categorically. 'It isn't natural to be so reserved. Sadie should take her somewhere to get professional help; a child psychiatrist perhaps.'

'Oh, Harriet. Now you really are being ridiculous,' he admonished. 'She isn't shy as such. She just has her funny little moments like any other child.'

'But you saw how she was with me.'

He didn't have the heart to suggest that the fault lay with her so he just said, 'Yes. She is a bit offhand with you at the moment, I agree, but I'm sure she'll grow out of it. There certainly isn't anything clinically wrong with her.'

'I sincerely hope it is just a phase,' his wife said crossly. 'But we shall have to monitor the situation very closely the next time we see her.'

'If you say so, dear,' sighed Gerald, keeping his eyes on the road ahead.

★ ★ ★

A couple of Saturdays later, after Ray had finished work at the shop, he went for a quick pint at the pub round the corner. It had been a busy day and he needed to unwind for half an hour or so before going home. Later on, when he had had something to eat and got changed, he would go round to the Bells to see Sadie. With a bit of luck Marge would go out with Cyril and he and Sadie would have the house to themselves. It wasn't ideal but it was the best there was when you were dating a woman with a child and no home of her own.

Standing at the bar, mulling over his day and anticipating with pleasure the evening ahead with Sadie, he noticed a familiar face further up the counter but couldn't remember where he had seen the young man before. Then it came to him and he left his beer and went over to him.

Slapping a firm hand on his shoulder so that the man turned around, startled, Ray said, 'Remember me?'

The young man — who was pale-faced and slight of build — looked blank. 'No, should I?'

'You'll remember me next time, I can promise you that,' Ray said, getting hold of his arm with such pressure the man winced. 'You're coming with me.'

'What are you doing?' the young man objected. 'I'm not going anywhere.'

'Oh, I think you are.'

Ray had plenty of muscle and the skinny younger man didn't stand a chance against him when he forced him towards the door.

'What the hell is this all about?' he protested outside the pub. 'Who are you and what do you want with me?'

'You really don't remember me, do you?' asked Ray in disgust.

'I've never seen you before in my life, so what is there to remember?' he said.

Frogmarching him into a side street to avoid the attention of passersby, Ray pushed him up against a wall and said, 'I'm the owner of the record shop. The one you ruined the reputation of and got me dragged off to the nick. Remember me now?'

'No, not really.'

'Oh, come on, you are up on a drugs charge. Has your case come up yet?'

'Oh, that,' the young man replied. 'No, it hasn't yet.'

'You haven't forgotten that then.'

'It was just a laugh,' he said carelessly. 'As far as I can remember we heard the music and wandered in. It seemed like a good idea to have a smoke and let our hair down. We didn't mean any harm. It isn't as if we robbed the place or did any damage.'

'You robbed me of my reputation and I don't know if I'll ever get it back,' Ray said. 'Some people still think I had something to do with it because it was on my premises.'

'Will it help if I say I'm sorry?'

'It'll be a start.'

He shrugged. 'Sorry.' He looked at Ray, puzzled. 'I still don't recognise you.'

'And if you carry on as you have been you won't only forget the face of a shopkeeper, you won't even remember your own name. Your brain will be about as effective as an ice-cream cornet.'

'Calm down, man,' he said. 'You need to relax a bit more and take it easy on yourself.'

'Like you do, with the help of illegal substances.'

'There's no harm in it. It's only pot.'

'It's what it leads to that's the problem,' said Ray. 'Harder, more dangerous drugs.'

'You've been in the pub and I don't suppose you were drinking lemonade,' the young man came back at him. 'That doesn't mean you're going to become a helpless alcoholic.'

'No, of course not,' Ray was forced to agree.

'But in case you are too far gone to remember, using drugs is illegal.'

'I know that but I happen to believe that what a man does in his own time is his own business,' he stated.

'I quite agree. But you weren't in your own home, were you?' Ray pointed out. 'You were in my bloody shop.'

'Oh yeah,' said the man. 'There is that.'

Ray shrugged.

'Anyway, just tell me what you want me to do to make it up to you and I'll do it,' said the man. 'If it's some stuff you want I can get it, no problem.'

At this point Ray realised that he was completely wasting his time.

'Get lost and don't come near my shop again,' he said and walked away in frustration.

Drugs were outside of Ray's personal experience. It was only the last few years they had featured so prominently in the culture and it was still only a small minority who used them as far as Ray knew. But he understood enough to know that they were bad news. Each to their own and if people wanted to relax in that way, it was their own business. So that was an end to it.

But he felt depressed, maybe because the bloke he'd just warned to stay away was so young. He couldn't be more than about eighteen or nineteen. When he himself had been that age he'd been doing his national service in the army. Fat chance soldiers had had to misbehave. Their idea of mischief had been a few beers on a

349

Saturday night and sex if they could find anyone willing.

Oh well, that was all a long time ago, he thought, deciding not to go back into the pub but to go straight home, so he walked briskly through the streets, unable to lift his spirits.

★   ★   ★

'Is there anything wrong, Ray?' asked Sadie later that same night when they were ensconced on the sofa together.

'No. Why?'

'You seem a bit fed up.'

He put his arm around her, looking at her and seeing genuine concern. For some reason, he was still bothered about the bloke in the pub; worried for him, which was stupid since the boy was a stranger. It should have been the simplest thing to talk to Sadie about it, but he was used to keeping worries to himself so he just said, 'How could I possibly be fed up when I'm with you?'

'Aah, you say the sweetest things,' she laughed.

'I try,' he said lightly.

But she knew something was bothering him and she also knew he wouldn't confide in her because he kept his worries to himself. She was beginning to realise that Ray was a man it was impossible to know because he kept a part of himself back. She wondered what really went on behind those velvet brown eyes of his.

'I wondered if you had gone off me or something,' she probed. 'Only don't be afraid to say if you have.'

350

'Of course I haven't.'

'It would be easier for you if you had a girlfriend who was free to come and go as she pleased, wouldn't it?' she continued. 'A girl who didn't have a child to consider.'

'Yes, it would be more convenient,' he admitted. 'But I've never been one to take the easy option.'

'Perhaps we could have a night out soon,' she suggested. 'If I can get Mum to babysit.'

'That would be nice,' he said.

'You must get bored with staying in.'

'Not at all. I enjoy being with you and I understand your situation,' he assured her. 'So don't go asking your mum to babysit just because of me. Yeah, a night out would be good but it isn't essential. I don't mind either way.'

To be perfectly honest right now he would like to take her home to bed. He was twenty-nine and well past the age of sitting on the sofa with a girl who lived with her parents. He wanted a full-blown relationship. But that wasn't possible so he had to take what was available until he was ready to move things on to the next stage and commit to her in the only way a girl like her would accept. And the thought of the repercussions that could create made his blood run cold.

'Whatever happens, Sadie,' he heard himself say emotionally, 'I love you. Never forget that.'

The declaration had a valedictory sound to it which spoilt it and worried her. 'You make it sound like a threat,' she said. 'All this whatever happens business. And why would I forget it?'

'Things happen in life and people's feelings

351

change because of them, that's all I meant,' he said.

'It all sounds a bit ominous but, anyway, I love you too,' she said, 'and I know that that won't change.'

They kissed but a dampener had descended on the evening. For him because he knew he must make an important, potentially life-changing decision; for her because she knew he wasn't happy and she couldn't help him if he wouldn't tell her what was the matter.

★   ★   ★

In the park with Sadie and Rosie the following afternoon, Ray thought he had more than any man could expect of life. As he pushed Rosie on the swing and heard her childish laughter he realised that he had come to love her like his own since he had been seeing Sadie.

In his mind's eye he saw another swing in the garden of the house he wanted to share with Sadie and her daughter, a house that he would buy or at least take a mortgage out on. House-buying was no novelty these days. Even the most ordinary people were doing it. He'd never thought he would be able to consider such a thing but the business was doing well, despite the drugs incident.

It was just a simple thing; being here, doing this on a Sunday afternoon in the park on a cold February day with the low sun spreading its light over everything. But right now it felt like heaven.

'It's so lovely to be here with you and Rosie,'

he said impulsively to Sadie, who was standing beside him.

'You've got over the funny mood you were in yesterday then, have you?' she responded.

'Yeah, sorry about that.'

'That's all right,' she said. 'We all have our off days.'

'I've realised how very lucky I am.'

'Luck doesn't come into it,' she said. 'You've worked hard and used your head, that's why you've done so well for yourself, building a business from nothing. It's a pity your parents didn't live to see your success. They'd have been so proud, I'm sure.'

'I wasn't talking about the business. I was referring to the fact that I have you in my life,' he said. 'You and Rosie.'

'Oh, I see. Well that's lovely and I'm very touched,' she said, linking her arm through his in an affectionate manner, her cheeks suffused with pink from the cold. 'But, even so, I meant what I said about your success in business. It isn't everyone from an ordinary background who can become an entrepreneur.'

'Oh, I don't know so much,' he protested. 'We're living in a meritocracy nowadays. All sorts of ordinary people are making their mark much more notably than I am. Pop stars, models, photographers. I'm just a boring shopkeeper. The day of common people has arrived.'

'You're not just a shopkeeper; you're an expert on the music retail business, and there's nothing in the least bit boring about you. I can promise you that.'

A lump rose in his throat. He knew he had a reputation as a bit of a hard man. No one would guess what an emotional being he really was, especially when it came to Sadie. He wanted to ask her to marry him and make the dream of a house with a garden and a family become reality. But this wasn't the time. It was too soon.

'Thanks, kid,' he said, squeezing her arm. 'You are so good for my ego; much more of that sort of talk and my head will start to swell.'

'Don't worry,' she laughed. 'I'll soon bring you down to earth if you get conceited.'

The conversation was interrupted by Rosie asking to come off the swing. Ray slowed it down and lifted her off and the three of them walked away from the playground together, Rosie skipping between them. He was happy but he wasn't content. These two people were all he wanted from life but there was always a snag. In this case it was that he wanted more of them than just the park on a Sunday afternoon and seeing them in someone else's house. He was impatient to share his life with them properly.

★   ★   ★

It was manic at the surgery the following week because Edith was off sick. Dr Russell's mother came in to give Sadie a hand but she didn't know the job in the same way as Edith did, now that they had expanded. Sadie couldn't go so far as to call Edith a friend but she missed her about the place, much to her surprise. The woman was outspoken and snappy but when she wasn't

354

around you realised how good she was at the job when she wasn't being rude to the patients.

On Friday after work Sadie called at her house with her wage packet.

'Yes,' said the person who answered the door, a balding, thin-faced man with a moustache whom Sadie assumed was Edith's husband.

'I'm Sadie. I work at the surgery with Edith. I've come with her wages,' she said.

'Oh. Thanks very much,' he said, taking the brown envelope from her as she handed it to him. 'It's very good of you to bring her money round.'

'How is Edith now?' asked Sadie.

'She's getting a bit better.'

'Flu, isn't it?'

He nodded. 'One of those things that just have to take their course, I'm afraid,' he said. 'Not worth bothering a doctor with.'

'Can I see her?' she asked impulsively.

'She's in bed sleeping at the moment.'

'Oh, I see. Well, that can only be a good thing,' Sadie said. 'Any idea when she'll be coming back to work?'

'I'm not sure,' he replied. 'This particular strain of flu is very weakening.'

'Oh well, give her my best wishes. Tell her I hope she feels better soon.'

'Will do,' he said, seeming keen to close the door. 'Cheerio.'

'Ta-ta.'

She walked up the front path and as she turned to close the gate, she saw the net curtains downstairs twitch and Edith looked out, obviously wide awake and fully dressed. She disappeared even as Sadie raised her hand to wave to her. That's odd, she thought, as she strode off down the street. Some people hated any invasion of privacy and Edith was obviously one of them. She wasn't really surprised, knowing Edith as she did.

★ ★ ★

On Saturday mornings Sadie borrowed Don's car and took their mother to the supermarket for the main weekly shop — no small job with a family of six to cater for. With Rosie riding in the trolley they trawled the shelves, chatting and jointly deciding what to have for meals. Marge always enjoyed herself, despite the crowds, the queues at the checkouts and the fact that Rosie pestered them for anything that vaguely resembled sweets or biscuits. After years of shopping daily and carrying heavy bags home, the supermarket system was a godsend to her, especially with a car to take the shopping home in.

Foraging in the freezer for frozen peas, Sadie put them in the trolley and as she looked up she saw Edith across the aisle by the tinned beans. She looked towards Sadie, ignored her completely then strode off purposefully pushing her trolley.

'I've just seen Edith from work, Mum,' Sadie said. 'And she pretended not to see me.'

'Didn't you say she's been off sick?'

'Exactly,' she confirmed. 'There doesn't seem

to be anything wrong with her now.'

'That isn't to say there hasn't been,' said Marge, preoccupied with her shopping list.

'Why would she blank me?'

'Because she's been off sick, she probably doesn't want to be seen out and about in case anyone thinks she's been swinging the lead all week.'

'But she knows I've seen her so what's the point of ignoring me?' Sadie wondered.

'I don't know, love,' replied Marge. 'She didn't want to get into conversation, I suppose. We all do that sort of thing from time to time if we're in a hurry.'

'When I called at her house with her wages, her husband told me she was asleep and I saw her at the window, wide awake. Don't you think that was odd?'

'Not really, love. They obviously didn't want a visitor at that time and they needed an excuse not to ask you in,' suggested Marge. 'To us it seems peculiar because we are sociable and straightforward and people come in and out of our place all the time. But not everyone is like us. Some people will do anything to guard their privacy.'

'Edith loves her job. In fact she's passionate about it so she wouldn't stay at home if she wasn't ill, in case they might decide they can do without her at the surgery. She'd also be terrified that I was going to get one over on her at work.'

'So she was ill earlier in the week then she was feeling better and was well enough to go out shopping today,' said Marge. 'I don't know why you're spending so much time thinking about it. What does it matter to you what she's up to?'

'I don't know why it matters, Mum,' Sadie confessed. 'I just feel as though something isn't right.'

'Even if there is anything wrong it has nothing to do with you, so stop fretting about it.'

'You're right,' she finally agreed. 'It's none of my business, so I'll forget all about it. Yes, all right, Rosie, just one small packet of sweets when we've finished the shopping and no, you can't get out of the trolley because you'll run about all over the place and cause havoc.'

'I want Uncle Ray,' Rosie said.

'You can't have him at the moment because he's at work,' Sadie explained.

'I wanna see him,' the little girl persisted.

'I'll take you over to the shop to see him this afternoon, if you're a good girl now and stop asking for things,' Sadie said. 'But he'll be too busy to play with you very much. He'll come with us to the park tomorrow, I expect.'

'She's very fond of him, isn't she,' remarked Marge as they joined the end of the queue at the checkout.

'Very,' Sadie confirmed.

'So, do you reckon it will come to anything serious between you and Ray?' her mother asked. 'I know you wanted it kept casual at first but you do get on well.'

'I hope it does lead to something but I really don't know at this stage,' she replied. 'Ray is a dark horse. You never know what's going on in his mind. For me it would be wonderful if he asked me to marry him. I didn't think I would ever fall in love again but I have. It's been a very gradual thing, quite different to the mad whirlwind romance I had with Paul, but none the less powerful. I believe Ray's feelings for me are the same but I don't know about marriage. He used to be deadset against the idea, which caused problems between him and Brenda. He might still be of the same mind. We haven't discussed anything like that.'

'It would be nice if it led to marriage with him being practically one of the family anyway,' said Marge. 'You're so good together. I've seen how happy you've been since you've been seeing him. It's nice for you to be with someone again.'

'Yes it is, but as for the future, we'll just have to wait and see what happens. I'm certainly not going to rush him,' said Sadie, suddenly spotting Edith marching towards the exit weighed down with shopping bags. She didn't look as though she'd been ill for years. 'Look, Mum, there's Edith again. As fit as a flea.'

'Oh, will you stop going on about blinking Edith,' Marge exclaimed.

'Blinkin' Edith,' echoed Rosie.

Both women laughed. 'Now see what you've done. You've made your granddaughter swear.'

'That isn't swearing,' Marge said. 'But she shouldn't be saying it. She's a proper little copycat.'

'Copycat,' Rosie repeated and both women laughed again, the mystery of Edith cast aside.

★ ★ ★

Edith returned to work on Monday and was fiercer and bossier than ever, perhaps because she felt a little threatened by her absence, Sadie thought.

'Are you feeling better?' enquired Sadie.

'Yes, thank you. I'm right back on form,' Edith replied curtly. 'Any problems while I was away?'

'No.'

'Oh.' She looked disappointed.

'It was very hectic without you, of course,' Sadie added to please her, but it was also true.

'You managed though.'

'With a little help from Mrs Russell, yes, I managed.'

'Good.'

'As a matter of fact I saw you in the supermarket on Saturday,' said Sadie with a casual air.

'Oh, really, I didn't see you,' lied Edith. 'I must have been too busy with what I was doing. I was feeling a lot better by Saturday. Well enough to go out.'

'So I noticed.'

'What's that supposed to mean?' she prickled.

'Nothing in particular. Just that I could see you were feeling better.'

'I hope you're not suggesting that I haven't been ill,' she snapped, narrowing her eyes suspiciously.

'I'm not suggesting anything,' Sadie told her. 'I was just making conversation.'

'That's all right then,' Edith said. 'Now come along, let's get cracking and get the patients' notes out ready for surgery.'

Sadie was going to say, 'Yes ma'am', and salute but she didn't think Edith's fragile sense of humour could cope with it so she heard herself say, 'It's good to have you back, Edith.'

The other woman's eyes widened in surprise and a suggestion of pleasure. 'Oh, is it? Is it really?'

'Yes, it is, actually.' Sadie was as amazed as Edith but it was true. In a peculiar sort of way it was nice to have her back.

★　★　★

That evening, after work, Sadie found herself heading towards Edith's house again. This time it was because her colleague had departed from work in a hurry and left her glasses on the desk in the office and Sadie guessed she would want them during the evening as she needed specs for reading.

'Sadie,' Edith greeted her in a surprisingly pleasant manner when she answered the door.

'You left these at work and I thought you might need them,' Sadie said, handing the spectacles to her.

'Oh, thank you.' She opened the door wider. 'Come in.'

Sadie was eager to get home but she didn't want to seem rude so she said, 'Just for a minute then.'

She was shown into a sitting room that was well-appointed and had a deep bay window, but the furnishings were dreary and old-fashioned, which she would expect of Edith.

361

'I don't know how I came to forget my specs,' Edith said. 'That isn't like me at all.'

'We all forget things at times.'

'Would you like a cup of tea?' she offered.

'I expect you need to get your evening meal,' suggested Sadie, because she wanted to get away. 'I don't want to hold you up.'

'My husband is working late tonight,' Edith told her. 'The least I can do is give you a cup of tea after you've gone out of your way to bring my glasses round.'

'I'll have to make it a quick one though because my daughter will be waiting for me. She gets very excited when it gets near the time for me to get home.'

'Aah, bless her,' Edith said and Sadie could hardly believe that this was the same woman she saw every day at the surgery. This version was softer and warmer altogether. 'It must be nice to have a child.'

Sadie already knew that Edith didn't have children but she didn't know any details. 'Would you have liked a family then?'

'Oh yes, very much so,' her colleague replied. 'But we weren't blessed in that way.'

There was the sound of a key turning in the lock and Edith immediately stiffened and looked uneasy.

'Oh, so we have company,' said her husband, coming into the room, now dressed smartly in a business suit.

'This is Sadie from the surgery,' Edith explained tremulously. 'This is my husband, Bill.'

They exchanged greetings.

'I thought you were working late,' Edith remarked.

'I didn't need to after all,' he explained. 'I managed to get everything done in normal office hours.'

Edith nodded. 'Sadie called round to give me my specs,' she explained to him, almost apologetically, as though she had to give a reason why she had a visitor. 'I'd left them at work.'

'That was very careless of you,' he said critically.

'Yes . . . '

'Sadie has had to come out of her way to bring them round,' he interrupted, frowning at his wife.

'I know.'

'Have you not offered her a cup of tea?'

'Yes, I was just going to make it.'

'It's all right really,' said Sadie, feeling uncomfortable. 'I can't stay. My little girl will be at the window looking out for me.'

'You must stay for a cup of tea,' he said and Sadie instinctively baulked at his commanding tone.

'I won't, if you don't mind,' she said firmly, giving him a hard look. 'I'd like to get home as soon as I can.'

'As you wish.'

'I'll see you to the door,' said Edith, now clearly wanting Sadie to leave.

Seeing how pale and nervous the other woman had become, Sadie said as she was leaving, 'Are you all right, Edith?'

'Yes, I'm fine, of course I am, why wouldn't I

be?' she snapped, reverting to the sharp manner she adopted at the surgery. She opened the door and made it obvious that she wanted Sadie to go through it with all possible speed. 'I'll see you tomorrow at work. Goodnight.'

'Goodnight.'

Well, what was going on there, Sadie wondered, as she walked down the street. She had seen two other sides to Edith tonight; the warmer, nicer one and the humble one. She'd never seen anyone change as fast as Edith had when her husband came in. The woman was clearly terrified of him. The overconfident bully of a woman she worked with at the surgery was like a frightened bird when she was with her husband. There was something very dark going on in that house, and Sadie knew instinctively that it was connected in some way to Edith being off sick last week. She was still convinced that she hadn't been ill at all.

As worried as she was, she knew she mustn't mention her concerns to Edith, who would probably behave as though the visit had never happened. Somehow she knew that her colleague needed help but the last thing she would ever do was to admit or ask for it. So all Sadie could do was put it to the back of her mind. No doubt Edith would be at the surgery throwing her weight about as usual tomorrow and Sadie would probably never see the other side of her personality again. She felt very uneasy as she walked home.

14

The dark winter days brightened into spring and the world came to life again. At work Edith remained her usual domineering self with no mention of Sadie's visit or sign of a less confident side to her nature, so the incident gradually faded from Sadie's mind.

She had plenty to occupy her thoughts anyway as her relationship with Ray continued and her daughter grew and flourished and became a character in her own right. Now well into her fourth year, her physical resemblance to her father became even more noticeable and was sometimes breathtaking for those who had loved him. Her mother's genes were also evident as her personality developed and she became outgoing to the point where she even seemed to get over her reticence with her Grandma Weston.

Derek's girlfriend Christine slipped unobtrusively into the family circle. An unassuming brunette of Derek's age with warm brown eyes and a ready smile, she was popular with them all. In August the couple announced their engagement and the Bell family celebrated it in their usual party style with masses of food, drink and music. All the latest records were provided by Ray, the furniture cleared for dancing and by nine o'clock the place was buzzing.

They were drinking a toast to the happy couple when the telephone rang.

'Who's that, calling us at this time on a Saturday night?' wondered Marge.

'Let it ring,' suggested Cyril. 'They can call another time when we're not in the middle of a party.'

'We can't just ignore it because it might be important but you carry on and I'll go and answer it,' offered Sadie, going to the hall and closing the door behind her so that she would be able to hear the caller above the noise of the party.

'Sadie, it's Edith.' Her colleague's voice came down the line, sounding shaky and tearful. 'Please could you come over? I'm in terrible trouble and I've no one else to turn to.'

Sadie didn't ask questions. Edith needed her; that was enough.

'I'm on my way,' she said.

As she replaced the receiver her mother appeared on her way to the kitchen.

'Is everything all right, love?' she asked. 'Who was it?'

Sadie could hear that the toasts were over and the music was back on again. The Beatles' 'All You Need is Love' was blaring out and people were singing along. Not wanting to spoil the fun, Sadie said to her mother, 'It was Edith. I have to pop over to her place so I'm just going to slip off for a few minutes. Would you mind looking after Rosie for me for a little while, Mum? I'll be back before anyone even notices I've gone.'

'Course I will, but is something wrong with Edith to make you leave the party?'

'I'm not sure but she sounds desperate, so I

need to go and find out what's going on.' Sadie picked up Don's car keys off the hall table. 'I'm taking Don's car to speed things up. He won't mind as he isn't going to need it tonight.'

'Don't you want someone to go with you?'

'No, they're all having a good time, so leave them to enjoy themselves,' she said. 'I won't be long.'

'See you later then,' said Marge.

★   ★   ★

Edith was whey-faced and trembling violently when she answered the door to Sadie.

'I've killed him,' she announced, her voice wobbling. 'I've finally gone and done it. He's been asking for it for years and now he's got it. He's dead and good job too.'

She led Sadie to the kitchen where Bill was slumped on the floor, against the fridge, frighteningly still, a trickle of blood coming from his head.

'Blimey, Edith. You have gone and done it too,' cried Sadie, shocked and not sure what to do in the panic of the moment. Common sense told her they must call the police immediately and leave everything exactly as it was until they got there.

But Edith seemed to need to unburden herself. 'Years of insults and put-downs, of bullying and treating me like scum has finally worn me down,' she said, wringing her hands, her voice guttural with emotion. 'That time when I was off from work sick, I wasn't ill at all.

367

He wouldn't let me go to work. He had a week off so he physically stopped me from going. Locked me in for the whole of the working week.'

'Oh Edith, how awful for you.'

'It was too. My job is the only escape from him I have; the only time I feel as though I might be worth something as a human being is when I'm at work, and if he had his way I'd give my notice in so that I never saw another living soul and he was the total breadwinner and I had to rely on him for every single thing,' she went on in anguish. 'Tonight he was on and on at me here in the kitchen when I was clearing up after our meal, telling me how useless I was at everything. I just couldn't take any more so I picked up the nearest thing to hand, a heavy saucepan, and hit him over the head with it.' She held her head as though in pain. 'I just had to stop him; his voice was going right through me and I couldn't stand any more.'

'He didn't hit you then.'

'No, he never does. I think that would have been easier to cope with over the years than the constant drip, drip, drip of criticism and mockery. Every minute of every hour when we are together he's at me. On and on and on.'

'Did you never think of leaving him?' enquired Sadie, very frightened and eager to call the police, but needing to calm Edith down by letting the conversation continue.

'I've thought about it many times but was always too much of a coward when it came to actually doing it,' she admitted. 'I'd have nowhere to go. We've no kids and he made sure I lost touch with all my relatives and friends.'

'Yes, these things are easier said than done and I can imagine how hard it was for you,' said Sadie. 'I'm sorry to have to say this, Edith, but we must call the police right away.'

'Yes, yes, of course,' she agreed. 'Sorry, Sadie, to have got you involved in this. I'm so scared.'

Edith looked so utterly forlorn, Sadie put her arms around her instinctively. 'I'm sure you must be but it will only make things worse if we don't tell the police what's happened right away,' she said gently. 'If you tell them what's been going on and how you were driven to it, I'm sure allowances will be made. I'll make the phone call if you like?'

But she didn't get the chance because Edith was suddenly dragged away from her and held in an iron grip by her husband. 'You make one move and she gets it,' Bill threatened Sadie. 'I'll break every bone in her body one by one, so don't even try it.'

'You're not dead,' gasped Edith.

'Obviously not but it's no thanks to you, you violent cow,' he said. 'I could have you done for attempted murder.' He touched the gash on his head. 'It's a miracle you didn't kill me instead of just knocking me out.'

'Why don't you go to the phone and report her to the police then?' Sadie challenged him, though she was feeling very nervous of the situation herself.

'Because it doesn't suit me,' he replied in an

arrogant manner. 'I want my wife here, not stuck in some prison.'

'So that you can go on making her life a misery,' accused Sadie bravely.

'If you say so.' As Sadie made a dash for the door, he pushed Edith to the ground and went after Sadie, pulling her back, locking the door and putting the key in his pocket before dragging Edith to her feet and holding her with her arms behind her back. 'Right, no one is going anywhere. Is that understood?'

'You can't hold me here against my will,' objected Sadie.

'You just watch me. It's your own fault for getting involved in someone else's business,' he told her. 'You should never interfere between husband and wife.'

'She didn't,' said Edith. 'I asked her to come over. It's my fault she's got caught up in all this.'

'She's been to the house a couple of times before this as well,' he observed. 'How many times have I told you not to ask anyone here? No one, not relatives, friends or work colleagues come to visit us. I won't have it.'

'She came with my wages and then my glasses,' his wife reminded him. 'She was doing me a favour.'

'Nobody comes to this house,' he said again, his voice distorted by anger. 'We don't need anyone but each other.'

'You might not, but I'm sure Edith does,' Sadie dared to suggest. 'It isn't natural the way you carry on. You can't cut her off from the outside world.'

'I would if I could but I can't because she defies me and goes to that stupid job,' he said.

'There's nothing stupid about the job,' Sadie pointed out, 'and I can tell you that she is very good at it.'

'She isn't good at anything except looking after me,' he came back at her. 'That's what her full-time job should be. She's my wife; that is her role in life.'

'You're sick,' accused Sadie, 'and she must be very sick of being married to you.'

'Why hasn't she left then?' he asked.

'Because you've shattered her confidence, you bully.'

'That isn't the reason,' he disagreed. 'She has old-fashioned values and knows that marriage is for life through thick and thin, that's why she's stayed.'

Sadie now accepted that even if she could get out of here she wouldn't leave Edith alone with him. Not while he was in this mood. Ray and the family at home would be worried if she didn't arrive back soon and she realised that they didn't know where Edith lived so they couldn't come and find her. But she couldn't desert Edith, so she was stuck here until this monster of a man decided otherwise and anything could happen in the meantime in this explosive situation.

★ ★ ★

'She said she wouldn't be long,' Marge said to the others when Sadie had been gone for over

371

two hours. 'I can't imagine what's held her up. She didn't expect to be gone more than a few minutes, which is why she didn't stop to tell you all.'

'She wouldn't stay away from a family party unless something had happened to her,' said Derek. 'Why hasn't she phoned if she's been held up? There are plenty of phone boxes around.'

'Where does this friend of hers live?' asked Ray.

'I've no idea,' Marge replied. 'Sadie doesn't know her very well. They're not friends as such. They just work together.'

'Oh, that's just brilliant,' said Ray with irony, as his anxiety grew. 'Sadie goes missing in the middle of a party and we haven't a clue where to start looking for her.'

'She just said she needed to go and see if Edith was all right,' said Marge.

'That sounds a bit ominous in itself,' suggested Don.

'She's probably fine,' said Ray in an effort to defuse the rising panic, especially for Marge, who he realised was on the verge of tears. 'So try to keep calm. I know someone who will know where this Edith person lives. Dr Russell is sure to have her address.'

'But he doesn't live at the surgery now.'

'He still lives at the same house though even though the surgery has moved, so I'll go and ask him,' stated Ray in a positive manner. 'Out of hours or not, I'm going to pay him a visit. There is probably a simple explanation and we are all worrying over nothing but I'm going to look for her.'

And he was off before anyone could offer to go with him.

⋆ ⋆ ⋆

Still trapped in Edith's kitchen, Sadie had been ordered by Bill to make some tea.

'Why don't you let Sadie go, Bill?' begged Edith, who was sitting on a chair next to Sadie's, her husband seated facing her by the locked door. 'It isn't fair to involve her in our private business.'

'You involved her,' he said. 'You asked her to come. It had nothing to do with me.'

'I thought I'd killed you then, didn't I?' she pointed out. 'Unfortunately I hadn't so why can't you let her go home so that we can all get back to normal, or what passes for normal in this house?'

'Don't worry about me, Edith,' said Sadie, pouring the tea. 'My family will track me down sooner or later and I wouldn't want to be in Bill's shoes when my boyfriend and brothers get hold of him. They are all more than twenty years younger than he is and, apart from Derek who has a heart condition, they are very fit. But I expect they'd rather leave it to the police to deal with him.'

'Oh, not the police, Sadie, please,' begged Edith. 'I'd sooner be dead than live with the shame of people knowing our business.'

'She's afraid you'll tell them she tried to kill

me, aren't you, Edith?' taunted Bill.

'No. Not especially,' denied Edith. 'I just don't want people to know about the peculiar way we live.'

'They'll hear nothing from me about it but my family won't take kindly to the idea of my being held here against my will.' It had occurred to Sadie that between them she and Edith could probably overpower Bill and unlock the door. But she had to consider Edith, who would be here with him on her own after she'd gone. If he let her go of his own accord when his rage had burned itself out, it would probably be better for his wife. 'Anyway, Edith, you might like to talk to someone about the way this man has been abusing you all these years.'

'Oh no, Sadie, please don't tell the police.'

'There wouldn't be any point in telling the police,' Sadie pointed out. 'There's nothing they can do unless you make a charge against him. You'd have to give evidence. Anyway, he doesn't actually use physical violence, does he? He's far too crafty for that so the police wouldn't get involved. But there are people you can talk to about this sort of thing.'

'I don't want to talk to anyone.'

'In that case you'll just have to put up with him,' said Sadie wearily. This was all very frustrating because she knew that Edith would let the situation continue simply because it was easier that way. And she could see her point. If she was to leave she would lose her home and a certain standard of living. But surely nothing could be worse than living with a bully. Still,

Sadie was in no position to judge as she had never been in the same circumstances. All she knew was that Edith was in a hopeless situation. In a distant corner of her mind, too, she wondered if the older woman did actually want to banish her husband from her life. She probably loved him, despite everything.

Edith looked sheepish. 'I'm very sorry to have ruined your evening and got you involved,' she said.

'I'm not involved, not really,' Sadie responded. 'How the two of you choose to live your life is up to you. Edith, you don't want to do anything about it and you, Bill, obviously have no intention of mending your ways, so you'll have to sort it out for yourselves.' She paused, mulling the situation over and deciding that there was nothing she could do here to help. 'But now you know that I'm not going to the police can I go home, please? There really is no point in my staying and my family will be very worried.'

Bill thought about it for a while then took the key out of his pocket and unlocked the door.

★　★　★

Ray was driving slowly along the road where Edith lived. The doctor had known the name of the street but not the number without going to the surgery to look at the files. So Ray was looking for Don's car. As he spotted it and drew into the kerb, Sadie came out of the house and ran down the path.

'Sadie,' he said, leaping out of his car and

375

dashing over to her. 'Oh, thank God. We've all been so worried.'

'Sorry,' she said.

'There's no need to apologise but what happened? It isn't like you to just take off like that and stay away for ages.'

'I'll tell you all about it later, but for now I'd better go home before they send out a search party.'

'I can't tell you how relieved I am to find you safe' he said emotionally, taking her in his arms. 'I don't know what I'd do if anything happened to you.'

Realising how genuinely worried he had been and remembering how he had lost Brenda, she said gently, 'Nothing will, I promise you. You don't get rid of me that easily.'

'I would never, ever want to get rid of you, Sadie. I love you and want you in my life forever,' Ray said with passion. Completely caught up in the emotion of the moment and without any prior intention he added, 'Will you marry me?'

'Oh.' She was taken aback and lost for words.

'It isn't the way I planned it,' he told her, 'with a romantic dinner and all the trimmings, but it does come from the heart. Please say you will, Sadie?'

'Yes, of course I'll marry you,' she said, melting into his arms.

★ ★ ★

'So are you saying that Edith's husband held you captive in their kitchen?' demanded Marge, when Sadie tried to explain why she had been so long. The other guests had already left and just the family and Christine remained.

'Yes, that's right,' she replied.

'We could have him done for that,' said her outraged father.

'But why would he do such a thing?' Marge wanted to know.

'He's got a screw loose, I think,' Sadie replied. 'Edith had hit him over the head with a saucepan and knocked him out though, so I suppose that would upset anyone. That's why she phoned and asked me to go over. She thought she'd killed him and was in a panic. We were just about to report the murder to the police when he came back from the dead and kept us both captive. He said he would harm her if I tried to get away.'

'Hit him over the head with a saucepan,' repeated her mother incredulously. 'Good grief! What sort of people are they?'

'They have problems,' Sadie replied.

'They sound like the sort you need to steer clear of,' put in her father, while there was a murmur of agreement from the others. 'I've never heard anything like it.'

'Plenty of domestic violence goes on behind closed doors, Dad,' Sadie informed him.

'But not among people we know.'

'That doesn't mean it doesn't happen.'

'I've a good mind to go and give the fella a pasting for holding you against your will,' declared Don hotly.

'You won't because I'm not going to tell you where they live,' she said, asking Ray with her eyes to keep quiet about Edith's address. 'Edith has enough problems without you adding to them. If anyone intervenes, he'll make her life even more of a hell than it is now.'

'We should report it to the police,' said Derek.

'No, definitely not,' Sadie insisted. 'It's over and done with and I came to no harm. I promised Edith I wouldn't involve the law. Anyway, let's change the subject because I have something very exciting to tell you all.'

They waited in eager anticipation.

'Ray has asked me to marry him and I've said yes,' she announced joyously. 'So I guess that means that we're engaged.'

There was a communal whoop of delight and a loud outpouring of congratulations.

'Oh, wonderful,' said Marge. 'But how, when? I mean, you haven't been here with Ray.'

'Spur-of-the-moment thing just now, Marge,' explained Ray.

'He was so relieved when he found me safe and well, he popped the question,' Sadie told them. 'It's only just happened, so there's no point in asking me when the wedding will be because neither of us have a clue at the moment.'

'Get some drinks, someone,' suggested Marge, noticing how radiant Sadie looked despite her ordeal, and was delighted for her. 'Let's drink a toast to the happy couple. Two engagements in one day. Yippee!'

Sensitive to the feelings of others, Sadie turned to her future sister-in-law. 'Sorry to muscle in on your party, Christine,' she said. 'It was completely unexpected.'

'That's all right,' said the amiable Christine. 'Our celebrations are over anyway.'

'As long as you're sure,' said Sadie, wondering how such a disastrous evening could end up so wonderfully.

'Did he give you a ring, Sadie?' asked her mother.

Such had been the events of the night she hadn't even given that side of it a thought. 'No, he hasn't actually.'

'I didn't intend to do the deed tonight so I don't have one,' Ray explained. 'But we'll go to the West End to choose one together as soon as possible, if you would like that, Sadie.'

'I would love that,' she said, smiling at him excitedly.

'Whoops, hang on to your wallet, mate,' joshed Derek. 'That's going to cost you.'

'I'll pay it willingly,' said Ray.

* * *

As the toast was made and they all raised their glasses, Ray was looking at Sadie and thinking how happy and gorgeous she was. He couldn't believe what he'd done. He'd intended to propose at some point but not now, not yet. Not until a certain matter had been dealt with. But he'd done it and there was no going back. He loved her and that was all that mattered for the moment. Nothing could spoil the deep joy and love for her that he felt right now.

* * *

'Do you fancy going for a run out to the country to Box Hill tomorrow, Ray?' Sadie asked when she was saying goodnight to him at the front door. 'It's such lovely weather at the moment, we might as well make the most of it. I could do with some country air. We could take a picnic. Rosie would love that.'

'Box Hill, eh?' he said in a questioning manner. 'But I thought that might be off limits to us together as it was special to you and Paul.'

'We did a lot of our courting around there and it does remind me of him, but I can think of him without pain now and I want to go there with you because I adore the place for itself,' she said. 'It will be nice for Rosie too.'

'That's okay with me then,' he told her. 'Will you want to call in at your in-laws' as we'll be so near to their place?'

'No, not this time,' she said. 'I want it to be just you, me and Rosie. I'll take Rosie another time to see the Westons. It isn't all that long since our last visit.'

'How will they take the news, about you and me, do you think?' he wondered.

'Gerald will be fine about it. He understands that people need to move on but Harriet won't like it one little bit,' she predicted. 'She wants me to be Paul's widow forever.'

'They'll probably be afraid it will interfere with their relationship with Rosie, and it's understandable,' he remarked. 'But you can assure them that it won't make any difference as far as I'm concerned. I'm not going to come the heavy stepfather. Would you like me to go with you when you tell them?'

'I think it might be better if you're not there,' Sadie replied. 'Harriet is an expert at making people feel uncomfortable. So you leave it to me.'

'As you wish,' he conceded. 'When shall we tell Rosie?'

'When the right opportunity arises; maybe tomorrow, maybe another day,' she suggested. 'She's too young to understand properly anyway. To her marriage is all about princesses and Prince Charming out of her story books.'

'How will she feel about having a new dad?'

'You won't be a new dad to her; you'll be the only one she has ever known,' she reminded him. 'Because she hasn't started proper school yet she doesn't realise that most of the other kids have them. Living with me and the family is the norm to her. But she loves you to bits, so I'm sure she'll be very happy to have you in our lives properly. We'll have to make sure she doesn't have her nose put out of joint by my having someone else to look after, of course, but she'll be fine as long as we're careful. At first we'll concentrate on the wedding and bring the rest in gradually.'

'That will probably be best,' he agreed. 'But we'll have to start thinking about where we will live after we're married. I've been considering buying a property for a while.'

'Slow down, Ray,' she said in a jovial manner. 'I haven't even got an engagement ring yet. Let me enjoy the fun part before we get to the serious business.'

'That's my girl,' he laughed. 'That's the Sadie I used to know; always in pursuit of fun.'

'Yes, I was, wasn't I?' she said, remembering. 'All of that seems a very long time ago.'

★ ★ ★

The weather was glorious as they parked the car at Box Hill, then walked for a while through beech and yew woodlands and found a quiet grassy spot for their picnic.

'It's like another world up here,' enthused Sadie, as they spread the tablecloth on the grass and set out the food. 'You come off the main road to Dorking with all that traffic and suddenly you're here in this glorious place.'

'Yes, it is really lovely,' Ray agreed. 'And so speaks a committed urbanite.'

'This is one of England's favourite beauty spots apparently,' Sadie told him. 'People have been coming here for centuries; famous, some of them, too. Jane Austen set a scene in one of her novels here on Box Hill. They had a picnic; it all turned out disastrously in her story.'

'Let's hope ours doesn't do the same.'

'Ours will be perfect,' she said.

She shouldn't have tempted fate. The first flaw in the plan for perfection was the hardboiled egg that hadn't been boiled at all and spilt all over the cloth when Sadie cracked the shell to peel it.

'Mum was supposed to have boiled the eggs,' she said, giggling.

'She obviously missed that one out,' chuckled Ray.

Rosie found the whole thing hilarious and laughed like mad.

'We'll have to share the eggs,' said Sadie, only to find that none of them had been boiled. 'I'll have something to say to Mum when I get home. That's what comes of having a hangover. She was like death warmed up this morning after the celebrations last night but insisted on preparing the picnic for us.'

'What else have we got to eat?' Ray enquired.

'There are some cheese and tomato sandwiches,' she told him, at which point the sliced tomato slipped out on to the grass as she got them out of the bag. 'Just cheese then in some of them.'

Being the time of year for wasps, they came after the jam sandwiches in swarms; there was no milk in the tea flask and the bottle of lemonade they had brought for Rosie exploded. The whole thing struck Sadie and Ray as funny and Rosie picked up on it and chuckled along with them. They did manage to sate their hunger with some fish-paste sandwiches which were surprisingly normal and some chunks of Marge's homemade sponge cake, which tasted delicious.

The mood was so wonderfully warm and light-hearted Sadie said to Ray, 'Do you think this is the moment?'

He nodded.

'Rosie,' she began. 'Something really lovely is going to happen soon.'

Rosie looked at her mother in that rather unnervingly intense way young children have. 'What is going to happen?' she asked.

'Mummy is going to get married.'

The child's face lit up. 'Like Cinderella. Will you have a pretty dress and a glass slipper? Will you be a princess?'

'I shall feel like a princess,' Sadie said. 'I am going to marry Uncle Ray.'

'Is he Prince Charming then?'

'He's my Prince Charming,' she said, 'and you will be my bridesmaid, so you will have a beautiful dress and flowers in your hair.'

The little girl's dark eyes were wide with awe. Then she said, 'Can we go to the swings now, please?'

'There aren't any swings here, darling.'

'Can we go home and go to the swings there?'

Sadie laughed. 'Honestly, I try to bring the countryside into her life and all she wants are the swings.'

'She's a town girl,' said Ray.

'Okay, we'll get packed up and be on our way. We'll stop at the duck pond on the way and you can feed the ducks, Rosie, with some of the leftover sandwiches.'

'Goodie,' said the child.

Sadie and Ray had cleared up and packed the bag when Rosie let out a whoop and shrieked, 'There's Fergus,' and hurtled towards a small white dog.

'It isn't Fergus, love,' Sadie told her. 'It's just a dog that looks like him; there are lots of them about. Grandma and Granddad never go walking here.'

'It is Fergus,' insisted Rosie. 'Look at his collar.'

'Oh no,' groaned Sadie, recognising the blue-check collar. She'd thought they were safe since the Westons didn't like to walk at Box Hill because of the slopes and the fact that it attracted so many visitors from London. But where there was Fergus there would be his owners, and sure enough they were trudging up the hill towards them.

★ ★ ★

'Hello there,' said Sadie as Rosie ran towards her grandparents. 'I didn't think you enjoyed walking here.'

'We don't as a rule,' responded Gerald. 'We thought it would be a change for Fergus.'

'You didn't tell us you were coming over this way,' said Harriet, managing to sound accusing.

'It was a spur-of-the-moment decision,' explained Sadie.

'Surely you wouldn't come all this way and not call in to see us,' said Harriet, looking hurt.

'We were going to surprise you,' fibbed Ray in the interests of good relations.

'Oh, oh I see,' she said, sounding a little less grim.

'But as you won't be there we'll go straight home,' said Sadie quickly, and before Harriet had a chance to suggest rushing off to make them tea or anything added, 'It's time we started to make our way back anyway. It's a long journey home and Rosie will be getting tired. I'll bring her to see you some time soon.'

'It's very nice to see you anyway,' said Gerald,

supervising Rosie, who was on her knees on the grass making a fuss of the dog. 'Are you both well?'

They exchanged pleasantries for a while longer and were just about to leave when Rosie said, 'My mummy is getting married and she's going to be like a princess and I'm going to have a lovely dress and flowers in my hair.'

The silence was breathtaking.

'I was going to tell you,' said Sadie, burning with guilt though she knew she had no reason to since she had done nothing wrong. 'It only happened last night.'

'Congratulations,' said Gerald, hugging Sadie then shaking Ray's hand. 'That's wonderful news.' He looked at his wife. 'Isn't it, Harriet dear?'

'Of course. Congratulations,' she said dully and without a smile. 'When is the wedding?'

'We don't know yet,' replied Sadie. 'It's all so new we haven't had a chance to make any arrangements.'

'I'm going to be er . . . er, what am I going to be, Mummy?' asked Rosie.

'My bridesmaid,' said Sadie.

Up went Harriet's brows. 'Oh. You're having a proper wedding then, are you?' she said.

'All weddings are proper, aren't they?' responded Sadie. 'But Rosie will be bridesmaid whatever type of wedding it is.'

'In a church?'

Her question brought to Sadie's mind the fact that this would be the first time for Ray. Having been through it all before she didn't want a big

386

fuss with church bells and the rest of the paraphernalia but she had to consider his feelings on the matter.

Luckily Ray came to her rescue. 'We don't know yet. We need to talk about things. It really is very early days.'

'I'll have more details when I see you next, so I'll tell you all about it then,' Sadie told them. 'But for now, we'd better get going or the traffic will be horrendous as people make their way back to town. I'll give you a call and make arrangements to bring Rosie over.'

'When you can, that will be lovely,' said Gerald reasonably. 'You know we're always pleased to see you.'

Goodbyes were said and Sadie and co. made their way down the hill to the car park. The meeting had cast a shadow over the day for Sadie. She was annoyed with herself for allowing Harriet to have this effect on her and pushed thoughts of her from her mind and joined in the fun with Ray and Rosie.

★　★　★

'I know you're upset, dear,' said Gerald as he and Harriet went on their way through leafy glades and grassy planes. 'But it was almost certain to happen sooner or later and Sadie will still bring Rosie to see us, I'm sure. It's important to Sadie that Rosie keeps her links with her father through us.'

'She says that now,' said his wife miserably, 'but it'll be a different story when they're married. Once he is legally Rosie's stepfather he can do what he likes.'

'He seems a nice enough chap to me,' Gerald remarked. 'I'm sure he won't want to do anything to hurt us or Rosie.'

'It's all right for you,' she snapped. 'You don't feel as strongly for Rosie as I do.'

'Oh, is that right?' He halted in his step and frowned at her. 'How do you know how I feel about Rosie?'

'You never seem to worry whether we see her or not.'

'Just because I don't spend all my time going on about it doesn't mean I don't care,' he said, sounding rattled. 'I am not obsessed about how much time we have with her now and in the future but I am very fond of her.'

'Oh, so I'm obsessed, am I?'

'You are rather, yes.'

'You don't understand the strength of my feelings.'

'Obviously not,' he said. 'But I do know that we must take what we can and cherish the time we do have with our grandchild. We must also treat Sadie with care. If we badger her to see Rosie and disapprove of her marriage too openly, she'll stop coming altogether.'

'By we you mean me, I suppose.'

'Well, you could have been more gracious about her engagement back there.'

'I congratulated her.'

'Through gritted teeth, yes,' Gerald said. 'Your feelings couldn't have been more obvious. There was that crack about a 'proper' wedding, as though you were expecting her forthcoming nuptials to be some sort of a sham.'

'I meant because she's been married before,' Harriet explained. 'Anyway, what am I supposed to do when my son's widow decides to remarry?'

'Be pleased for her and if you can't manage that, pretend,' he suggested. 'Sometimes when Sadie comes to visit, I hold my breath at your attitude towards her. I'm afraid that one day she's going to walk out and never come back.'

'Am I such a bad person, Gerald?'

'I am not saying you are a bad person in general but when it comes to Sadie you can be Satan himself,' he said. 'And all because she happened to be married to your son.'

'Our son.'

'Oh, so you acknowledge the fact that he was my son too then?' he said.

'What do you mean by that?'

'You know very well what I mean.'

They walked on in silence, the dog trotting alongside, sniffing around in the undergrowth from time to time.

'A mother is always more emotionally involved with her child than the father,' she said. 'It's the way of things.'

'All right, Harriet, if you say so,' he said with a sigh of resignation. 'Let's drop the subject, shall we.'

'Yes, I think that would be best.'

He took her hand. 'Cheer up, dear,' he said. 'You've always got me by your side.'

'Thank you, Gerald,' she said. 'We ought to be heading home now anyway.'

They walked down the hill with their adored little dog, too engrossed in their own thoughts to notice the stunning views.

★ ★ ★

Such a lot had happened since Saturday night, the incident at Edith's house had been pushed to the back of Sadie's mind. But when she arrived at work on Monday morning, naturally it came to the fore even though Edith was behaving as though nothing had happened at all. Sadie could tell that she was tense, though, by the sharpness of her attitude and when things quietened down towards the end of morning surgery she asked her how things were at home.

'Fine,' Edith said in such a manner to suggest that Sadie had imagined the goings-on of Saturday night.

'No more problems then.'

'Of course not,' she replied tersely.

'All right, there's no need to bite my blinkin' head off,' Sadie came back at her. 'Having spent a large part of Saturday night trapped in your kitchen against my will when I should have been at a party, I think I'm entitled to ask how things are, don't you?'

At least Edith had the grace to look sheepish. 'Yes, of course. I'm sorry, Sadie.'

Sadie nodded her approval.

'I'm also sorry about what happened,' Edith said, sounding sincere. 'I'm so embarrassed about the whole thing, I suppose I'm just trying to forget it and pretend that it never happened. I

390

feel awful that I involved you and I'm very grateful for your help. Thank you.'

'It's all right.'

'No one would ever have known about it if I hadn't got out of control and hit him with that damned saucepan.'

'I think it might be as well that someone else does know what you have to put up with. But you can consider it forgotten as far as I'm concerned,' Sadie assured her.

'Oh, I would be so grateful,' the older woman said.

'It never happened then.' She looked at her thoughtfully. 'On one condition.'

'Which is?'

'You don't take your personal problems out on the patients,' she began, 'snapping their heads off and so on.'

'I'll try not to and I'm sure I can rely on you to pull me up about it if I do,' Edith said with a wry grin.

'Absolutely!'

Sadie sensed a new understanding between them and knew that if Edith ever asked for her help again she would give it willingly. But, unfortunately, she could never offer it unsolicited. Her colleague didn't have a lot going for her but she did have her pride and Sadie respected that.

15

'Can I stay in the water for a little bit longer to play, Mummy, please?' asked Rosie, who was in the bath.

'Just a few more minutes then,' agreed Sadie, sitting on the stool holding the towel ready for her daughter to be wrapped in. 'Then you've to come out without making a fuss or you'll get cold.'

It was a Saturday evening in October and two months had passed since Ray's proposal. Sadie now wore a diamond solitaire ring on her wedding finger and they were planning to marry in the early summer of next year. Ray agreed with her choice of a small family wedding. Economically as well as emotionally, it made sense.

Obviously Sadie didn't expect her parents to foot the bill the second time around and she herself lived hand-to-mouth, so Ray was funding the wedding. He was also intent upon buying a house locally for them so a reasonably priced event was the sensible option.

It had been a blissful time for Sadie as she'd enjoyed the romance and security of her engagement. She hadn't been looking for love but as it had come her way she welcomed and embraced it, careful to make sure that Rosie was included in her new-found joy and plans for the future. Indeed the little girl seemed very excited and happy about the forthcoming changes.

Therefore it seemed extremely odd to hear her daughter say now, 'I don't want you to marry Uncle Ray because I don't want him to be my daddy.'

Sadie shot her a look, trying not to be overly concerned and reminding herself of the random nature of children's comments. 'Yes, you do, of course you do. You love your Uncle Ray,' she said, noticing the physical perfection of the child at this tender age, her dark hair damp at the ends, olive skin shining as she squirted bathwater from her plastic duck on to herself.

'I do love him but he's bad,' announced Rosie. 'So I don't want him to be my daddy. Can you find somebody else to marry?'

'It doesn't work like that, sweetheart,' Sadie told her. 'But why are you saying such nasty things about Uncle Ray when you know they aren't true?'

'They are true. If he's my daddy and lives in my house he'll hurt me and make me cry,' she said, looking soulfully at her mother.

'Now you're just being silly. Of course he isn't going to hurt you,' said Sadie, beginning to feel uneasy. 'Whatever is making you say such things?'

'Grandma Weston told me,' she replied.

'Oh, I see.' Sadie felt winded with shock. 'What exactly has she been saying?'

'She said that he's not a good person and I'll be sad if he's my dad. So I don't want him to be.' Rosie paused, squeezing water out of the duck and pondering. 'Can I still be the bridesmaid and have the pretty dress, Mum, even if Uncle Ray isn't going to be my dad?'

'Yes, you can still have those things,' Sadie said, deeming it wise to play along with her for the moment.

'Good. Can the dress be pink?'

'Yes, I'm sure that can be arranged.' She paused for only a moment. 'Did Grandma Weston say anything else about Uncle Ray?' she enquired, thinking back over today when she had taken Rosie to Surrey to see her grandparents, going on a Saturday to leave Sunday free to see Ray. She remembered that Harriet had taken Rosie out into the garden to play with the dog. They'd been out there on their own for quite a while so Harriet could have said anything and obviously had, because Rosie wouldn't have invented this.

The child thought for a moment then turned her huge eyes on her mother. 'She said lots of things. She doesn't like Uncle Ray because he's a bad person. She said that you shouldn't be getting married to him because he'll be nasty to me.'

'He isn't bad, I promise you, darling,' Sadie said, careful not to show her fury with Harriet in front of her daughter. 'He isn't going to hurt you, *not ever*. I wouldn't marry anyone who would do that, would I? You know Uncle Ray, he would never do anything to make you sad.' She held out the towel and lifted her daughter out of the bath, wrapping her in the soft, fluffy material. 'Uncle Ray is a very good man and he loves you, I promise you.'

'But Grandma Weston said . . . '

'She was just teasing you,' she fibbed. 'So forget all about it. You and me and Uncle Ray will have a great life together.'

The child seemed pacified but Sadie was incandescent with rage. Harriet had gone too far this time and Sadie wasn't prepared to let it go, she decided furiously, as she dried her little daughter and helped her into clean pyjamas.

★　★　★

'Sadie.' Gerald greeted her with a smile as he opened the front door and ushered her inside, later that same evening. 'We weren't expecting to see you again today.' He spotted the fury in her eyes and frowned. 'Is anything the matter, my dear?'

'Yes, there certainly is. Very much so,' she replied hotly. 'Is Harriet around?'

He led her into the living room where Harriet was sitting in an armchair in her dressing-gown, watching the television.

She looked surprised to see Sadie. 'Oh, you're back,' she observed in an insouciant manner as Gerald went over to the TV set and turned it off. 'Did you leave something behind? You should have telephoned to let us know and Gerald would have met you halfway to cut out some of the journey.'

'I haven't left anything behind and I'll come straight to the point,' Sadie said in a definite manner. 'You have overstepped the mark this time, Mrs Weston, and as a result I shall make sure that Rosie doesn't see you again until she's old enough to make up her own mind about it.'

Harriet leapt out of her chair and glared at Sadie. 'What on earth are you talking about?' she demanded.

'I've put up with more than enough from you over the years but now that you are putting evil ideas into my daughter's head, it ends. *Right now!*'

'Evil ideas? I don't know what you mean.'

'You have been telling Rosie lies about Ray and frightening her,' Sadie said sharply.

'Frightening her?' Harriet looked puzzled but Sadie could see right through her pretence.

'Oh, don't come the innocent with me. You've been telling her that Ray is a bad man and that he will harm her in some way if he becomes her stepfather,' she said. 'How sick is that?'

'Oh Harriet, you didn't,' groaned Gerald, turning pale and looking worried.

'No, I didn't.'

'Liar,' shouted Sadie, seething now. 'Rosie wouldn't make something like that up. She isn't old enough to have the guile. So don't make things worse by denying it. You told her that Ray is a bad man and will do horrid things to her when he is her daddy and make her sad. At least have the grace to admit it.'

'I'm sure I didn't say those exact words,' the older woman prevaricated. 'I may have mentioned the fact that I don't want you to marry him.'

'You and I both know exactly what you said and I have had it verbatim from Rosie. You're a mature woman, a grandmother, for heaven's sake. Can't you see how irresponsible it is to put ideas like that into the mind of a small child?'

'I only . . . '

'You took Rosie outside into the garden with the deliberate intention of poisoning her mind against Ray because you think that he will somehow come between you and Rosie,' Sadie cut in. 'Well, he wouldn't have and neither would he ever harm a hair on Rosie's head. So all you've done is hurt yourself because it's over, Harriet. You won't be seeing Rosie again.'

'Oh no.' She looked stricken, eyes filled with tears, face suffused with pink.

'It's no good looking like that now,' Sadie admonished. 'You've done it to yourself.'

'You promised you would always make sure she was a part of our lives,' she said feebly.

'Yes, I know I did, but you've broken the rules and forced me to reconsider and take this step.' She turned to Gerald. 'I'm so sorry. I know that this is none of your doing and you've been an absolute dear to me ever since I first came to this house. You will be welcome to come and see Rosie if you wish but I won't bring her here again.' She turned back to Harriet. 'You won't be welcome to come with him. I don't want Rosie exposed to your vile tongue ever again. It's too dangerous now that she's growing up.'

'But I love her.'

'You call that love? The only person you love is yourself,' Sadie stated categorically. 'You want Rosie to fill the gap left by Paul. You want to own and possess her as you tried to do with Paul.'

'Please . . . ' begged Harriet.

'I'm sorry but I can't take the chance.' Sadie was adamant. 'I'm getting married next year and Ray will be Rosie's stepfather. I can't have you poisoning her mind against him. It's a dangerous game you're playing, interfering in people's lives through a child.'

'I wasn't . . . '

'Oh, don't deny it.' Sadie was impatient now with Harriet's shabby denials. 'I suppose you thought if you planted these ideas in Rosie's mind, she would start to object to the wedding and I would call it off. That's pure evil and I have no time for that in my life or my daughter's. Now I must go. I dropped everything to come over here when I realised what had been going on. I couldn't leave it and I couldn't do it on the telephone. It was far too important. So I'm going and I won't be back.'

Leaving his wife sinking down into her armchair looking stricken, Gerald went with Sadie to the door.

'I really am sorry for you in all this,' she said with sincerity. 'I know none of it is your fault.'

'I'm sorry too.' He sounded sad but Sadie knew that loyalty to his wife would prevent him from making further comment. 'Take care driving home.'

'Will do,' she said and hurried out to Don's car, which he had allowed her to borrow. She was trembling so much she had to sit for a few moments before driving away and her vision was blurred by tears as she headed towards London.

'I suppose you're going to blame me for that tirade of abuse, are you, Gerald?' said Harriet accusingly as he sat down wearily in his armchair.

'Well, she didn't come all this way after dark because of anything I've done,' he responded.

'Such a fuss over nothing,' she complained. 'As if a child of that age would understand the goings-on of adults.'

'She obviously understands enough to change her mind about Ray,' he pointed out.

'The silly girl,' said Harriet crossly. 'I told her not to say anything to her mother about it.'

He threw her a look.

'All right. I admit I said those things and I regretted it afterwards. I spoke in haste and I guessed it would lead to trouble.'

'Why say wicked things like that in the first place, Harriet?' he asked emotionally. 'In heaven's name, why?'

'I don't know why. I suppose I am so upset at the thought of a replacement for Paul, I spoke without thinking.'

'Rosie never knew Paul so Ray isn't a replacement for him. He'll be the first father she's ever known and it will be good for her and for Sadie,' Gerald said. 'He's going to buy them a house with a garden, so Rosie will be able to have her own room, which will be much better for her as she grows up than being crowded into that small place with Sadie's family. They are going to be a proper little family unit. I wish you could find it in your heart to be happy for your granddaughter if you can't be pleased for Sadie.'

'It's all right for you. You can go and see her whenever you like,' she said nastily, adding meaningfully, 'Depending on where your loyalties lie.'

He chose to ignore the latter part of her dialogue because there were more important issues to deal with. 'It was only a matter of time before something like this happened anyway, the way you carry on towards Sadie,' he pointed out. 'I've warned you about it often enough. For me, knowing that Rosie is loved and being well looked after is far more important than seeing her, as much as I enjoy that.'

'It isn't like that for me.' A sudden darkness engulfed her as memories from the past, stifled for so long, flooded into her mind. She forced them out because they were hardly bearable. 'It's very different for me. Very different indeed.'

'Yes, I realise that,' he said sadly. Whatever the reason for her unhealthy behaviour he knew she would never confide in him about it. Sometimes he felt almost as though he didn't know his wife at all.

★ ★ ★

'What is it with you and Saturday nights?' asked Ray in a light-hearted manner when Sadie finally got home around midnight to find the family in bed and Ray waiting for her. 'That you feel the need to disappear. It was a Saturday night when you went to Edith's.'

400

'Sorry, Ray. I just had to go. Mum said she'd look after Rosie and I twisted Don's arm into letting me borrow his car. I asked Mum to apologise to you on my behalf.'

'She did and it's all right. I was only kidding,' he assured her. 'Some trouble with the Westons, I gather.'

'With Harriet, not Gerald,' she explained. 'I never have any trouble with him.'

Sadie wondered if Ray would be hurt if she told him the details and decided that the truth would be the best thing. It wouldn't be a good idea to start their life together with secrets. So she told him exactly what had happened.

'That woman must be feeling really desperate, to plant ideas like that in Rosie's mind,' was his reaction.

'Desperate? Evil is what I call it.'

'Yes, it is evil but she's motivated by the fact that she fears losing Rosie because of me, and that's the last thing I would ever want to happen. She's very twisted though, I must admit.'

'Very. Which is why I'm not going to allow her to see Rosie any more. I can't take the chance, Ray. If she can tell Rosie lies about you, what will she think up next? I just can't take that risk.'

'No, I suppose not,' he said with a hint of sadness in his tone.

'Do you think I did wrong then?'

'You had no option under the circumstances but it's such a shame she can't be a proper granny like your mum is. It would be better for her and easier for us all,' he said. 'I must say I

401

don't like to think that she would have Rosie afraid of me.'

'Exactly. That's why I can't have her in Rosie's life any more. She could put all sorts of dangerous notions into her head about other things if something happens that she doesn't agree with. Rosie is just a little girl. What an adult says, especially someone as authoritative as a grandmother, is taken to be the truth. Fortunately her memory span at this young age isn't very long so, hopefully, she'll soon forget Harriet's mischief.'

'Mmm, that's true.'

'Anyway, I'm sorry I ruined our evening together,' Sadie said. 'Did you go for a pint to help pass the time?'

Ray nodded. 'I knew you wouldn't be back until late because of the journey so I went down the pub with Don.'

'Thanks for coming back here to wait for me,' she said.

'It never occurred to me to do anything else,' he told her, taking her in his arms. 'I couldn't bear not to see you at all until tomorrow.'

★ ★ ★

Sadie lay in bed with Pickles beside her, thinking over the events of the evening and agonising over her decision to stop Harriet seeing Rosie. Now that her anger had subsided it seemed so cruel but what else could she do, since her priority must be her daughter's well-being? Despite the logic of the situation on her part, she felt

402

desperately sad. Harriet was a pathetic character for all her high-and-mighty attitude. She must be very troubled to behave as she did. Sadie's intellect told her she'd had to take this drastic step because she had to protect her child but her emotions were in turmoil.

Even after all the anguish Harriet had caused her over the years, she pitied her because she was the loser in all this. Sadie's own mother was a fantastic granny to Rosie so the child wouldn't suffer by not seeing Harriet, who didn't have Marge's gift with children anyway. What was it that gave Harriet the need to possess rather than just love? Poor old Gerald; he was a saint the way he put up with her. Sadie doubted if he would come to see Rosie as he would judge such an action to be a betrayal of his wife. For all her faults he was staunchly loyal to her. Was it just duty or did he actually love her? Oddly enough she thought the latter was probably the case.

'Oh well, Pickles,' she said, finding the cat's weight alongside her oddly soothing. 'There's no accounting for some people; all any of us can do is what we think is right and hope for the best.' She gave him a gentle nudge. 'Now move across a bit so that I can turn over. You're taking up half the bed.'

★   ★   ★

'The 'Sergeant Pepper' album by the Beatles is number one in the chart again this week,' Ray remarked to Derek, looking up from some paperwork. 'It's been there for twenty weeks.'

'It's a great album, that's why,' opined Derek, who was becoming very knowledgeable in the music retail trade and enjoying it immensely. 'The Beatles' music is getting better all the time. It seems different to their earlier stuff.'

'They've matured as musicians,' said Ray. 'They've changed in appearance too with their longer hair and moustaches. Their songs are more meaningful now.'

'The punters still love them whatever they do,' Derek pointed out. 'They're having a long run for pop stars, aren't they? Some of the others are a five-minute wonder.'

'The Beatles are more than just pop stars really; they are a phenomenon and very good for our sales figures,' declared Ray. 'Long may it be so.'

Derek looked at Ray, who was wearing a smart suit, white shirt and tie rather than the sweater and casual trousers he usually wore for work. 'Aye, aye, what are you all dressed up for?' he asked in a light-hearted manner.

'I've got to go out for a couple of hours, mate,' Ray explained. 'On a spot of business. So I need you to hold the fort for me while I'm away. Is that all right?'

'Sure,' agreed Derek.

They were good friends as well as colleagues and normally Derek would ask where he was going if Ray hadn't already offered the information. But something about Ray's attitude today made him hold back.

When a man went out all dressed up, smelling of Old Spice and keeping shtum about where he was going, there was usually a woman involved. Derek hoped to God it wasn't the case with Ray, because he couldn't begin to imagine what he and his brother would do to their friend if he cheated on their sister.

* * *

Ray's stomach was churning horribly as he left the shop and headed towards the station. Finally he was doing something he should have done a long time ago and he was as nervous as hell about it. He had no idea what the outcome would be but he did know that it could be avoided no longer. He walked into the booking hall and bought a return ticket to a station near the end of the line in Essex. But instead of heading for the platform, he paused, tempted to turn back. Then he took a deep, calming breath and hurried towards the stairs. He couldn't truly move on with Sadie until this had been done. He had to face up to his demons.

* * *

Time was passing. Christmas was over and the days were lengthening. Rosie was now turned four and old enough to play outside in the street with the other children, something she adored. Even though there were a good few car owners around locally these days, they always travelled slowly along Fern Terrace so the youngsters were still able to do what kids in this street had done for generations.

As parks, gardens and grass verges were resplendent with the colours of daffodils and tulips, Sadie's mind was on her forthcoming nuptials and naturally she wanted to talk about the wedding rather a lot. Ray didn't seem to share her enthusiasm.

'There's ages to go yet,' he said when she broached the subject after the family had gone to bed one night in March.

'Only a couple of months.'

'But it isn't as if we're having a big do, is it?' he said sharply. 'There's no need to go on about it *ad infinitum*.'

'All right,' she retorted. 'There's no need to bite my head off.'

'Sorry.'

'What's the matter with you, Ray?' she asked. 'You've been in a funny mood all evening and you've been odd towards me for a while.'

'Have I?'

'Yes, you have and you must know that, so don't pretend otherwise,' she told him firmly. 'Look, if you're having second thoughts about the wedding, tell me now. Don't humiliate me by leaving me waiting at the registry office.'

'Of course I'm not having second thoughts,' he insisted. 'It's just that . . . well, I thought everything was arranged. Wedding talk is more of a woman's thing.'

'Typical man,' she huffed. 'Arrangements are made, so let's not talk about it any more. Honestly!'

'Come on then, let's talk.'

'I don't feel like it now,' she said with a wry

grin. 'You've spoilt the mood.'

'Oh, come on, I'm sure you can get back into it,' he said, teasing her. 'Tell me again what colour Rosie will be wearing.'

'Now you're just humouring me.'

'I'm trying to make you smile,' he said.

'You've succeeded,' she said, grinning. 'Now about the wedding flowers . . .'

★ ★ ★

Ray walked home deep in thought. Although he'd denied it, Sadie had been right about his mood. He was feeling tense because he hadn't been straight with her. He just couldn't bring himself to do it. It should have been done before the proposal. Now the wedding was looming ever closer and she was still in the dark.

★ ★ ★

'Are you not seeing Ray tonight, love?' enquired Marge of Sadie one evening a week or so later when she settled down on the sofa after dinner.

'No, not tonight. He's staying in to catch up on some paperwork,' she explained. 'He's going to take it all upstairs to the flat and work on it in comfort.'

'If you want to go round and see him I'll listen for Rosie,' offered Marge.

'It's tempting but I suppose I'd better not disturb him. He needs to get his work done.'

'An hour or so won't hurt, surely,' Marge pointed out. 'He'll probably be glad of a break.

407

There's no need to stay long.'

'I'll ring him. See what he thinks.'

'I'd surprise him if I were you,' suggested her mother. 'That will be much more fun.'

'Yeah, maybe I will,' she said after thinking it over. 'I'll pop round there about nine o'clock. He should have done a fair bit of the work by that time.'

* * *

Sadie never ceased to be grateful to her mother for the support she had given so unstintingly since she'd had Rosie. Everything was done with such a willing heart. The last thing Sadie had in mind tonight was a visit to Ray while he was working but Mum had come up with the idea, so why not? Even if she just stayed for half an hour.

She was smiling as she turned off the main shopping street and headed towards Ray's door. That was odd. The shop window was lit as usual but the flat upstairs was in darkness. The office at the back of the shop was used as a stockroom so he wouldn't be working in there because there was no spare space. Puzzled, she rang the bell even though she knew there would be no answer because the place was obviously deserted.

He must have gone out unexpectedly, she told herself. Probably nipped out for a pint to give himself a break. Anyway, he didn't have to account to her for his every movement. She waited for a while, hoping he would come striding down the street. But there was no sign of him. Unwanted thoughts came rushing into her mind. Maybe he'd lied to her about staying in. He had been moody and withdrawn lately. Was this just another symptom of his having fallen out of love with her?

Telling herself she was just being paranoid, she made her way home.

★   ★   ★

The next day she called at the shop in her lunch break on her way home. Ray was serving a customer.

'Hello, sweetheart,' he said, smiling and seeming pleased to see her. 'I'll be with you in a minute. Derek's gone for his dinner break so I'm on my own. Turn the sign to closed for me, would you, love, while I have something to eat?'

He finished with the customer and came out from behind the counter and put his arms around her.

Sadie hated herself for what happened next but she heard herself say, 'How did the paperwork go last night?'

He hesitated and she held her breath, hoping he would give her the explanation she wanted.

'Pretty good, thanks,' he replied, dashing her hopes. 'It needed to be done so I'm glad I got on with it.'

'Did it take long?'

'Yeah. All evening.'

'You didn't even go out for a quick pint for a break then?'

'No, I was here all evening.'

His lie felt like a physical blow because her

409

trust in him had been complete until last night. Ray had been around forever, a trusted family friend long before she had fallen in love with him. It had never occurred to her to doubt him about anything.

'I came round here last night to surprise you,' she told him, moving away. 'So I know that you weren't here.'

The blood drained from his face; he was obviously taken aback. 'Oh, I see. So you were spying on me, were you? We're not married yet, you know,' he said gruffly.

'No we're not, thank God,' she retorted. 'The last thing I want is to be married to a liar. You knew you wouldn't be at home last night, didn't you? You lied to me when you said you were staying in.'

There was a brief hiatus then he said, 'Yes, that's right.'

'You're not even going to try to deny it then.'

'There's no point since I've already admitted the truth.'

'I knew there was something wrong these past few months,' she said through dry lips, holding back the tears. 'You've been behaving oddly towards me for a while.'

Ray stared at her, his face pale and set in a grim expression. He made no attempt to deny it or give any sort of explanation. He just stood looking at her in silence.

'You didn't even have the courage to be straight with me and admit you want to call the wedding off,' Sadie said, twisting off her engagement ring and handing it to him so

410

forcefully she almost threw it. 'So I've done it for you. That must be a great relief to you, I'm sure. You can have the job of cancelling all the wedding arrangements, since you would have been paying for them.'

She rushed out of the shop and hurried down the street, turning to look back at the corner in the hope that he would be coming after her. But his shop door remained closed. It was over and he hadn't even tried to get her back.

★   ★   ★

Sadie spent the rest of the day hoping that Ray might contact her, first at the surgery and then at home. But there was no word. Naturally the family guessed there was something wrong.

'Is Ray coming round tonight?' asked Marge when they were all sitting around watching 'Coronation Street'.

'No.'

'Is there something wrong?'

'Yes, you could say that.' She waved her left hand about. 'It's all over between Ray and me,' she said, her voice breaking. 'The wedding is off.'

There was a communal intake of breath. 'You've had a tiff then,' speculated her mother.

'Far more serious than a tiff but I don't want to talk about it, so I'd be grateful if you could leave it, please,' Sadie told them, and rushed upstairs to the bedroom in tears.

★   ★   ★

411

Someone had their finger pressed on Ray's doorbell so hard that it was ringing continuously.

'All right, I'm coming,' he shouted, hurrying down the stairs and opening the door. 'Oh, it's you two.'

'Surely you must have been expecting us,' said Don, pushing his way inside followed by his brother.

'No. Why would I?'

'You upset our sister and you upset us,' explained Derek. 'Sadie is at home in her bedroom crying her eyes out and we don't like that, do we, Don; we don't like that at all. So what have you to say for yourself?'

'Nothing. It's a private matter between Sadie and me and I'm buggered if I'm going to tell you about it.'

'Oh nice, very nice,' said Don sarcastically, pushing Ray hard in the chest. 'So you break our sister's heart and we're not allowed to know why.'

'That's right,' said Ray. 'I admire the family solidarity but it isn't anything to do with you.'

'Of course it is,' said Don. 'It's family business.'

'Who do you think you are? A member of the Mafia or something? Sadie is a grown-up. She doesn't need you two rushing about like overgrown schoolboys in her defence.'

They stared at him menacingly.

'You can hit me if you like,' Ray invited them. 'It might make you feel better but it won't mend things between Sadie and me because only she and I can do that.'

'I knew you were up to no good when you started taking time off from the shop all dressed up every now and again. Swanning off drenched in aftershave,' said Derek. 'You dirty bugger.'

Ray looked at them but made no comment.

'Sorry, Ray, I know you're a mate and all that but I've got to do this,' said Don and threw a punch at Ray, which sent him reeling against the stairs.

Ray sat on the bottom stair holding his jaw, making no move to retaliate. 'Feel better now, do you?' he asked.

'Not really,' said Don.

'How about you,' he said to Derek. 'Do you want to have a pop at me too?'

'What with my heart condition, I'm not that stupid,' he replied. 'And there's also the fact that you pay my wages.'

'Oh, so you're prepared to carry on taking my money despite your disgust with me for breaking your sister's heart?'

'You've got to be realistic about these things, mate,' Derek said. 'It doesn't need two of us to show our loyalty to Sadie.'

'I'm glad your common sense hasn't deserted you altogether while you rush about doing a bad impression of the Kray twins.' Ray looked from one to the other. 'Anyway, if you've done what you came to do you can bugger off and leave me in peace.'

Derek opened the front door then turned to look at Ray. 'You must be mad to screw things up with Sadie. You'll never find anyone better than her,' he said.

'Do you really think I need you to tell me that?' said Ray, sounding grim.

Neither of the brothers knew what to say after that so they left quietly, closing the door behind them. Ray stayed where he was on the stairs for a long time, lost in thought. Then he went up to the flat and turned the television off because he couldn't bear the noise. It aggravated his sensitised nervous system even more.

* * *

Even Pickles couldn't soothe Sadie tonight, though he was ensconced on the bed beside her. She lay still, listening to her daughter's even breathing and thanking God for her. Whatever else was inconsistent in her life, her love for Rosie remained constant. The feelings of a mother for a child were the strongest love of all, in her opinion. Nothing else compared to it.

But the love for a man was powerful too and her thoughts turned again to Ray and she decided that the most obvious explanation for his dishonesty was another woman. Yet somehow this didn't fit her idea of him. Maybe, because she didn't want to face up to it, her mind told her it couldn't be true. She supposed that was how it was for anyone who had been cheated on. But he was a man and these things happened.

Whatever he'd been up to wasn't the point. He'd lied to her and that was what she couldn't take. She herself was straightforward in the way she lived her life; it was how she had been brought up. So lies were anathema to her.

In an effort to take her mind off her aching heart, she tried to concentrate on the practicalities of their broken engagement; the fact that Rosie would be so disappointed not to be a bridesmaid and the money she had spent on the dress and other things was wasted. She would have to make sure that Ray cancelled things or he would lose money too. But none of this seemed to matter. All she could think of was the expression in Ray's eyes when he'd told her that he was lying. There was anger and guilt, even a touch of defiant arrogance, but there was something else too that she couldn't quite identify. It had seemed to be a profound sadness. She supposed he was sorry he had burnt his boats. But it was more than that, she was sure of it. Yet because of the way Ray was, she would probably never know.

Obviously she would have to see him because he lived locally and was her brothers' friend, so it wasn't going to be easy to put the whole heartbreaking business out of her mind.

★ ★ ★

Marge piled some mashed potato on top of the mince she had cooked with onions, carrots and seasoning to make a shepherd's pie for lunch. She looked at the kitchen clock and saw that it was half an hour until Sadie was due home from the family planning clinic so the potato should be nicely browned by the time she got in and ready to eat. She put some cabbage into a saucepan of salted boiling water and opened the back door to let the steam out. The front door was always left open when Rosie was playing out so a fresh breeze blew through the house.

It was a lovely spring day; just the weather for Rosie to play outside. Marge frowned as she remembered Sadie being so upset, having broken up with Ray recently. She was putting on a brave face but her tired, shadowed eyes indicated that she wasn't sleeping. It was such a pity this had happened because she and Ray had been so good together. They had seemed very happy, so Gawd knows what had gone wrong.

Still preoccupied with thoughts of Sadie, Marge went to the front door to tell Rosie that she must come in soon and get ready for her meal. The last time Marge had looked out the pre-school kids had been sitting on the front wall. They weren't there now so they must have moved up the street a bit to play outside one of the other houses. Going to the gate she saw that the street was devoid of children. They'd all gone in to next door but one to play inside with little Melanie who lived there, she guessed.

''Ello, Dot,' said Marge when Melanie's mother answered the door to her. 'Rosie's got to come for her dinner now.'

'Rosie's not here, love,' said Dot.

'Oh, the kids must have all gone in somewhere else then.'

'Melanie came in ten minutes ago,' said Dot.

'Really.' Marge was beginning to feel uneasy. 'Could you ask her if she knows where Rosie is, please?'

Dot called into the house and Melanie

appeared and said she thought Rosie had gone in for her dinner.

'We all said we were going in for dinner 'cause we were hungry,' she said. 'We're going out again after.'

Panic was beginning to rise but Marge managed to stay in control. 'Oh,' she said. 'I'll call at the other kids' houses. She must have gone in somewhere.'

Seeing how worried Marge had become, Dot said, 'I'll help you look for her, love. Just give me a minute while I turn the gas off under the gravy and I'll be there.'

Rosie wasn't at the homes of any of the other children. She wasn't round the back alley or anywhere in the street. Marge was just beginning to accept the awful truth, that Rosie had disappeared, when Sadie came hurrying down the street to see her mother and some neighbours gathered outside the Bells' house.

'What's this?' she asked lightly. 'A mother's meeting?'

'Oh Sadie, love,' said Marge, trying not to frighten her by showing the depth of her concern. 'I'm sure there's no cause for alarm at this stage but . . . '

'What's happened, Mum?' Sadie asked, looking worried now.

'Your Rosie has gone missing,' Dot blurted out.

'Missing?' She couldn't take it in. 'What do you mean?'

'She was playing out and when I came to bring her in for her dinner, she'd gone,' her

mother explained. 'She must be around somewhere but . . . ' Her voice tailed off.

'Oh no, please God, not Rosie, not my little
girl.'

Sadie thought she might pass out as the word
every mother dreads hearing rang and resounded
in her head. Someone supported her as her legs
seemed about to buckle. She wanted to be sick
and couldn't get her breath. Somehow she
managed to stay on her feet as she gasped, 'I'm
going to call the police.'

16

Ray felt a buzz of excitement in the near-certainty that he was about to close the sale of an expensive electric guitar. The customer — a part-time musician and guitar enthusiast who worked in an office by day — had been in the shop drooling over the instrument every Saturday for ages. Now he seemed ready to buy; he'd even faked a dental appointment to get time off from work to come to the shop during the week when it was less busy.

'It's a fabulous piece of gear,' he sighed adoringly, gazing at the red and white Gibson, which was similar to the type used by the Shadows.

Ray nodded. 'I won't argue with you about that.' He had invested a great deal of time and effort in this customer, over the course of several weeks, and was hopeful of a lucrative conclusion. 'Anyone would be proud to own it.'

'You did say you can fix me up with HP, didn't you?' asked the young man. 'Only I can't afford to pay outright.'

'Yes, we can arrange all that for you,' Ray assured him.

A woman came into the shop and went straight over to the counter where Derek was waiting to serve her. She'd come to collect a record her son had ordered.

'That will please my boy when he gets in from

work tonight,' she said chattily as Derek put it into a paper bag for her. 'He loves the Rolling Stones.'

'He isn't the only one, judging by the amount of their records we sell,' remarked Derek in a friendly manner.

'Their music is just a blinkin' racket to me but that's because I'm old, according to my boy. Honestly, you can't hear yourself think in our 'ouse when he's got his records on. Me and my ole man are always going on at him about it but he takes no notice.' She raised her eyes, sighing. 'Teenagers, eh!'

Derek nodded politely.

'He made less noise when he was little and screaming the place down,' she went on. 'I never thought I'd ever say this but I'll be glad when he leaves home.'

'Don't believe you,' Derek kidded her. 'You'll miss him like mad when he goes.'

'Yeah, I expect you're right.' She took the paper bag from Derek. 'Kids, what can you do with them, eh?' She paused for a moment, her manner becoming serious. 'Terrible business about the little girl who's gone missing from round here, isn't it?'

'We don't know anything about it,' Derek told her. 'What happened?'

'She disappeared from right outside her own house; there one minute, gone the next,' she informed him gravely. 'Four years old, the poor mite. I mean, what sort of a person would take an innocent little thing like that?'

'Some sick bugger and there are a few of those

about.' Derek drew in his breath, shaking his head. 'I've got a niece of that age. It makes my blood run cold to think of her getting taken. The kiddie's family must be going through hell.'

The woman nodded in agreement. 'She could have just wandered off, of course, and not been taken at all,' she suggested. 'It's too early to say for sure. It's not long happened. I only know about it because my neighbour has a sister living in the same street and she'd been visiting there.'

'Are the police out looking for the little girl?'

'Oh yeah, my neighbour said the cops are everywhere.'

'Let's hope they find her soon then,' he said.

'Not half,' the woman responded. 'My thoughts will certainly be in Fern Terrace until they do.'

'Fern Terrace,' gasped Derek.

'Fern Terrace,' echoed Ray, who had been half-listening and now deserted his customer and came over. 'Any idea what the missing child's name is?'

'I'm not sure,' the woman said, thinking about it, 'but I've got an idea my neighbour referred to her as Rosie.'

Derek turned pale and Ray said to his customer, 'Sorry, sir, but I have to go.'

'Go . . . but you're in the middle of serving me and I want to buy the guitar.'

'Can you come back another time, please?' he asked quickly. 'I really am very sorry but something extremely urgent has come up and we are closing the shop.'

The customer looked peeved. 'I took time off

work specially to come here,' he grumbled.

'I know you did and I wouldn't do this if it wasn't absolutely vital,' said Ray, the much-wanted sale having lost its importance in the light of events.

'Oh well, if you don't want my business I can easily go elsewhere,' the customer said gruffly.

'That's up to you,' said Ray in an even tone. 'I really am sorry but we have to be somewhere else.'

The two men ushered the people out and hurried to Ray's car and drove like fury to Fern Terrace. Derek was so distracted he forgot he had his own car parked at the back of the shop.

★ ★ ★

Every knock at the door and ring of the phone was like a sharp knife scraping on a plate to Sadie's shattered nervous system. She wanted news but was terrified of what it might be. The police had been to the house to take details and a photograph so that they could mount a search for Rosie. Sadie wanted to go out looking herself but they asked her to stay at home in case the little girl turned up. She had never been much of a churchgoer but she was praying like mad now.

Her mother was riddled with guilt and blamed herself entirely as Rosie had been in her care when it had happened. But, as Sadie pointed out to her, it had been Sadie's own decision to let Rosie play in the street as she herself had at that age. This was a friendly neighbourhood. It had never occurred to anyone that it wasn't safe.

She'd tried to assure her mother that she had nothing to blame herself for but Marge didn't seem convinced.

There was talk of Rosie having wandered off but Sadie knew there was more to it than that. 'Don't go away' had been drummed into the child too deeply and she knew she had to stay close to home. Anyway, none of the other children had disappeared and Rosie wouldn't have gone off on her own. So Sadie knew in her heart that she had been taken and the thought of it made her feel physically ill.

When Derek burst in followed by Ray, she collapsed into tears.

'There there, sis,' said her brother, putting his arms around her. 'We'll find her, won't we, Ray? Why didn't you give us a bell? We'd have been here sooner.'

'We were going to,' she told him, struggling to stop crying. 'We just hadn't got around to it. We were hoping they'd find her and it wouldn't be necessary.'

Ray took in the scene: Sadie in tears, her mother whey-faced with anguish, Derek distracted with worry. Ray himself was distraught but, not being family, he was slightly less emotionally involved and saw it as his duty as their friend to stay strong and give them the support they needed.

'Would you like me to fetch Don from work and let Cyril know?' he offered.

'I think you'd better,' replied Marge. 'Thanks, Ray.'

Ray went over to Sadie, who was standing by

the window. Derek had now moved away.

'I won't tell you not to worry because I know that would be impossible,' he said. 'But everybody is doing all they can. When I've got your dad and Don we'll go out looking as well as the police. Rosie will be back.'

'She's been taken, Ray,' she said. 'I know she has. She wouldn't just wander off. That isn't the way Rosie is.' She mopped her streaming eyes. 'She'll be so scared, she's only little. She'll be wanting me and missing all of us. I can't bear to think about what her abductor might be doing to her.'

'Hey, steady on.' He held his arms out to her and she went into them without hesitation. 'Shush,' he said softly. 'We don't know what's happened yet.' He kissed the top of her head. 'I'll go and get your dad and brother and we'll be back soon so you'll have all your family around you.'

'Thanks, Ray,' she said, her eyes red and swollen. His lies and the reason for them seemed long ago and trivial compared to what had happened since.

There was no room in her life at the moment for anything except the disappearance of her darling daughter. All her mental and emotional energy was channelled into that.

* * *

The afternoon ticked by slowly, every minute long and agonising. The policemen came back to tell them that they were doing everything they

424

possibly could to find her, searching alleyways and garden sheds and allotments as well as the streets. Ray came back with Cyril and Don and they all went out looking for her. Marge made endless pots of tea and Sadie stood by the window looking out and longing for her daughter to appear.

When darkness fell the men came back and a policeman called to inform them that they would be calling off the search until morning. Sadie reached her lowest ebb, nightfall seeming like a loss of hope. She could hardly bear to guess where her daughter might be but couldn't stop her imagination running riot with visions of a pervert who might do God only knows what to her. Everybody was doing all they could to help and support her but she felt isolated and alone.

★ ★ ★

Gerald Weston was surprised to see the house in darkness when he got home from work because Harriet was always there to greet him. In fact he couldn't remember ever having returned from the office to find it otherwise. He was alarmed by the break in normality, fearing that she was ill and had collapsed.

'Harriet,' he called as he entered the hall and turned on the lights. 'Harriet, where are you?'

Silence washed around him. He rushed from room to room, calling her name. Upstairs, downstairs and in the garden. No sign of her. Heart pounding and sick with worry, he was about to go next door to see if the neighbours

425

had seen her today when he noticed a folded piece of paper in the kitchen by the kettle.

Dear Gerald,
    I'm sorry to have to leave you but I must put my duty to our granddaughter first and I am taking her to a better place.
    Harriet

'Oh my God, Harriet, what have you done,' he said to an empty house and hurried to the telephone in the hall, searching for the Bells' number in the address book with trembling hands.

* * *

'Have you any idea at all where your wife might have taken Rosie, Mr Weston? Any favourite haunts?' asked one of the policemen who had come back to the Bells' house when they had telephoned to tell them that there was a new lead. The family had been asked to leave the room so that Gerald could be on his own with the officers for the interview.

'I'm afraid I haven't. The whole thing is a complete mystery to me,' said Gerald worriedly. He had come over immediately after he'd spoken to Marge and discovered that Rosie was already missing, checking only to see if his wife had taken any clothes with her. 'I can't think of anywhere at all she would have gone. It must have been a spur-of-the-moment thing because she doesn't seem to have taken any of her things.'

'And your wife had given no indication that something like this might happen.'

'No, but she has been very depressed lately.' He paused in thought. 'She's never really got over the death of our son, and since we stopped seeing our granddaughter she's been very low indeed. She's obsessed with the idea that the child's future stepfather will not be good to her and she can't let it go.'

'Would you care to enlarge on that, sir?' asked the policeman.

Gerald told them what had led up to Sadie keeping Rosie away and filled him in on the background.

'Mmm, I see.' The officer looked at the note again. '"To a better place",' he read thoughtfully. 'An ambiguous message, wouldn't you say?'

'Yes, I would,' agreed Gerald. 'It could mean she's taken the little girl to another town or . . . she could have some sort of suicide thing in mind.' He put his hands to his head in despair.

'Do you think her state of mind is such that she could be capable of something like that?'

Gerald thought back to the time since Paul's death and Harriet's increasingly odd behaviour: her reclusiveness, her obsession with Rosie and her attack on Sadie that had caused Rosie to be a premature baby. He thought of how — time and time again — he had tried to reason with her about things and she had become beyond sensible communication on the subject of Rosie.

He looked across at the policeman. 'I don't know for sure but I think it might be possible for her to have something like that in mind.' To his acute embarrassment Gerald felt tears running down his cheeks and he took a handkerchief out of his pocket and wiped his eyes. 'We have to find them.' He stared at the floor. 'You see, I know my wife is a very difficult woman and everyone is concerned about Rosie, as indeed I am, but I'm worried about my wife too, even though she's done this terrible thing.'

'Naturally.'

'I think she must be ill,' he went on, 'and she only has me. She's driven everyone else away.'

'I see.' The policeman looked at some notes he was holding. 'I understand that you live in Surrey. Do you think your wife would be likely to have taken the little girl to somewhere near to where you live or further afield?'

'I really don't know, officer,' Gerald said, spreading his hands in a helpless gesture. 'I feel as though I don't know my wife at all. She never goes to London on her own but she must have done so to have taken Rosie. She must have been waiting and watching by the house for a chance to snatch her. The woman I know wouldn't have had the courage to go into London on her own, let alone abduct a child. She normally doesn't go further than our village without me. Although she is outspoken and given to rages, she is actually very lacking in confidence.'

'Well, we need to find her and the little girl with all possible speed so if you can cast your mind back to anything she might have said over the last few days that may give us a clue. Let us know if anything comes to mind.' He paused. 'One last thing; do you have a photograph of

428

your wife so that we can get that circulated along with that of the little girl?'

'Yes, I have one in my wallet,' he said, taking it out of his inside pocket.

★ ★ ★

In the other room Sadie was wondering which was worse, imagining her daughter with some vile pervert of a man or with her crazy mother-in-law, and decided that they were both equally as terrifying. Sadie knew what Harriet was capable of; she'd experienced it first-hand in the toilets of the courts. Surely she wouldn't hurt an innocent child though. For all her faults she did love Rosie in her own twisted way. But Harriet couldn't be in her right mind to do a thing like this, so who could say what she might do while so disturbed? And the worst part was that no one had any idea where she might have gone.

Gerald came back into the room followed by the policemen who said they were going back to the police station with the new information, which they thought would help with the search. 'We'll see ourselves out,' one of them said and they left.

Sadie looked at Gerald and saw the defeated stoop of his shoulders. All the pain and worry of the last few hours culminated in uncontrollable anger towards him.

'Why didn't you put your foot down with that crazy wife of yours?' she shrieked. 'If you'd not been so weak and stood up to her she might have been a half-decent human being instead of an evil old witch, completely devoid of empathy. As it is, she's taken my child, my baby, and God only knows what she'll do to her.'

'Sadie, that's enough,' admonished her father. 'It isn't Gerald's fault.'

But Sadie was beside herself and out of control. 'She's taken my daughter,' she screamed and lunged towards Gerald with her fists clenched.

'All right, Sadie,' said Ray, and gently but firmly led her from the room and into the kitchen, where she sat at the kitchen table with her head in her hands and sobbed.

'Oh, what have I done?' she wept, her voice ragged with emotion. 'Laying into poor Gerald like that.'

'He knows you're upset and you didn't really mean it,' he said soothingly.

'I don't know what came over me,' she sobbed. 'I must apologise to him.'

'Later,' he suggested. 'When you're feeling calmer. For now, just sit here with me for a while.'

She blew her nose and managed a watery smile. 'As long as you don't offer me a cup of tea,' she said thickly. 'I'm swimming in the stuff.'

'I won't, I promise,' he said.

★   ★   ★

Nobody wanted to go to bed. Sadie suggested that the others go, just to rest if they couldn't sleep, but she herself couldn't face that room

430

without Rosie and the thought of all those silent hours staring at the ceiling, plagued by her fertile imagination. So she opted for a blanket and an armchair in the living room. Ray took the other chair and stayed with her. His presence was as comforting as anything could be at this terrible time. He was the only person she wanted with her. Every now and then she dozed, only to feel even worse when she awoke with a start and remembered. Her mouth was parched, her insides in knots and her head aching. Oh, please bring my little girl home safe, she cried silently as the grey light of dawn crept through the curtains.

★ ★ ★

'When can I go home to my Mummy, Grandma?' asked Rosie nervously the next morning when she awoke in a hotel bedroom she was sharing with Harriet.

'When I say so, dear,' Harriet replied.

'But I want to go now.'

'Don't keep on pestering. Grandma will look after you. We are going to have such a lovely holiday.'

'But I miss my mummy and my pussy Pickles and Uncle Ray and everybody.'

Harriet experienced a moment when all of this seemed unreal and for a second she couldn't remember where they were. Of course, she thought, when the feeling of unreality passed, we are in a bed-and-breakfast hotel at the seaside, which she'd thought was the best place to take a

431

child as the sea air would be good for her health. It was certainly a better place for her than London with the threat of an evil stepfather looming.

The last twenty-four hours or so was something of a blur but she remembered thinking how easy it had been to take Rosie. She'd waited at the end of the street where Rosie had been playing and when the other children had gone in she'd walked up to her, taken her hand and told her they were going on a holiday to the seaside. Because she wasn't a stranger, Rosie had gone with her without argument.

Later it had become much more difficult because the child was asking to go home to her mother and snivelling more or less constantly. Harriet was confident that it would pass as Rosie's other life faded from her memory. Meanwhile she had to get her breakfasted and deal with the practicalities, such as clothes and toiletries for them both. Having acted on a sudden impulse, she had walked out of her home with nothing except her handbag, purse and cheque book.

'We're going downstairs to have breakfast and then we are going to go to the shops and buy some new clothes for us both,' she said. 'Won't that be lovely?'

'I want my mummy.'

'Don't be silly, Paul,' she said. 'I am your mummy. Now come along. Let's give you a wash and get some breakfast.'

'My name is Rosie. Not Paul.'

'Yes, yes of course it is,' Harriet said absently.

'Now come along and no more of that silly crying.'

She led the sobbing, homesick child along the landing to the bathroom.

★　★　★

Rosie had been missing for more than two days and, unable to stand being at home with nothing to take her mind off her thoughts, Sadie had gone to work though she felt ill with despair and her concentration was patchy. Edith was kind and covered for her and the doctors were very understanding.

When Sadie got home at lunchtime on day three, her mother handed her the newspaper.

'Surely someone will see this and recognise them and get in contact with the police,' she said as photographs of both Rosie and Harriet leapt out at Sadie from the front page under the heading *MISSING*. 'It's one of the nationals so has a huge readership. It was well worth your giving that reporter an interview.'

'I only did it because I thought it would help, even though I didn't like the idea of it being splashed across the papers,' Sadie said, made tearful again by the picture of her little girl. 'Oh Mum, I'm so scared that Harriet will harm her.'

'We'll just have to hang on to the fact that she's her grandmother and does seem fond of her.'

'I'm clinging to that but it's her state of mind I'm bothered about,' she said. 'If she is sick enough to abduct a child, who knows what else she might do, especially as she left that frightening note.'

'Try not to think about that,' advised Marge, 'and hope we get some news soon.'

'Yeah. Okay.'

Derek and Ray came in with a copy of the paper and a positive attitude.

'Someone is bound to see them and recognise them now,' said Ray, who had been a rock to Sadie these last few days. He was the only person who seemed able to give her any comfort. Their broken engagement wasn't mentioned; physical contact was affectionate rather than romantic or sexual. Everything was put to one side because of the current crisis. 'This is just what we need. Good solid nationwide coverage.'

Sadie's nerves jangled as the phone rang. It turned out to be Gerald, who called every day for an update. He had also seen the paper. Her father and brother arrived simultaneously, using their dinner break to see how things were. Despite the depth of her distress Sadie was still able to feel profound gratitude towards her caring family. She also valued Ray's support enormously. Whatever happened between them in the future, she would always be grateful to him for the endless strength and comfort he had bestowed upon her during this terrible time.

★ ★ ★

It was a bright and sunny Sunday, and Brighton seafront was awash with brightly dressed day trippers, the beach a mass of deckchairs.

Harriet and Rosie were among the crowds on the seafront. The latter had seemed off-colour this past couple of days. She'd been complaining of feeling sick and had barely eaten a thing, something Harriet put down to homesickness and therefore assumed that it would pass. In Harriet's present state of mind, empathy was almost non-existent but she did feel bad when the child cried herself to sleep at night. She'd tried everything she knew to soothe her but Rosie had been inconsolable.

Knowing that she had done the right thing in removing her from an environment which wasn't good for her and which was soon to include a stepfather, eased Harriet's conscience. She had, after all, brought her granddaughter to a much better place. What could be a healthier environment than a seaside town for a child? Rosie's negative feelings would soon pass.

In occasional moments of rational thought, Harriet wondered about accommodation in the long-term since they couldn't stay in a hotel indefinitely and needed their own place. But as she couldn't let anyone, not even Gerald, know where they were it wouldn't be easy. She had a cheque book for their joint account but she had no idea how much was in it, which was why she'd gone to a cheap guest house rather than a good-class hotel. Gerald looked after their finances and she had a feeling he had larger amounts of money invested elsewhere. Fortunately, these worries were short-lived because she soon retreated into a dreamlike world where she didn't look much beyond the current moment.

'Can we go on to the beach, Grandma?' asked Rosie.

'Yes, we certainly can,' she replied, heartened by this show of interest.

'And perhaps you'd like an ice cream.'

'Yes, please,' the little girl said.

That was more like it, thought Harriet. 'Would you like a cornet or a wafer?'

'A cornet, please.'

At least that would get some nourishment inside her, thought her grandmother, as she handed the ice cream to her. She'd eaten so little she would be ill if she didn't have something to sustain her.

'Come on then,' she said. 'Let's go on to the beach and find somewhere to sit.'

Making rather an odd-looking couple — Harriet in a frumpy grey jumper and longish dark skirt completely incongruous with their surroundings, and Rosie in a frilly frock that was too long for her and more suited to a party than Brighton beach, chosen by Harriet who had no idea about modern dress and had thought a special sort of outfit might cheer her up — they made their way across the pebbles and found a couple of deckchairs.

'Do you want to go for a paddle, dear?' asked Harriet when Rosie had finished her ice cream.

'No, thank you, Grandma.'

'There are lots of children at the sea's edge for you to play with,' suggested Harriet.

'I don't want to go.'

Leaning back in the chair in the sunshine,

Harriet felt exhausted suddenly. It had been a hectic few days and the extra physical activity had taken its toll on her. Her lids began to droop and she drifted off to sleep. Rosie stared at the sea and the children playing; they reminded her of how she played with her friends in the street at home. She started to cry quietly, not wanting to wake her grandmother, who got cross when she cried. She was too young to define such feelings as loneliness but she was old enough to ache for her mother.

★ ★ ★

There was a middle-aged couple wearing 'kiss me quick' hats and eating fish and chips out of newspaper sitting next to Rosie and Harriet. The man, who had taken his shirt off and rolled his trouser legs up to catch the sun, was looking out to sea; the woman was watching the odd couple nearby.

She was particularly struck with the little girl, who looked so desperately sad. It was no wonder, making a kid wear a dress like that to the seaside. It would look more at home on a bridesmaid. The poor thing started to cry and the onlooker wanted to go and comfort her.

'Now Bet, don't be nosy,' warned her husband when she drew his attention to her.

'But she looks so miserable, George,' she said.

'She'll go off and play in a minute, I expect,' he suggested. 'That'll soon cheer her up.'

'The old lady has gone to sleep and she should be watching her,' Bet told him in concern. 'She can't be more than about four. She could run off and get drowned in the sea.'

'She doesn't look as if she wants to go anywhere. Anyway it's nothing to do with us,' he said, holding a chip ready to eat. 'So stop staring at them and eat your food.'

Bet did as he said.

'Do you think the woman is her grandma?' she enquired after a while.

'She's knocking on a bit so I expect she is her gran,' he responded without a great deal of interest.

'I wonder where her mother is.'

'Who knows? The gran is probably looking after her so her mum can have some peace or something.'

'But the girl is so miserable.'

'So did I used to be when I was left with me gran,' he told her. 'She was a right stickler for making us do as we were told. We were terrified of her. It'll be the same with that little mite.'

'She's just sitting there and that ain't natural for a kiddie on a beach; look at all the others playing.'

'Oh, give it a rest, Bet, will yer?' he urged. 'We're supposed to be having a nice day out together, not poking our noses into other people's business.'

'Do you think the old woman is mistreating her and that's why she's sad?'

'Go over and ask her if you fancy the idea of a black eye,' he suggested. 'People come here for recreation, not to have nosy parkers like you watching their every move.'

'Yeah, I suppose you're right,' she said. 'Looks as if they're going now anyway.'

'Thank Gawd for that,' he said. 'Perhaps you'll shut up about them now.'

She watched as the little girl walked past; such a pretty little thing with the most gorgeous dark eyes. It was a pity they'd been filled with tears for most of the time she had been here.

★ ★ ★

'Where are we going now, Grandma?' asked Rosie.

'Back to the hotel, dear. Your grandma needs to rest for a while. I'm very tired.'

'I wish I had someone to play with,' said the little girl.

'You wish that, you want that,' snapped Harriet, irritable with weariness. 'Try being grateful for what you already have for a change and stop whining.'

'Sorry, Grandma,' said Rosie miserably as they headed away from the seafront towards the town.

★ ★ ★

'We'll make a move soon, shall we, Bet?' suggested George. 'The pubs will be open by now and we can have a few drinks before we get the train home, can't we?'

'Not half.'

He stretched lazily and looked at his arms and legs. 'I've got a nice bit of colour on me anyway.'

'Not as much as I have,' she grinned, putting

439

her arm against his to compare. 'I've cooked very nicely this afternoon.' She looked at her scarlet legs, her skirt pulled well up over her knees. 'It's stinging a bit but it's worth it.'

'The pubs will be packed,' he remarked, seeing people heading off the beach as he rolled down his trouser legs and put on his socks and shoes. 'We'll have to wait ages to get served.'

'Don't matter. It's all a part of the day out,' she said, slipping her feet into her sandals.

'I suppose so,' he conceded. 'There would be no atmosphere without the crowds.'

'Exactly!' She stood up and gathered her things together. 'If you could carry the bag, George, I'll take the rubbish to the bin and catch you up.'

'Righto, love.'

★ ★ ★

Trudging across the pebbles to the litter bin, she found it was full up. She'd have to roll the fish and chip paper into a smaller ball to get it in. Having screwed it tighter, she pushed it in, and it was as she was trying to secure it that something caught her eye and she took it out and stared, her eyes bulging. On the outer part of the newspaper ball was a photograph of someone she had seen quite recently. Unravelling the rest of the paper she read the print, her heart racing.

'Oh, my good Gawd,' she said out loud. 'George, George, wait for me. George, look at this.'

* * *

Every evening the Bell family plus Ray sat around in the living room waiting for news, and every night the telephone and the front door knocker remained frighteningly silent.

'Why don't you boys go down the pub for a break later on,' suggested Sadie on Sunday night. Her nerves were raw and almost at breaking point in the evenings. All day she lived in hope and tried to stay positive but as darkness fell yet again with no news, her spirits plummeted and she found it a strain having to put up a front for the sake of the others. 'There's no need for you to stay in every night.'

'There might be news,' said Don.

'We'll soon let you know if there is,' said Sadie. 'The pub is only down the street.'

'We can't desert you,' said Derek.

'You won't be deserting me,' she assured them. 'Not if I tell you to go.'

'I think she wants us out of the way,' said Ray.

'I want to break this awful nightly pattern,' she admitted. 'This terrible routine of waiting every evening is making nervous wrecks of us all. I think it would do you good to go out. You and Dad can go as well if you like, Mum.'

'I'm not going anywhere and leaving you at a time like this,' declared Marge.

'And neither are we,' added her father.

'Oh well, see how you feel later. But please don't think that you have to stay in because of me.'

Watching her daughter, Marge's pride in her

441

was renewed yet again. Sadie had been so brave throughout this whole terrible ordeal; keeping going and trying to stay positive. Even now she was thinking of the others though Marge suspected she found it wearing having everyone around. It hardly seemed possible that Marge had despaired of her daughter's selfishness and lack of empathy when she was younger. But she'd risen to the challenge of motherhood magnificently and changed almost overnight. So Marge thought she must have done something right in bringing her up, even if she had had to fight to stop the men of the family from ruining her altogether.

* * *

'I think you're being over-dramatic, Bet,' said George when his wife smoothed the crumpled newspaper out on the pub table, having been going on about it ever since she'd spotted the photograph. 'It would be too much of a coincidence for the people in the picture to be sitting next to us on the beach. I mean, things like that don't happen, except in the films.'

'But you must agree the little girl in the picture looks like the one we saw on the beach.'

'She looks a little bit similar,' he admitted. 'But the woman in the photograph is a lot younger.'

'They probably used an old photograph,' she suggested. 'I think we should contact the police. There's a telephone number here and they want people to use it.'

442

'Now you really are being ridiculous,' he admonished. 'It probably isn't the same child and it's nothing to do with us anyway, so throw the chip paper away and forget about it.'

'How can you be so unfeeling?'

'I'm not. I'm just being realistic,' he explained. 'If I thought it was the missing kiddie I would be down the phone box like a shot but it probably isn't.'

'It might be so we have to do something,' she insisted.

'There is such a thing as wasting police time, you know, Bet, and that's an offence, so will you shut up about it.'

'I suppose I'd better,' she said. 'It probably isn't her.'

'At last. So now that's settled I'll go and get us some more drinks, then we'll make our way to the station.'

'Okay, love,' she said, reluctantly screwing the paper into a ball.

★ ★ ★

Tension in the Bells' living room grew more intense by the second that same evening as they all sat round supposedly watching the television, but no one was paying any attention. When her mother suggested making yet more tea Sadie said, 'I really think you lot should go out for a drink like I said earlier.'

The pressure was obviously getting to her father and he said, 'I think so too, love, after all, if you're sure you don't mind.'

There was a murmur of agreement from the others who clearly welcomed the idea of a break, though were reluctant to admit it because it seemed disloyal.

'Thank goodness for that,' said Sadie to her mother when the door closed behind them. 'They were like caged animals and putting my nerves on edge.'

'Mine too.'

'It's so hard to stay optimistic all the time and I try to for them,' she said. 'I can let myself go with you, Mum.'

Marge was about to reply when the telephone rang. Simultaneously they both rushed to the hall to answer it.

★　★　★

Sadie tore down the street and caught the men as they were about to go into the pub. They all looked stricken when they saw her because it had to be important for her to come after them.

'What's happened?' asked her father warily.

'They've had a possible sighting of them,' she said.

'Oh, thank God. Where?'

'Brighton. A couple saw the photos of Rosie and Harriet in the paper and think it might be the same two who were sitting next to them on the beach. They were hesitant about contacting the police because they are not sure but the woman decided to take a chance and do it. The police are going to follow it up.'

There was a general outpouring of relief.

'Nothing can be done until the morning, obviously,' said Sadie. 'But first thing tomorrow they'll start a search in Brighton.'

'It's Bank Holiday Monday so there will be crowds, which won't help matters,' Sadie pointed out. 'Anyway, we mustn't get our hopes up too high because it might not even be them and they still have to find them but I'm keeping my fingers well and truly crossed.' She paused for breath. 'I'm going to go there. I want to try and find her. Another pair of eyes can only be a good thing. I'll get an early train.'

'You'll do no such thing,' insisted Ray. 'You'll go with me in my car. You and I are having a day out in Brighton.'

'Thanks, Ray,' she said, feeling brighter than she had since before Rosie went missing but still afraid to be too optimistic.

'You lot can go and have your drink now,' she told them. 'There's nothing you can do until tomorrow morning so go and enjoy yourselves, please.'

'Enjoy ourselves when Rosie is missing?' said Derek. 'You must be joking.'

'Just give yourselves a break,' she urged.

'We'll have half an hour then,' agreed her father.

'Take as long as you like,' she said and turned and headed back towards Fern Terrace, hope swelling in her heart, despite all her reservations.

17

The Bank Holiday crowds were already building up when Sadie and Ray arrived in Brighton, even though they were there early. Hordes of day-trippers were piling off the London trains and heading towards the seafront.

'Needle and haystack come to mind,' said Sadie after they had parked the car, called at the police station to tell them they were here and agreed to keep in touch, and finally arrived on the crowded promenade. The masses were loud and exuberant, moving slowly in groups, laughing and shouting to one another. Enjoyment was their aim and they were really in the mood for it. A multitude of traders plied their trade vociferously. 'Get your Brighton Rock 'ere', or 'the best cockles and whelks on the South Coast'. Ice cream, candy floss and souvenirs were just a few of the traditional seaside goods on offer here. 'How will any of us ever find them in this lot?'

'It does make you wonder but the police are experts at locating people, especially when a child is involved; they'll have a special system, I expect,' Ray said to encourage her. 'They are probably checking all the hotels and boarding houses as we speak. The bobbies on the beat will be looking for them, too.'

'I suppose it was a bit impulsive of me to want to come here,' she admitted, 'but I couldn't just sit at home waiting now that we've had a lead.'

'It's only natural you would want to be here,' he said, 'and every little helps in a case like this.'

'Exactly.'

'Before we start scouring the streets let's go to that café over there and have a cup o' tea or something,' he suggested, pointing to a seafront eatery. 'If we can get a seat by the window we can sit and watch the people go by.'

'And maybe spot them,' she said.

'It's a long shot but they have to be somewhere, so why not on the seafront?'

She agreed so they made their way to the café.

'Why did Harriet bring Rosie to Brighton, I wonder,' mused Sadie, looking out of the window at the passersby in brash seaside hats printed in large letters with comical sayings. 'It's the last place on earth I would expect Harriet to head for. It's far too common for the likes of her. And as for her sitting on the beach, that is completely beyond my powers of imagination.'

'Maybe that's why she came here, because it's the last place anyone would expect to find her,' he replied. 'That and the fact that it isn't far from London. Perhaps she thought Rosie would like the seaside and this is the nearest one.'

'It could be that they just came for the day yesterday and we are on a wild-goose chase here today,' she went on. 'We don't even know if it was them on the beach. The couple who reported it weren't sure.'

'That's true but we are going to stay positive, aren't we?' he said determinedly. 'It's much too soon to lose heart. We haven't even started yet. I

447

don't think she would have brought Rosie here just for the day. If Harriet is a home bird and not used to travelling around, she'll want to stay put wherever she is.'

'Yeah, there is that but there are such a lot of people and we don't know where to start.'

'I think we should check out the parks when we've finished our tea,' he suggested, 'keeping our eyes peeled in the streets as we go along. If we have no luck with that we'll concentrate on the beach this afternoon. If they were there yesterday they could well be there again today. The weather is still nice so the beach is the most likely place later on.'

'I haven't seen many policemen around, have you?' she observed.

'No, but they won't be marching the streets in dozens looking for her,' he pointed out. 'They'll be around and about though. Don't forget they have their normal policing to do as well as looking for a mad old woman and a little girl. They'll have plenty of Bank Holiday drunks to deal with later on too, I expect.'

'Who knows what Harriet might do?' Sadie said, as fears niggled at her. 'I would have put money on her not travelling to London on her own to snatch Rosie, let alone Brighton. Oh, Ray, what is she doing to my little girl? She's very stern and impatient. Rosie will be so scared and miserable.'

'Try to calm down,' he said, putting his hand on hers reassuringly. 'Kids are more resilient than you might think.'

'I expect you're right,' she said, far too

preoccupied with Rosie's safety to notice an odd expression pass fleetingly across his face.

★ ★ ★

Harriet had forgotten what hard work looking after a young child was. It was especially difficult in a strange town without the comforts of home or anyone else to share the responsibility and a lack of other children to keep Rosie amused. There was also the fact that Harriet was twenty-odd years older than she'd been when Paul was little.

Trying to keep Rosie entertained all day and some of the night because she wasn't sleeping properly was both trying and exhausting and Harriet was missing her comfortable Surrey home. But she felt compelled to soldier on with her mission for Rosie's sake.

'What would you like to do today, Rosie?' she asked after breakfast on Monday morning.

'Don't know.'

'What about the park if we can find one?' suggested Harriet.

Rosie shrugged.

'I thought you usually liked going to the park.'

'Will it have swings?' The child was very subdued.

'I expect so; they usually do.'

'All right then,' she said without enthusiasm.

'Right, the park it is, and perhaps we'll go to the beach this afternoon.'

'Yes, Grandma,' said Rosie in a small voice.

Her granddaughter had always been a little

quiet when she'd come to visit her and Gerald. But now Harriet could hardly get a word out of her and she was still very tearful. Naturally she'd be missing her mother but Harriet had expected that to have lessened by now. She felt a pang as thoughts of Gerald came into her mind. She missed him terribly and knew he would be worried about her and Rosie. Still, he would understand why she had to do this. He was a good sort. She had a kind of ache in the pit of her stomach, which made her long to be at home with everything normal. But she dismissed it at once. This was no time to get sentimental.

The real and far-reaching consequences of her actions didn't occur to Harriet. If she did occasionally think that Sadie might be anxious, she told herself it was entirely her own fault for getting mixed up with another man. Paul was her husband. The fact that he was no longer around didn't come into it. She had no right to inflict another father on Rosie.

'Come on then, dear,' she said wearily, 'let's find ourselves a park with some swings in it.'

★ ★ ★

Sadie and Ray were sitting on a bench in the park near to the playground watching the kiddies play.

'This turned out to be a dead end then,' said Sadie, who was made tearful by the sight of the children on the swings because Rosie wasn't one of them.

'Give it time.'

'We've been here for most of the morning,' she said. 'I think we should go and look somewhere else.'

'Maybe you're right,' he agreed, rising to his feet. 'Let's go back to the seafront. We can keep a look-out and have a bite to eat or just a cup of tea if you can't manage any food, then try the beach this afternoon.'

'Yeah, okay,' she said, wondering how it was possible to find anyone in this crowded town with everyone seeming to be constantly on the move.

* ★ *

A few minutes after they left the park through one gate Harriet and Rosie arrived through another.

'The swings are all in use, dear, so we'll have to wait until one becomes free,' said Harriet, feeling jaded. 'You stand near the swings and grab one when it's empty and I'll sit on the bench.'

Rosie stood rather shyly near the swings and Harriet flopped down on the seat, glad to get the weight off her feet. She'd never done so much walking in her life and her legs and feet were throbbing. It wasn't even lunchtime and she was exhausted. The warmth of the sun felt good on her face and she longed to sleep. But she managed to keep her eyes open and watched her granddaughter standing by the swings where there were a couple of youngish women, presumably the mothers of the children occupying the swings. Time passed and they swung on and still Rosie waited.

With energy born of outrage, Harriet got up and marched across to them.

'It's my granddaughter's turn to have a go now,' she said to the boy on one of the swings. 'She's been waiting for ages. So, off you get and give someone else a chance.'

'Oi, don't you dare speak to my boy like that,' objected his mother. 'He isn't ready to come off yet.'

'Well, it's high time he was; he's been on there for more than long enough,' declared Harriet.

'He'll come off when he's ready.'

'This is a public park,' Harriet reminded her sharply. 'It's meant for us all and a bit of consideration would be appreciated.'

'It's all right, love, we're going now,' said the mother of the other child. 'So the little girl can have this one.'

'Thank you,' said Harriet and held the swing for Rosie as she got on.

'You old cow,' said the stroppy mother to Harriet as she finally removed her son from the swing.

Harriet almost took a swipe at her but decided it would be far more dignified and in keeping with her status as a grandmother to simply ignore her.

'Mummy usually pushes me,' Rosie was saying. 'I can't get the swing up high by myself.'

Harriet had been planning on having a sit down while Rosie played but she dutifully pushed the swing.

'Higher,' said Rosie. 'Higher . . . higher.'

It was such a relief to see any sort of enthusiasm from the child, Harriet carried on pushing even though she thought she might collapse with fatigue at any moment. She kept going though her bones and muscles ached like never before. She had to carry on. It was her duty. The beach this afternoon — crowded with the noisy, beer-drinking masses — would be a treat after this. At least she could sit down there, provided they could find a couple of deckchairs.

★ ★ ★

Sadie and Ray were tired too. Sadie had barely slept since Rosie disappeared, and because of the worry and the walking they had done today, they were both footsore and weary as they trudged up and down along the promenade peering at the crowds here and on the beach in the hope of seeing Rosie and her grandmother. But it was almost impossible to pick anyone out in the crowds.

'I think we should take a break,' suggested Ray. 'Let's get a couple of deckchairs and have a sit down. Just for a short time. No need to stop looking round. But we do need to rest for a while and there are no empty benches to sit on along here.'

Sadie knew he was right so they got a couple of chairs, paid the man and trekked across the pebbles where there was barely room enough to get through the crowds. It was only just possible

453

to get a space to sit down so they went quite close to the sea to find somewhere to park themselves.

★ ★ ★

Never in a million years did Harriet ever think she would be pleased to sit in a deckchair among the hoi polloi on Brighton beach with the reek of fish and chips and candy floss mingling with the pungent whiff of the ocean. But she was so worn out that afternoon, it felt like bliss.

'Are you going for a paddle, Rosie dear?' she asked, taking off the child's socks and shoes. 'I'll watch you from here. As long as you stay near the edge you'll be quite safe.'

'I'll get my frock wet,' said Rosie.

Harriet noticed that most of the other children were wearing bathing costumes, which was the last thing she'd thought of when she'd bought Rosie some clothes.

'We could tuck your dress into your knickers,' she suggested, desperate for some time alone to rest. 'That would keep it out of the water.'

'I want my mummy,' said Rosie out of the blue, her eyes filling with tears.

It was infuriating for Harriet. Just when she thought she was making progress and Rosie was beginning to get used to her, she was put right back to square one when the wretched child suddenly started to fret for her mother. It happened all the time.

'You can't see Mummy today.'

454

'I want her, I miss her,' she sobbed. 'Please let me see her.'

'Now stop making such a silly fuss,' admonished Harriet sternly. 'Grandma is very tired. If you're a good girl and let me rest I'll buy you an ice cream later.'

'I don't want an ice cream,' Rosie spluttered, tears falling. 'I just want my mummy.'

'Well, you can't have her, so stop making that horrible noise, at once,' Harriet snapped viciously.

Rosie's weeping became silent instantly because she was frightened of her grandmother when she was cross. The child's body shook and she made little gasping noises as she tried to hide the fact that she was crying.

Harriet was too weary to even try and comfort her. She'd stop the awful whining eventually. Meanwhile Harriet leaned back and closed her eyes.

★ ★ ★

Having finally managed to stop the flow of tears, Rosie stared at the sea, feeling miserable. But her interest was suddenly aroused by some older children who were playing with a red ball in the water, throwing it to each other and squealing with delight. She turned and looked at her grandmother who was snoring gently, eyes closed and mouth open. Rosie got off her chair and walked towards the sea and the red ball.

The water felt cold to her toes at first but it was nice when she got used to it so she went in further, heading towards the children with the ball. The waves felt strong against her little body and pushed her back so she tried even harder to get further out and near to the red ball, her frock dragging her down. She began to feel really cold and wanted to go back to the beach but a wave pushed her so hard she lost her footing and fell backwards, her head sinking under the water filling her with panic because she couldn't breathe. Not quite sure what was happening to her, she was terrified and wanted her mum . . .

* * *

'Wake up, missus,' said a man who'd been sitting near to Harriet. 'Your nipper is in trouble in the water.'

Her eyes snapped open. 'What . . . what's happened?' she asked, disorientated by her nap.

'Your little girl wandered off into the water while you were asleep,' he explained. 'I've been keeping an eye on her and I saw her get knocked over by a wave and go under. A couple of men who were swimming around there are trying to get her but I thought you should know what's going on.'

'Oh, my God,' she exclaimed, wide awake now as she hobbled across the pebbles towards the sea fully dressed; she even had her stockings and shoes on. 'Rosie, where are you? Rosie . . . Rosie . . . '

With no concern for herself or the fact that she couldn't swim, she waded into the water.

* * *

'What's all that shouting about,' wondered Sadie, looking towards the sea and shading her eyes from the sun with her hand. 'I thought I heard someone calling Rosie. All the stress is wreaking havoc on my imagination.'

'Someone's in trouble in the water by the look of it,' observed Ray, also looking towards the sea. 'There seems to be something going on over there anyway.'

Then Sadie saw the top of a bedraggled figure in the sea, the water up above her waist. It wasn't possible to be sure from this distance but Sadie knew from the incongruity of the person who it was. 'Oh, my God, Ray, it's Harriet,' she cried, getting up and running towards the water with Ray close on her heels, already starting to undo his shirt.

People gathering around the water's edge were saying that a little girl was drowning. Some men were trying to rescue her. Sadie and Ray both plunged into the water and waded over to Harriet. 'Please, please tell me it isn't Rosie,' begged Sadie.

'She went out too far,' Harriet told them, her teeth chattering from the cold water. 'I told her to stay at the edge. I have to find her.'

'You can't swim, can you?' said Sadie.

'No, but I'll find her or die in the attempt,' she said and plunged into the waves, splashing and coughing.

Ray dragged her back and turned to Sadie. 'Can you take her to the beach and keep her out of the way?' he asked. 'I'm going after Rosie. There are already people looking for her. We don't want to make it into a circus. We'll lose all hope of finding her if there are too many.'

'I have to find her,' shrieked Harriet again.

'Shut up,' shouted Sadie. 'You've already caused enough trouble by stealing my daughter and allowing her to get carried out to sea, so the least you can do now is to keep quiet and out of the way while they try to rescue her.'

As the two women reached the beach, first-aid workers were already hurrying towards the water's edge and an ambulance was on the promenade.

'Are you all right, ladies?' one of the medics asked, since they were both fully dressed and sodden. Harriet was shaking and crying and on the verge of hysteria.

'I'm okay,' said Sadie, looking at Harriet. 'But she's in a hell of a state.'

'Come on, my dear,' said one of the medical team kindly. 'Let's get you over to the ambulance and dry you off.'

Sadie had never hated anyone as she hated Harriet at that moment. She *never*, *ever* wanted to see her again for as long as she lived.

★　★　★

Back at the water's edge the medical team were asking the crowd to move back to leave the way clear for the rescue.

'It's my daughter they're looking for,' Sadie

458

explained. 'I have to be here when they find her and bring her out.'

She was beyond fear and despair. It was as though she had been crushed inside and all she could feel was an ache of longing for her daughter to be brought back from the jaws of death. Was this a punishment for the selfishness of her youth? First her husband, then her best friend and now her daughter. How much more pain could she take?

It was hard to stay on the beach and not go in the water and help Ray. But such an action could hinder his efforts. She could see heads bobbing above the water then disappear, then two heads appeared together and Ray swam towards her with his arm under a small head. Reaching shallower waters, he stood up carrying Rosie and Sadie's heart rose.

But her joy was short-lived because when he reached her she could see that her daughter was limp and ominously still. Oh no, please God, no!

★　★　★

Tension filled every corner of the Bell household as the family waited for news from Sadie. Marge thought she had never known a Bank Holiday Monday to pass so slowly. They went through the motions of normality. Marge made some chips to go with the cold meat from yesterday's joint, the same as usual, and they all sat round the table and tried to eat. But there was a great deal of food left on the plates.

When the phone finally rang in the early

459

evening, they all rushed to answer it but Marge got there first. She was trembling and her hands were clammy as she picked up the receiver and gave the number.

'Hello, Mum,' said Sadie.

'Have you found her?'

'Yes, we've found her.'

'Is she all right?'

'Yes, she's safe,' said Sadie.

'Oh, thank God.'

'I'll tell you all about it when we get home. We'll be back later. Not sure when; it depends on the traffic.'

'Okay, love.'

'See you later. Bye.'

'Ta-ta.'

★ ★ ★

Sadie came out of the phone box and walked across the road to the seafront where Ray and Rosie were sitting on a bench waiting for her. She was still feeling quite shaky from the ordeal, but so relieved she vowed not to ask anything more of life *ever* as Rosie had been spared.

She'd been convinced she had lost her when Ray got her to the beach but the medics had worked on her and she'd vomited up large amounts of the English Channel and eventually regained consciousness. She'd been checked over in hospital — where they had dried all their clothes — and they had said that they didn't need to keep Rosie in, but Sadie was to keep an eye on her.

Harriet had also been at the hospital being examined after the drama. She and Sadie had met in the foyer after being given the all-clear. Harriet had been full of contrition for taking Rosie and so nearly causing her to lose her life. But although Sadie wasn't going to press charges — because Harriet was Rosie's grandmother and obviously unbalanced — she could barely bring herself to speak to her and wasn't planning on seeing her ever again. She certainly wasn't going to let Rosie anywhere near her.

Poor Gerald was beside himself when he arrived to take his wife home, and managed a few quiet words with Sadie.

'I don't know what to say, my dear, except I'm very sorry,' he said to her.

'None of it is your fault, Gerald,' she assured him. 'So don't go blaming yourself. Harriet is an adult and therefore responsible for her own actions.'

'Yes, but she's my wife and we have been together for many years, so anything she does is my problem as well as hers,' he told her.

'With respect, I think she needs professional help,' Sadie suggested, 'for her own sake as well as everyone else's. We won't want to let Rosie out of our sights unless your wife's behaviour becomes more stable.'

'Yes, I can understand why you feel like that,' he said sadly. 'I must go now. Cheerio, my dear.'

'Ta-ta,' she said, saddened by the fact that she probably wouldn't see him again, given his devotion to his wife.

Now Sadie turned and looked at Ray and

461

Rosie sitting on the seat together, looking at the sea. They were both eating ice creams and obviously at ease with each other. Sadie paused for a moment just enjoying the sight of them, and loving them both so much it brought tears to her eyes.

'Hello, you two,' she said, sitting beside Rosie.

'I got you a cornet, Sadie,' said Ray, handing it to her. 'It's melting so you'll have to lick it quick.'

She laughed at the not particularly funny rhyme and the other two both joined in. She didn't know if it was caused by the relief but they were all in fits for ages.

★ ★ ★

Life seemed to return to normal over the next few days. Ray was right when he said that children were resilient because Rosie didn't seem to have sustained any serious harm, though she was much more clingy than usual towards her mother. Gerald telephoned to say that Harriet had gone voluntarily into a psychiatric hospital and no charges were brought by the police because of her state of mind.

With Rosie safely at home, Sadie's thoughts turned to another matter of major importance: her relationship with Ray. He'd been magnificent throughout the whole abduction ordeal and she had told him so on several occasions. She decided that — being the man he was — he must have had a very good reason for lying to her and she wasn't going to say any more to him about it.

462

'So now that Rosie is safe, we can think about our own plans,' she said a week or so after the dramatic events of the Bank Holiday when she called at the shop in her lunch break. 'I'm so sorry I ever doubted you, Ray. I should have known better. So can we go back to the way things were before the argument?'

'No,' he said bluntly.

'What!' she gasped. 'Oh, Ray, after all we've been through together this past week. Why are you turning me down?'

He looked at her grimly, his brown eyes penetrating and unblinking. 'Can you arrange babysitting for this evening?' he asked. 'I want you to come somewhere with me.'

'I'm not sure about tonight,' she replied. 'It's short notice for Mum and Rosie's still a bit weepy when I leave her.'

'I wouldn't ask if it wasn't really important,' he said. 'I haven't been honest with you.'

Please, please, please don't let it be another woman, she thought, but said, 'Oh, I see. It all sounds very ominous.'

'It is,' he said.

'Ray, you are the most straightforward person I know, so why are you being so mysterious?'

'Maybe I'm not as straightforward as you think,' he told her grimly. 'You can make your own decision about that and our engagement after you've been with me tonight.'

'All right, Ray, I'll come so long as Mum doesn't mind,' she said, wondering what on earth was in store for her. 'I'm sure Rosie will be all right with her for a few hours tonight.'

Ray said the journey would be quicker by train because of the traffic on the roads, so they walked to the tube station and he bought tickets to a stop near the end of the line in Essex. Very little was said on the journey and Sadie was feeling nervous about the reason for all this.

'Am I allowed to know where we're going now, Ray?' she asked when they came out of the station and walked down an ordinary suburban street.

'We're going to my home,' he said.

'Where you lived with your grandparents?' she asked.

'Not exactly, no.'

As they walked on there was some open space then they came to a large old building set back from the road and iron gates at the end of the entrance path.

'St John's Home for Boys,' she read from a board inside the gates.

'It was called St John's Home for Destitute Boys in my day,' he said. 'They must have thought that wasn't appropriate in these more affluent times.'

'You lived here?'

'That's right. From birth until the age of fifteen.' He pointed towards the big house. 'They built more dormitories at the back. There were a lot of kids in care back then.'

'I thought your mum and dad were killed in the war and your grandparents brought you up.'

'It was all a pack of lies,' he told her. 'A

complete and utter invention.'

'But why, Ray?' she asked. 'Why?'

★ ★ ★

'It must be hard for someone like you with a loving family to imagine how it was for me when I came to Hammersmith at the age of fifteen with no one at all,' said Ray when they were seated at a table in a nearby pub. 'The people at the home thought I should go into a trade and fixed me up with an apprenticeship as a car mechanic. They found me lodgings and after that I was on my own in a world full of families, or that's how it seemed to me. At the home we were all in the same boat — unwanted — and there were always plenty of kids about so I was never lonely because we were like a family in a way. Alone in Hammersmith it was very different. Every friend I ever made had a normal home and family. I was, and I now realise wrongly, ashamed of my background so I invented a story.'

'I'm disappointed that you didn't feel able to tell me the truth,' Sadie said.

'The lie was too old, too well-established,' he explained. 'I felt like a fraud. That's why I never wanted to get married because I would need to produce my birth certificate. There's a blank space where the names of my parents should be. I was left at the gates of the orphanage when I was a few days old. The people at the home gave me a name and got it made legal.'

'Oh Ray, how dreadfully sad.'

'That's exactly the reaction I never wanted,' he told her. 'Having a fictional background protected me from sympathy as well as shame.'

'And no relatives ever got in touch?'

He shook his head. 'I never had a visitor the whole time I was at St John's,' he said. 'I hated Sunday afternoons when most of the other kids had someone visit them, sometimes at least. I never did.'

'Have you never wanted to find out why you were abandoned?' she asked.

'Maybe when I was younger I might have been curious from time to time but not now. If my mother wanted to know how I was doing she could easily have found out. But she didn't bother. So I don't want to know about her.'

Sadie could understand his feelings and she now knew how damaged he must have been. She was in such admiration of him for the way he had turned his life around.

'She's the loser,' she said adamantly. 'She doesn't know what a fine man you turned out to be.'

'Give over, Sadie,' he admonished. 'You know how I hate that sort of talk.'

'I'm only saying it because it's true,' she said. 'You looked after yourself through your teen years and you built a life and a business from nothing with no help or support from anyone. That's something to be really proud of.'

He shrugged. 'My sort of background makes you tough. As I told you the other day, kids can be very resilient.'

'You certainly were.' She thought for a

moment. 'But if we hadn't had that argument that's led to all of this coming out, how were you going to get on when you had to show your birth certificate for the wedding?'

'I would have had to tell you somehow before then,' he explained. 'I've been trying my hardest to pluck up the courage ever since we got engaged.'

'Did you really think I would change my mind over a thing like that?' she asked.

'It isn't a small thing, Sadie,' he pointed out gravely. 'I don't know who I really am. I could be the son of bad people. Who knows what's in my background if we have children . . . '

'Do you really think they would grow up bad with someone with your strength of character as their father?'

He wasn't happy with compliments so just lowered his eyes.

'The reason I lied to you that night I was out when you came round to the flat was because I had been to St John's and I still couldn't bring myself to tell you the truth,' he went on. 'I'd already been back several times recently after years of turning my back on the place altogether since I left at age fifteen. I was very nervous the first time I went back because I knew I had to face up to reality and admit to myself that St John's was the only home I had ever had, and stop hiding behind the background I had invented for myself. I realised that I had a lot to thank them for too. All right, so it was a hard life but they fed and clothed me, made sure I was educated, albeit it very basically, and they taught me the rudiments of how to live a decent life. I decided it was time I gave something back. So with the approval of the powers that be at the home, I've been taking some of the boys swimming at the local baths after school. Some of them enjoy boxing so I've been taking them to a local club.'

'How come I didn't get to know about it,' she asked, 'as I see you in the evenings?'

'Except for the night I pretended I was doing paperwork, I've been going early; taking a few hours off from the shop and being there when the boys finish school,' he explained. 'I've been back in time to see you without you being any the wiser, but that night I was having talks with the administration at St John's so I was out all evening.'

'I see.'

'I would like to go some Sunday afternoons to visit the boys who, like me, have no one from outside come to see them. But I couldn't do that without you knowing.' He looked at her. 'So now that you know what a devious sod I am, I expect that marriage is out of the question.'

'I'm sad that you didn't feel able to be straight with me but I can understand your reasons, knowing the sort of man that you are,' Sadie said. 'I think I love you even more now that I know the truth. You are so special, Ray Smart. So brave and tough and caring all at the same time. As for visiting on Sundays, I'll go with you.'

'So you still want to marry me.'

'You bet I do,' she said, smiling. 'And I can't wait to get my engagement ring back.'

'You won't have to wait long,' he said, digging into his pocket. 'I brought it with me just in case . . .'

They both laughed and he slipped the ring back on to her finger then took her in his arms.

★ ★ ★

The wedding took place as arranged. It was a small register-office do, which they both thought was appropriate as Sadie had been married before and Ray had no family. They didn't want the razzmatazz; only to be together with Rosie in their own little semi just a few minutes away from the Bells.

Sadie looked lovely in a pale blue dress and jacket that matched her eyes. Rosie was resplendent in a pink satin bridesmaid's dress with white edging and a pretty floral headdress. She was carrying a small basket of flowers. They booked a meal at a local hotel and, apart from family, there was Edith who had become a good friend to Sadie, and some of the staff from St John's who had known Ray all his life. Sadie felt a pang that Brenda wasn't there. She still missed her.

When Sadie threw her bouquet, Christine caught it, which caused great hilarity because her wedding to Derek was planned for the end of the year.

'I'll only have one of you left at home soon,' Marge was heard to mention.

'And you'll never get rid of me, Mum,' laughed Don. 'I know when I'm well off.'

'You do an' all,' she smiled.

Because of the abduction, Sadie and Ray didn't want to leave Rosie while they went away on honeymoon so were spending their wedding night in a West End hotel, then coming back tomorrow to start their new life in their own house with Rosie.

As they were driven away in a taxi, waving out of the back window to all the well-wishers, Sadie felt blessed. Life was a mixture of good times and bad, and she had experienced the other side of happiness as well as the joy. Now her life was set fair and she was enjoying every moment and looking forward to the future with her new husband.

★ ★ ★

Six months later a letter arrived for Sadie from Gerald at the Bells' house because she hadn't sent a change-of-address card to the Westons. In the interests of Rosie's safety she'd not thought it wise to let Harriet know where she was.

Dear Sadie,

I don't expect you ever want to hear from us again after what happened but I am writing to ask a very big favour of you, though I know I have no right. Harriet has had a spell in hospital and is much calmer and more reasonable now. With drugs and regular out-patients' visits she should be able to stay stable, especially as they have found out why she has been so troubled. She really wasn't in

470

her right mind when she abducted Rosie, as I think you have probably guessed.

Anyway, now to the favour. Harriet very much wants to see you; something I know will not be reciprocated. But she has things she wants to say to you, so I wonder if you might do this one thing for me. I don't think any of us can truly move forward unless the two of you meet to clear up the loose ends from the past. Just you. She knows you wouldn't agree to her seeing Rosie.

If you could find it in your heart to do this for me, I would be very grateful.

Kind regards,
Gerald

Sadie was feeling extremely emotional; maybe because she was fond of Gerald, perhaps because the Westons were a part of her life with Paul, which would always be important to her. Whatever the reason, she had tears in her eyes when she showed the letter to Ray.

'You're not going to go, are you?'

'Yes, I think I am.'

'Why? After everything that woman put you through?'

'Because good or bad, Harriet is Rosie's grandmother,' Sadie said. 'And I want to hear what she has to say.'

'We'll go at the weekend.'

'No. I'll go on my own one evening if you don't mind, Ray,' she replied. 'If you could let me use your car, and babysit Rosie, I'd be very grateful.'

'It's our car, not just mine, and of course I'll look after Rosie.'

'What did I do to deserve you?' she said, smiling.

'I regularly ask myself the same thing about you,' he replied tenderly.

★ ★ ★

'I asked you here because I want to tell you something which might explain why I have behaved as I have towards you,' said Harriet after greetings had been exchanged, profuse apologies offered and Gerald sent from the room. 'The doctors seem to think it is something in my past that has affected my adult behaviour.'

'I'm listening,' said Sadie.

'When I was fifteen I found myself pregnant.'

'Oh,' said Sadie, surprised but not sure how this was relevant.

'It was considered a terrible disgrace back then.'

'It still is, up to a point.'

'Not as much as when I was young. It was really shocking; the worst thing that could happen to a girl in those days,' Harriet explained. 'Anyway, my parents forced me to have an abortion and I never got over the guilt. When Paul was born I felt blessed to have been granted a son after what I had done, and I wanted more children. But after a series of miscarriages I had to have a hysterectomy and I saw this as a punishment for killing my first child.

'But I had Paul. He was my gift and I never wanted to let him go. I was possessive, I can see that now. I couldn't accept another woman in his life, which is why I never warmed to you as I should have.' She paused, tears coming into her eyes and she emitted a small gasp. 'His death all but destroyed me and I blamed you initially in an effort to ease my pain. I couldn't admit it then but I can now.

'Anyway, when Rosie arrived it was as though my child had been given back to me. She was so much like Paul, I wanted her as my own, all to myself, and I wanted it with a passion. I hated the idea that I could only ever be in the background. When you decided to get married again, I feared I would lose her altogether and I panicked.' She paused thoughtfully. 'It was as though I had lost all control of my emotions and actions when I took her. It felt almost as if it was someone else doing it. It's hard to describe and even harder for me to believe that I did such an awful thing.'

Sadie was moved by the woman's confession, almost despite herself, but still extremely wary.

'So . . . what do you actually want of me, Harriet?'

'I just wanted you to know that I'm sorry.'

'And you also want me to let you see Rosie again, don't you?' Sadie suggested. 'That's what this is really all about, isn't it?'

'I can't deny that I would love that, of course, but I don't suppose you would . . . '

'Not yet, Harriet,' Sadie cut in. 'But maybe

473

later on when I feel I can trust you we'll talk about it again.'

'That's the best I could have hoped for,' Harriet said, leaning forward and putting her bony, veined hand on Sadie's. 'Thank you so much. I will do my very best to earn that trust.'

Even after all the awful things Harriet had done, Sadie felt deeply sorry for her. Sadie herself was happy and had a wonderful life with Ray and Rosie. Harriet just had Gerald. As important and good as he was, he could never change the fact that she had lost her son; the pain of that would never really go away. In her own twisted way Harriet did love Rosie. Maybe now that she had had treatment and her irrational behaviour had been recognised, in time some sort of a relationship with Rosie would be possible; under supervision.

'Are you going to put the kettle on now that you've got all that off your chest?' Sadie said with a wry grin. 'I don't know about you but I'm parched.'

Harriet recognised this as the first step in an effort to build bridges. 'What a good idea,' she said, smiling.

Sadie thought that was the first time she had ever seen her smile properly, and with genuine feeling.

We do hope that you have enjoyed reading this large print book.

Did you know that all of our titles are available for purchase?

We publish a wide range of high quality large print books including:
Romances, Mysteries, Classics
General Fiction
Non Fiction and Westerns

Special interest titles available in large print are:
The Little Oxford Dictionary
Music Book
Song Book
Hymn Book
Service Book

Also available from us courtesy of Oxford University Press:
Young Readers' Dictionary
(large print edition)
Young Readers' Thesaurus
(large print edition)

For further information or a free brochure, please contact us at:
Ulverscroft Large Print Books Ltd.,
The Green, Bradgate Road, Anstey,
Leicester, LE7 7FU, England.
Tel: (00 44) 0116 236 4325
Fax: (00 44) 0116 234 0205

Other titles published by
The House of Ulverscroft:

HARVEST NIGHTS

Pamela Evans

West London, 1920. The Great War is over and former land girl Clara Tripp is back home with her family. Although she's working and engaged to local boy Arnold, Clara longs for country life. She's thrilled when old flame Charlie Fenner offers her temporary work at his family orchard in Kent. She goes, taking her little brother, Cuddy. But living with the Fenners gives her reason to suspect that something isn't right . . . After a traumatic accident forces Clara and Cuddy to extend their stay, Clara makes a discovery that threatens to tear the Fenner family apart. And, struggling with forbidden feelings for Charlie, she's drawn into a darker conflict of guilt, shame and greed which she fears there is no way out . . .

THE TIDEWAY GIRLS

Pamela Evans

It's 1904, and close sisters Bessie and May live a happy but frugal life in the busy maritime village of Tideway in Essex. But trouble divides the family when May falls pregnant, and she is sent away to London. When war is declared in 1914, Bessie's life is shattered when her husband is killed in battle in France. Yet, when photographer Digby Parsons dies suddenly and leaves Bessie a camera, she is able to use it to set up her own photography business and support herself and her son. But Digby's jealous daughter, Joan, is enraged by her late father's generosity and will do everything she can to destroy Bessie and her business . . .

UNDER AN AMBER SKY

Pamela Evans

To the Porters and the Mills, family and friendship had been the glue binding everything together. But their lives are shattered when the Porters' home is destroyed in the Blitz. Only seventeen-year-old Nell and her little sister Pansy survive. Peg Mills welcomes them into her family and gradually the girls thrive: Pansy, evacuated to the countryside home of Peg's loving mother, and Nell in her new job at the local newspaper. But trouble looms. Nell discovers her suitor, Gus Granger, hides a dangerous secret and her childhood friend Ed Mills is declared missing in action. Nell is distraught that the war has stolen the man she cares about most. If only she'd told him how she really felt about him before it was too late . . .

WHEN THE BOYS COME HOME

Pamela Evans

As German bombs wreak havoc on West London, Megan Stubbs' father, Dai Morgan, is killed in an air raid. Coping with her loss, Megan takes over her father's milk round, and she and her mother, Dolly, brave the ravaged streets with the horse and cart. Comforted that her twin girls have been safely evacuated to Wales with her sister Hetty, Megan worries about her husband, Will, fighting abroad. And when Will's life-long friend, Doug Reynolds, returns, wounded and disfigured, she takes him in. However, Doug is not the man she thinks he is . . . When peace is declared in 1945 the boys come home. But the reunion for Megan and Hetty with their husbands brings heartache, especially for Megan, who is nursing her own battle scars . . .

IN THE DARK STREETS SHINING

Pamela Evans

After Rose Brown's husband is killed at Dunkirk in 1940, she is determined to pick herself up and start again. Wanting to help the war effort, she begins life as a postwoman on the Blitz-torn streets of London. And when she rescues a young boy from a bombed-out house and takes him back to the family home in West London, she finds a new sense of purpose. Traumatised from losing his mother and being trapped in the ruins alone, seven-year-old Alfie is rebellious and withdrawn. However, he touches the hearts of the family whose patience and special insight from Rose win his trust. But then a stranger, Johnny Beech, turns up on the doorstep looking for his son, and everything changes . . .